THE RISE OF
MALBECK

JASON L. MCWHIRTER

A Twiin Entertainment book

Books by Jason L. McWhirter

THE CAVALIER TRILOGY

Book 1: The Cavalier

Praise for THE CAVALIER, book one in this series

"The Cavalier (Book One of the Cavalier Trilogy) is a descriptively strong story, staying true to the style of similar fantasy novels. If you enjoy being drawn into a world laced with heroes, goblins, orcs and magic, then this is the story for you."
Fantasy Book Review (M.G. Russell)

Book 2: The Rise of Malbeck

Book 3: Glimmer in the Shadow
Soon to be out…the last book in the Cavalier Trilogy

Published by Twiin Entertainment
www.twiinentertainment.com

Copyright © Jason L. McWhirter, 2012
Library of Congress
All rights reserved

Cover and title page art by Christian Quinot
Oak tree drawing by Katherine Bronstad
Map by Jason McWhirter
Edited by Linda McWhirter and Sarah Finley

AUTHOR'S NOTE

This is a work of fiction. Names, characters, places, and incidents are the product of the author's imagination or are used fictitiously, and any resemblance to actual persons, living or dead, business establishments, events, or locales is entirely coincidental.

The Rise of Malbeck

Dedication:

I would like to dedicate this book to my wife, Jodi. She is the most incredible person I have ever met. I am thankful for her constant support. I am thankful for her amazing marketing and networking skills. She is my unofficial publicist and I couldn't ask for one that was more supportive and dedicated to helping me get my trilogy out to the public. She brings substance to my dreams. Thank you, my love.

Acknowledgements:

There is a long history to the process by which I decided to write a fantasy trilogy. I've read so many fantasy books and spent so much time thinking of adventures that it would be impossible for me to create my own ideas without giving credit to the very authors and artists who inspired me to write and create my own works of literature. Their stories helped inspire my own.

So let me start by thanking some of the authors that first turned me on to reading fantasy. Lloyd Alexander tops the list as one of the first authors I read when I was ten years old. After that I moved on to Tolkien, R.A. Salvatore, Simon Hawke, and Gary Gygax. Then in my college years I started reading David Gemmell, Terry Brooks, and Elizabeth Moon. In fact, it was when I had read Moon's Paksennarion books that I was inspired to begin formulating my own 'Paladin-like' story based on a similar character that I had created many years ago in my adolescent Dungeons and Dragons campaigns. I continued to read many of these authors as I got older, and I discovered new writers as well, writers such as Jim Butcher, Brent Weeks, Vince Flynn, and Wilber Smith. There are many more authors I'm currently reading, not just those in the fantasy genre, but also those who write action/adventure, and even some suspense/thriller novels. Each author has given me ideas and has influenced my style, providing me with a foundation from which I can learn, experiment, and improve my skills. It's a wonderful ongoing process by which I hope to continue developing as a writer

Lastly I'd like to thank TSR and all the creators of Dungeons and Dragons. I spent so many years in middle school and high school playing the game and dreaming of sword wielding heroes and fire breathing dragons, that it would be inconceivable not to acknowledge the impact that the game had on my writing today, providing me with a plethora of ideas for stories, themes, characters, and conflicts.

Maybe someday I, too, can inspire another writer, just as all these artists have inspired me. Thanks for the adventures, the journeys to other worlds, times, and places, and the ability to step out of myself for some precious moments in time!

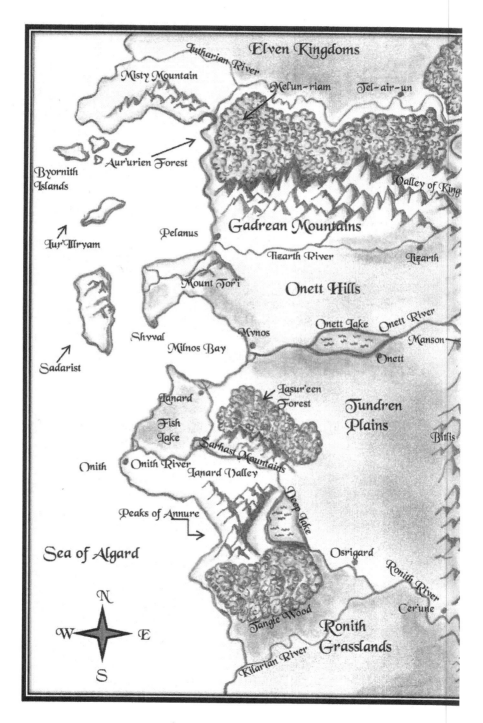

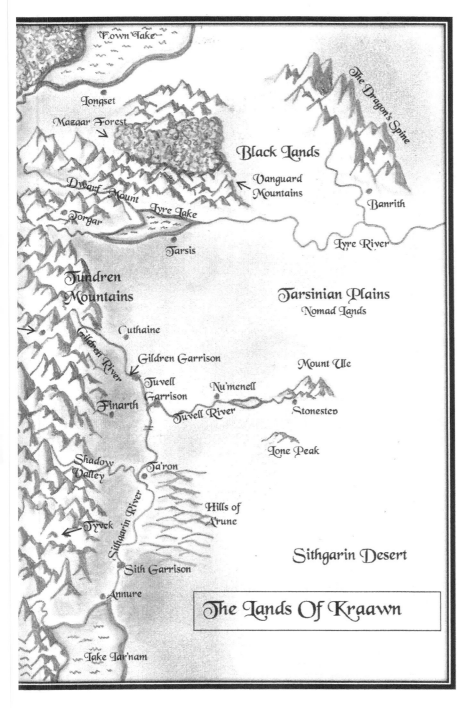

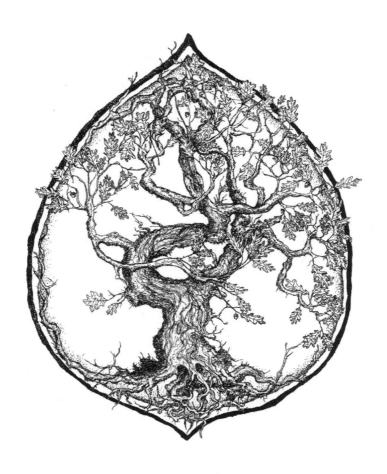

Shyann's symbol: Carved on the door at
the Annurien Kulam

Dated 4045 of the Kraawnian Calendar

Artist: Cureleon Amorst

THE RISE OF MALBECK

BOOK TWO OF THE *CAVALIER TRILOGY*

JASON L. MCWHIRTER

Prologue

The Sharneen warrior rode his horse slowly northeast, toward Finarth. It had been a long road for the assassin, the longest yet in his accomplished career. A month of hard riding had brought him to a distant land, a land forested with strange trees, steep mountains, and cold winters. These harsh lands made the foreigner eager to perform his task so he could return to the east where he was known and where his name was whispered with fear in taverns and dark alleys...*Uthgil, the quick blade.*

As he meandered along the trail, he looked inwardly, thinking about the job ahead, while his eyes scanned outward, always looking for some unseen threat. This was a task that he was being paid a king's ransom to perform, but one he would have done for free, just for the challenge of it.

He was simply the best. He had never met a warrior who could defeat him, nor equal his skill with a blade. The assassin could move as quietly as an elf in the forest, and he killed with a speed and precision that was unmatched. There was no castle he couldn't breach, no wall he couldn't climb, and no target that he couldn't kill.

Uthgil was of average height for his race, but short in comparison to the race of men in the west. His skin was brown, tanned from the hot sun of the east, and his hair was as black as a demon's heart. He wore it tied back in a knot at his neck. Dark oval eyes slanting at the corners gave him an exotic look, but it was the black pupils that gave someone pause. Devoid of emotion, they reflected an emptiness that was a warning to most that this man was capable of anything. His black leather armor had been enchanted by magic, making it as strong as plate mail yet as light and supple as a deer skin vest. Two unique blades adorned his hips, each about as long as his forearm, both razor sharp and double sided, with the pommels slightly curved to perfectly fit his hand. Each knife had a cross piece that extended on one side of the handle, wrapping around the hand and ending in a smaller razor sharp blade about the size of his finger. The guard was used to protect his hands and the short knife gave him a tool to deal death on both ends. They were unusual weapons that had cost him a year's wages to have crafted, and equally that much to have enchanted by wizards. A leather bandolier on each wrist carried three small throwing daggers, and his armor was equipped with several hidden sheaths at his chest which held four throwing darts, two that carried lethal amounts of poison and two that were laced with a sleeping draught. Strapped to the side of his horse was a light crossbow of his own design that could shoot two small bolts, one on each side of the stock. He could spin the weapon quickly, firing each bolt within a heartbeat. The Sharneen assassin had mastered every weapon conceivable and had perfected every known fighting style. His pursuit of martial excellence had occupied every moment of his entire life.

It had been one night, many weeks ago, while working in a city far to the east that an aged man had materialized in his room. Uthgil could tell that the man was a powerful wizard. He had encountered many powerful people in his life, but this man had an aura of power beyond any he had previously felt. So, keeping his blades sheathed, he had let the scene play out.

The old man had given him a name, a name he had heard of, a place, and a large bag of gold, much more than his normal price, and had asked that the man be eliminated. It was more a command than a request, but he took the job with a nod of his head, for the name alone sparked enough interest in the assassin that the exorbitant payment would not have been needed. The old wizard disappeared as quickly as he had arrived.

A silence in the forest alerted the Sharneen that he was not alone. His senses quickly took over and he cleared his mind, focusing on the disturbance he detected, gently stroking the crossbow strapped to the side of his horse.

When three men leaped from the brush no more than four paces away, he was not surprised. The lead brigand carried a sword while the two men behind him held short bows drawn tight. They wore heavy wool woodsmen's clothes that were dirty and tattered. Equally unkempt were their old and tarnished weapons. It was obvious to Uthgil that these men were mere thieves, not accomplished warriors.

Uthgil spat in disgust but said nothing as he slowed his horse to a halt. He sat casually on the saddle with his right hand resting gently on the pommel of his crossbow.

"We'll be having that fine horse and anything else of value," announced the bearded thief holding the sword. The man appeared to be around fifty winters. His face was haggard and his skin was tanned and leathery from exposure to the elements.

The Sharneen didn't move or speak, he simply lifted his dark eyes giving the leader a deadly glare so pronounced that the man stepped back a pace, pausing and taking a gulp before he spoke again. "Did you hear me? Give us your goods and you might walk from here alive," he demanded weakly, his voice having lost much of its former confidence.

"Shall we stick him like a pig?" asked one of the bowmen behind the leader. The man was young and beardless and his bow was shaking slightly, his eyes darting from his leader to the Sharneen like a nervous squirrel.

Finally Uthgil spoke up. His voice was low, but it carried the threat of a sword being slowly drawn from its scabbard. "The story of your pitiful lives can continue, or end here, it's up to you." He spoke in the common tongue, but his accent was thick and noticeable. "Sheath that blade, lower the bows, and return to wherever you call home," he paused, and then continued, "And that goes for the men behind me as well." The Sharneen spoke a bit louder on the last phrase so the two men hiding in the woods could hear him.

Since their hiding spot was now unveiled the two thieves behind the Sharneen slowly emerged from the forest. One held a pitted short sword, the other a long spear.

"He's a foreigner," spat the bowman with the spear. "Let's just kill him."

Uthgil looked down at the pitiful man with undisguised contempt. The bowman was thin as a rail with a face covered in pock marks. He then turned his attention to the leader, who shifted his feet nervously. Then the assassin saw it, the subtle clue he was looking for. The leader's feet stopped suddenly and his knuckles turned white as he gripped his sword tighter. He saw the man's jaw muscles flex and the weight of his body shift to his back foot, all signs of intended action.

"Bad move," the assassin whispered, his left hand whipping out and releasing a dart from the bandolier on his chest, his right hand bringing the crossbow up and in-line with the bowman on his right, letting the bolt fly just as the bowman released his arrow.

The bowman on the left was struck with the dart in the neck before he could release the shaft. Dropping the bow he grabbed at the dart, all the while falling to his knees, the deadly poison quickly doing its work.

The Sharneen ducked behind the horse's head as the arrow from the other bowman came whistling by, narrowly missing his shoulder, but his own bolt struck true, skewering the young man through the throat. Uthgil never missed.

The leader of the group of thieves swung his sword at the side of the horse hoping to take the assassin in the leg, but Uthgil pivoted the horse towards the warrior and the brigand's sword struck the horse in the neck. Whinnying in pain, the horse fell to its knees just as Uthgil leaped from the animal's back, landing on his side and rolling to his feet with the crossbow in his right hand.

The Sharneen assassin spun the small weapon, firing the second bolt into the warrior while whirling around and side stepping the spear tip as its wielder lunged forward. Uthgil felt the wind from the thrust on his face, but he never slowed. Dropping the crossbow he drew one of his knives and stepped into the spearman so quickly that the man didn't even have time to draw his spear back. He brought the blade across the spearman's abdomen and then back across his chest as he spun away to engage the swordsman.

The young swordsman stared at the Sharneen, eyes wide with fright. Then he turned and ran for the brush. Reaching to a wrist, the Sharneen flung a dagger side armed at the fleeing man, the move so fast that even if you were looking right at him you'd barely notice it. The dagger struck the man in the back, causing him to stumble forward at the side of the road.

Uthgil looked around to make sure that everyone else was down. Then he started walking toward the doomed swordsman. The man was moaning in pain and struggling to crawl forward across the muddy road. Uthgil reached down, grabbing the man's hair on the back of his head. He pulled back hard, bringing his razor sharp knife across the man's exposed and tightly arched neck. There was a release of pressure and the sound of blood splattering the ground. The young thief instantly stopped moving, his blood draining quickly from his body. Uthgil released the man's hair, dropping his face into the bloody mud, and turned to face the carnage, using his cloak to wipe the crimson from his blade.

"That warms the blood," he said, a smile of pleasure transforming his face.

One

A Calling

Jonas, cavalier to the goddess Shyann, led the warriors increasingly further from the city of Finarth. Mounted on Tulari, the magnificent horse given to him by Shyann, he led the men through the tall grass of the Finarthian hills. The cool winds from the north were brisk, but tolerable, and created an ocean of green waves in the gentle hills. Far ahead lay the thick forests of the Tundren Mountains, whose snow covered peaks, resembling giant fangs bursting from the earth, were clearly visible even at the immense distance.

Tulari could travel long distances without tiring, as could Kormac. Kormac was the mount of Taleen, cavalier to the god, Bandris, and she had been with Jonas ever since the fight with the Greever, the demon sent by Malbeck to kill him. She had arrived just in time, and together, along with Kiln, they were able to defeat the powerful demon.

Fil's horse, however, though strong and powerful, did not have the god endowed power of the cavalier mounts, and needed to rest. Nevertheless, their pace was strong and they had made good time over the last few weeks. As they neared the Tundrens, the grasslands began to melt into sporadic pockets of trees which eventually gave way to a thick growth of colossal timber.

Jonas, on Tulari, led the procession. Fil followed closely behind, with Taleen bringing up the rear. They had been riding hard all day, but now, later in the evening, they led their horses at a more leisurely pace, their riders pulling their cloaks around them hoping for some protection against the brisk evening air. Jonas, as well as Fil and Taleen, were lost in thought as he led his comrades toward the Tundrens. They were on a mission, sanctioned by Shyann herself, to find and save King Kromm of Tarsis.

13

Jonas's mind drifted from event to event, thinking about all that had recently happened. Soon after the army of Lord Moredin was defeated at the Lindsor Bridge, Jonas had received a calling from Shyann. He was instructed to go to Tarsis, in all haste, and find the warrior king. It was a task he eagerly embraced. Tarsis had been destroyed and the city's king and army had scattered into the outlying areas. Taleen, a second rank cavalier, was asked by Shyann to accompany him on this important task.

As far as they knew, they were the only two remaining cavaliers. This possibility had not been lost on Kiln, the new war commander of Finarth. He had, in fact, complained about losing these two powerful warriors, though he knew their mission must be of grave importance if Shyann sanctioned it. Kiln and the new king of Finarth, King Baylin Gavinsteal, had the formidable task of preparing Finarth for a siege, a siege that would be brought to them by Malbeck the Dark One, who, by all accounts, was now marching his army from Tarsis to Finarth, the last remaining stronghold in the East. The battle with Moradin's army was just a prelude to what was coming. Malbeck would destroy the holdings and towns alike along the southern path to Finarth. This conquest and the winter snows would surely slow him, giving Finarth plenty of time to prepare. Or so they hoped.

King Uthrayne Gavinsteal, Baylin's father, had been murdered by his own adopted son, Prince Nelstrom, who had become an agent of Naz-reen and a follower of Malbeck. The poor boy had been compromised long ago by the treachery of the Forsworn, their dark designs slowly poisoning him until he was nothing but a shell of his former self. He was also Kiln's real son, although few knew that. Jonas had defeated the demon prince, but not before Nelstrom had managed to slit the king's throat while he slept.

Now the throne was being guarded by his only remaining son, Baylin Gavinsteal, who had been captured, tortured, and nearly killed by Moredin's forces. Jonas, Kiln, and Alerion, the king's wizard, had been teleported into Lord Moredin's tent, where they had killed the occupants, including Lord Moredin himself, and succeeded in their mission to rescue the tortured prince. He had suffered grievous wounds, wounds that left more than just physical scars. Prince Baylin had lost his manhood, the flesh cut off by a Dykreel cleric, one that was now dead, dispatched by Jonas's swords.

There was no denying it now. Malbeck was back, and he had in his possession the Shan Cemar, a powerful elven book that contained secret words of magic, ancient words of power that enabled the one possessing it to access the power of the Ru'Ach, the energy of all things. No one knew how they would defeat this mighty army, nor how they would counter the magic of the Shan Cemar, but they had to try. Jonas had been told that King Kromm would be needed to defeat the Dark One, so he would do his best to find him.

The sun was beginning to set so Jonas slowed his mount, pausing by a small stand of low lying trees. He shivered from the cold as the shadows of darkness began to creep along the green grass. "Let's set up camp for the night," he said as he surveyed the terrain. He scratched his head, and was again surprised at his baldness. During his fight with the demon prince he had been badly burned. Taleen had healed him but his hair had hung in patches, so Taleen had shaved him clean. It felt strange under his hand, but already he could feel the stubble of new growth.

"Looks like a good place," replied Fil, as he moved his tired horse next to Jonas.

They all dismounted and took off their bed rolls and packs. As Taleen dismounted she asked, "Anyone up for a warm meal?"

"Aye, that would be nice," Fil said as he stretched his tired back.

Jonas and Fil gathered some dry wood and started a fire while Taleen prepared a meal of beans, slices of cheese, and several pieces of milt, a hard bread often used to feed soldiers since it could last weeks before spoiling.

The fire felt good, and the food was hearty and nourishing. Jonas looked up from his clean plate and gauged the descent of the sun. It was almost eclipsed by the dark peaks, but there was still enough light to see.

"We still have some sunlight left, would anyone like to spar?"

"I'm tired, Jonas. Don't you ever like to rest?" asked Fil.

"I rested the first fourteen years of my life." Jonas smiled, "Come, Fil, let's see how well Master Morgan has trained you."

"*I'd* be happy to cross blades with you, Jonas," Taleen said, standing up smoothly.

Fil looked at the two cavaliers, smiled, and shook his head. "Fine!" he said, reluctantly leaving the warmth of the fire to join them.

They walked into a grassy clearing and drew their swords, the rasping sound of steel sliding on steel echoing in the quiet evening air. Fil grabbed his shield since he had been primarily trained in formation fighting. He noticed Jonas's amused look when he grasped the heavy shield in his left hand.

"Well, you have two swords. Seems fair to me," Fil laughed.

Jonas smiled confidently. "Flat of the blade…one strike to the body, or two to an appendage?" he asked.

"Okay, but you better not cut me," Fil declared, turning to face Jonas while Taleen stood to the side to watch and wait her turn.

"Well if I do, I know a few people who can heal you," Jonas laughed.

"Very funny," Fil retorted, lunging forward with his sword, hoping to catch Jonas off guard. Jonas spun one blade, deflecting the sword easily, the other blade moving in low towards Fil's thigh. But Fil's shield was there to meet it. Their swords came together repeatedly, the clashing sound of metal on metal sounding out of place in the quiet wilderness. It wasn't long before Jonas scored a hit. Fil swung his sword hard in a downward chop. Jonas, quicker than thought, stepped to the side, both swords striking out, one low toward Fil's ankle, and one high toward Fil's head. Both blades tapped him firmly as he stumbled forward. They did little harm other than a small bruise on the side of his head.

"Not bad, Fil, you've improved a lot."

"Not enough it would seem. You've learned a lot from Kiln, haven't you?"

"I have. He is incredible."

"Did you ever defeat him?" Fil asked with interest.

"No, although I have scored a few light hits. Kiln said that I am good enough to earn the master mark, and yet I could not defeat him. But there would be many minutes of sparring before he could find an opening, something of which I am rather proud."

Taleen moved in to take Fil's place. "Kiln has had many years to perfect his skills; you are still young, just twenty winters. You have many years left to practice," she said.

"I guess you are right, Taleen. That is just what Kiln said," Jonas replied, lifting up his swords.

"In time you may even surpass him," she said, raising her sword at the ready.

The thought seemed impossible, but then again Jonas had experienced many things that had at first seemed impossible and yet had happened. Maybe in time, he could become that good. Jonas tucked the thought away, concentrating on their bout.

They circled each other slowly before Jonas stepped in with an offensive attack. Taleen parried his strike easily, launching an attack of her own. They traded blow for blow for several minutes. Taleen was more skilled than Fil, but that was to be expected since she had trained much longer. She was quicker, and had excellent defensive skills. Her experience in battle made her a difficult opponent for she did not make many mistakes, but after several minutes Jonas saw his opening and exploited it. Jonas noticed that she occasionally overextended herself as she swung her blade from right to left, her balance slightly off as she favored her lead leg. Jonas waited, and then capitalized on her error. She swung her blade as expected and Jonas leaned way back from the attack, but his speed and balance were so perfect that he was able to strike her blade as it came by, causing her to fall forward, slightly off balance.

Jonas, quickly snapping back from his sway like a bent bow, leaped forward and to the side, swatting her back lightly with the flat of his left sword as she stumbled by. Taleen quickly regained her balance and stood up smiling.

"Kiln *has* taught you well," she said, catching her breath.

Jonas smiled at her compliment as he sheathed his blades. "You are skilled, Taleen. I had to hunt for an opening."

"And how did you find it? What did I do wrong?" she asked sincerely.

"Occasionally you overcommit in your right to left attack. You lean too far forward on your lead foot, causing you to be slightly off balance. It was that error that allowed me to strike your sword as it came by, forcing you to stumble forward since you were already off balance. Next time, try to keep some weight on your back leg."

"I will remember that. Thank you for the advice. But why are you sheathing your swords...are you tired already?" she laughed. Jonas smiled and again drew his swords.

They fought for a few more rounds before the sun's light became too dim. At that point, Fil had the fire stoked and was preparing three mugs of tea. Jonas and Taleen sat down around the fire, taking comfort in its warmth, sipping the hot tea.

"How much farther do you think we have to go before we will find King Kromm?" Fil asked.

Jonas glanced up from the mesmerizing flames and swallowed some tea. Their supply of honey was low so it tasted a little bitter, but nonetheless it warmed his body and invigorated his tired muscles.

"Tulari seems to be on a confident course, but I don't know how much further we have to travel. I cannot sense anything yet," Jonas answered.

"Nor I," Taleen added. "But we should be halfway to Tarsis. If King Kromm is moving toward us, then we should be close, maybe several days to a week at the most."

"But we do not know for sure if he is moving toward us. He could have been captured, or could even be holding up somewhere," Fil countered.

"True," Jonas admitted.

"In that case it will be longer. We just have to keep moving," Taleen said, taking a sip from her mug.

They were silent for a while as they enjoyed their tea and the dancing warmth from the fire. Fil broke the silence again.

"Jonas," he hesitated a bit, "do you miss Manson much?"

"Of course, but not so much the town...I miss my mother, and our home." Jonas paused and seemed to drift off in thought as he again gazed at the hypnotic flames.

"What else do you miss, Jonas?" Taleen asked gently, afraid she might be prying.

Jonas looked up at her and answered her softly. "It sounds strange, but I miss my life," he replied sheepishly.

"What? I don't understand. You were a cripple and now you are a powerful cavalier. What is there to miss?" Fil asked incredulously.

"I miss the solitude, and the peace that I had with my mother. My life was quiet. I don't miss being a cripple and I certainly don't miss the pain and ridicule that the people of Manson threw my way, but I miss what I had with my mother. I miss the quiet evenings together, the walks in her garden, and the warm hearth as her rabbit stew boiled above the fire." Jonas paused for a moment looking at Fil. "Does that make sense?"

"Yes, I guess so," Fil answered, thinking about what Jonas had said. "But surely your life is better now."

"Yes, I guess it is," Jonas replied.

"I think I understand, Jonas," Taleen interjected. "Your life was simple and it was mapped out for you. There was naught that you had to think about, but now you hold great power, and that comes with responsibilities, as well as the unknown. You don't know what will happen to you, or your loved ones, and that is unsettling," she finished.

"Yes, you describe my feelings well. Do you ever feel that way?" Jonas asked.

"Of course," Taleen replied. "Sometimes I wish I were a farmer and that my life was more simple; hard, but simple. I wish I had a man to share the warmth of our hearth and I wish I could hear the laughter of our children while I made bread. But then I think of all I can do with my power and it makes me proud. I can leave a beneficial imprint on this world, and I plan to do so. If I am to die, I want to die fighting the evil that threatens us. I don't want to die in a small home with dirty hands from working the fields. I would rather rot in my armor holding my sword than have my crops rot untended in a field because Malbeck's forces marched through and killed everyone."

"You make farming sound so insignificant," Fil said a little sharply. "Our town survived on hunting and farming."

"As did mine, young warrior, I mean no disrespect," Taleen added gently. "I just mean that some people are destined to mold the world, while others simply live within it. We three are the former, and to not embrace our role would simply strengthen our enemies. I will not let that happen, nor will I spend precious moments of my life questioning it. I don't mean to make light of your words, Jonas," Taleen added, glancing across the fire at him. "You are young. You should question things as all young people do, as I did when I was your age, but rest easily tonight, and every night, knowing that your presence saves lives."

Jonas was silent, taking in her words. After a few moments he spoke again. "How old are you, Taleen?"

Taleen smiled softly. "Surely you were taught not to ask a woman that question."

"I was…just…"

"I have seen twenty nine winters," Taleen interrupted Jonas's mumblings. "It is okay, Jonas, I was just teasing you."

Now it was Jonas's turn to smile. "You are not that much older than we are."

"Nine years is a long time when those years were forged with a sword in your hand and a warhorse beneath you," Taleen said.

"Indeed, I can imagine so," Fil said.

"What about you, Fil, do you miss Manson?" Jonas asked. Jonas and Fil had not been able to talk much since they had been reunited. Events had progressed so quickly that down time to relax and talk had been virtually nonexistent.

"I miss my family. I never even found Cole's body, or the rest of them," Fil paused as he looked away briefly, "the images of their ripped and torn bodies will never leave my mind. I miss the sound of my mother's voice and the smell of my sister's hair. It's the things that seemed so mundane that I miss the most." Fil wiped a tear from the corner of his eye. "It's a weird feeling when your family is no more. It's like a part of you died with them. Sometimes I wonder who I am. So yes, Jonas, I do miss Manson."

"Home has a strong pull within us all," Taleen said softly.

"We will just have to make a new home," Jonas said gently, smiling at Fil and Taleen.

Taleen met his smile with her own. The glow of the fire brought out the whiteness of her teeth, and gave a warm iridescence to her amber hair. Jonas could not keep his eyes off her, and he did not try. Their eyes met, lingering for a moment before she glanced away, nudging a stick into the fire.

***

Hagar yanked again at the heavy chain that held him, the sturdy iron links clashing together making a harsh sound in the quiet clearing. The chain would not give. It was so strong and securely attached to his manacles that even Hagar's immense strength was not enough to break the chain or dislodge it from the stout cart to which it was attached.

Hagar was an ogrillion, half ogre and half orc. He knew nothing about his father and very little about his mother. An adult ogrillion was twice as tall as a man and their thick skin was like leather with bony plates covering much of their body, giving them a natural defense against most bladed weapons. Their facial features were usually a blend of the two races, large bony heads sat atop even wider necks, big misshapen noses, deep set eyes hiding under shelf-like brows, and sharp teeth that could rend flesh from bone. Like both ogres and orcs, they were fearsome in battle and evil in nature, hating all and killing without question. Hagar, however, was an exception. As big and powerful as any ogrillion, he could fight if necessary, but he did not enjoy causing pain. He was quiet and gentle, his evil appearance not reflecting what he felt in his heart.

When he was young, maybe ten winters, he ran away from his ogre clan. He was never sure of his age, his reckoning of time different than humans. Things were bad for him there; he was beaten and used, made to do menial tasks beneath the pure bloods. He knew at a young age that he did not fit in with the fearsome creatures that surrounded him. Instead, he chose to live alone in the wilds, away from those of his kind.

Life was not easy. Hagar struggled to learn to survive in the wilderness alone. He ate berries, dug up roots, and scavenged dead animals. Eventually he grew to love the woods, as well as the creatures living there. Unlike his own kind, they let him be and did him no harm.

Through trial and error, Hagar learned to throw stones with immense power and accuracy, enabling him to fell deer, elk, and wild boar. This allowed him the luxury of having fresh game to eat, though having never learned to make fire, he was forced to eat it raw. Their furs and hides kept him from freezing in the winter and his naturally tough constitution and thick skin made the bitter cold bearable. Hagar was dirty and haggard in appearance, and had the look of a terrible beast, but inside he was gentle and lonely. He did not feel the bloodlust that was so apparent with his brethren. Hagar was an anomaly.

He grew tall and strong but never learned real language since he had no one to talk with. He remembered a few words in ogrish, but most of those disappeared from his mind as time went on. He could say his name; that was one thing he hadn't forgotten.

Slave traders had captured him several suns ago, by Hagar's limited reckoning. He had seen humans before, at a distance, and typically avoided the trading caravans that sometimes traveled through the forests in which he lived. The slavers came into the forests looking for ogres, but this time they came across Hagar instead. Ogres were often used as slaves in the diamond mines around Mt. Ule. Their immense strength and small brains made them powerful and useful servants, but they had to be watched carefully, and their will had to be beaten down until they were mindless laborers. The slavers were good at that.

Hagar had already been beaten several times, the slavers starting the slow process of crushing his will until eventually he would become a mindless worker. The thick leather whip barely penetrated his tough skin, but it did sting. It wasn't long before they had moved on to long flexible staves capped with heavy balls of iron. The slavers could swing the 'clubs' from a distance, the flexible wood sending the heavy ends smacking into his flesh with painful thuds. They hurt, and Hagar's body was covered with welts and bruises.

Hagar was not an intelligent creature, but he could comprehend basic truths, like knowing that these men were bad, for they had hurt him, and that they were hurting the other human slaves they had captured. There were four carts, three filled with a handful of humans, women and men both, and the fourth filled with supplies and provisions. They were all chained to the bars and only let out once a day to eat and relieve themselves in the woods. Hagar couldn't count, but he knew that there were as many slavers as he had fingers and toes. Anger did not come to him easily, but his beady eyes narrowed intensely every time he saw one of the slavers. A low ominous growl rolled out between razor sharp teeth every time the slavers whip, or stave, came close to him. The urge to inflict harm was not a normal feeling for him, and he struggled with the emotion every time he saw a slaver treating their captives cruelly or come near him.

The procession had stopped to make camp for the evening. As the sun began to set, a handful of the slavers were already cooking their meals over the open flames of their fires. They stayed behind, eating their meals and preparing the parties food while the rest of the men had split up into groups and gone off into the woods to hunt while there was still some light. The men ranged in age from their early twenties to their fifties. Some were ex-soldiers who had seen hard times. Others were wandering vagrants finding work where they could. Some were even criminals running from the law in Finarth, Tarsis, and Cuthaine. They were men who had seen hard times and did not expect anything to be handed to them, so they learned early on that you had to take what you wanted. And that was what they did.

Four of the men at the fires finished their meals, got up, leaving the others to finish the cooking, and approached Hagar who was chained and leaning against a large oak tree. They wore mismatched pieces of plate mail, leather armor, and chainmail. They looked like poor and unkempt mercenary soldiers who seemed to take little pride in their appearance. Hagar growled as they drew near, his large chest emanating a powerful warning. They were laughing and pointing at him in jest, and although he could not understand their words, their meaning was clear enough. One of the humans, a short squat man with curly red hair and several missing teeth, threw him an old stale loaf of bread. The bread hit Hagar in the head and the men laughed. Hagar narrowed his eyes in anger, but he was hungry; he reached out and grabbed the dirt covered loaf, eating it in two big bites.

Soon tiring of harassing the ogrillion, the slavers turned their attention to the wagon to which Hagar had been chained. The wagon held a large cage made with thick bars of wood lashed together by boiled leather strips. Inside, seven human males and three females were chained to the interior of the prison. They were all dirty and their simple clothes were in disarray from their long forced journey. The four men sauntered over to the wagon. The red haired man, who had thrown the loaf at Hagar, then reached into the cage, grabbing a young female by the hair. He pulled her head back hard against the wood bars. Hagar could not understand the words but he recognized the girl's fright as she screamed and cried.

"Ello my pretty," the red haired man hissed through clenched rotten teeth. He yanked her hair back harder, aligning the side of her face with his own. He ran his tongue across her cheek and she screamed with fear and disgust. "I've been eyeing you for a week. Tonight is your lucky night."

"Leave me alone!" she yelled.

One of the men in the wagon struggled to protect the girl but his chain allowed for little movement.

"Leave her alone. She has done nothing to you," the man said sternly.

"No…but she soon will. Sarin, open the door and unlock this pretty."

"With pleasure," Sarin replied, moving toward the wagon. Sarin, a skinny middle aged man, wore chain mail over worn wool leggings and an equally ill kept tunic. A broadsword and dagger dangled from his hip. His long, dark, and greasy hair, framed a thin, bearded face with high cheekbones. An overbite with large front teeth gave him the appearance of a weasel. Sarin lifted himself into the wagon, and unlocked the girl's shackles from the chain. Roughly he grabbed her by her hair, dragged her out of the wagon, and threw her to the ground.

The girl was young, no more than eighteen winters, and very pretty. Old tattered leggings did little to hide her shapely legs. Likewise, her dirty cotton blouse, thin and worn, was not effective at covering her feminine attributes. Her face was strong and narrow, more angular than soft looking, a face that could melt you with a smile but still somehow radiate a sense of underlying strength. Her bright green eyes shone with life, contrasting sharply with her otherwise bedraggled appearance.

She landed hard, but quickly regained her footing, standing up to face the four men. Frightened eyes were looking upon the men as a child might look at a monster in the darkness, but there was something else behind those scared eyes, something strong, and deep, a defiance that she was not yet aware of, like a burning ember waiting for air to fuel it to open flames.

"Stay away from me!" she screamed, backing up slowly. The four men easily surrounded her, leaving her no place to go.

One of the slavers, a heavy set man wearing black leather armor and matching breeches with several holes, spoke up, "Landers, if you hurt her or bruise her face, Korgan will have your tongue."

"That is why you will hold her down. We shall all have our fun. We shouldn't have to hurt her then," the red haired man replied. "What do you think, boys?"

Sarin leered at the lovely prisoner with lust in his eyes. "Aye, I'll savor the young lass, but let's hurry before Korgan comes back from his hunt."

The fourth man was young, maybe twenty winters. He looked around uncertainly. He wore padded leather armor, metal shoulder guards, and forest green breeches. Like his companions, he looked as if he had stolen bits and pieces of other's armor, randomly attiring himself, which is exactly what they had all done.

"I don't know. What if Korgan comes back?" he asked.

"Tyvol, when are you going to grow up and act like a man? There is a perfectly good woman here, in fact, she is better than good. My bet is she will be sold as a whore to some wealthy merchant at Stonestep. When will you ever be able to afford a warm piece of flesh like this? Take advantage of it now," Landers advised.

The young slaver looked agitated and unsure. He glanced to Glave, the heavy set slaver, searching for some confirmation.

Glave, looking about nervously, nodded his head. "Okay, let's take her behind the tree." The three men glared at Tyvol with their unspoken challenge.

Finally the young man broke down. "Okay. Let's be done with it," he said reluctantly.

The young girl crouched defensively as the men advanced, fear constricting her voice. "Leave me alone! Stay away from me!"

"We won't hurt you, lass, we are going to make you feel real good." Sarin's voice was hoarse with anticipation as he reached out to grab her. But she surprised the skinny man by stepping into him and kicking him as hard as she could in the groin. Sarin groaned in pain, falling to the ground just as Glave wrapped his arms around her from behind.

In their excitement they had forgotten about Hagar who was behind them watching the whole event play out. Hagar lacked higher intelligence, but their intent was quite clear to him. The girl was young, and most likely had done nothing to the men, as he had done nothing. Growling, he stood up from the tree. The chain used to bind him to the cart was long and the excess was wound up on the ground by the men. Hagar pulled the excess chain toward him as the fat human grabbed the screaming girl. He pulled the chain tight, lifted it in the air, and with immense strength, flung the thick chain into the red headed man's face.

Landers, seeing the chain rise in the air, was about to yell a warning when the heavy metal links came crashing into his chest. Flying backwards he slammed into the side of the wagon. Hagar began pulling on the chain again until he had several feet of the links in his hands. One big stride put him right behind the heavy set man just as the man was turning to face him. Hagar, wrapping the loose chain around Glave's neck, easily lifted him into the air. Glave's eyes opened wide with shock and fear. He dropped the flailing girl to the ground, choking as the chain links tightened. The chain was thick, about as big around as Glave's wrist, but Hagar's powerful arms easily cinched the links tight around his neck. It only took a few seconds before they heard a sickening crunch of bone and Glave's body went limp. Hagar flung the man easily aside, and reached down to pick up the young girl. She screamed in fright. But when Hagar gently set her behind his broad body to protect her, she realized what he was doing and stopped screaming.

Tyvol and Sarin both stepped away from the dangerous Ogrillion as Landers slowly got up from the ground. His right arm was hanging useless at his side and his face was a mask of pain as he regained his footing.

"He broke my shoulder," the red haired slaver moaned, his face ashen in shock.

"Well, he killed Glave! What should we do?" Tyvol wailed.

A commotion down at the camp alerted the men that their mishap had not gone unnoticed. A handful of slavers led by a tall blonde warrior wearing shining banded mail briskly made their way toward them. The leader wore a long sword and short dagger at his belt, both of high quality. He strode over to the wagon with an air of strength and authority, his long forest green cloak billowing behind him. His clear blue eyes sparkled against his tanned skin.

Hagar was crouching, holding his muscled arms out wide, ready for any attack. He felt the young girl behind him, one of her hands gently touching his thick leg. The tall blond warrior stood before the beast, his blue eyes scanning the scene quickly before landing on the red haired man that Hagar had injured.

"Let me guess, Landers, your loins were in need of attention and you thought to take advantage of my departure?"

"I was going to do what every man here is thinking. Come on, Korgan, you have no right to take away our spoils," Landers mumbled, grimacing from the pain in his shoulder.

"First of all, Landers, they are not *your* spoils. They are mine, and they are mine because you are too stupid to know that if this young girl is raped or harmed in any way then I will not be able to sell her as a palace slave. I will be forced to sell her to the common brothels for a pittance of what I could have received."

"Money that WE will not see, money that we should..."

Suddenly Korgan's arm shot forward and a small dagger appeared in Lander's throat, cutting off his next word. Lander's eyes reflected shock and disbelief as he spit up blood and stumbled to his knees. He then fell face first onto the ground, a crimson pool surrounding his head. Everyone stared at the body for several seconds in silence.

"Does anyone else have the desire to sample the flesh from this young lady?" demanded Korgan. The rest of the slavers looked away, saying nothing.

"Now, this is quite a sight…an ogrillion protecting a young human. He should be eating her, not helping her. Cully, do you have the crossbow?" Korgan asked.

"Yes sir," replied a tall warrior moving up to Korgan with a short small crossbow in his hand. Korgan took the crossbow as Cully drew a short dart from a quiver strapped to his thigh. The dart was shorter than a man's forearm and tipped with a razor sharp point. Cully then took out a small metal container with a cap. He unscrewed the cap carefully, dipping the dart into the vessel. Withdrawing the tip from the container, he handed the dart to Korgan. The silver tip was now coated with a black sticky substance. Cully, replacing the cap, dropped the metal container back into a small pouch hanging from his sword belt. Korgan, placing the dart laced with the sleeping drought into the crossbow, faced the ogrillion.

Hagar wanted to charge and crush the little humans, but was afraid they would hurt the girl. So he stood his ground growling loudly as the blonde human pointed the tiny weapon at him. The weapon made a light click as Korgan pulled the trigger. The small dart shot from the weapon, hitting Hagar in the chest. Hagar hardly felt it. He looked down at the dart jutting from his body. The weapon had barely penetrated his thick skin and Hagar easily reached up and batted the dart aside. He lunged forward toward the blonde warrior but the long chain connected to his leg went taut, pulling him back hard. Then his vision began to blur and a strange dizziness overcame him. Growling, he shook his head to try and clear it, but it did nothing to help. Stumbling left and right his vision became even more blurred. His eyelids felt heavy and he dropped to his knees, no longer able to hold himself up. He felt the girl rush to him, grabbing hold of his thick arm. She was saying something in his ear but he could not understand it. Then everything went black as he fell face first onto the ground.

"Put the girl back in the wagon," Korgan ordered, spinning on his heal and marching back to camp.

***

The tired trio slept well that night, waking early the next day, eager to get on the road. Shyann had stressed to Jonas the urgency of their mission and they pushed themselves physically to the point of exhaustion. Jonas and Taleen would wake up each morning refreshed and ready to travel, but the long hard days of riding were beginning to take their toll on Fil, who did not have the magical endurance of the cavaliers and their steeds. But he was tough, both physically and mentally, and he did his best to keep up with the two warriors and not complain.

Riding hard that day, they reached deep into the forests that surrounded the Tundren Mountains. Fil was tired and his mind had begun to wander just as his horse came to a stop. Looking up, he noticed that Taleen and Jonas had both stopped and were gazing intently into the thick forest to his left. Fil rode up next to them.

"What is it?" he asked.

"I don't know. Tulari stopped suddenly and acted as if he heard something," Jonas whispered softly. They all paused and listened. Suddenly, from a distance, they heard a faint roar. They had to strain to hear it, but the sound was unmistakable. Something, or someone, had roared in anger, or pain.

"What was that? I do not detect any evil," Taleen said, looking at Jonas uncertainly.

"Nor I," he replied puzzled, looking intently into the dense forest. "It sounds far away. And whatever it is sounds as if it needs help." Jonas looked at Taleen, his gaze lingering for a moment before she nodded at him in confirmation. "Good", he said. "Let's leave the horses. We'll climb that ridge on foot and take a look."

The three dismounted and Fil tethered his horse to a nearby tree. Quickly they began plodding their way up the ridge. It was steep and the dense brambles made the ascent slow going.

Once they reached the top they dropped down a gentle hill before beginning another climb up an even bigger rise. The thick undergrowth gradually gave way to more sparsely growing brush, making the climb a bit easier. As they neared the top, they heard another roar, this time much closer, followed by the sound of human voices. Slowing their pace they crept quietly up to the top of the ridge. At the top they hid behind some trees and positioned themselves to look down into the clearing at the bottom of the valley.

Below them was a caravan of four large carts, each carrying a wooden cage packed with over twenty ragged looking men and women. There were eight oxen and ten horses tied to various trees grazing silently on the forest shrubs and grasses. Scattered throughout the camp were over twenty men, eating at fires, and tending to the animals and slaves.

What drew their attention was a large creature looking similar to an ogre, shackled to a large oak tree. It was roaring and pulling on its chains while the men in the clearing ignored it, going about their evening tasks.

"What is that?" Jonas whispered softly.

"That is an ogrillion, half-ogre, half-orc. Very rare and very dangerous," Taleen answered, gazing down upon the scene.

"Looks like a slave caravan. And by the looks of it those slavers have not just captured that ogrillion. I see at least twenty men and women shackled in those carts," Fil whispered, glancing over at Jonas. "What should we do?"

"Slavery is not illegal outside the Finarthian lands," Taleen stated bluntly.

"But it is wrong, nonetheless," Jonas answered quickly, his hand unconsciously moving to one of his blades.

"Jonas, we have a mission to fulfill. We are outside Finarthian lands and we have not yet entered the lands of Tarsis, therefore those men have broken no laws." Taleen was looking at his hand on his sword hilt. Jonas raised his eyes to meet hers.

"Tell that to those men and women chained to the carts. You know very well that those men will be used to work the metal mines in Stonestep, and the women...well...you know what will happen to them."

"But there are twenty men down there. You want to risk our mission by aiding those slaves?" Taleen asked calmly, not against the idea but unsure if it was the right choice considering the urgency of their mission.

Jonas sighed in frustration, looking away in indecision and gazing back down at the scene below. After a few moments he glanced at Fil.

"What do you think, Fil?" he asked.

"I'm not sure what we can do against twenty men, but I would have a hard time departing knowing what will happen to those people. I would also have a hard time shedding the blood of those men when they have broken no laws." Fil shook his head. "I'm not sure, Jonas."

Suddenly a loud roar broke their train of thought and they all turned to look back down into the clearing. A handful of the slavers had surrounded the ogrillion and they were carrying long whips. The loud snap of the whips rang in the clearing and Jonas cringed, the howl of pain from the ogrillion was like a shot of adrenaline, causing his heart to beat fast with anger. They continued to whip the beast until it was on its knees, no longer struggling to break the chains. They were playing with it, causing the beast to suffer just for fun. The giant creature was moaning in pain, the fight beaten out of him. Jonas could take it no longer.

"I will not sit up here and watch these men beat this helpless beast. No creature, not even an ogrillion, deserves such treatment!" Jonas hissed through clenched teeth as his hand returned to the hilt of his sword.

"Nor will I. What do you have in mind?" asked Fil, now determined to help the people below.

"Okay Jonas, but remember, these men may be simply trying to earn a living. I do not detect the kind of evil that opposes us on this mission," Taleen reasoned.

"I understand that, but what they are doing is still wrong and I cannot sit here and watch. Those men may not be truly evil, like the followers of the Forsworn, but their actions are a start, a small stain on their souls that left unchallenged will grow into the very evil against which we fight. It is our duty to protect those men and women. Are you with me?"

"I am," she sighed. "What do you want to do?"

Jonas looked down into the clearing and saw that the ogrillion was now lying on the ground, either asleep or unconscious.

"We go back and get our horses, ride into that clearing and simply ask the men to release the slaves."

"And why would they do that?" Fil asked incredulously.

"We are cavaliers. They will not want to defy us, or fight us. We must hope that will be enough," Jonas stated calmly.

"And if it's not?" asked Taleen.

"We will have to convince them. They will not want to fight cavaliers, so perhaps we can get them to disband without a fight. Then we free the slaves ourselves."

It took them a while to hike back to their horses and then find the trail that led to the clearing. By the time they neared the camp the sun was almost completely behind the high peaks of the Tundrens. They agreed to use no stealth, making their arrival known by riding directly into the clearing, calmly, and with authority.

Jonas led Fil and Taleen into the clearing. Tulari pushed his way through some brush, entering the camp with Fil and Taleen right behind him. Jonas sat tall and proud on the impressive animal, his armor shining with brilliance. He had the appearance of one of the kings of song and legend. The surprised slavers immediately stopped what they were doing, hesitantly drawing their weapons as the trio boldly rode into their midst. Shocked into silence at the presence of two cavaliers, they looked about, unsure of what to do.

Jonas called on Shyann's magic, and immediately felt the pleasant warmth of it rise up inside him. Bringing forth his light, he let it shine subtly, just enough to show without a doubt who they were, and to hopefully ease the tension reflected in the faces of the slavers. He carefully harnessed more magic, using it to enhance his voice. He had used this skill once before during the battle at the Lindsor Bridge, near Finarth, but it still felt a bit awkward using it. His voice, now loud and powerful, hit each man with force, causing them to step backwards and lower their weapons.

"Who is the leader here?" he asked, gazing at the group. His antlered helm covered his head but there was no hiding his dazzling blue eyes that burned with authority and power at the men congregated around him.

"What brings two cavaliers and a soldier of Finarth into my camp uninvited?" asked a blonde haired man to Jonas's left. Korgan stood up from his fire, moving directly in front of Jonas as his men parted behind him. They still held their weapons in their hands but it was obvious that they were unsure if they would even use them, and Jonas's light seemed to have calmed them, at least momentarily.

The man was obviously not as taken aback by Jonas's power as were his men. Jonas, releasing the magic from his voice, withdrew the light, and looked down at the warrior. The man stood casually, his right hand confidently resting on his long sword.

"What you are doing is wrong, and we have come to ask that you free the slaves and the ogrillion," Jonas announced smoothly as Tulari pivoted from side to side.

Korgan looked at the animal and was clearly impressed, but he stood his ground, returning his gaze to Jonas. "Young cavalier, surely you know that slavery is not illegal here. Besides, many of these prisoners are brigands and thieves and the magistrates of Gildren and Torgar have sentenced them to a lifetime of slavery,"

34

he said firmly, indicating the slave carts to his right. "You have no jurisdiction in this matter, but if you like you may eat with us until you feel the need to depart."

The man spoke well and his cleverness and calm demeanor somewhat flustered Jonas. He hesitated, looking at Taleen for support. She gave him a, *this was your idea* stare that did not go unnoticed by Korgan, his lips curling slightly into a triumphant smile.

"What of the ogrillion?" Jonas asked, returning his gaze to the slave leader.

"An evil beast being sold to the diamond mines at Stonestep. If I were to release it, the animal would attack us and I'd be forced to kill it."

"I sense no evil in him, slave holder," Taleen spoke for the first time.

Korgan raised his shoulders in mock uncertainty. "Cavalier to Bandris, I have never known an ogrillion to be anything but evil. But if you see it best to release it, then so be it, but I will not be responsible for what it does."

Again the canny man had manipulated Taleen into a corner and she did not know how to respond. They were both silent for a moment until a young girl's voice shattered the stillness.

"He is lying! We were taken from our homes and our children and elders were murdered!"

Jonas, jerking his head toward the noise, saw a beautiful young woman from inside one of the cages yelling through the bars. A slaver standing next to her punched her in the face and she fell back into the cage. The other slaves caught her and began frantically yelling at the cavaliers, corroborating her statements with similar stories of murder and capture.

Jonas's eyes flared with anger as he turned to glare at the tall warrior who merely shrugged his shoulders nonchalantly.

"I was hoping you wouldn't have to hear that, but it matters not; slavery is not illegal here and it is against your godly ethics to kill us when we have done nothing wrong. So it is your call, Cavalier, how will this play out?"

"Nothing wrong? You think killing innocent people and masquerading your actions under the absence of law is nothing?" Jonas's voice rose with anger, his eyes panning the group of men facing him.

Korgan had stepped back and away from Jonas, giving him more space. His men spread out and were nervously looking at the three mounted warriors and back to Korgan. Uncertain, they looked to Korgan for leadership, as they always had.

Jonas knew that they were afraid to take on two cavaliers. He did not miss their glances as they looked to Korgan to solve this predicament for them. Jonas also knew that Korgan probably did not want to fight them, but then again he did not know this man, nor did he know his capabilities. Jonas felt he had to act quickly before Korgan did something stupid, causing his men to react in violence.

Jonas made a quick decision. He would use his cognivant powers. He began focusing this magical energy around the man, gradually gathering it in a translucent shell. It took a few moments but he pushed the energy together, compressing it around the warrior, freezing him in place.

The tactic was not difficult for Jonas, but it did take a little time…time that he would not normally have in a fight. Luckily Korgan was not aware of Jonas's use of magic and could not sense the energy coalescing around him, ready to press in on him at Jonas's command. For all he knew Jonas was taking a few moments to weigh his options before he spoke. But as he felt himself constrained and compressed by this invisible force, his eyes widened in shock and fear.

The slavers watched their leader in disbelief. He struggled to move but failed miserably in his attempts. Jonas then easily lifted the man in the air. His men jumped back with fright. Jonas wanted them to see his power, to deter them from raising their blades. If things went well, perhaps they could part ways with no blood shed.

He spun the man in the air so he was parallel to the ground and then he slowly and gently laid the man down on his stomach, while simultaneously speaking to the crowd. Again he used Shyann's power to amplify his words. Her magic made his voice dance around the clearing with tremendous power, and it seemed to drain the tension away from the men. They were listening intently, slowly lowering their weapons.

"None of you will be harmed, nor will your leader. We will free the slaves and the ogrillion and then be on our way. You will do nothing. If you follow us or the men and women we free, we will see it as a threat and be forced to fight, and that will be a fight that you will not walk away from. By the grace of Shyann and the strength of my blades, I will see it so. Am I understood?"

The men all nodded, slowly moving away from the three warriors and clearing a path to the slaves' carts.

"Fil, tie this man's hands and legs," commanded Jonas. Fil dismounted, withdrawing a length of rope from his saddle bag. He proceeded to tie Korgan's feet and hands. When Jonas saw that he was secured he released the energy surrounding the leader.

Korgan immediately began thrashing about, struggling to escape his constraints. He flipped over to his back, lifted his head, and glared at Jonas with undisguised malice.

"You are making a grave mistake, Cavalier. Many of these men have wives and children to feed. These slaves would bring them money to buy food for several months. Now they will go hungry and we will be forced to enslave more people. You have just prolonged the inevitable and doomed the lives of other innocents."

"You may be right, slaver, but no matter how you try to justify it, no good can come from doing evil. Destroying the lives of these men and women," Jonas said as he gestured toward the captive slaves, "to better your own lives will not make the world a better place. This is how evil starts. It grows and festers inside you until it is so colossal that you can no longer control it." Jonas again used Shyann's magic, bolstering his voice so all could hear. Many had sheathed their weapons and were gazing intently at the warrior, listening to his every word. "Slavery is wrong, and it lessens you to participate in it. If you continue on this path, you will be judged, in this life, or the next."

Jonas then quickly pivoted Tulari around, away from the men, and rode over to the ogrillion who was now pushing his wounded body up on one knee. Taleen and Fil followed closely, continuing to scan the slavers, looking for any sign of trouble.

Hagar watched the human ride up to him, but his armor was so shiny that it momentarily blinded him as the last rays of sun reflected of its polished surface. Hagar slowly stood, facing the man on the horse. The animal was so big that it put the human at eye level with the ogrillion. Hagar was in obvious pain from the lacerations on his back, but more than the pain, he felt a fierce anger toward the men who had hurt him.

He growled as the human neared but the ogrillion did not attack. The human held no weapon and there was something about him that diminished his anger. Suddenly the warrior began to glow with a bright white light that pulsed outward from his body, gradually blanketing Hagar. The light stunned him and he was forced to shield his eyes, but it caused him no pain. In fact, it felt warm and rejuvenating. His anger vanished, replaced by a calm feeling of peace. Then, as quickly as it appeared, the light vanished.

"Taleen," Jonas stated. "This ogrillion is not evil. In fact I sense an overwhelming goodness in him. Quite strange really." Jonas seemed bewildered. Taleen rode up next to Jonas, and gazed at the ogrillion.

"That would be rare indeed, but I, too, sense no evil in him." Taleen then pointed at herself and said, "Taleen." Next she pointed at Jonas and said, "Jonas." The ogrillion looked confused but it was obvious that the beast was trying to comprehend Taleen's words. Taleen repeated their names and the ogrillion looked back and forth between them.

Fil ambled over to them, leading his horse by the reins and carrying a set of keys with his other hand. He was moving slowly so as not to startle the ogrillion. As he neared them Taleen pointed at him, stating his name loud and clear. Finally the ogrillion lifted his lips in a smile, if such an expression could be called a smile. His wide mouth was filled with teeth and the expression looked strange, almost evil, the vicious fangs suggesting a hunter who killed for warm flesh. The ogrillion banged his meaty hand against his chest, and in a deep guttural voice he growled, "Hagar!"

Jonas and Taleen replied simultaneously, "Nice to meet you, Hagar," even though they knew the beast probably didn't understand them.

Jonas dismounted, grabbed the keys from Fil, and began to slowly approach Hagar. He held the keys out in front of him, pointing at the beast's manacled foot. Hagar seemed to understood his intent, and stepped his huge foot out so Jonas could free him. Jonas knelt slowly by the beast, intently aware of his own vulnerability. One kick from the powerful ogrillion could kill a man, armored or not, but Jonas felt sure that Hagar was of no danger to him, so he brought his gaze down to the lock, slowly working the key into the mechanism. There was an audible click and the manacle fell away leaving behind a sore and bleeding abrasion on the ogrillion's ankle.

Jonas stepped away as Hagar squatted down, rubbing his sore ankle. He looked up, smiling at Jonas. But then his gaze swung to the slavers, his smiling expression becoming an icy glare. He stood up slowly, and looked as if he were about to charge them.

"No, Hagar! They are not to be harmed!" Jonas ordered. The beast didn't understand his words, but his intent and tone were clear. He looked down at Jonas and seemed to calm down. Jonas smiled at him, and then turned, striding toward the carts with the keys in his hand. As he neared the cages he counted about fifteen young men and women, all dirty and ill-kempt, but otherwise strong and fit. They greeted him with smiles and praise.

"Thank you, sir!"

"Thank you, Cavalier!"

"You saved our lives!"

"Bless Shyann!"

As Jonas unlocked the doors on the carts, the people stepped from their prisons, crowding around him giving their thanks. They turned to Taleen and Fil, thanking them as well, their smiling faces animated with open joy and relief at their new freedom.

The beautiful young girl who had shouted at them earlier approached Hagar as Jonas was remounting Tulari. Hagar looked down at the petite girl as she boldly reached out and touched his thick hairy leg. Hagar moved back a little, unsure of the touch, but the girl did not move away. She reached out her hand toward the ogrillion again, touching his leg a second time. This time Hagar did not move away, and slowly squatted next to her. His massive body dwarfed the girl even while kneeling.

"Thank you, Hagar," was all she said, gently stroking the side of his arm. Hagar smiled broadly, moving his huge hand toward her face. Jonas moved Tulari closer, unsure if it was wise for her to get that close. But the girl did not flinch and Hagar took one of his thick fingers and gently touched her cheek. The touch looked odd, for the same hand that could crush her head in an instant barely grazed her soft face. The girl smiled and Hagar smiled back saying, "Hagar" for a second time. Touching her chest with her hand she said, "Myrell". Hagar, standing up to his full height, repeated her name, this time much louder.

Myrell turned from the smiling beast, and approached her rescuers. The three were all mounted and had been watching the exchange between her and Hagar with interest.

"Thank you very much for intervening. What I said was the truth. These men raided our villages and killed our elders and our children. We are not thieves and brigands as that scum would have you believe."

The girl was young, maybe eighteen or nineteen winters, but she carried herself with the maturity of one much older. She was beautiful, with golden brown hair, which despite its current unkempt state, still shimmered in the sunlight. Her skin was smudged with grime and her clothes hung on her like rags, but her disheveled appearance did little to mask neither her figure nor her beauty.

"You are welcome, Myrell. I am glad that we happened by when we did," replied Taleen.

"The sun is setting. When was the last time you have eaten?" asked Jonas. Myrell looked at Jonas, her dazzling eyes searching his features, and he couldn't help but think how attractive she was. Despite what she had been through, she held herself with pride and dignity, and Jonas did not miss that strength in her stare. Her confidence and poise seemed odd for a young girl born in a mountain village.

"They fed us once a day. We are tired and hungry and I think I can speak for all of us."

"Let us set up camp. I'm sure these men have enough food to feed you well. Let's talk more over full stomachs and a hot fire," Jonas replied warmly.

The slavers wanted no part of the present situation and departed quickly, gathering their meager belongings and riding the horses and carts into the forest. Before they left, Jonas confiscated some clothing, food, supplies, and even weapons for the freed slaves. They would need all the help they could get to move on with their lives. Jonas allowed the slavers to leave with enough to survive until they could get to the nearest settlement.

But he could not free the leader, Korgan, afraid that he would bring the slavers back and attack them in the middle of the night. So he kept him tied up, sitting up against a tree several paces from their warm camp fire. They roasted some of the venison that had been taken from the slavers, and accompanied it with some of their bread. It was hard and stale, but hearty, and it tasted good smeared with the venison fat and juices.

Hagar would not come near the fire but he sat on the ground near Korgan and watched the scene intently. Myrell approached him several times and gave him meat and bread, which he gratefully swallowed in a few big gulps.

After they had all eaten, one of the young men, a short stout villager, spoke first. He looked at the three of them and announced, "My name is Kilius, and I thank you all for saving our lives." The young man had long brown hair and a short scraggly beard. In fact, all the men had facial hair since they had not had the luxury to shave for quite some time. Thick, long eyelashes framed his dark brown eyes, giving his face a slightly feminine look. But his thick and powerfully built body gave him a look of strength and maturity beyond his years.

"You are welcome, Kilius. My name is Jonas and I am a cavalier to Shyann. This is Taleen, cavalier to Bandris, and my friend Fil, soldier of Finarth."

"We owe you our lives," interjected Myrell as she sat sipping from her tin cup. "We were lucky you were near us. If I may ask, what are you doing so far in the Tundrens away from civilization?"

"We are on a mission, Myrell, a mission from Shyann herself. It is very important and we must leave first thing in the morning. I'm sorry that we must depart so soon, but it is paramount that we make haste. What will you do now that you are free?" Jonas asked, wishing that he had more time to help them get to safety.

"I do not know," answered Myrell softly, looking into the flames. The firelight reflected the glistening tears that appeared in her eyes, and the men and women around the fire suddenly became solemn. There was a long uncomfortable pause before Kilius broke the silence.

"Sir, the slavers destroyed our village and killed many people. Most of us do not know which, if any, of our family members survived the raid."

Jonas did not miss the anger lacing his words, nor his glare toward Korgan and his emphasis on the word *most*.

"Kilius, do you know what happened to your family?" Taleen asked softly, obviously coming to the same conclusion as Jonas that maybe Kilius's own family had not survived the raid.

Kilius looked at Myrell, dropping his head sadly. After a few moments he looked up at Taleen with glistening eyes. A lone tear dripped down his dirty face leaving a trail of clean pink flesh.

"Yes, I know. Our father," he said, gesturing towards Myrell, "was the village leader, by blood and deed. Korgan killed him as he was trying to protect our mother. Then he raped her and slit her throat." Kilius's voice was shaking with emotion but he was able to hold back the wave of tears. But he was unable to hold back the look of hatred in his eyes as he glared at Korgan who was sitting at the edge of the firelight. Though visibly shaking with rage, Kilius turned his face to stone as he fought to restrain the urge to leap across the fire and kill the man that had brought him, and the others, so much pain.

"I'm sorry, Kilius. No one should have to bear witness to such an atrocity," Taleen replied softly.

Myrell was crying openly now, but she managed to regain her composure and quickly wiped away her tears. Kilius reached out, briefly touching his sister's hand before returning his gaze to Jonas. His eyes were hard and determined.

"Sir, my sister and I would like to accompany you on your quest. We have nothing left here."

Jonas was just about to respond when Kilius quickly added. "I can fight." Kilius didn't miss Jonas's eyes flicker toward Myrell. "And so can my sister. My father taught us well. We will not be a burden."

Jonas looked down into the fire momentarily before glancing over at Taleen and Fil. They offered no resistance or advice and it was clear that they were leaving the decision to him.

"Sir, my name is Jangar and I too would like to travel with you. My family died long ago and I can fight as well." The man that spoke was older, around forty winters, with a few streaks of gray highlighting his impressive beard. He was powerfully built, with strong square shoulders and thick muscular limbs. A life of hard labor had kept these villagers in shape.

"Before you make this decision, you should know what we face. You may wish to change your minds after you hear of our mission." Jonas's eyes scanned the group as he spoke. They listened intently and Jonas even saw Korgan in the shadow of the fire lean in to hear of their tale. "Malbeck the Dark One has returned. His armies have already taken Tarsis and are now preparing to march to Finarth, the last stronghold in the east. The king of Tarsis is still alive and we've been told he is somewhere in these mountains. Shyann has asked me and my companions to find him and to bring him back to Finarth. He is being pursued by evil minions of the Forsworn and we are his only chance of survival. If you join us, you will be marching toward the greatest evil that has threatened the lands since the great wars. You may very likely be marching toward your deaths."

There was a pall of silence around the fire as the men and women digested his words. Taleen and Fil looked from person to person as they thought about what Jonas had said. Finally Kilius spoke up again.

"Cavalier, I am not afraid of death. I was taught by my father that no man is worthless, that all men can do something to further the cause of good. Your cause is just, and I would like to be a part of it; however, I will not have my decision influence my sister or the others here. I suggest we all think on it and make the decision by morning."

"Words spoken like a leader, young Kilius. Decisions like this should not be made in haste when anger and revenge still weigh so heavily on your heart," counseled Taleen.

"I agree. Your judgment is sound and full of reason. We will speak of this in the morning. Let us rest now, for we will rise before the sun does and you have some thinking to do," replied Jonas, standing up from the fire, and ending the conversation.

***

Fil opened his eyes slowly as something far away in his mind interrupted his sleep. It was a sound, something out of the ordinary. Slowly he rolled out of his bed-roll and scanned the dark clearing. The previously roaring fire had disappeared, leaving behind a pile of burning embers. The light was minimal but it was enough for him to see Jonas, Taleen, and a handful of the freed slaves lying near the dying fire.

Fil heard the sound again, the sound of bodies shuffling in the tall grass. His eyes adjusted more to the darkness and as he scanned the clearing he saw a few men creeping through the tall grass about fifteen paces away. They were moving away from the fire toward the tree where Korgan was chained. Just as the scene registered in his groggy brain, he heard a yell followed by more sounds of a struggle.

Fill grabbed the short sword that he kept by his side, and hurriedly ran toward the commotion. It was dark, but his eyes adjusted enough to see three men struggling with Korgan while a fourth stood before him with a sword in his hand. Fil wouldn't have seen the blade if the man hadn't turned slightly causing the moonlight to sparkle from the polished surface. Then he understood. Four of the villagers had decided to enact their revenge on the slave trader.

Fil hesitated; he did not know what to do. He would not strike down a villager who was just looking for their revenge. Who knows what atrocities happened to these men and their families at the hand of this slave trader. Fil did not know the details but he assumed that their anger must be insurmountable. But he could not just let them kill the man. That did not seem right either.

Korgan was struggling and yelling furiously, but his chains limited his movement. The three men holding him were hitting him with abandon, but the slaver was tough and he continued to struggle violently against his attackers.

Suddenly a bright light filled the clearing and the men instantly stopped their attack. Fil glanced behind him as Jonas quickly strode forward, his body emanating beams of white light. The men holding Korgan instantly relaxed, as if the light had sucked away all their killing rage. The man with the sword lowered the weapon, his features softening, replaced by calmness that he didn't think possible at that moment. Jonas stepped near the man holding the sword.

"I understand your anger, but you cannot kill him like this," Jonas addressed the men loudly. More of the villagers were now up and moving closer to the scene.

"But sir, you do not know what this man did to our families, you were not there. He deserves to die." The villager that spoke was the same man carrying the sword. He was tall, thin, and middle aged. Jonas had learned that his name was Byranoll.

"Byranoll, you're right. I was not there, but I do understand your anger. My entire village, including my mother, was completely wiped out, massacred by boargs. I do not know what to do with this man, but I do know that if we kill him like this, then we become just like him."

"Sir, everyone here witnessed his atrocities. He would be found guilty in any court, and he would be sentenced to death," Byranoll continued, his voice softening, losing some of its anger under the pressure of Jonas's words and magical light.

"You are wrong, slave! We are in frontier lands, lands that are not under dominion of either Tarsis or Finarth! In these lands the strong survive, and that is me!" Korgan was yelling loudly, his bloody and bruised face contorted in killing rage. "You are nothing, and under frontier law I have every right to impose my strength on those beneath me!"

Suddenly, Korgan bolted forward unexpectedly, there being enough slack in the chain to allow some limited movement. The man holding the sword, caught by surprise, didn't have time to react before Korgan grabbed his wrist, slamming his other fist into Byranoll's stomach. Byranoll pitched forward as Korgan ripped the sword from his grip. Korgan, quick as a cat, reversed the momentum of the sword in one smooth motion, and brought the razor sharp edge down on Byranoll's neck.

Jonas screamed as Korgan attacked. The surprise move was so quick that he didn't have time to react. No one did. Byranoll's head separated from his body, his blood spilling across the forest grass.

The other two villagers were closest and they reacted first, simultaneously leaping forward to grab the slaver. But the man

46

was a whirlwind. As one of the villagers reached for him, Korgan shot his foot out like a kicking mule. The man flew backward as his friend simultaneously tried to grab the swordsman. Korgan, ducking under his reach, sliced the sharp edge of the blade across the villager's belly, spinning away quickly as the villager fell to the ground, moaning in agony.

Korgan had turned to face Jonas and Fil when an arrow suddenly flew from the surrounding darkness, burying itself halfway to its fletching in the slaver's forehead. Korgan's eyes crossed momentarily trying to see the arrow that had pierced his brain. He fell to his back, the stillness of death embracing him.

Everything had happened in a matter of seconds. Fil and Jonas ran forward to see if the other villager was dead. It only took Jonas a few seconds to see that the man's wounds could not be healed. His bowels had been completely cut in half destroying too many of his vital organs. His blood had soaked the ground and even if Jonas could heal the wounds, the loss of blood would surely kill him anyway. The dying man moaned in pain, rolling briefly on the ground before losing consciousness. As his blood pooled around him, death rescued him from his agony.

Jonas, briefly stunned, was angry at himself for not seeing the attack coming. Frustrated and saddened, he stood up and glanced behind him, looking for the bowman. His body, still glowing, allowed him to clearly see many of the villagers standing at the edge of his magical light. Jonas caught their expressions and followed their gazes to Myrell, who was standing calmly with one of the slaver's bows in her hand and a quiver on her back. Her face was hard and impassive.

"That's justice," she said, her eyes devoid of emotion.

Jonas said nothing, mostly agreeing with her. He was saddened by all the death. But he could certainly empathize with the villagers and Myrell's action. Not knowing what else to do, he simply walked away.

Two

The Hunters

G ullanin stood before Balzrig, war leader of the Gould-Irin orcs, and was amazed at the sheer size of his creation. Orcs were known to be strong and thick of limb, but Balzrig was a Gould-Irin orc. Using the magic of the Ru'Ach, Gullanin had created him to be significantly larger and stronger than his cousins. He was even larger than the other fifty Gould-Irin orcs that stood behind him. Balzrig, several heads taller than a big man, towered over Gullanin, who looked frail and pitiful in comparison. But Gullanin had created the Gould-Irins to be submissive to him, and to serve him without question. When Gullanin looked up at his warrior, Balzrig would did not make eye contact.

That is good, thought Gullanin, *he knows his place.*

The huge war leader wore enchanted plate mail, and in the center of his chest plate was the embossed image of Gould's white eye. His long arms, bare and muscular, ended in large clawed hands protected with steel gauntlets. A skirt of banded steel hung to mid-thigh, his large muscled legs protruding from it like thick tree trunks. Balzrig's shins were covered with steel greaves and his huge feet were encased in sturdy leather boots wrapped with bands of steel. His wide neck, nearly as thick as his thighs, supported a knobby and bony head, and though more or less human in shape, the resemblance ended there. His massive square jaw filled with long yellow teeth, his pig like nose, and his mane of greasy black hair that grew all the way down his neck to the base of his muscled back, gave him a distinctly animal-like appearance. Strapped to his broad back was a huge two handed sword and a quiver of black arrows, each as thick as his thumb. In his right hand he held a short black curved bow, the stained wood as thick as a human wrist, tapering to two re-curved ends that had been capped with human bone and carved into points. The bow was shorter and stockier than a woodsman's bow; it looked more like a cavalry bow, but much thicker and heavy in appearance. All in all, when compared to their smaller cousins, the Gould-Irins looked more human. The other fifty Gould-Irin orcs, though similarly outfitted, did not possess Balzrig's great size or power.

Crouched behind Gullanin were the Hounds of Gould, three beasts spawned from the blood of the recently murdered high priests to the Forsworn. Gullanin chuckled to himself thinking about the gruesome role he played in their destruction. He had simply followed Malbeck's orders and slit their throats as they were immobilized by his master's magic. He did enjoy it though. The three priests had always competed for dominance, and it wouldn't have been long before the power struggle turned into all out violence. With three easy strokes from his knife he had eliminated his only threats, making him Malbeck's right hand man in the struggle of the Forsworn to dominate Kraawn. Gullanin had a long history with Malbeck. He knew him originally as Malbeck Dysander, ruler of Banrith and conqueror of all the lands north of the Lyre River. Gullanin's father had served Malbeck's father as his court wizard, and Gullanin, following in his father's footsteps, as was typical of court wizards, became the next court wizard after his father's death. No one, not even Malbeck himself, knew that Gullanin had killed his own father so that he could take his place prematurely. Gullanin, even at the young age of thirty, had surpassed his own teacher and father in the art of magic. His thirst for power even surpassed his love for his father. But that love was minimal at best, and their relationship was primarily based on their service to their lord, Malbeck's father, King Brandus Dysander, who by all accounts was a decent man and an even better king. But the same could not be said for his son, who, after his father's death, began the downward plunge into becoming the man, the king, who had plagued his kingdom in wars, taxes, and slavery. Gullanin, whose temperament and lust for power paralleled Malbeck's, became his right hand man in these endeavors. When Malbeck sold his soul to the Forsworn, Gullanin did the same, and together they strived for more power. Magic, combined with the power of the Forsworn, kept them alive well past the average lifespan of a human, but it all came with a cost. Malbeck became the Dark One, changed into half man and half demon, and after his defeat during the Great War, Gullanin stopped at nothing to try and bring his lord back. After hundreds of years, nearly a thousand in total, he had finally succeeded. Now they were at it again. This time it would end differently.

The hounds, each the size of a large bull, stood on four thick legs ending in dragon-like paws tipped with three curved claws, as black and shiny as obsidian, each as long as a man's middle finger. Strong and razor sharp, they were capable of rending steel. The beasts' legs twitched with anticipation, waiting for the orders to begin the hunt. They growled menacingly, a deep low rumble which caused the orcs to shift uneasily. Baring their razor sharp teeth they looked to the dense forest, the draw of the hunt and the smell of their prey causing them to salivate, thick spittle dripping slowly from their gaping jaws.

Gullanin absently thumbed the amulet hanging around his neck. It was this magical talisman, given to him by Malbeck, which enabled him to control the hounds. He was thankful for that, for he felt that these demon hounds would rip him to pieces if they had the chance. Perhaps there were remnants of the three priests left in some part of their brains. Indeed, there were times when he felt that they eyed him knowingly, as if waiting for him to make a mistake, so they could tear him to shreds and consume his flesh.

Gullanin pushed the thought away, turning his attention to his war commander. "Balzrig, are you ready to serve me?"

Balzrig continued to stare straight ahead, avoiding eye contact with his master. "Yes, my Lord, what are your commands?" Balzrig's voice was gravelly and deep, some of his words difficult to understand through his tooth filled mouth.

"You are to follow the demons into the mountains, and find the king of Tarsis and destroy him. Can you keep up with the hounds?"

Gullanin saw Balzrig's beady yellow eyes glance toward the beasts for a quick second. "Yes, master, we can run all day and night."

"Good," replied Gullanin, turning his back on his Gould-Irin, and facing the hounds. "I will be traveling with you, but you will not see me. Do you understand?"

"Yes, Master."

Gullanin knew that the orc probably didn't fully understand, but he was trained well and he did not question his master.

Gullanin, holding the magical amulet in one hand, whispered his commands to the beasts. *You may hunt now, search for your prey and destroy him. Make sure the orcs can follow your trail.* As Gullanin's thoughts drifted to the hounds, he momentarily felt them collide with the demons' minds. The sensation repulsed him and he unconsciously stepped backwards a few paces. Their demonic thoughts quickly wrapped around his brain, stroking his mind with tendrils of suffocating hatred. Their thoughts, dark and heavy with despair, were filled with hatred for him and everything around them. He heard them whisper.....*Yesssss......*and then the connection was broken. Their mental touch had lasted only moments, but it left a foreboding stain of darkness deep within him. He shook it off and watched the hounds leap into the trees, disappearing into the dark forest with incredible speed. They sprang from one shadow to another, Gullanin barely able to follow their movements.

Lifting his right hand he pointed after them. "Go, Balzrig, do not lose the trail," he ordered. Balzrig simply nodded his head and bounded down the hillock with long powerful strides. The rest of the Gould-Irin followed, the only sound being the rhythmic pounding of their boots as they disappeared into the forest.

Gullanin smiled as he turned around to look at the smoldering city of Tarsis. He could hear the thousands of orcs and goblins howl and scream as they continued to loot the mighty city. The sun had just set and he could see dancing campfires spring up all across the grasslands before the burning city. Smoke and fire still rose into the night air days after the city's destruction. Tarsis was a large city and it would take days to loot it and burn it to the ground. There were still remnants of the Tarsinian army roaming the countryside, but they were small, dispersed groups without any form of leadership. The surprise attack on their city was so complete that they barely had time to prepare for battle before Malbeck's army destroyed them.

Malbeck, using the power of the Shan Cemar, was able to move his entire army under the cover of a sinister fog, a mist that masked their visibility as well as any noise they made. The Tarsinian scouts who had got caught in the evil mist were suffocated by the toxic miasma. Gasping for air, they inhaled the vile fumes, which burned their eyes and lungs as they died in agony.

With the scouts dispatched, there was no one to warn the garrison that Malbeck's forces were so near. Silently his army marched to the city's gate in the middle of the night. Malbeck then sent the evil mist into the walled city itself, killing any guards who were no doubt diligent at their posts. The mist, being a short term weapon, slowly dissipated as the magic shaping it unraveled. Despite Malbeck's power, he could not maintain a spell that powerful for too long. He then sent Gullanin himself in to open up the huge iron doors that denied them entrance. Gullanin's magic easily accomplished that task, given the fact that there were no living guards to stop him. With the gate open, the massive army quickly overran the surprised Tarsinian forces, a feat that proved much more costly than expected. Gullanin was grudgingly impressed with the Tarsinian Knights' valor on that night, and the king himself was something to behold. He fought like a mad man, killing any enemy that neared him. He did not tire and not a single orc or goblin could reach him with their blades.

As the fighting commenced throughout the city it became obvious that Malbeck would eventually prevail, and this knowledge did not escape the king and his elite guard whose job was to protect him. They fled through a secret tunnel into the mountains as the city was ransacked and destroyed. No one who remained in the city was left alive. Furious at the king's escape, Malbeck immediately ordered his forces into the woods in pursuit. But the king and his small guard managed to elude the enemy, while small groups of fleeing knights continued to use hit and run tactics against the invaders, giving their king time to retreat further into the Tundrens. At one point in the fight, Gullanin thought he had the king slain, but the annoying Blade Singer intervened, shielding him with magic that deflected his lightning attack. A Blade Singer with the king, that was not to their advantage. But even her skill with a blade, and her magic, would not keep the Hounds of Gould from their prey. King Kromm was a dead man.

***

Dandronis was a farmer turned soldier, a private in the Tarsinian army. Why did they want him to lead? At least that is what he thought as he looked at the fifteen warriors before him. These warriors were all privates; their lieutenant had recently been killed as they tried to evade a patrol of orcs. They escaped the patrol and had been running frantically deeper into the Tundrens. When they felt confident that they had eluded the orcs, they stopped to rest. They knew they needed a new leader and had unanimously chosen him.

Dandronis was a good man, a silent man that people seemed to trust, although he was not sure why. His family had died of the scratch fever, a fever that caused horrible welts that itched immensely, and in the victims' delirium they would scratch their body so frantically that they would soon be covered with bleeding and festering wounds. They would often have to be restrained so they would not claw themselves to death. If the victims managed to survive the fever, they were still likely to die from infection or loss of blood. It was a horrible thing to witness. Dandronis had to watch his wife, son, and daughter succumb to

53

the disease. After that, nothing would satiate his anger toward Shyann, once his goddess. How could she let this happen? Twice a year, on the winter and summer solstices, he had left her corn, barley, and potatoes in thanks for his harvest. Even when food was scarce, he left her something, and this was how she repaid him. He grew solemn and withdrawn, filling his days and nights with drinking and brawling in the town's local tavern. He had no desire to farm, and he could no longer bear to live in his own home. He was falling apart. That was when he decided to join the king's army, a place where he could direct his anger, and focus his energy, to lessen the pain of his loss. That had been four years ago.

Dandronis turned out to be a good soldier. He was strong and an above average swordsman, but his real strength was his courage. He was utterly fearless, and pain for him was just an inconvenience. He had already lost everything he cared about, including his sense of self. The light inside him had been extinguished, leaving behind a shell of a man who had no interest in making friends, who didn't want anything for himself. Most of the time he was a perfect soldier, hardworking, strong, quiet, fearless, but at times his demons took over and he succumbed to fits of despair and anger that manifested itself in bar room brawls and fights which kept him from being promoted. But there was something about him that commanded respect from the soldiers of his modrig. Somehow they saw him as a leader, *their* leader, and so he was elected.

They all voted for him to lead, a position he did not want. Like everyone else, he didn't know what to do. Things had not gone well for them or their comrades. Two days ago the alarm had been sounded within Tarsis, and thousands of soldiers awoke to find themselves fighting for their lives. They fought furiously to defend themselves and their people, but it was to no avail. Thousands died that night, and the few that didn't barely escaped with their lives. Pockets of resistance formed and fought the orcs and goblins as the beasts chased them into the forests, but nearly all of them perished, and as far as Dandronis knew there were only small groups of survivors left, groups like his own. No one knew what had befallen their king, but they did know that he escaped and he was alive, as of two days ago anyway. They were part of the surviving group that had stayed behind to slow down Malbeck's patrols as their king escaped. There were several hundred of them that were fighting a series of skirmishes against the invaders, but they couldn't hold back the orcs and goblins, and after their officers had been killed they were all forced to split up into smaller groups as Malbeck's army attacked them. It was disorganized, and the chaos forced what was left of the king's warriors farther and farther apart. Their group fought all night until finally the stragglers that were still alive escaped Malbeck's skirmish lines. The question on all of their minds was, now what do we do?

"I am a soldier, I do not want to lead," Dandronis had adamantly announced. Dandronis, tall and lean, wore hardened leather armor over a chain mail shirt, the traditional footman's garb in the Tarsinian army. Covered with the sweat and grime of battle, his overall appearance was haggard. His hair was cut short, almost to his scalp, and his facial hair was also trimmed close, so that he constantly appeared to have several days of growth. Piercing turquoise eyes dominated his face. They had no give in them. Looking into them was like looking at an impenetrable wall of iron, a wall that you could not easily crack. When peopled looked at him they saw something in his eyes that said, *move on, this is not a man to trifle with*. The joy that had once been there had disappeared with his family's lives. His square jaw looked too big for his head, giving his face the appearance of a block of stone, which matched the feeling in his heart.

"That is why we want you to lead, Dandronis," one of his men announced. "You just want to fight. You have never desired power or glory. Besides, you are the best fighter here and you know it," said Tyful, a short and stocky veteran soldier.

"You are our best chance for survival," added Lypus, a young recruit who had recently joined the army.

"I know how to fight, but to lead? Come on, Tyful, you have more experience in these matters. Why don't you lead us?" asked Dandronis.

"Because I was not voted to lead, you were. Dandronis, we can do this together, I will help you. You were voted to lead and under our laws you must do so. You know this to be true." Dandronis gripped his sword hilt in frustration. He knew Tyful was right. Their military laws were clear; if the sanctioned leader is killed in battle and there is no person of rank to lead, the men in question must pick their own leader, and that leader must lead to the best of his ability.

"Alright, I will lead, but I will take council with you all before I make a decision. Is that clear?"

"Yes sir!" all the men replied in unison.

"Good. Now, what do we do? The forests are filled with Malbeck's minions. We do not know if King Kromm is still alive or where he is located. Our options are limited. Any ideas?"

"Sir, we have to assume that our king is still alive. There is no better fighter in Kraawn, and the elite Tarsinian Knights, plus the Blade Singer, guard him. There is a good chance that they have evaded detection," Tyful said hopefully.

"Besides, we cannot go back to Tarsis. Our homes are destroyed," added Willock, another young recruit with long scraggly blonde hair. Willock was tall and powerfully built. He looked like he had some tribal blood in him from one of the barbarian tribes that lived deep in the Tundrens. There were at least ten different tribes that were scattered throughout the northern regions of the Tundrens, all tall, fair skinned, with long blond hair. They were as big as mountain bears and as tough as the unforgiving lands in which they lived. Willock was a spitting image of the fearsome barbarians.

"Then we try to find our king?" asked Dandronis. The men all looked around at each other and there was silent agreement apparent on their faces. "Okay, does anyone have any tracking skills?" The warriors looked around at each other for several moments before one man spoke up.

"Aye, I do," replied a veteran warrior, Kye. "I hunted these hills when I was a boy and my dad was a trapper. He taught me some skills, although I would not say I'm an expert." Kye was heavily muscled, thick around the belly with wide shoulders. His black hair was long and thick and he wore an unruly beard that was wet with moisture from the evening air.

"Your skills will have to do. What supplies do we have? Any food, bed rolls, tinder boxes?" asked Dandronis.

The men went through their packs that they had hastily packed the night they were attacked. Some didn't even have time to grab anything other than their weapons. As they laid out their supplies it became apparent that their situation was pretty grim. They had two tinderboxes, five bed rolls, some dried hard bread, salted ham, and a bag of oats. It was enough food to last several days. The men looked at their meager possessions and then eyed Dandronis uncertainly. He didn't like their stares; it was as if they expected him to fix their problem. He hadn't asked for this, but he decided he would do his best to get them out of their predicament. He just hoped that he would find some orcs along the way, so he would have someone on which to take out his frustration.

"This will be difficult. We will have to try to track our king in woods that will be swarming with the enemy. Along the way we need to hunt and gather food or we will starve. I don't know about you, but I'd sooner die by an orc's sword than starve to death in these cold mountains. Our chance of survival is slim, but we have no other choice. Are you with me?"

"Yes sir," the men replied with new purpose in their voice.

***

Kromm knelt by a small fire that had been hastily built at the base of a rock wall. There were four other fires along the wall giving off a bit of warmth to the remaining Tarsinian Knights. The group consisted of forty men, in addition to the Blade Singer, Queen Sorana, the king's wife, their son, Prince Riker, and the Tarsinian court wizard, Addalis. Building the fires was risky, but winter was approaching and the cold was sapping what little strength they had left after all the hard fighting and their subsequent flight as they evaded Malbeck's forces the last two days. Kromm decided that a fire and warm food were necessary under the circumstances. Hopefully the rock wall and the dense forest before them would shield most of the smoke and light. It was risk, but a justifiable one.

Kromm was a giant, several heads taller than most other big men. Lean and strong, one could see the striations of his muscles beneath the skin of his long arms and legs. His thick muscular neck, broad powerful shoulders, and huge thighs were in relative contrast to his narrow waist. Long blond hair framed his clean shaven face, giving him the appearance of youth even though he had seen more than forty winters. His sky blue eyes perpetually shone with an inner determination. It was whispered among his men that he shared blood with one of the barbarian tribes that lived among the Tundrens surrounding the lands of Tarsis. Kromm's lineage, being rather important for a king, was widely known. But there was a commonly told story that one of his ancestors had a secret liaison with a barbarian chief and bore a child that was brought up as a prince. Such an act was not allowed, of course. The king, a long dead ancestor to Kromm, raised the boy as his own to save their name from disgrace. No one knew if the story was true, but Kromm certainly bore a striking resemblance to the tall and powerful blond haired barbarians

Kromm's armor consisted of a silver chest plate with matching shoulder guards, all bearing the Tarsinian mark, a decorative T, which had been engraved into the expensive metal crafted by the best dwarven metal smiths. The mark had been the Tarsinian family emblem for many generations. His hands were covered with supple leather gloves that stretched tight over his thick forearms all the way up to his elbows. Attached to the leather were steel plates cinched tight and strapped down with strong leather straps. Underneath the armor he wore a steel shirt that hung to mid-thigh made with interlocking links of chain.

Around his narrow waist was a thick leather belt adorned with silver pieces of steel from which hung a long hunting knife. The king's legs were covered with thick but supple leather breeches, and strapped to each thigh was another silver plate of armor. His breeches were tucked into knee-high boots made from boiled hardened leather shaped perfectly to his feet.

The king was tired, and covered with dirt and spatters of blood that he could not wash off, luckily, none of it his own. Yet despite his battle fatigue, he continued to radiate power and authority. His very presence on a battlefield uplifted his men and gave them courage. His size, strength, and charisma commanded complete and utter respect from all that stood before him. It was rumored that he had not yet met a man, or beast, that could defeat him in single combat.

Sitting with him at the fire was his queen, Sorana, Allindrian, the Blade Singer, Kromm's general and leader of the Tarsinian Knights, Farwin, and lastly the court wizard, Addalis. Queen Sorana, tall and lithe, had the grace of a dancer. Her golden blonde hair was pulled tight into a braid that was wrapped around her head and fastened at the back with jeweled pins. Her elegant face was considered beautiful, but she was not particularly curvy or voluptuous, the physical attributes most commonly admired by men of royalty. And though she appeared stunning when attired in sparkling jewels and draping gowns, she felt more comfortable in clothes most often worn by common women, which was closer to what she was now wearing. She wore form fitting leather breeches, dyed black, and her torso was covered with a tight green cotton shirt laced up around her small breasts. Over her shirt was a light green wool tunic cinched tight with a brown leather belt that matched her knee high woodsman's boots. Draped over her shoulders and pulled tightly around her for warmth was a forest green woolen traveling cloak lined with cotton. Strapped to her waist was a curved short sword that was bladed on one side. The razor sharp blade was made for her by the dwarfs at Dwarf Mount as a wedding gift.

Queen Sorana had been raised as a commoner and was accustomed to strenuous physical activity; in fact she was partial to it. She had spent much of her time riding the grasslands flanking Tarsis or hiking deep into the Tundrens on hunting excursions with her husband. She could hold her own with a sword and she was skilled with the light woodsman's bow that was leaning against the rock wall next to her.

Lord Farwin also wore plate mail common for a Tarsinian Knight. Around his shoulders draped a wool traveling cloak. His shoulder length hair was thick and dark, highlighted by streaks of silver. A bushy mustache covered his upper lip. He appeared younger than his fifty winters, and he had fought with King Kromm for more than twenty of them. The king trusted Farwin with his life. He was a hard, stern man, but his men respected him as a leader, because he was demanding, yet fair, nor did he ask more of his men then he would of himself. Like his men, dirt and grime was encrusted on his sweaty body. His right arm was wrapped with a strip of brown wool that had been ripped off his own traveling cloak. Blood had soaked through the wool, staining his arm red, but the wound was not severe and he ignored it.

Allindrian sat cross-legged next to the fire, her long thin sword gently resting on her thighs. The unique blade was slightly curved, and at the base of the blade, where it fastened into the hilt, were a series of shapes cut into the steel. It was an intricate design of triangles cut into the metal, decreasing in size as it extended up the blade. The spine of the blade was left untouched by the designs and it too was razor sharp. The tip of the blade also had a triangular shape cut into the metal. Normally, a sword smith could not do this because it would weaken the weapon. But this blade was elven made, forged by Tsillerian Cho Andorin, an ancient elven blade smith whose weapons were unmatched in beauty, strength, and power. Even the dwarves accepted her weapons as masterpieces. A Blade Singer's sword was also enchanted by Ekahals, elven wizards who knew the old words of magic, giving them more power than any other wizards in Kraawn. These shapes cut into the blade gave the weapon its incredible lightness, as well as its unique *singing* sound as it spun through the air.

This blade would not *sing* for just anyone, however. In order to make it sing, its owner must wield the blade a certain way, a way that had been developed and taught only to Blade Singers, sword wielders who train for many years. Specialized positions and movements, combined with techniques for maintaining complete concentration and mental control, would bring out the true power of the blade. The blades are magically linked to each Blade Singer, allowing only the blade's owner to unleash its full potential. The blade itself is unbreakable, and the vibrations of the *singing* enable it to cut through any substance known in Kraawn.

Allindrian wore clothing typical of a ranger, forest green breeches and light elven chain mail under a green tunic covered with elven symbols. Around her neck draped a flowing brown elven cloak that enabled her to be virtually invisible in the forest. Her brown leather boots, laced tightly up to her knees, and the matching leather gloves similarly laced around her forearms, had been magically enchanted, enabling her to run and climb without making a sound.

Addalis, the fourth member of the tired group by the fire, was a wizard whose family had served the Tarsinian royal family for many years. He had short brown curly hair and he wore a trimmed beard that was separated into two short braids. He was still young, just thirty five winters, but already powerful in his own right. He had been groomed and trained since he could walk to master the arcane arts in order to serve the royal family. Wizards were rare. In fact, it was difficult to find any outside of royalty. The time and cost it took to master the art was so great that most people could not undertake the training without the backing and funds associated with royal families. Court wizards were typically tied to the royal family through bloodlines. They were usually lords themselves, passing on their skills and knowledge to their own sons who could then continue to support the royal family with their magic. Addalis's face looked older than his years. It was not uncommon for wizards to look older than they were;

prolonged use of magic had a way of speeding up the aging process. But ironically, that same magic could also be used to prolong life if the wizard had the skills to do so.

Addalis wore simple gray breeches and a thick, long sleeved tunic cinched tightly with a brown leather belt. To protect him from the mountain air he also wore a long green hooded cloak made of wool. Dangling from his belt were a number of pouches containing spell components and other tools that a wizard might need to cast his spells. Strapped to his right thigh was a baldric of six small, razor sharp throwing knives. Most wizards were not proficient with swords or other weapons because they didn't have the time to train and still master the magical arts. But Addalis had been trained by his father, who had always stressed the need for a wizard to not rely on his spells alone. He had given Addalis the baldric of knives when he was ten years old, and as an additional gift, he had enchanted the knives himself. He imbued the knives and the baldric with a homing spell, a spell he created that enabled the knives, once thrown, to magically reappear back in their sheaths. Addalis had worked diligently to master these weapons, eventually developing an accuracy that was uncanny.

The most important possession that Addalis carried was his spell book, a book that had been passed down over many generations and was finally given to him by his father. In the book were all the spells of his ancestors, hundreds of years of history and work, all compiled into one leather bound tome strapped to his back in a thick protective case made of leather and wool. The book was enchanted with its own magical wards to protect it from fire and the elements. Anyone attempting to open it, other than he, would find themselves writhing on the ground in pain from electrical shock. It was his most prized possession, and he protected it with his life.

"My Lord, what are your orders for the morning?" asked Farwin.

King Kromm, looking up from the fire, made eye contact with his commander. The king's eyes reflected his sadness and lacked their usual luster. "We have lost everything, my friend;

everything my family has built for countless generations. This is the first time in my life where I can honestly tell you that I know not what actions I should take."

Queen Sorana gently touched her husband's thigh, looking into his sad eyes. She smiled softly as if to say, *everything will be okay*, but she knew that things would not, and her eyes betrayed this to her husband. He caressed her hand softly, trying his best to smile.

"We can rebuild, my King. There is nothing we cannot do," announced Farwin, trying hard to muster the confidence that he did not feel.

"I thank you for your resilience, Farwin, but we have nothing left to rebuild. Yes, we have the smoking remains of a city that can be rebuilt. But stone walls do not make an empire. People do. They are the blood and strength of Tarsis. My army and my people were destroyed; all that remain sit here as outcasts in their own lands. The people that my army tried to protect are no more, tortured and murdered by Malbeck and the Forsworn. If we were to rebuild the city then I'd be the king of an empty land. What would be the point?"

"They couldn't have killed everyone. There must be thousands of refugees that fled the lands who would return if word spread that you were alive," the queen said softly.

"King Kromm, may I interject?" asked Allindrian.

"Of course, Blade Singer. Because of you we are still alive. I welcome your council and I will forever be in your debt."

"And I," added Sorana sincerely.

"You owe me no debt," Allindrian replied. "But I have some advice. In time, rebuilding Tarsis may be possible, but that time is not now. I believe that Malbeck will move his forces south, to Finarth. He will take out any cities or towns along the way, including Cuthaine. Once he arrives at Finarth's gate he will raze that city to the ground, just as he did Tarsis. Malbeck knows that the combined armies of Annure and Finarth will assemble to fight him at Finarth. That city will be the last major stronghold east of the mountains to stand in his way. Once it is destroyed then I believe he will move over the mountain passes into the West. This is just the beginning; he will not stop until all of Kraawn is smothered with the blackness of the Forsworn. As his domination and power increases, he will finally take out the last threat to his power."

"The elves and the dwarves in the North," Kromm concluded.

"Yes, I believe that to be the truth. We cannot let that happen, and I believe that all of us here can be an integral part of the plan to stop him," she added.

As a Blade Singer, Allindrian's job was to protect her home at all costs. The elven kingdoms to the north generally stayed out of human affairs. But that was the job of a Blade Singer, to interact with the rest of the races, especially the humans, so that the elven rulers could feel the pulse of the rest of the lands around them. Being a reclusive race, it is important that the elven kingdoms know what is happening in the lands around them. Are there any rising threats or political unrest that could threaten their lands? These are questions that can only be answered by the information gained from Blade Singers. Allindrian had been a Blade Singer for over a hundred years, and her training to become one took half of that time. Her mother was a Blade Singer before her, and her father, who was human, died long ago. Her parents met during her mother's travels, and although their time together was short, by all accounts it was filled with passion and love. Her mother had been killed when Allindrian was just a girl, slain in a far off place. She was told that her mother died while protecting a family from raiding orcs near the Sarhast Mountains, west of the Onith Kingdom. Not many details were known, but Onith troops said that there were nearly fifty dead orcs scattered around her body. They said that her body was pierced four times by arrows before she was cut down. The entire family she fought to protect was massacred and everything was taken, including her mother's armor and sword. Her lonely death saddened her, but she barely knew her mother as the life of a Blade Singer was not to raise children, but to fight, to learn, and to protect. Allindrian was raised in the Kufaro, the training grounds for elven warriors.

From there she worked her way up, spending over fifty years serving in the elven legion, then another hundred years in the Silvarious, an order of elven rangers who guarded the borders of their forests. Then, after excelling in this role, she attempted to follow in her mother's footsteps. After many years of training, she became a Blade Singer, an elven warrior whose job was to protect their home by leaving it, the highest honor that an elven warrior could achieve. But it was a lonely and arduous path, for a Blade Singer really had no home. You roamed the land gaining information and looking for areas of unrest, learning about the lands and collecting information that her elven rulers would want. Everything she did was in service of her people.

"What do you have in mind, Blade Singer?" asked Farwin.

"I think we should travel south, to Finarth and…"

"You wish us to leave our ancestral home?" Addalis interrupted, a hint of concern in his voice.

"I do. Right now you must look past the walls of Tarsis and attempt to see all the kingdoms of Kraawn. All of Kraawn is threatened and we must make a stand."

"And you think that stand should be made at Finarth?" Addalis asked.

"I do, Addalis. We must combine our strength to defeat Malbeck."

"Will the elves and dwarves join in that fight?" asked Farwin skeptically. Allindrian looked at Farwin and she did not try to mask her worried expression.

"I do not know, Farwin. As you know, the elves have always stayed hidden in their forests far to the north, away from the intrigue of humans. I cannot speak for my king or queen, but I can only hope that they would see Malbeck as a threat and help where they may. We may have a better chance with the dwarves, considering Tarsis is one of their major trading partners."

"That relationship is built primarily on the desire for gold. Convincing them to join the fight may not be that easy," added the king.

"It may be if the demand for their metal work disappears," Addalis replied.

"Good point, Addalis," Queen Sorana spoke up. "If Tarsis and Finarth are destroyed, they will have lost their most valuable market for their weapons. Their coffers will dry up and you know how dwarves love their gold."

"That argument may work." The king smiled briefly as he paused to think. "So we travel all the way to Finarth, with the winter season upon us as we are being pursued by Malbeck's army?" The king looked at each man and woman as he spoke. They looked back at him, their faces set with determination.

"That is exactly what I propose," Allindrian replied. "My skills should keep us clear of the orcs and goblins that are sure to be hunting us."

Addalis then spoke, "And I have some spells that will also help. I am only sorry that I do not have the power of teleportation, a spell that would serve us well now. I think that under the circumstances we have few options, therefore I support Allindrian's plan...if that is your wish, my Lord," he added, bowing his head slightly to his king.

"I agree, Addalis. We need a plan of action...the men need a purpose. Blade Singer, how do we send out scouts to Dwarf Mount and the elven kingdoms? The mountain passes will be snowed in and not passable. How would you suggest we get word to them?" asked the king.

"Right now I think we should concentrate on staying alive. When we reach Finarth we can contact them by use of magic. They may know what has happened already. I only hope that there will be enough time for potential allies to come to Finarth's aid before Malbeck's forces arrive at the city's gate," Allindrian replied somberly.

"Very well. Farwin, assemble the men, I want to address them personally to explain our plan," ordered Kromm.

"Yes, sir," replied the knight, as he rose and walked toward his men who were huddled around the other fires nearby.

Queen Sorana leaned in and kissed Kromm gently on the cheek. He looked into his wife's eyes, gently holding her hand. The king's massive hand, like a bear's paw, completely engulfed hers.

Allindrian, glancing at the pair, was amazed at how such a large man, so fearsome and powerful in battle, could be so gentle. She envied the two; it must be nice to find solace in the comfort of another's arms, especially in the midst of such loss and destruction. Allindrian shook the thought away, and stood up briskly by the fire, its flames illuminating her silver sword pointed at the ground.

"I need to scout the forests. Get some sleep. I will be watching the perimeter of our camp."

"Thank you, Allindrian, but you don't..." the king stopped in mid-sentence as Allindrian leaped into the forest, disappearing in the blink of an eye. Addalis shook his head, smiling as the king gazed at the spot where Allindrian had been.

"She sure is fast," Addalis chuckled, catching the king's amazed expression.

***

Durgen Hammerhead led a small group of dwarves up the gentle rise of a well-traveled trade route. The road was dry and the ground was hard and frozen from the frigid night, making it easy for the sturdy dwarves to guide the pack mules and carts. Ten dwarves guided three carts heavily laden with dwarven made armor and weapons. Durgen had traveled this path many times, and looked forward to getting to the peak of the rise so he could gaze down the valley toward Tarsis just as the morning sun was rising above Lyre Lake.

Durgen was of average size for a dwarf, about as tall as a man's chest, but much thicker. Dwarves were like walking boulders, sturdy and tough as the stone in which they lived. His large head was covered with wiry blonde curls, and he wore his mustache braided on each side as it descended into his dense beard. He wore beautifully crafted plate mail and dangling from his belt was a heavy dwarven hammer that he had forged himself. The dwarves traveling with him were similarly outfitted, but they also carried short sturdy crossbows to protect the caravan from possible brigands. They rarely encountered outlaws on this road since King Kromm was vigilant in patrolling the trade routes from Dwarf Mount. In fact, Durgen wondered why they had not run into any Tarsinian Knights yet. Usually by this time they would have been greeted by a patrol from Tarsis.

The answer to Durgen's question soon became apparent as he crested the gentle hill. Stunned, he stopped, staring down in disbelief at the burning remains of Tarsis. He was still standing there, his mouth agape, as the caravan made its way to his vantage point.

"Is me eyes playing tricks on me?" Durgen asked as his men moved around him, shocked into silence at the sight before them. Durgen's son, Olaf, the youngest dwarf in the caravan, stood next to his father. He set the front of his crossbow on the ground, leaning on it with both hands as he gazed ruefully down the valley to the smoldering city.

"Father, ye seeing the same as us, Tarsis is no more." Olaf bore a striking resemblance to his father, though his beard was shorter and more blonde. Strapped to his back was a magnificent battle axe that Durgen had crafted for him the day he made Trader rank, a difficult task requiring five years of training. It wasn't just military training that was required, but knowledge of forging, metals, stones, as well as language skills, business knowledge, and other talents necessary to interact with neighboring kingdoms with which they traded. Olaf was the youngest graduate to pass the tests in quite some time and Durgen was immensely proud of him for that. All caravans were led by a Master Trader and the guards that accompanied them were required to be of Trader rank. These Traders were the best of the dwarven fighters, and Durgen, being the Master Trader, was one of the elite. They trained as a unit of ten, each Trader knowing his place in combat. Olaf had just made Trader rank and this was his first trip with his father.

Olaf's axe head was made from Mithril silver and the shaft was adamantiam, a light powerful metal that only the dwarves knew how to smelt. The weapon was blessed and imbued with dwarven magic by the most powerful of their clerics. The handle was wrapped in leather and the razor sharp edge sparkled in the morning sun.

"Who did this?" muttered a burly red bearded dwarf standing next to Durgen.

"By me own eyes, I know not, Ballick, but it smells of orc. We best get turned around and back to Dwarf Mount. Our king will want to hear of this."

Durgen had just turned to give the order to turn the carts about, when he heard something in the forest to his left. He instinctively reached down to the hammer strapped to his belt as he peered into the thick brush. He caught a glimpse of something sparkle, just as he heard the unmistakable 'twang' of a bow string.

"To arms!" he yelled, un-slinging the shield on his back. He quickly glanced toward his son just as the young warrior was doing the same. And in the space of an instant, he saw the whole world crumble as a black shafted arrow took his son in the throat. Olaf, thrown backward against the cart, locked eyes with his father, staring at him in shock and stunned disbelief. Weakly, he lifted his hands to the feathered shaft buried in his throat. As blood bubbled through his fingers and trickled from his mouth, his wide eyes dimmed and glazed over as he fell to the ground.

"No!" Durgen screamed. He brought his shield up, frantically looking for an assailant, any outlet for the boiling rage within him. The dwarves, all veterans, moved quickly into formation, five shield bearers in the front, the rest standing behind them with loaded, duel firing crossbows. Their backs were to the carts which offered them some protection from the rear.

Black arrows peppered them from the forest as a group of orcs ran from the undergrowth, dark swords and spears leading the way. Two more dwarves were hit before they could get their shields up.

"Stay in formation!" yelled the enraged Durgen. Fifteen orcs, screaming for blood, ran toward the remaining seven dwarves. As the orcs advanced, the dwarves held their position. Then, just when they were about five paces from the locked shields, Durgen yelled, "Now!" The 'click' of the dwarven made crossbows could be heard over the screaming orcs, and four thick bolts rocked into them with tremendous power, launching four orcs backwards as if they had been hit by a dragon's tail. The four dwarves then expertly spun the crossbows so that the bottom bolt was now on top. In half a second they had four more bolts in the air and four more orcs falling to their deaths. The crossbowmen then dropped their weapons, un-slinging their shields and close formation weapons, and joined their brethren to continue the fight.

The shield bearers closed formation again as more orcs came crashing into them. These dwarves were experts at close formation fighting, and the fearsome orcs learned that lesson quickly. The orcs brought their weapons down upon the steel shields with little effect. Blocking the strikes, the dwarves attacked the orcs' knees and ankles. Their short size enabled them to lift their shields above their heads, protecting them from the orcs' attacks while allowing them to cut into the orcs' legs like they were cutting down a field of wheat. The orcs howled in pain as hammer and axe crushed and cut at their legs.

Durgen roared in fury as he swung the head of his hammer forward into the knee cap of an attacking orc. He heard the knee crack as the beast screamed in agony, crumbling to the ground. He then lunged forward bringing his hammer down hard on the beast's chest, cracking its sternum and crushing its heart. Another orc attacked him with a long spear, but he blocked the thrust with his shield, and quickly counterattacked by leaping in toward the attacker. The orc, astonished at Durgen's speed, nonetheless tried to raise its spear so it could bring the jagged point down on the fearsome dwarf. But the orc was too slow, and Durgen, screaming maniacally, smashed the edge of his shield into the orc's knee. The knee shattered, snapping inward and causing the orc to fall to his good knee. Durgen then quickly cracked his hammer into the side of the orc's head, crushing it like a watermelon.

He looked up as more orcs were pouring from the forest, swarming toward them like angry hornets. There were too many of them, and despite the orc bodies piling up around them, there were still only five dwarves remaining.

"Come on, orc scum! Come feel the might of dwarven steel!" Durgen yelled as an arrow whistled from the forest taking him in the thigh. His armor deflected the arrow but a second pierced his forearm, penetrating deeply into his muscle. He laughed, yanking out the arrow as three more orcs charged him. He fought tirelessly, as if possessed. He felt no physical pain. He felt only an overwhelming anguish and fury at the loss of his only son. No pain could penetrate such grief. Orc bodies continued to pile up around him, and though he had received several wounds, he felt nothing but the intensity of his anger, an anger that fueled his arms as he wielded shield and hammer in a deadly barrage of devastation upon any orc unfortunate enough to come within his range. He glanced to his right and saw Ballick nearby, the only other remaining dwarf. They moved back to back as fifteen more orcs surrounded them.

"Good place to die, eh Durgen," Ballick growled, holding his blood covered shield and axe in front of him. Durgen noticed that Ballick was bleeding from several wounds but did not seem to notice the pain. It would take more than a few superficial wounds to make Ballick grimace.

"Aye, but let's bring a few more of these 'yellow fangs' with us," Durgen rumbled in reply, his voice low, laced with the anger still boiling within him.

Just as they had reconciled themselves to their fate, while taking out a few orcs along with them, they saw a flurry of spears flying from the woods, slamming into the backs of several orcs, causing many of the beasts to turn around and face their invisible assailants, exposing their backs to the two remaining dwarves. Durgen and Ballick didn't wait to see who threw the spears. They attacked the orcs ruthlessly with hammer and axe, cutting down several before the orcs turned back toward the more immediate threat. As they did so, fifteen armored men stormed in from the forest. Well disciplined, and in close formation, they cut into the astonished orcs with practiced precision.

Durgen brought his hammer down hard on an orc's reinforced boot. The force of the blow crushed the screaming orc's foot, causing the beast to lift its injured foot off the ground, exposing the other leg, its only support. Durgen, swinging his hammer sideways, took out its leg, snapping it in two, causing the howling monster to fall to the ground where Durgen finished it off with a blow to its head. Durgen roared to Moredin, their dwarf god, "Moredin, give me strength!" He called upon the dwarven god as he turned to face yet another foe just as he heard a man shout.

"Hold, Dwarf, we are not your enemy!"

Durgen stopped momentarily, and looked quickly about to see who had addressed him. He was stunned to see all the orcs had been slain. Next to him stood Ballick, as exhausted as he was, but miraculously still alive. Surrounding them were a group of men, all bearing the Tarsinian mark on their armor. They stood, panting from the exertion of battle, gripping weapons that dripped with orc blood.

Durgen lowered his shield and re-slung the hammer at his belt. The man who had spoken approached him. Tall, clean shaven, and almost bald, his intense blue eyes seemed devoid of emotion.

"Well met, I am Durgen Hammerhead, Master Trader and emissary from Dwarf Mount. I thank you for your assistance," Durgen replied, his anger gradually diminishing. A feeling of utter exhaustion overcame him as his gaze returned to the body of his dead son lying next to the cart.

"I am Dandronis of the king's men. We were moving south when we heard the fighting. We arrived just in time it would seem."

Durgen turned away from Dandronis, stepping over the numerous dead to get to his son. Olaf was sprawled on his back, his shield lying next to him, his axe still strapped to his back. He hadn't even had time to un-sling his weapon. The crude orc arrow was embedded all the way to the fletching just under his chin. Durgen dropped to his knees before the body, his shoulders heaving with grief as he looked upon his son. He reached out with one hand, gently closing his eyes. Then he unfastened the strap holding the axe to his back, and removed the weapon from underneath him.

Ballick approached Dandronis as the Tarsinian warriors took in the tragic scene.

"Well met, Dandronis, I am Ballick, and the dead boy is Durgen's son."

Dandronis's expression softened as he thought about his own slain family. His heart ached for the dwarven warrior as he recalled his own intense pain at the loss of his loved ones.

"I'm sorry for your losses. These are indeed grave times. I wish we had arrived earlier," Dandronis replied.

"What happened?" asked Ballick. "As we speak Tarsis smolders."

"The Dark One is back and he brought his army to our gates with no warning, using some type of magic. We were overrun in our sleep. Few escaped with their lives."

"And the king?" Ballick asked, trying to digest this sobering news.

"Alive by all accounts, but we do not know how he fares, or where he is located. There are remaining pockets of resistance but Malbeck's minions are swarming over the kingdom. We are trying to find King Kromm and join with him."

"I'll be joinin' ya'," growled Durgen as he walked briskly toward Dandronis. "And I'll be bringin' me son's axe to the fight. It still shines bright and is needin the smear of orc blood."

"And your axe will be welcome, Master Durgen," Dandronis replied easily.

"What of me, Durgen?" asked Ballick.

"I'll be needin' ya to return to Dwarf Mount. The king must know what happened and take further action."

"Aye, I be thinkin' you're right. Although me axe craves more blood."

"Blood you will surely shed, in good time. Now, Dandronis, would you be needin' some of the best weapons and armor ever made?" Durgen flicked his gaze over to the three carts. Dandronis and his men smiled, realizing what Durgen was offering. Dwarven armor and weaponry were of the highest quality. Their weapons were made from special blends of metals, secret amalgams that other weapon smiths could not duplicate, though not for lack of trying. There weapons were lighter, stronger, and could hold an edge through many fights. The superior armor and weapons in the cart were reserved for Tarsinian Knights only, and the cost for a suit of armor alone was more than one man earned in a year. "Take it all, outfit your men, everything already bears the Tarsinian mark. We have food as well. We'll call them gifts from my king for coming to our aid."

"A mighty gift, Master Durgen," replied Dandronis, as his men hastened toward the carts, eager to inspect their new possessions.

"Aye, it is," replied the dwarf as his mind drifted back to his son and the magnificent battle axe that he had crafted for him, the same axe that was now strapped to his own back. Silently he promised his son that his axe would soon feed on orc blood.

Three
Companions

The six riders had been traveling hard. They had put four days between themselves and their encounter with the slavers and Jonas had spent a significant portion of that time contemplating the choices he had made that day, and the days that followed. He had agreed to take Jangar, Kilius and his sister, Myrell, with them on their mission. He did not yet know if this was a good choice. More swords would be needed, that much he reasoned, but he knew little of their capabilities, or whether they would have the resolve necessary to face the enemies they would surely encounter. He was also keenly aware of the risks of the mission, and that by allowing them to come, he may have very well signed their death warrants. Maybe he had been swayed by the fact that he understood their anger, and could relate to their desire to take action, to do anything to distract them from the pain they felt at the loss of their family. Whatever the reason for his choice, he was gratified that they were holding their own so far. The three newcomers had outfitted themselves with pieces of armor and various weapons confiscated from the slavers, as well as three sturdy horses complete with tack and saddle.

Hagar, the ogrillion, did not want to part with them the morning they left. He was clearly agitated and he would not leave Myrell's side as they readied their gear. Myrell had tried to tell the beast that they were leaving, but he didn't seem to understand her. There was no way they could take on the task of allowing him to come with them. It was a liability they could not risk. After all, he was ogrillion. They knew nothing of him, nor what he was capable of. No one knew if his gentle demeanor would continue or if he would suddenly revert to his aggressive and evil nature. They could not communicate with him either. All of these things made it too risky to have him along. Myrell had approached him, touched his hand, and said goodbye. Jonas had laid a pile of food at his feet and said farewell as well. The entire time Hagar was silent, looking at everyone with wide eyes, unsure why they were leaving him. So they finally had to just mount up and ride off, leaving him alone. It was a hard parting; the huge beast just stood there with sad eyes and watched them depart. It was strange watching an animal that big and ferocious standing alone with slumped shoulders and uncertain eyes.

Tulari had led them far beyond the Finarthian Hills to the outer edges of the Tundren Mountains, the great mountain range that extended thousands of miles from the deep north into the south, far into the foreign lands beyond the great Lake Lar'Nam. Neither, Jonas, Fil, nor Taleen, had been this far north before. Kilius informed them that they were now at the outer edges of the Tarsinian Empire. The paths and trading roads they traveled were flanked by massive stands of timber and dense brush.

The sun had recently dipped behind the tall mountain peaks, the subsequent shadows accompanied by the sudden chill of the night, which crept through the forest like a hunting cat. Rays of brilliant pink and red shone behind the tall peaks as the last of the sun's light remained. It wouldn't be long before they would be bathed in darkness. Jonas, stroked by the fingers of an icy breeze, wrapped his blue cloak tightly around his shoulders for warmth. They would have to make camp soon.

Suddenly Tulari slowed, shaking her head from side to side. Then Jonas noticed it, the scent of smoke, something burning. Though the sun had set, it was not yet dark, and light still filtered through the canopy of the colossal trees.

Jonas, peering ahead, saw white smoke drifting through the trees on the back of a cold fall breeze. Tulari stopped and Jonas waited for the others to catch up.

Fil, seeing Jonas halt ahead, rode up and positioned his horse next to Tulari. "Smoke," he said. "What could be causing it? It looks to be more than a few campfires."

"I don't know," Jonas said worriedly.

The other four rode up slowly with Taleen bringing up the rear.

"Are we to make camp here, sir?" asked Jangar, one of the three villagers who had lost his family when the slavers attacked their home. "What is that?" he asked quickly, as he too noticed the smoke.

"Campfires?" Kilius asked, a bit apprehensively.

"No, too much smoke for that. Something bigger," replied Jonas, staring intently toward the smoke. The smell of something burning was stronger now; the smoke was being pushed by the cool air right towards them. "Are there any villages around here?" asked Jonas, addressing Kilius and the other villagers.

"These forests are peppered with many small settlements like our own. Mostly farmers, hunters, and herdsman trying to make a life for themselves," Kilius answered.

"Why so far out, so far away from anything?" asked Fil.

"Land near Tarsis is expensive, and the taxes can be overwhelming for a small farmer. This land," Myrell indicated the forest around her with a swoop of her hand, "is more or less free as the king's tax collectors do not come this far out."

"I see." Fil certainly understood that reasoning since he had grown up in similar circumstances. As a young boy he did not question why someone would live far from major cities. Living in Manson was all he knew. "You think a village is burning?" Fil asked Jonas.

"I don't know, but let's proceed cautiously and find out," Jonas replied, nudging Tulari forward.

It didn't take them long to find the source of the smoke. They rode over a gentle rise in the trail and came upon a vast prairie abutting a small cliff face. A gentle creek meandered through the grass and a rough bridge made of thick timber stood before them. Beyond the bridge were the remains of a small farming village. Smoke was still rising from the burnt husks of the buildings, blowing southwesterly on the evening breeze. As they neared the bridge, a ghastly scene came into view. Jonas's throat constricted in revulsion at what he saw. On each side of the bridge a naked villager was impaled on a pole as thick as a man's arm. The stakes had entered the decimated bodies through the bowels exiting at the top of the head. Covered with blood and gore, their limbs hanging at grotesque angles, it wasn't until they got close that they could see that both the bodies were women. The carnage was beyond anything Jonas had ever seen.

"May Ulren's eye protect us," whispered Jangar as they crossed the bridge and neared the corpses. It looked as if their arms, legs, and hands had been broken before they were impaled. The bodies of the women were cut repeatedly and it looked as they had been bitten numerous times. *Who could do something like this?* Jonas thought as he scrutinized the unbelievable scene. It would require immense strength to impale a body in that way. Jonas then noticed something that made his heart beat faster. Cut into the abdomen of each woman was Dykreel's mark, a ring of barbed wire.

"Jonas, do you see it?" asked Taleen, her soft voice hoarse with emotion.

"Dykreel's mark," he whispered. "It seems the talons of the Forsworn have reached further south than we thought."

"What should we do?" asked Myrell, her voice shaking with fear at the mention of Dykreel's name.

"We split into two groups. I will take Fil and Myrell while Taleen takes Jangar and Kilius. We will search the village for any survivors. Do not touch anything unless Taleen or I say it's safe. Something dark and evil destroyed this town and we do not know what it left behind, or if it has even left at all. I do not sense any immediate danger, but be vigilant, and bring your weapons forth."

As he spoke Jonas drew one of his swords. The rest of the group followed suit.

"Taleen, you take the east side of town and I will take the west. The village is small so we should be within hearing distance of each other. We'll meet at the north end momentarily." Jonas felt Tulari move impatiently under him. His great steed was clearly agitated, and rightly so.

The two groups split up, slowly riding through the burned and looted village. Jonas led Fil and Myrell down a muddy road flanked by burning and smoldering homes. The houses were simple, made of logs and covered with thatch. They had burned quickly.

"Hello! Is anyone here?" Jonas yelled, his sword held low to the side. Myrell carried a small short sword and Fil firmly gripped his long spear. They came to a home on their left that was partially burned. The front entrance still stood, held up by thick logs that were now more charcoal than wood. There was the body of a man nailed upside down to the wooden door. Metal spikes had been hammered through his ankles and wrists. The man was unrecognizable, for his skin had been flayed open on his bare thighs, arms, and belly. A knife had slit open his chest and something, or someone, had ripped open his stomach and pulled out his entrails. Some of the glistening mess lay on the ground by his head and some had been stuffed into his mouth. Jonas heard Myrell gagging behind him as he took in the grisly scene.

As they meandered through the village they came across many more bodies. Some looked as if they had been eaten while others had been tortured and killed. And no mercy had been shown for the women, children, and elderly. They continued through the carnage veering northward towards Taleen.

Jonas wrinkled his nose in disgust as they came around a corner. The smell of burnt flesh hit them hard as they approached a smoking hay barn. Jonas stopped, flanked by Myrell and Fil. They stared in horror at the sight before them. Myrell moaned in anguish as Jonas ground his jaw in anger. Fil looked around nervously, hoping that whatever had been responsible for this horrible carnage was long gone.

A pile of smoking bodies, charred and no longer recognizable, lay before them. Crisp black husks of flesh were fused together in death. Staked into the ground near the pile was a tall pole bearing a dirty red flag lightly billowing in the breeze, Gould's white eye painted crudely in the center.

But that was not the worst of it. Off to the side of this ghastly pyre was a circle of more bodies, five total, all staked to the ground on their backs. There was a man in the middle with his arms and legs tied to two thick poles stuck into the ground. The ropes were pulled tight, forcing his arms and legs to be splayed wide. His naked muscular body was covered in blood and his head was hanging to the side. Staked to the ground in front of him were four bodies, a woman and three children. The blood and dirt that covered their naked bodies could not conceal the many wounds that had been torn and sliced into their flesh, nor did it hide the black brand seared in the middle of their chests. Even Fil, who had little faith in the gods, made the sign of Ulren's four pointed star as he gazed down at the mark of Dykreel.

"Jonas, it looks like the man was forced to watch these people being tortured," Fil whispered, his throat constricting from shock and disbelief.

"It was his family, his wife and children. In Ulren's name, who would do this?" Myrell asked, not really wanting an answer. Her voice shook with fear as she glanced around the clearing half expecting Dykreel himself to emerge and slay her.

Fil looked at the bodies staked to the ground and thought that Myrell could be right. He flexed his fists instinctively thinking about the pain these people suffered.

"Look, there are four dead orcs," Jonas said using his sword to point out four large bodies littering the ground behind the man. Jonas moved Tulari closer to get a better look. The orcs were heavily armored but they were obviously killed by a blade. "This man was a warrior, and a good one judging by the dead orcs behind him. He may have been the village leader," Jonas said as he continued to survey the scene.

"They made an example out of him. They made him watch the torture of his family and left him to die," Fil added in disgust.

"Fil, cut him down," ordered Jonas, "he deserves a decent burial."

"What about the rest of the villagers?" asked Myrell as Fil dismounted, moving towards the tortured man.

"Regrettably there is no time. We must move on and find camp elsewhere before the sun's light is no more. I will burn the flag while you two bury this man." Jonas dismounted and strode over to the evil talisman as it tauntingly flapped in the breeze.

Fil drew his short sword, slicing through the two ropes holding the man's arms. As the tension was released the man fell heavily to the ground. Fil stood, dumbstruck, as he heard the man grunt when his face struck the muddy ground.

"He is alive! Jonas, the man still lives!" Fil shouted, quickly kneeling by the man and rolling him gently over onto his back. Fil quickly cut the ropes holding his legs. Jonas and Myrell rushed over and kneeled by the man. Fil stepped back to give Jonas a better look.

Jonas put both his hands on the man as his eyes fluttered open. Instantly he sent Shyann's power into the warrior, searching for his injuries. What he found set him back on his heels. He had been beaten so badly with a blunt object that most of his ribs had been broken, and his internal organs had been ruptured or damaged beyond repair. His insides were filled with blood and Jonas could feel the faint beginnings of infection. It would take him too much time to heal the amount of wounds this man sustained, and by that time, he would be dead. This man should not be alive. Jonas knew that he could do nothing. He was too far gone.

"Orcs...Forsworn warlocks...killed everyone," the man sputtered softly. He was so weak that they could barely hear his voice. "My family...," He was interrupted by a spasm as he coughed up dark blood.

"I know. I am sorry," Jonas said. It sounded so inadequate, but Jonas did not know what else to say to the dying man. "Do you know why they came here?" he asked.

"To...kill," whispered the man. Jonas could feel the last of the man's strength leave him, his eyes focusing on something else while his body went limp. Jonas stood up with determination.

"Bury him and let's depart quickly. This place is making me sick," he said as he marched over to Gould's flag, intent on burning it, destroying it with fire, the same weapon that had destroyed the village, and its inhabitants. If only the destruction of this vile symbol of Gould could somehow compensate for the great loss that had befallen this poor village.

Taleen, Kilius, and Jangar guided their horses through the destruction, stunned to silence by the devastation that surrounded them. Taleen's anger rose steadily as she observed the men, women, and children that had been cut down and murdered. The trio was filled with revulsion by the sight of so much carnage. The villagers' murdered in their homes was bad enough, but many had also been tortured or eaten beyond recognition. As they rode slowly through the devastated town, they saw remnants of a cooking fire with a half-eaten corpse spitted across the black embers. The blackened corpse, missing much of its flesh, looked more like a skeleton with bits of skin hanging from its frame. Kilius had to look away, bile rising in his mouth.

By the time they made their way to the north section of town Taleen was visibly shaking. She took a deep breath, calming her beating heart. She held her sword to the side, looking down at the bright silver blade. Her shaking sword arm slowly calmed and she held her blade steady, taking a few more deep breaths.

"My lady, I have never seen such horrible deaths. Why would they do this?" asked Jangar.

"Jangar, I am no lady. I was a soldier before I came to be a cavalier. Please, call me Taleen." They had played this game several times already but it was proving difficult for Jangar to refer to her by her name. He had never seen a cavalier before and he was totally in awe of her.

"Yes, Taleen, I'm sorry, it just rises to my tongue so quickly."

"As for why, I do not know. They may have been looking for something. Or they simply were looking to kill and destroy.

Followers of the Forsworn need little reason to murder and torture. They thrive on chaos."

"Do you think they are still close?" asked Kilius, nervously looking around the darkening clearing.

"I do not detect any evil near us. By the looks of the destruction they were here maybe a day or two ago. I think we are safe for the moment," Taleen replied with a reassuring, but grim, smile.

They decided to set up camp in a clearing an hour's ride from the destroyed village. It was getting cold, as winter was beginning to set in, and a fire became necessary to keep them warm at night. They worried about being spotted so they kept the fire small with a few hot coals rather than large bright flames.

They ate a meal of hot oats, dried venison, and chunks of a strong tasting Finarthian cheese they had taken from the slavers. Taleen cooked up some potent aromatic tea and they sat around the fire discussing what they had seen earlier.

"We must be getting close to Tarsis if minions of the Forsworn are patrolling the area," Taleen said thoughtfully as she sipped her tea.

"I'm not sure, but you may be right. Kilius, do you know how far Tarsis is from here?" Jonas asked the young villager.

"Not exactly, sir. I have never been to Tarsis."

"My best guess is that we are a week's ride from Tarsis," added Jangar. "It is possible that the Blackhearts are crawling out of their holes now that Tarsis is destroyed."

"Blackhearts? What do you mean?" asked Fil.

"Followers of the Forsworn, that is what we call them," said Jangar.

"Are there many Blackhearts in the area?" asked Taleen.

"I don't know. But we were always told stories of witches and warlocks who lived in the mountains. My father told me that Blackhearts were everywhere, hidden amongst the populace, doing their evil whenever possible," Jangar said as he sipped his warm tea.

"And now that Tarsis is no more, and the cavaliers are gone, they are becoming bold and more aggressive. Is that what you mean?" asked Fil.

"I do. It makes sense to me, but what do you mean that the cavaliers are all gone?" asked Jangar. "We are presently graced with two sitting before us."

"He means that we are the only two left, that Malbeck has spent the last two years hunting and killing cavaliers," Jonas stated.

"Ulren's star, that cannot be," muttered Myrell.

"I'm afraid it is," added Taleen.

"How will we defeat them? Without the cavaliers we are lost. What can mere men do against such odds?" asked Kilius, shocked by the news.

"I don't know, but the good people of Kraawn will find a way. We have to," added Jonas weakly.

They were all silent for a moment, their minds wandering, bringing up images of what they saw at the village and what they might soon be facing.

Finally, Taleen spoke up. "Jonas, if we are a week's ride from Tarsis we may find the king sooner rather than later."

"If he still lives," Fil said somberly.

"He lives." Jonas said. "Tulari can sense him and I can feel the connection through him. Shyann has linked Tulari to the king, how, I do not know, but he is alive. I agree with you Taleen. I would think that he would be moving south quickly, directly towards us, cutting our travel time in half."

"But we cannot be sure of that," Taleen replied.

"No, we can't, but with Tarsis gone, he has but few options. South is the direction I would go. We must stay vigilant. The closer we get to the king means the closer we get to our enemies. They are hunting him just as we are."

"Let's just hope we get to the king before they do," said Kilius.

***

Jonas held himself perfectly still, his knees balancing steadily on his elbows and his mind drifting within himself. His torso was bare, but the cold breeze could not penetrate his mental state.

He had awoken early, the sun not yet climbing out of its nightly hiding place, and had decided to practice Ty'erm in the cool morning air. The scene at the village had shaken his nerves and he needed to meditate, to calm his inner being and refocus his energy.

He had been resting in the position of power for forty five minutes and yet it seemed like only a few moments. Finally, his mind gradually returned to the present and he slowly lifted his legs straight in the air. He stood on his hands perfectly still, his fine-tuned muscles keeping his body straight and rigid. Finally he pushed up with his hands, bringing his feet under him in one smooth motion.

He walked over to his twin sabers that were leaning against an old rotten log and unsheathed them smoothly. It was still dark, but the rising sun was painting a streak of pinkish light over the craggy peaks of the Tundrens, just enough light to see his surroundings. He raised both blades straight up above his head, taking a deep breath. Then he brought them down quickly, moving from one sword form to another. He started off slowly, focusing on every move. Then he began to pick up his speed, moving from one sword position to another with lightning quick, precise, movements. His body was glistening with sweat despite the cool air that surrounded him. Leaping and spinning, his swords wove an intricate pattern of death around the clearing.

He kept up his pace for half an hour until finally he stopped his movement just as quickly as he had begun it, both swords aimed at the sky and his body fully erect. He breathed deeply, as sweat dripped from his forehead. He slowed his breathing and relaxed his body just as he heard a quiet clapping behind him, followed by a melodic voice.

"Very impressive."

Jonas turned to see Myrell sitting on a log intently watching him. She was beautiful despite her dirty and disheveled appearance. Her clothes were too big and her leather armor was mismatched, making her look every bit the mercenary, but her face was clean and her tanned skin as smooth as an infant's. Her green eyes sparkled with energy and her wavy brown hair was pulled back, tightly wrapped with a strip of leather.

"I have never seen anything like that," she continued. "Where did you learn to do that?"

"From a friend, a great swordsman," he replied, moving towards the log she sat on to retrieve his shirt.

"He must be."

There was a moment of silence as Jonas pulled his shirt over his head and sheathed his blades.

"Why did you agree to take us with you?" Myrell asked bluntly.

Jonas sat down on the log next to her, wiping the sweat from his face with the edge of his shirt.

"I've asked myself that same question several times," he replied.

"And?"

"I could relate to your desires, to your predicament. I understood your reasoning…and your pain," he added, looking into her beautiful eyes.

"And what are my desires?" she asked softly. Jonas looked away from her for a moment before returning to her questioning gaze.

"Revenge, I should think. You want to avenge your family and your town. To stand up to those who do evil."

"And?" she urged.

"To feel useful in the struggle. To do something, anything, to help balance the fight."

"You see a lot, Jonas."

"It is not so hard to see, to empathize. My family and my village were also destroyed, killed by boargs over three years ago."

"I'm sorry. I did not mean to bring up painful thoughts," she said, gently touching his arm.

"Do not concern yourself. It is good for me to think about my mother. I don't want to forget her."

Myrell smiled at him warmly, both becoming silent for a moment, thinking about their parents. After a few minutes Myrell looked back at Jonas.

"Can you teach me to use a sword? My father taught me a little, but most of his time was spent with Kilius and I'm afraid I am not very good."

Jonas grinned at Myrell.

"What's so funny? Do you doubt my ability to learn?" she said with mock anger.

"No, I was just thinking back to a time when I asked the same question to someone else."

"Who was he? A cavalier?"

"She; she was a Blade Singer."

"A Blade Singer? You were trained by a Blade Singer?"

"Not really trained. When I was fifteen my village was destroyed. Fil and I were traveling to Finarth to join the king's army. We met a caravan on the way and there was a Blade Singer traveling with them. She taught Fil and me a few positions, that is all."

"You are full of surprises, Jonas."

"More than you know," Jonas laughed, standing up from the log. "And yes, I will give you some training, but let us pick up camp and be moving. Time is pressing and we must find the king."

***

Tandris moved quietly through the brush, his sharp eyes scanning the forest around him as he moved slowly south. Four other Tarsinian scouts were near, bringing up the rear of King Kromm's small force. He was a knight, a position achieved through years of hard work, not by possessing royal blood. But he had learned to hunt and track as a young boy, taught by his father, a well-known hunter who had provided meat for the royal family, at least until he had died over ten years ago. It was this connection to the royal family that had enabled him to get sponsored when he was fifteen. His tenacity and skills allowed him to achieve knighthood by the time he had reached his twenty fourth winter.

The king had set scouting lines behind him as he moved his small force south. Tandris led one group, while two other groups were flanking him east and west. Their goal was to watch for pursuit and warn the king if need be. They were several hours behind the main group. Tandris and the rest of the scouts wore only leather armor, allowing them to move faster and be more invisible in the forest undergrowth. They all carried short swords and long bows, and each man had also been handpicked for their skills as woodsmen. Though Tandris felt somewhat vulnerable without his gleaming plate armor, he did like how light he felt. He was so accustomed to wearing the heavy armor that when he didn't have it on he felt like he could fly, like he was lighter than the air around him.

A sudden noise jolted Tandris to attention. Coming from his left, it sounded like something running through the undergrowth. He halted in mid-stride, his senses alert, listening intently. Sure enough, he heard it again, and he began racing silently through the forest, leaping over logs and brush, stopping every few moments to listen, as he picked up the sound again. The noise continued to his left. Tandris knew that Pyell's group was in that direction, but there was no way of knowing who, or what, was making the noise. Tandris continued to leap and dodge from tree to tree until finally he saw a form flying through the brush with no attempt at stealth. Tandris recognized the man's gait, and ran after the fleeing form.

The man was fast, but not as fast as Tandris. He had not won the foot race four years in a row at the king's games for nothing. He was the swiftest man in Tarsis and it wasn't long before Tandris was close enough to see that the racing form was indeed Pyell, tall and lanky with long straight hair, black as oil.

Tandris raced to intercept him. Pyell was running so frantically that he didn't notice Tandris until he was nearly on top of him.

"Pyell!" yelled Tandris, "What is it?"

Pyell, leaping away from Tandris, frantically drew his long sword, an expression of terror on his sweat covered face. That's when Tandris noticed the blood on his shoulder and the crude black shaft protruding from it.

"Tandris! Orcs, they are near! Morg and Dillion are dead! We must warn the king!"

At that moment the underbrush suddenly parted and three more scouts emerged from the woods. It was Ballin, Finn, and Chondis, each gripping their longbows, sweat dripping from their brows.

"We heard the commotion. What is it?" asked Chondis, a big blonde haired archer who could move with surprising stealth for one his size.

"Orcs are upon us! Pyell is wounded, and Morg and Dillion are both dead. How far back are they, Pyell?" asked Tandris, trying to calm the agitated Pyrell by using a more reassuring tone.

"Not far, and they are moving fast. These orcs are larger and quicker than any I have ever seen," Pyell gasped, trying to catch his breath.

As if on cue, an ominous rumbling reverberated through the ground at their feet. They looked back as the sound got louder.

"Pyell, how many orcs?" asked Finn, nocking an arrow.

"I'm not exactly sure. I think it was a scouting party, maybe ten."

"Tandris, you have to get to the king," Pyell continued weakly, sagging slightly from loss of blood. Tandris reached out, catching him before he fell.

"I will not leave you."

"You must. I cannot run much further, and you are the fastest of us all. You know it to be true. It is an order."

Tandris looked to his comrades, not wanting to leave them, but Pyell was right, and he did out rank him.

"Tandris, you must leave. We will hold them back as long as we can," added Finn, his face stern and determined. Chondris nodded his head in agreement and Ballin confirmed the order with a friendly pat on Tandris's shoulder.

"Run for us all, my friend," Ballin replied, jumping up on a fallen log to get a better view of their surroundings. "We will keep them at bay for as long as we can."

As the sounds became louder, it became clear that something quite large was crashing through the forest with no attempt at stealth. Ballin looked back, smiled reassuringly, before turning back to the threat. "Here they come," he said, as he quickly drew his bow back, took aim, and fired.

Finn and Chondris leaped into the forest on either side of Ballin, leaving Tandris with Pyell, who quickly unsheathed his sword with his left hand. "Good thing I'm left handed," he said with a slight smile towards Tandris. "Now be off with you."

Suddenly the underbrush exploded in front of them and a massive orc crashed through, a huge black sword raised above its head. Tandris heard more commotion from the other side and reasoned that the orcs must have been flanking them the entire time, a maneuver not expected from creatures known more for their strength and brutality than for their intelligence. They generally didn't think much about tactics.

The beast was a giant, at least a foot taller than most orcs, and far more heavily muscled, with arms thick and bulky like thin sacks stuffed with big rocks. The orc wore dark plate armor with Gould's white eye painted on the breast plate. He roared loudly, the sound echoing off the steep gulch in which they traveled.

Tandris, an accomplished archer, nocked an arrow quickly, releasing the shaft without aiming. He had no time to sight in the beast, but luckily the orc was close enough that he didn't need to. The shaft took the orc directly in the forehead, stopping its momentum dead, and dropping it to the ground like a sack of bricks.

They heard fighting and yelling nearby just as a second orc rushed at them from behind a nearby tree. Pyell, revitalized by a surge of adrenaline, shoved Tandris aside as the orc's blade whistled by, cleaving into the ground. He swung his long sword down onto the orc's back. The blade hit its armor, sliding down the metal and making a shallow cut on the base of its neck.

Tandris stumbled to the side as Pyell engaged the orc. He knew Pyell was right, that his duty was to get to his king and warn them, and that he was the only man who could make it. So with an ache in his heart for his friends, he extracted himself from the fight, leaping over a log and sprinting through the underbrush with as much speed as he could muster.

The orc swung its meaty arm sideways and took Pyell in the side, launching him backwards into a large tree. Then it turned, aiming a vicious looking weapon, similar to a meat cleaver, at Pyell's head. Pyell ducked under the blade just in time, and it embedded itself several inches into the thick wood. He then lunged forward, hoping to skewer the beast through one of the seams in its armor. His aim was true and his dwarven made sword sliced into the orc's thick shoulder, stopping as the tip hit the armor on its back.

The orc roared in pain, and with savage fury grabbed Pyell around the neck with its left hand, driving him back into the tree. The orc's weapon, thick and bladed on both sides, was bad luck for Pyell, as it was embedded in the tree at the same height as the back of his head. With its tremendous strength, the beast easily slammed Pyell's head into the back of the blade, embedding the black steel six inches into the base of the knight's skull. Pyell's body instantly went limp as the blade severed his spine.

Tandris did not look back as he dodged and bounded through the forest like a frightened deer. He raced through the game trails spurred on by the sound of pursuit. Several black arrows whistled by him, some thudding into nearby trees. But after several minutes the noise lessened and all he heard was the pounding of his own heart as he pushed his body to run even faster. He knew that his friends were giving their lives as they fought to give him time. All he needed was a few more minutes, enough to give him a wider lead. If he got that, no one could catch him. He knew he could run for hours, maybe even all day at this pace, but he wouldn't need that much time, so he pushed himself even more. He only needed a few hours to reach the king and the rest of the knights. He could do it. He concentrated on his breathing and the pumping of his arms and legs. He must warn the king.

He was startled by a sudden sharp pain slamming into his shoulder, causing his body to stumble to the right. He managed to keep his footing and continue running, but when he glanced back at his shoulder he saw a splotch of red materialize on his tunic. Something had hit him, penetrating the flesh by his shoulder, though he could feel that it had not hit bone or a major artery. It must have been an arrow shot by a powerful bow, luckily only grazing him, passing right through flesh and landing somewhere in the forest. It was a shallow wound and he ran on, his fear and adrenaline masking the pain.

He had no sooner regained his rhythm when, from the dense brush, a huge orc jumped at him from the side, swinging its heavy sword in a deadly arc. Tandris knew that if he lost his momentum, all would be lost. He dodged by the blade, spinning around the monster. He was quick, narrowly evading the deadly attack, but not fast enough to avoid the edge of the orc's blade that whistled just past his arm. It was unlucky really. Tandris had used his arm to balance his spin, and because of that his hand was stretched out wide, right in the path of the orc's weapon. He felt a sharp pain as the orc's thick sword severed three of his fingers at the second digit.

Tandris didn't acknowledge the pain. He just kept running as blood from his injured hand splattered the forest around him. The oversized orcs were extremely powerful, and dauntingly inexhaustible, but they could not match his speed and agility. He would make it through them he thought, gritting his teeth and running on.

***

King Kromm pushed aside the fir branch, stepping down a rocky animal path. His giant frame still moved with grace, and despite how hard he had been pushing himself, he did not seem to tire. He focused his mind on his destroyed city and dispersed people, channeling his anger into every step and movement. Generations of his family had built Tarsis from the ground up. And now, after one horrible night, it was all gone. Why was it so hard to build something great, but so easy to destroy it? What is it that drives someone like Malbeck to do what he does, to destroy when it is so much more rewarding to create? As he contemplated these questions, he made a silent vow to make things right, and he knew that he was willing to die trying to achieve that goal.

It was mid-day and the air was brisk, but nevertheless he was sweating under his polished armor, as were all the men as they pushed themselves hard, hoping to break clear of the low lying mountains, dropping down onto the Tarsinian plains. From there they would try to commandeer horses from mountain villages and make haste to Finarth. It was a long journey that was sure to be filled with many struggles.

The soldiers were tired and dirty but their determined faces reflected years of training and combat. They were the king's best fighting men and they would not let him down.

Allindrian, the Blade Singer, scouted ahead while three groups of scouts brought up the rear. They had fought hard to break through Malbeck's picket lines and now they hoped they were home free.

"Father, do you think they are following us still?" asked Riker, the blonde youth following close behind the king. The boy was only sixteen but he was already bigger than a grown man. He was not an experienced fighter, but his father had started his training when he was young and he was exceptionally skilled with all weapons, more skilled in fact than most veteran warriors, but lacking the confidence that comes from actual combat. Riker wore a shirt of chainmail covered with huntsman's leather. His long blonde hair and blue eyes made him a spitting image of his father. The only difference was that Riker did not have the girth of his father, which meant he was still more muscular than most men. But in comparison to his father, he was more slim and lithe, attributing those characteristics to his mother.

King Kromm continued to push on as he talked with his son. "I do, my son. The Forsworn will be relentless in their hunt, but have no fear, we will escape them."

"I do not doubt it, but why do they put so much effort in hunting you?" asked the youth.

"Hard to say. My bet is they know I am capable of uniting the people again, something they do not want. Malbeck will want to destroy all leaders who have the strength and power to stand up to his injustices. They are hoping to lay a path of destruction for the darkness of the Forsworn."

"But we will fight them, right Father? Riker asked, worry evident in his voice. "We will not let that happen."

The king stopped in his tracks, turning to face the prince. "Son, I will not stop until Malbeck is destroyed."

Riker smiled, placing his hand on his sword. "I will help you, Father. I am not afraid."

"I know, but remember, fear is your friend. Harness it and use it, but don't let it override your courage. Men of courage know fear, but they control it. Do you understand?"

The boy looked at his father, thinking about what he said. "I do, and I will remember your advice."

"Come on, you two," chided the queen, "you chatter more than my hand maidens." The queen moved up behind them, getting closer to hear their conversation. Forty knights marched behind them in groups of two as they made their way down the narrow animal trail.

The king smiled at his beautiful wife. He thanked Bandris every day that he had escaped from Tarsis with his family. Now, more than ever, he was thankful that she was not the typical woman of royalty pampered in her great halls with silks and jewels. She looked at home in her huntsman's clothes and wool traveling cloak. Her short bow stuck up behind her back, nestling in a leather quiver with several hands of arrows. Strapped to her side was a beautiful curved saber that she could use quite well for a king's wife.

They continued moving down the trail, coming to a large clearing that opened onto a tranquil mountain lake.

"Take some water and quick rations," the king said to his men as they funneled into the clearing. "Take rest, we will depart shortly."

The men gathered in groups, resting on rocks, logs, and the soft grassy ground. They drank from their water bags and ate strips of salted meat. General Farwin ordered the men to replenish their water from the lake as he wandered amongst them speaking words of encouragement. The men were tired, for they had traveled and fought hard for days, but their eyes still reflected the passion and energy they had for their mission. They would see their king to safety, or die trying.

King Kromm drank from his water skin as a man yelled in the distance.

"My Lord!"

His men were up quickly, weapons out, moving into defensive positions. Years of formation drilling had enabled them to adapt to the fighting ground quickly. Men with bows were up and standing high on rock formations while spearman ran to the front, backed by men with swords.

All eyes turned toward the sound of a man sprinting down the trail from which they had come. It was one of their scouts. The king quickly advanced towards the scout as the man stumbled down the rocky path.

"My King!" cried Tandris. "Orcs are rapidly approaching!" Tandris stumbled, his tired legs finally giving out on him. He had run full out for two hours and his injuries were taking their toll. Though his wounds were not serious, he had been slowly losing blood as he could not risk slowing to mend them adequately.

Kromm caught Tandris as he stumbled into him. His mighty arms held him up with ease as Tandris tried to regain his balance on wobbly legs.

"Easy, Tandris. What happened?" the king asked calmly.

"My King, we were set upon by orcs, huge beasts that fight like they are possessed. Pyell and the rest of the scouts stayed behind to give me time to warn you. I barely got out alive."

"How many and how far back are they?" the king asked tensely.

"Pyell said it was just a scouting party, ten in total. He believed they were part of a larger force but I do not know how many. These beasts can run like the wind. I could barely stay ahead of them, my King. I imagine they will be here shortly."

"Very good, you did well, Tandris. Here, drink some water," ordered the king as he gave his water bag to the exhausted scout. "Tolben, see to his wounds."

A short knight with cropped gray hair moved from behind the spearman to help Tandris. The king turned away from the scout and faced his men.

"Men, orcs are near! We must find better ground in case we are forced to fight! Gear up! General Farwin, Addalis, to me!" he ordered, moving toward his wife and son.

The knights gathered their gear, preparing for departure with military precision. Addalis and General Farwin met with their king and his family near the edge of the lake.

"Any ideas?" the king asked them quietly.

"My Lord, your suggestion about finding better ground is sound. These hills taper down to this lake. I would not want to be here when the vermin arrive. We would be sitting ducks to archers and spearmen, if they have any."

"My King, we need more information on who follows us. I have an idea," Addalis said.

"I agree. I need to know their numbers, what their strengths may be. What is your idea?" asked the king.

"I have a potion that will enable me to scout their numbers unseen and return to you promptly."

"Addalis, I cannot afford to lose you. Will it be safe?"

"I will be fine, my Lord."

"Very well, see to it. General, what is your suggestion. Do we run, or do we fight?" The king turned his blue eyes on his commander.

"Sir, I do not suggest a fight until we know their numbers. Let us proceed south down the mountain and reevaluate after Addalis returns."

Kromm nodded in affirmation, having already come to the same conclusion. "Very well. Hopefully the Blade Singer will return. We could use her skills. General, give me your five best fighters. I want them with my family. Pick ten more to bring up the rear. Have them stay within shouting distance," ordered the king.

Addalis stepped away from the king, fishing around in a bag at his belt. Because the bag was enchanted, all he had to do when he reached into it was to think of the object he wanted. Instantly a small glass bottle materialized in his hand and he brought it forth. The bottle, a cerulean blue, was filled with a small amount of clear liquid. He removed the lid, bringing the bottle to his mouth.

"My King, I shall return shortly," he said quickly.

The king turned from his wife and gazed at the wizard with concern. "Be safe, my friend, and return soon."

Addalis nodded his head and drank from the bottle. The bitter fluid slid down his throat and immediately he felt its effects. His body felt warm as he concentrated on the form that he wished to take. Within a few moments his body had melted into the form of a raven, its black wings flapping in mid-air. Addalis flew off as the knights began to make their way down the mountainside.

The men moved with haste and purpose, their eyes constantly scanning the area for enemies. The east side of the lake was blocked by tall steep cliffs that grew into the clouds, completely blocking travel in that direction. The ground gradually sloped away from the lake on the west side, so that was the direction they took. They had already made their way to the base of the mountain and the scenery was starting to open up into meadows of lush grass peppered with patches of fir trees. Even if they chose to find high ground, there was none nearby that was accessible. The natural incline of the rocky cliffs funneled them further down the mountain. Besides, the plan now was to wait for Addalis to return from his reconnaissance trip before they made any tactical choices. What they did know, however, was that they could not sit there and wait.

The king walked briskly in front of his wife and son while the five guards moved quickly behind them, alert and ready to give their lives for the king and his family. Kromm carried a massive two handed long sword strapped to his back. The blade had been made by the elves and imbued with the energy of the Ru'Ach. It had been given to his great-great-great grandfather and passed down from father to son for several generations. It was a sentient weapon, named Cormathian by the elven wizard who spun the magical weaves of the blade. The weapon had been given as a wedding gift to Kromm's ancestor, King Lybidus. Sentient weapons were very rare, as the magic used to imbue a sword with human characteristics was beyond even most court wizards. Cormathian had thoughts, made choices, and could interact with Kromm in a way that no other magical sword could. It was part of him, an extension of his very self. Together they were an indomitable force. Luckily for Kromm, his ancestors had been as large as he, and were capable of wielding such a massive sword. The blade was almost as tall as a man with a two foot handle wrapped in silver wire. The cross piece was wide and simple, free of intricate carvings, and at the base of the blade, where the pommel met the cross piece, a sapphire, with a milky white interior, had been embedded, giving the stone a life of its own as the milky interior swirled around inside the stone like a mist caught in a glass ball. The sparkling silver blade, despite generations of battles, was unmarred and perfect in shape and form. The weapon, simple in design, was made for destruction, not appearance.

Suddenly a black bird flew down from the sky and landed in front of the king. Within moments it transformed back into

Addalis, whose sudden appearance startled the men behind them into drawing their weapons. Once they saw that it was Addalis, they slid their blades back into their scabbards.

"Addalis, I'm glad to see you. What news do you bring?" the king asked anxiously.

"My Lord, I counted close to fifty orcs moving at a rapid pace."

"Only fifty? One of my knights can kill five orcs easily." As the king finished his sentence, General Farwin quickly stepped up beside him. The king turned toward Farwin, smiling as he spoke. "General, fifty orcs approach, shall we have some fun?"

"My Lord, if I may interrupt," interjected Addalis.

"Go on," replied the king, turning his gaze toward the agitated wizard.

"These orcs are not normal. They are abnormally large, heavily armored, and they move with a precision not typical of their species. They run with no evidence of exhaustion. I have never seen their like."

"I see," the king replied, his smile disappearing.

"A new breed I believe. They will be upon us sooner rather than later," added the wizard.

"My King, perhaps we should look for a location from which to ambush them. I'd rather bring the fight to them than get stuck in the open where they could attack us at will," added the general.

"My thoughts exactly," replied Kromm thoughtfully as he gazed up the path they had just traversed. Behind them was a narrow trail a few paces wide flanked by two walls of rock spanning a stone throw's distance north and south, and at least twenty paces high on both sides. The rock faces were not straight up and down, but rather sloped at a steep incline, interspersed with several large stone ledges. It was a perfect choke point for an ambush. The problem was that the king did not know if the orcs would channel through the trail as a group, or move in several groups, some flanking the narrow gap and moving around it through the rocky terrain. It would be a gamble, but either way, it was a good location to make their stand, and a better one might not present itself before the orcs arrived.

General Farwin smiled knowingly, following the king's gaze up the hill

Four

Stand and Fight

It was a simple strategy. Ten knights with bows would conceal themselves in the rocks just above the trail where it narrowed to a span only wide enough for two men at a time. As the orcs moved through the choke point, they would hammer the beasts with arrows from above. In the meantime, ten knights with spears would be hiding in various locations on the upside of the trail. Hopefully the orcs would move past them in haste, getting stuck in the narrow chute while the archers slaughtered them. Then the spearmen would come from behind to block their retreat, while Kromm led ten more men at the front, completely boxing in the orcs. In the narrow confines of the choke point the orc's massive size would hinder them, allowing only one or two to fight at a time. At least that was the hope.

"My Lord, we are taking an enormous risk by assuming that our men won't be seen above the trail. If they are sniffed out then our plan will crumble and our men will be at the mercy of the entire orc patrol," the wizard said worriedly as he looked around at the battleground.

"I know, Addalis, which is why I am moving to the front. I'm going to lure them in. After all, it is me they are after," the king said calmly, lifting his giant sword off his back. Queen Sorana, standing nearby, protested immediately.

"You cannot, my love. It is too dangerous," she said, grabbing his arm with concern. Turning to face her he gently covered her hand, smiling reassuringly.

"I will be fine. It will take more than fifty orcs to bring me down. Besides, I will not be alone," the king said, turning to face his knights who were preparing themselves for battle. "What five men will join me as bait?" he asked.

Three of the swordsmen that were given the honor of guarding the queen and the prince stepped forward immediately. One was a tall warrior with a cleft chin and eyes as dark as a demon's heart. He nodded his head in affirmation. His name was Gylow, a warrior well known for his courage and his skill with a blade.

Another was Vilnos, a short burly man with an ugly face that looked like it had been kicked numerous times by a horse. He smiled through several broken teeth. "I would be honored, my Lord."

"And I," added Kandoron, an aging veteran who fought like a berserker with his two hand axes.

"Father, I too wish to fight with you," Riker announced, stepping next to the king. His eagerness to test his blade and be a part of the fighting was apparent in his expression.

"I'm sorry, son. You need to stay here and help the general. I need your sword near your mother. Will you protect her for me?" the king asked gravely.

Riker set his jaw, fire flaring in his eyes. "I will, Father, with my life."

"It's your sword she needs, my son, not your life. Our family must survive, do you understand?"

Riker simply nodded in affirmation, gripping his sheathed sword tighter.

Two other men moved toward their king to join the fighting group. Both were archers carrying long bows and swords strapped to their sides.

"Good, we will need your bows. I have a plan," announced the king, turning toward General Farwin. "General, be ready. We will lead them through the gap in all haste. Tell the archers not to fire until we are well past the narrowest point. If they fire too early the orcs will back up and we will lose the advantage."

"I understand, my Lord. Are you sure it is wise to be the hen for the fox? Your safety is paramount."

"Do not fear," interrupted the king. His eyes were hard and focused. His anger had turned to rage and adrenaline coursed through his veins as he anticipated the coming battle. "I have not yet quenched the fires of revenge."

General Farwin had seen that look many times and knew that the king's mind would not be changed. And he knew his men would follow their king to Dykreel's torture chamber with nothing more than their fists for weapons if need be. They loved the king dearly, for he treated them as his equal, as brothers in combat, and he would not ask them to do anything that he would not do himself. That kind of respect was earned, and in so doing, was returned tenfold.

The king kissed his wife good-bye, and then ran up the trail with his five men trailing closely behind. They ran past the spearmen as they were selecting suitable concealed locations at the top of the chute. They wanted to be far enough away from the main trail that they would not be detected, but not so far that they couldn't sprint into the gap to quickly close it. The spearmen pounded their fists against their armored chests in salute to their king and his men as they sprinted by.

Balzrig stopped momentarily, sniffing the mountain air. His pig-like nostrils flared open, seeking the scent of man. They were near; he could smell them and his mouth salivated at the thought of destroying them and devouring their flesh. His massive chest heaved in and out as he breathed deeply. But he was not tired. He could run for days on little food and still fight like the enraged beast that he was. His brethren were the same, but they did not quite have his strength and size, which was why he led. They were all encased in thick black armor, and carried bows and giant swords capable of cleaving a man in two with one fell stroke.

The fifty orcs stopped with him, their yellow eyes scanning the forest while they waited for their leader's command. He roared something in orcish at a large beast to his right. The orc, growling in acknowledgement, conversed briefly with the beasts near him. The sounds were guttural and harsh, a reflection of their breed.

103

Quickly, twenty orcs raced off to the right while thirty stayed behind with Balzrig. Balzrig tightly gripped his stout bow in his huge hand, signaling them to continue on. They were off immediately, their heavily muscled legs moving them steadily through the forest.

"Do you hear that, my King?" asked Vilnos.

"Aye, they are near. Men, stay hidden. As soon as they see me, Jarvis and Orion, I want you to use your bows. The path here is fairly open so you should be able to get a few shots off. Then we run. We must get them to follow us, but do not fall behind or they will overrun you. Am I understood?"

"Yes, sir," the men replied in unison.

"Very well, now move off, and be careful," ordered the king. The men jumped into the nearby cover of brush while Kromm stood in the open trail casually gripping his massive sword. He looked up the trail, his eyes scanning the forest for their pursuers. He had to hope they lived up to their characteristic stupidity for the plan would only work if they did not divide their forces. They had to get the orcs to pursue them into the choke point. From there, devastation would rain down on them in a barrage of steel tipped arrows.

Kromm suddenly tilted his head, hearing the faint sound of muffled footsteps. It was a distant sound, barely audible, but it did not take long for the sound to rise to a crescendo as booted feet hammered the forest floor.

Balzrig's long muscular legs carried him quickly down the mountain trail. Thirty orcs followed closely behind him. They were all close to eight feet tall and half again as wide. As the orc leader came around the corner of a switchback, he came to a halt. Standing on the trail ahead of him was a large human, almost as large as he, casually holding a giant two handed sword.

Balzrig sniffed the cold air as his orcs came up behind him, some standing in the trail and others stepping into the undergrowth fanning out as they saw the human before them. It was the king, Balzrig could smell the man. He growled deeply, showing his long yellow teeth.

"Flank the human, and look for more. He is not alone," he growled in orcish. As he spoke, he nocked an arrow, slowly walking down the path. Several orcs stayed behind him while the others fanned out, moving through the brush like stalking cats.

"Damn," whispered Kromm to himself. They had spread out and they were not charging him as expected. They were not acting like orcs, and that made Kromm nervous. They would be circled and trapped, something that he could not allow to happen.

Kromm waited for them to get closer before making his move. They were just as Addalis had described, gigantic, much larger than their more common brethren. Heavily armored and outfitted for war, their weapons also appeared to be of much better quality than those of their cousins. They also seemed to move with a precision and focus uncharacteristic of their race. And their leader; he was a giant. And though he was only a bit taller than Kromm, his wide girth made him look larger than the king.

"We must retreat! Archers, take the leader and everyone fall back!" bellowed the king.

Just as Kromm ordered the retreat, Balzrig drew back his stout bow, releasing a black shaft right at him. The archers had jumped from the brush, standing in front of their king, and bringing their bows to bear simultaneously.

Jarvis, one of the archers, took the orc's arrow in the chest before he could release his own. The impact of the shaft from the powerful bow launched the man backwards, crashing into Kromm, who caught him easily, easing him to the ground, his lifeless eyes staring at nothing.

Orion got one shot off before another arrow took him in the leg, the impact spinning him around in a complete circle before he landed on the ground in a crumpled heap. The arrow had completely pierced his thigh, the barbed tip creating a grievous wound that bled profusely.

Orion's arrow covered the length of the trail in the blink of an eye, hitting the orc war leader just below his armored shoulder. The arrow penetrated his pasty green flesh, but did little damage. His skin and thick muscles proved to be a tough barrier and the arrow only sunk in several inches. Balzrig stopped, yanking the arrow from his arm as if it were nothing more than a bee sting.

Kromm surged forward, lifting up the wounded archer as if he were a baby. Flinging Orion over his shoulder he raced down the trail with the three other swordsmen right on his heels. As arrows whistled by them Kromm heard several grunts of pain from behind. Although he did not look back he could only assume that several of his men had been hit. He didn't want to break stride by turning back, so he kept his head low and vaulted down the trail. Clearly they were being chased as he heard the roar of the orc leader and the stomping of booted feet behind him.

As they ran by the opening of the rock face, Kromm yelled for the spearmen hidden there. "Men of Tarsis, retreat with me to the choke point!"

Kromm heard, rather than saw, the spearmen emerge from their concealed locations, following their king down the trail that was cut into the cliff face. They raced past the choke point coming to the location of General Farwin's men.

"Men, form up, groups of three, four rows deep! We must hold the orcs here! Protect your queen!" the king roared.

Instantly men came from around the rock wall at the end of the choke point. Their swords were out and their faces were set with determination. General Farwin moved to his king as several men took Orion from him.

"I will stand by you, my King," the General replied, moving into position. Kromm grabbed his shoulder, turning him about.

"My friend, I need you to stay back with the queen and the others. If they break through I can't have them taken. You must run and lead them to safety. Take the five best swordsmen with you!" General Farwin was just about to protest when the king added solemnly, "I am trusting you to watch over all that I care about in this world."

"Yes, my King," replied Farwin. "It will be as you say." He gripped the king's hand. "Be careful and may Bandris guide your blade," he said as he moved behind his men who were now forming a barrier between the rock faces that formed the natural bottle neck at the bottom of the trail.

The king looked beyond his men, making eye contact with his wife just as the pounding of running feet forced him and his men to turn and face back the onslaught storming down the path. Orcs raced toward them, roaring and bellowing their war cries.

"Form up! Behind me!" yelled the king, moving forward to the narrowest part of the path. The rock walls tapered to a part of the trail no more than a few paces wide. Two to three men could fight there at a time, and not more than one or two orcs could return their thrusts. It was the perfect place to stop their charge. Kromm swung his huge blade from side to side and the spearmen stood just behind him, their long weapons pointing towards the attacking orcs. Kromm glanced up, hoping that the archers had remained hidden. "Come on you whoresons! Come feel the might of Tarsinian steel!" he yelled up the trail.

The orcs, led by their giant leader, were pouring into the narrow path. Kromm looked up, expecting to see arrows fly down upon the orcs, but instead he heard the commotion of battle from above. He caught glimpses of men turning from their hiding places to fire their weapons at unseen assailants in the forest behind them.

"We make our stand here!" roared the king, filled with fury and desire to wreak vengeance on those who had destroyed his kingdom and threatened his family. His muscles tensed and his body swelled with an intensity fueled by his rage. He stored it in every thread and strand of his being, releasing it with every sword stroke and surge of his powerful muscles. He had always felt a huge rush of power when he fought. He seldom tired and his strength was prodigious in battle, allowing him to perform feats well beyond those of a typical soldier. He could fight through most wounds and he seemed to heal faster than the average man. He had the charisma and a constitution born for war.

Balzrig ran at Kromm, swinging his mighty sword in a powerful arc. The men flanking Kromm jabbed their spears forward, and several tips were sheared off by the orc chief's vicious strike. More spears jabbed forward from the ranks of men, skewering several beasts near the orc chief.

The king hefted his mighty sword, aiming for the orc chief, but instead hitting another orc in the shoulder. The blade drove through muscle and bone, burying itself against its spine. The orc's eyes widened in shock at the tremendous power of the strike, which killed the beast instantly and caused it to fall back into its comrades, who were now stuck two by two in the bottleneck.

Balzrig saw the king lodge his sword into the orc's shoulder and tried to take advantage of his enemy's predicament. He brought his sword up and across, aiming at the king's stomach, hoping to disembowel him by starting at his hip and moving all the way up his body to his shoulder. He held the heavy blade with both hands, aiming the stroke with tremendous power.

Kromm, sensing the attack, let go of his sword, pivoted to his left and kicked his huge leg out, snapping his booted foot into the orc leader's lead sword arm. The massive orc bellowed in rage as the power of the strike hyperextended its elbow, causing the sword to clatter helplessly to the ground.

Kromm then drew his dagger in one smooth motion, ramming the blade into the orc's side, seeking the seam in its armor and finding it with precision. The orc roared, snapping his other arm forward, hitting Kromm in the face. Kromm's head rocked back, his nose exploding in blood.

The fighting was chaotic. Orcs, flanking their leader on both sides, were beating the spearman back. A handful of knights lay dead, cut down by the powerful orcs, as the next knight moved in to replace them. Normally, a battle with orcs in this type of killing ground would be over quickly. But these orcs were beyond the strength and endurance of even the great Tarsinian knights who were desperately struggling to keep from being overrun.

As the bloodied king and his knights fought furiously against the formidable orcs, Goran, one of the archers given the task of ambushing the orcs in the bottleneck, was suddenly ambushed himself by the beasts that had separated from the main force to flank the narrow path. Hearing commotion behind him, he had quickly turned and launched an arrow directly into the face of a charging orc, simultaneously leaping to the side and drawing his long sword. An orc arrow, fired from the concealment of the brush nearby, had struck his thigh. Despite the pain, he managed to jump out of the way of the dying orc as it fell toward him. His arrow had taken the beast between the eyes, snapping its head back and killing it instantly. Goran reached down, gritted his teeth, and snapped the shaft off so it wouldn't snag on anything as he moved. Growling in pain, he looked up, quickly assessing the situation. As the archers had prepared to fire their weapons at the orcs below, more orcs had suddenly attacked them from the forest behind them. It was total chaos as the men frantically tried to defend themselves. He saw three knights fall, killed instantly by the deadly arrows that had taken them by surprise.

The situation looked bleak. As Goran saw several of his outnumbered brethren go down, he rushed forward, struggling over rocks and brush to help a nearby comrade. The man brought his sword up over his head to block a downward strike from a snarling orc. The strength of the beast was astounding and the force of blow knocked the knight to his knees. But the seasoned warrior quickly drew his knife, aiming for the gap just under the orc's breast plate. The orc had lifted its sword high for another strike, which lifted its breastplate, widening the gap enough for the knight to thrust the razor sharp blade into its flesh. The beast howled in pain as the warrior buried his blade to the hilt, jerking it to his right. He gutted the orc the length of the blade just as the beast kicked out with its powerful foot.

Goran heard the crack of the man's jaw as it broke, and saw him collapse unconscious. He lunged forward with his sword, attempting to spear the orc in its injured stomach. But the orc managed to bring its blade down, batting the long sword away.

Goran moved with the parry, using the momentum of the orc's strike to spin and slide the razor sharp sword across the orc's exposed thigh. The blade bit deep into its leg just above the kneecap. The orc howled again, stumbling forward as the pain of its stomach wound caused it to falter. Goran didn't waste any time. Jumping forward with his good leg he swung his sword as hard as he could. The blade sliced through the orc's throat, nearly separating its head from its shoulders. As blood sprayed from the wound, Goran leaped away, quickly reaching down and lifting the unconscious warrior who lay at his feet. He hefted him up with a grunt, pain lancing through his wounded leg as the weight of the man settled on his shoulders. Gritting his teeth, he quickly moved down the forested rock face toward the rear of the choke point, hoping to meet up with the rest of the knights. As the sounds of screams and growls surrounded him, he could only hope that some of his comrades had gotten away.

Kromm reacted to the strike quickly, faster than any man could. The strength of the blow would have killed the average man. He fought back the stars in his head, kicking out with his powerful leg as hard as he could, which was considerably hard. The orc war leader grunted in astonishment as Kromm's foot connected solidly with its breast plate, launching the huge creature backwards into its own comrades. Kromm, reaching down, ripped his blade from the dead orc at his feet just as more orcs surged forward to take their leader's place. Kromm fought them all; the size of his sword swinging left and right in the narrow gorge shielded his men behind him. They stayed back in the narrow gap ready to defend their liege if he were to fall, or to protect his flanks if need be, but nothing seemed to stop the colossal warrior. Orcs stepped forward, and orcs fell dead at his feet.

Then, in the midst of the battle, the air surrounding the king suddenly cooled to a freezing chill. It happened so quickly that the air was sucked from his lungs. The orcs felt it too, hesitating momentarily as the piercing cold gripped them. They suddenly began to slip, falling over each other and landing hard on their backs.

Kromm was surprised to see that the ground under the orcs, and the narrow rock walls, were covered with a sheet of glittering ice. Growling in frustration, the orcs tried to move but fell helplessly over each other. Every time they reached up to the rock wall to stabilize themselves, their hands slipped on the ice and they sprawled to the ground again.

"My King, the queen is being attacked, fall back!"

It was Addalis's voice yelling from behind him. He must have cast the ice spell to give them time to retreat. His voice sounded strained and Kromm's heart pounded with fear at what he said. The men around him also heard the warning, turning around as well. Only four of the original nine remained.

They quickly ran back to their queen, shocked to see that at least fifteen orcs were battling the remaining knights. They must have circled around, dispatched the archers and then attacked the group from the rear. The orcs had surrounded nine knights, the queen, Prince Riker, and Addalis, all of whom were frantically fighting for their lives, which were now hanging tenuously under the relentless onslaught of the orcs. It was clear they were about to be overrun. It was then that Addalis cast his next spell.

As Kromm and his remaining men sprinted toward their queen, they saw the ground, underneath four orcs who had surrounded the queen and her son, suddenly erupt with green thorny vines. In a matter of seconds the vines had grown as thick as a man's arm, snaking forward and grabbing the orc's legs and arms, entangling them in a knot of vine and limb. Growling in fury and frustration, the orcs struggled against the magical vines, but they could not break away. Several had their sword arms free and tried to hack their way out of the vines. But for every one they cut, two more slid into place, securing the large beasts even more firmly.

Kromm and his four knights stormed into the orcs that had not gotten caught up in the vines, scattering them and evening the odds. Thirteen knights, including the king, now faced eleven orcs, whose numbers would increase as soon as their brethren freed themselves from the ice on the trail. And Kromm knew that wouldn't take long.

"Addalis, take the queen and prince away! We will hold them off! Get them out of here!" the king bellowed as he parried a strike from an orc, then rammed his blade forward with such strength that it punched through the beast's armor, bursting out its back in a shower of blood. Kromm pushed the dead beast off his blade, propelling it backwards into another attacking orc. He took a second to look back at his wife, just in time to see her fire an arrow from her bow into a nearby orc.

"I will stay and fight!" she yelled.

Just as she spoke, another orc barreled through a man it had just killed and rushed at the surprised queen.

"No!" screamed the king as he struggled toward her.

The queen quickly dropped her bow and smoothly drew her sword, which looked no larger than a knife when compared to the giant creature that was soon to crush her.

Kromm frantically parried another attack, stumbling backwards to get near his wife. He risked another glance back and saw Riker, his son, step in front of the queen with his sword held before him.

But the glance was brief as Kromm was forced to bring his attention back to his attacker. The orc was relentless, bringing its heavy sword down again and again with tremendous power. Kromm, forcing himself to focus, carefully timed his next move. As the beast again swung its sword, Kromm pivoted forward and to the side as the orc's blade came whistling by him. The momentum of the swing carried the sword forward and toward the ground, knocking the orc off balance. The king then leaped forward, bringing his blade down on the orc's exposed back. It crumpled to the ground as Kromm's powerful blow cut through its armor, driving his sword through its spine.

Riker's blood pounded in his ears as he tried to calm his fear. He remembered what his father had said, that fear was his friend, but it had to be controlled. He tried to force it down deep into his body, concentrating on his sword and the charging orc. He had fought men many times in training, but he had never before shed blood or faced an opponent as large and ferocious as the charging orc. He saw his attacker come at him as if in slow motion. His mother screamed as he pushed her aside. Then, just as he raised his sword to meet the charge, two daggers flew past him, burying themselves into the orcs exposed neck. The knives must have come from Addalis who was standing just behind him.

Riker reacted on instinct as the injured orc tried to skewer him with its blade. Parrying the thrust he pivoted to the side, swinging his blade low and at the back of the orc's leg as it stumbled by. The move was perfectly executed and his strike was true, his blade easily severing the orc's unprotected hamstring, causing it to roar in pain and fall to the ground.

The queen was there to finish the beast off, jumping onto it and ramming her blade through the base of its neck, severing its spine, killing it instantly.

Kromm battled his way to his queen as she yanked her blade from the orc's neck. "You must flee! I cannot protect you! Addalis, can you get them to safety?" roared the king.

"I will not leave you!" the queen yelled frantically.

"My King," Addalis responded, "I have a spell that will do as you ask, but I can only take the queen and prince with me. I was hoping to save it but I think now is the time."

Just as Addalis spoke, the sound of twanging bows and the howling of more orcs caused the men to turn toward the choke point they had left, and saw, to their horror, a barrage of arrows flying at them. One took Kromm in the shoulder, causing him to stagger back a few feet. He yanked the arrow from his shoulder, showing no sign of pain, and then quickly threw himself in front of Sorana as more arrows came at them. He saw several of his men fall as the arrows found their marks. Within seconds another arrow struck his right forearm, penetrating the thick leather wristband he wore and piercing all the way through his thick muscle. He growled angrily, broke off the tip, and ripped out the arrow, throwing it on the ground.

"Get them out of here! Now!" Kromm yelled frantically, using his huge body to shield his wife and son. But the order was not necessary. He heard Addalis chanting behind him as the orcs that were delayed by the ice spell joined the fighting.

Kromm roared in defiance as an orc ran towards him. The mighty king lifted his sword over his head, flinging it with all his might. The blade spun once, striking the charging orc in the chest. The strength of the throw propelled the weapon through the orc's body, launching it backwards onto its back. Kromm ran forward, yanked the blade from the dead orc, and engaged the next adversary.

The snarling creature swung its heavy sword in a sideways arc, hoping to cleave the king in two. Kromm ducked under the blow, dropping to one knee, swinging his heavy blade with one hand in a vicious arc, completely disemboweling the beast. Kromm's wounds stung, but they did little to hamper his movements. His anger fueled his body and he felt little pain or fatigue. A normal man would have been severely compromised by injuries such as he had sustained, but Kromm was not a normal man, he had never been *normal* in battle.

The orc collapsed, writhing in agony as its blood poured from the gaping wound on its abdomen.

Kromm glanced back to check on Addalis and his family. All he saw was the form of Addalis stepping through a shimmering door floating several feet off the ground. The edges of the door were a glowing line of white while the interior was as dark as night. Addalis stepped into the portal and then the door disappeared in a white flash. Kromm looked around and there was no sign of his wife or son. He did not know where they had gone, but he had total trust in his loyal friend. They had grown up together, their childhood forming a bond that was solidified with the honor bound oath between a king and his court wizard. They were like brothers; each would die for the other. Kromm knew that Addalis would protect his family with his life.

The king quickly scanned the battle scene. Things were not faring well. Ten orcs remained, including the powerful leader who had just ripped his sword from the remains of the archer, Orion. Six loyal knights were still alive and fighting, plus Kromm and General Farwin. There was no organization to the battle and each man was fighting furiously to defend himself. But they were the best fighters, the finest swordsmen in Tarsis, and would not be as easily killed as their comrades.

Kromm gritted his teeth, clenching his jaw in fury. He leaped over the dead orc he had just killed, and charged the orc leader. The beast lifted his bloody sword to block the king's strike. Kromm attacked the orc repeatedly, roaring in anger with every powerful strike. After taking several blows straight on, the orc angled its blade, causing the king's sword to slide to the side, simultaneously kicking his right leg into the side of Kromm's knee. Kromm's leg buckled and he dropped to the ground. The beast then lifted its bloody blade above its head preparing to crush his skull.

The king, with his right hand, gripped the long handle of his sword while quickly drawing forth a hidden blade with his left hand. The second half of the sword's pommel was the handle of a stiletto that was sheathed in the first half of the pommel. Before the orc could bring its deadly blade down, Kromm rammed the blade into its groin, burying it to the hilt. The orc dropped its blade, howling in pain as it stumbled backwards, its hands clutching at the vicious wound.

The king, despite his injured knee, managed to jump up, swinging his sword with one hand, and completely severing the orc's arm at the elbow. The war leader howled, ripping the knife from its crotch with its remaining hand. Kromm reversed his swing, coming back at the orc with frightening force, striking its other arm, cutting it badly and leaving it hanging uselessly at the beast's side. The stunned beast roared in pain and anger, leaping at the king with its bared teeth, snarling angrily and desperately seeking Kromm's blood with the only weapons it had left. Refusing to give up, the beast flew at Kromm, trying to bite into his neck and tear out his throat. But the king countered the attack by bashing the end of his pommel into its face, causing the beast to stumble backwards. Then, gripping his sword with both hands, he swung the blade through the defeated orc's neck, severing its head and sending it flying into the air.

Kromm looked quickly around to assess the battle, and saw that there were only three of his men left. They were standing back to back facing six orcs. The men were bloody and exhausted and the king could tell that it would not be long before the struggle would be over.

As the king rushed over to join the fight, two of the orcs suddenly dropped as arrows pounded into them. Kromm caught some movement in the rocks nearby, and his heart soared with hope as he saw Allindrian fire her bow with lightning speed. She had two arrows in the air while she nocked a third. It was amazing to watch. Every arrow hit its mark.

The orcs were distracted, to say the least, by the relentless barrage of the Blade Singer's arrows. The tired knights took advantage of the confusion, attacking the distracted orcs furiously, rejuvenated by the sense that victory was near.

Allindrian dropped two orcs quickly, her magic arrows easily penetrating their armor and flesh. She then fired into the remaining four, hoping to kill them or at least injure them and give the warriors time to finish them off. The beasts must have thought there were ten archers firing at them as Allindrian's arrows rained endlessly down upon them. As the arrows fell, many hitting their marks, the beasts howled, frantically looking for the source of the onslaught.

Meanwhile, the king's men cut them down mercilessly. It was over in minutes. The three remaining warriors moved toward their king, blood dripping from their swords. Though bloodied and exhausted, they carried themselves with determination, scanning the area for more enemies.

Allindrian bounded down the rocky face like a mountain goat, to join the remaining warriors, her face flushed and sweaty.

"Blade Singer, it is good to see you," said the relieved king, as the tension of battle slowly dissipated from his body.

"King Kromm," she replied, "I would have arrived sooner but I was delayed."

"Aye, we could've used your blade," the king responded as he looked at his men. What he saw filled him with sadness. The battle had been fierce and the destruction nearly complete. He had lost most of his men, including his general and close friend. The last he had looked, his friend had been alive. But in the last few moments of battle he had taken a sword to the side of his neck, nearly decapitating him. And now his wife and son were gone and he did not know where. He felt sure they were safe, but not knowing their whereabouts filled him with worry. Kromm took his eyes off his friend's body and looked at the survivors. Three men stood before him, and he acknowledged each of them with a grateful smile and a nod. "Good work, men, you fought well."

Gylow, one of the swordsmen, was holding a sword at his side and leaning heavily on his left leg. Kromm noticed a black shaft protruding from his leg and blood had stained his leather breeches. Next to Gylow was Lieutenant Tyn and he was using his traveling cloak to wipe the blood off his long sword. Lastly there was Evryn, a giant axe man who was almost as large as the king. The man had cuts that crossed his forearms and one deep laceration across his cheek. He bowed his head as he made eye contact with his king.

"Check the men for survivors and then see to your wounds," the king ordered, turning back to Allindrian.

"Yes, my King," replied Lieutenant Tyn.

"Lord Kromm, we must make haste, there is a bigger threat hunting us," said Allindrian.

"What do you mean?" asked the king as he perused the destruction, haunted by the blank stares of his dead men.

"I was delayed because I was tracking three beasts that were tracking you. They are watching us now, from the cliffs above. I do not know why they hesitate to attack. I assume they were waiting to see what happened here. Now that your forces are weak, they are sure to attack. But I know this…we cannot defeat them with our present force. We must flee, but I'm afraid even that may not be possible. I do not think we can outrun that which hunts us."

Kromm stopped in his tracks, hearing the news. "Blade Singer, I must find my wife and son. Addalis took them from the battlefield through a portal of some sort. I do not know where they went. I do not know if they are safe. We must survive and find them. What do we do?" asked the distraught king.

"Could be a dimension door spell. They could be anywhere but it must be somewhere that is known to the wizard. Do you have any ideas about where Addalis might go if he had a choice, would it be somewhere nearby?"

Kromm thought for a moment. "He has family in Cuthaine. It is the only place I can think of since Tarsis is no more."

"The free city of Cuthaine?" Allindrian asked.

"Yes, but it is a long way from here. It would take weeks to reach the city, while all the while being chased by beasts that we cannot defeat. Our choices are few and none are desirable," replied the frustrated king.

Allindrian pondered something briefly. "King Kromm, I may have a way to get you to Cuthaine quickly, but it will not be without risk."

"What do you suggest?"

"We can take the Hallows Road," she replied quietly.

Kromm looked up at her as he inspected the wound on his arm and shoulder. "The Hallows Road? But isn't it sure death to enter that realm?"

"Not if you know the way. We elves can walk the dark paths of the Hallows. I have done it before. Besides, I think the threat of the Hallows is not as dangerous as the threat that follows us now."

"I see. And you can get us to Cuthaine quickly?" he asked.

"Yes. Time spent in the Hallows is just a fraction of time here. It may take us days within the Hallows but when we arrive at the gate of Cuthaine it will only have been hours, a day at the most."

Kromm's features changed from one of despair to eagerness at this news. "How do we enter the Hallows?" he asked eagerly.

"We must find a gate, a portal into that realm, and I know of one no more than a half day's march from here," she replied. "I do not know if we can make it before the hunters are upon us."

"We must. If not, then we must fight," Kromm said with determination. "Men! Prepare for hard march!" shouted Kromm. "Take us to the Hallows, Blade Singer," the king said, turning his gaze back to the half-elf warrior.

"We are being hunted!" Allindrian yelled, addressing the men who were attending the wounded and seeing to their own injuries. "I will be moving fast and you must be vigilant! We are being pursued by something of great evil. If we elude these hunters then we enter a place of shadows and darkness, a place where death lurks behind every corner. Stay close, and make haste," she said in a softer voice as the surviving men were now nearby, adjusting their gear with fixed purpose.

Just as she finished speaking, an eerie howl echoed off the canyon walls. The men needed no further encouragement. They began running with all speed after the fleeing Ranger, eager to distance themselves from whatever was hunting them.

Five

Finding Them

The five warriors moved quickly down the mountain side. Their wounds had been hastily patched up and blood stained their clothing, but the significance of their mission pushed them beyond the pain and exhaustion. The Blade Singer led them from animal trail to rock strewn path, running and leaping like a hunting cat, pushing the men hard. They were alert, scanning the landscape for their enemies that they knew were near. Allindrian had told them so. Evil beasts were hunting them and it was likely they would be found before they reached the gate to take them into the Hallows, a place of darkness and death. But it was the only way to get to Cuthaine quickly enough to find the queen and prince. And they all were willing to risk their lives to achieve that goal.

Gullanin stood high on a cliff face overlooking the fleeing men. They resembled ants scurrying over a green landscape that was brushed with dabs of gray and brown from the mountain stone. Deep growls reverberated through the rock as the three Hounds of Gould, crouching beside him, peered down at their prey. Each was the size of a horse, but with the bulk of a bull in its prime. They growled ominously, exposing dagger-like teeth, barely able to contain the desire to jump off the ledge towards their feast.

It was all Gullanin could do to control them. Their desire to hunt and rend the flesh of the men below strained Gullanin's hold over them. Thumbing the amulet in his hand, he whispered calming words to the beasts. Gullanin had hoped that the Gould-Irin Orcs that he had created would destroy the king, allowing him to take credit for Kromm's defeat, since it was his creation in

Gould's name that would have destroyed the remnants of the Tarsinian royal family. But it was not to be. The meddlesome Blade Singer had intervened again. She had saved the men just as Gullanin was about to bask in his victory. He grinned evilly as he thought about what the hounds would do to her petite body. It was not often that he got to witness the body of an elf, even a half-elf, being torn to pieces.

"Let us go," Gullanin ordered, "it is time to taste the flesh of our prey."

The demon beasts growled again, pivoting their heads toward Gullanin. The wizard rubbed the amulet while focusing on his command. The beasts' yellow eyes narrowed and they bared their vicious fangs as they felt the pull of the amulet's power. Their razor sharp claws clicked on the rough stone as they eagerly flexed their massive muscular bodies. Moving like birds, quick and jerky, they bounded down the rocky hillside as if it were nothing more than a flat cobblestone road.

"Time to die," Gullanin whispered to the wind as he glanced back down at the fleeing forms below. The wizard then brought up his right hand, splaying his fingers in front his face. On his index finger was a plain gold ring. Bringing the ring closer to his mouth he softly repeated several words of power, activating the magic of the ring. Instantly Gullanin felt a tremendous wind howling around his body, creating a powerful vortex into which his body melted. In just a few seconds his body had dispersed into the swirling air; he had become the wind itself. The sensation was odd. His body felt like it was everywhere at once, but he could see and hear as if he were still in human form. With a quick thought, Gullanin spun off the cliff face, blowing rapidly toward his enemies.

***

Tulari whinnied loudly, shaking his head from side to side, his nostrils flaring as puffs of steamy breath rose in the cool air. Tulari was agitated and that worried Jonas.

"I think we are close," Jonas announced to the group as they rode up behind him. They had been riding hard and Tulari was now starting to lead them farther up the mountainside. Jonas was worried that the terrain would become more hostile and un-navigable for the horses. They already had to slow their pace as the horses stumbled up rock strewn paths and were forced to pick their way around fallen timber and rockslides. It was slow moving and Tulari seemed tense under his legs.

"Maybe we should leave the horses and go on foot," suggested Fil, his steed struggling over some loose rocks.

"I've thought about that. What do you think, Taleen?" asked Jonas.

"A sound suggestion," she replied. "We could probably move faster without them at this point."

"But how do we find the king without Tulari to guide us?" Kilius asked as he rode up next to Fil. The young villager had done well so far and Jonas was impressed with his stamina. In fact, all three of the villagers had pulled their own weight, including Myrell.

"It is Shyann who guides us and she will continue to do so," Jonas answered, confident that she would lead the way.

"It is a risk," put in Taleen. "But we must be close. Tulari is clearly agitated. My bet is that Shyann or Bandris will lead us to the king without Tulari's guidance. They will find a way to show us the correct path."

"I agree. I'd rather die by an orc blade than fall off this blasted horse and break my neck," said Fil.

"I second that," added Myrell, who was riding with Taleen in the rear. Jonas had spent several nights working with Myrell on her sword work. She was a quick learner and had been given a solid foundation by her father. But she still had to work on her strength and speed. Jonas remembered his first lessons with Allindrian, recalling having to learn similar lessons himself. She had scolded him constantly on how important it was to build strength, speed, and stamina; without them a skilled swordsman was nothing more than an actor playing a part.

"Then it is agreed. We will leave the horses in the next meadow. Tulari and Kormac will stay close and we will have to hope that the other horses follow their lead. We can come back and get them once we find the king and his family," Jonas said as they continued to slowly advance up the mountain trail.

***

Dandronis knelt by the huge decapitated orc leader. At least it looked like the leader to Dandronis. The orc was gigantic, larger even than the other large beasts sprawled in death along the mountain path. Bodies were strewn all around them, orc and human alike. The men had traveled hard, tracking the orcs in hopes that they would lead them to their king, and by the looks of it, they had. But was it too late? They searched the bodies, relieved that they did not find King Kromm or any of his family members, but General Farwin was among the dead and that did not bode well with Dandronis.

As he further inspected the scene, it became pretty apparent what had happened. The orcs had caught up with them and the Tarsinian Knights had tried to trap them in the narrow confines of the trail. By the looks of it, it was successful, but it came at a huge cost. Dandronis counted forty seven dead knights. He had never seen or heard of orcs that could do that type of damage, especially against such elite knights and the battle hardened king. They were huge, heavily armored and obviously capable of holding their own against the toughest fighting men in Tarsis. Many of the men that lay dead around him were warriors that he recognized, and some that he knew personally. He had seen many of his comrades die the last few weeks, but this time it seemed to anger him even more. These men were the best warriors in Tarsis, forged by countless battles, years spent with sword and shield in hand, defending the land against all who threatened it. And now they were dead, rotting along the mountain trail without a proper burial.

Dandronis, filled with barely contained rage, stood up from the orc leader's body and looked around him. His newly acquired dwarven mail glinted in the afternoon sun. His emotions ranged from anger to sorrow as he viewed his comrades lying in death, their bodies already rigid. The stench of death drifted around him, a smell he loathed, the coppery odor of blood combined with that of the men's emptied bowels, a common side effect of death. The stench of a battlefield could be overwhelming, and anyone who had experienced it knew there was no dignity in battle. War brought out the animal nature of men.

"Any sign of the king?" Dandronis asked the men who were searching the battle grounds. Several 'nays' followed as the distraught men continued their search. There were a few bodies here and there that they, too, recognized, and that realization, combined with the amount of death they had seen over the last few days, engulfed them in a dark cloud of despair. Dandronis could see by their expressions that they felt as he did.

Kye, their tracker, broke the momentary silence. "Sir, it appears that a group of men continued down the trail. By the looks of the tracks I'd say one was King Kromm. I know of no one else who has the size of his foot print."

"What of the queen and prince?" asked Dandronis.

"We found no bodies, so that is good news. As far as tracks, I cannot be sure."

Durgen the dwarf approached Dandronis.

"These orcs, I have not seen the likes of them. It's a shame we missed the fightin'. What's yer plan?" he asked brusquely.

"Follow the king," Dandronis replied simply.

***

Allindrian ran with the speed and grace of a fleeing deer. The men behind her were tiring; the recent battle and their wounds were taking their toll. The king, however, seemed unfazed by his ordeal. His great strides kept him right behind the Blade Singer. Allindrian could hear his breathing as his giant lungs sucked in and expelled the crisp mountain air. She could clearly hear the thudding of his booted feet as they carried his massive body across the terrain.

She was in a deep state of meditation, focusing intently on her surroundings. Every sound was clear and every smell acute. Nothing went unnoticed as her trained eyes scanned her surroundings.

Suddenly she heard a faint clicking noise carried on the wind. It was barely audible and anyone else would never have noticed it. She knew the sound was out of place in this environment, and to Allindrian it was as obvious as the stench of an orc in an elven flower garden. She stopped running and tilted her head to listen. Kromm abruptly pulled up next to her as did the panting knights.

"What is it?' Kromm asked through deep breaths as he instinctively reached for his great sword that was strapped to his back. Allindrian held up her hand to silence him.

They were in a large meadow surrounded by fir trees. To the west was a gentle rise of rocks and ledges along the mountainside. She heard it again. It was a clicking noise, coming from the rocks. She scanned the ridges and ledges looking for the source of the noise. What was that sound? She had heard it before.

Then it came to her in a flash. It was the sound of claws on stone! Reaching back she drew an arrow from her quiver. Her move was faster than a striking snake, and the men were momentarily taken aback by her sudden movement. But it was only seconds before the seasoned warriors saw her action for what it was…an alarm that danger was near. Within heartbeats they had all brought their weapons to bear. The sound of scraping steel on scabbards echoed off the rock face.

"Prepare to fight!" she yelled, bringing her bow up and drawing back on the string. Instantly, two large beasts leaped from a ledge, sprinting down the rock face. They moved as easily as lizards down the rocks and in a few seconds they were on the soft meadow floor running on all fours toward the astonished men.

The creatures were as large as bulls in their prime, with huge dog-like heads. But because their thick skin seemed to take on the hues of their surroundings, Allindrian had looked right over

125

them thinking they were nothing but part of the rocks that surrounded them.

She was astonished at their size and speed, but her training took over and she reacted instinctively, firing arrow after arrow into one beast, hoping to take it down and even the odds. Incredibly the beast dodged two of her arrows, but the third and fourth slammed into its thick shoulders. Allindrian's arrows were magical, but even so they barely penetrated the animal's hide. And then the beast was on her.

Kromm drew his sword, surging toward the threat with no hesitation. Any other man would have fled, for the terror that these creatures engendered was overpowering. Each beast emanated a magical fear stronger than anything these men had ever felt. Though the king's men held their ground, their swords shook with the fright that was enveloping them.

Kromm could not believe the size of the beasts. Even he seemed small compared to their massive bulk. His men fanned out to both his flanks, giving him room to use his sword. They stood, grasping their weapons in trembling hands as the demon hounds charged them. It was an eerie sight, for the beasts did not growl or make any sound as they sprinted across the grassy ground, which seemed completely out of the ordinary for an animal of that size. It made them seem as if they were floating across the meadow.

But as they rapidly drew near, Kromm could see that they were not animals at all. They were demons. Their skin shifted in colors and their eyes glowed red. Their teeth and claws were black, like coal, and abnormally long.

They fanned out as they charged the group. One was targeted on Allindrian while the other two bore down on Kromm and his men. The nearest demon hound was ten feet away when it pivoted, jumping to Kromm's left. It was so quick that Kromm registered the move several seconds after the beast was tearing into Gylow. The creature hit the swordsman in the chest, remaining on top of him as he hit the ground. The impact alone had crushed his sternum, but when the beast landed on top of him it continued attacking, using its knife-like talons to rip and tear through armor, muscle, and bone, completely tearing his chest apart. Then, in mere seconds, it had leaped away from the torn body of Gylow, and had charged toward the astonished king.

Allindrian drew her sword, quickly whispering the words to a spell. As the last word was uttered, six glowing bolts appeared next to her, floating in mid-air. With a quick mental command, she sent all six into the demon just as it jumped towards her. The magical bolts slammed into the flying animal as Allindrian dove forward under the beast. The giant hound flew over her as she came up from a roll, standing to face the snarling monster.

The demon spun and roared, the sound causing all the men to stumble as they held their ears in pain. Even Allindrian reacted by bringing her hands to her ears, trying to block out the assault that was pounding at her head. Her vision momentarily blurred and her head swam, but she managed to shake off the audible attack just in time to see the demon hound strike with both front claws. She brought her sword up quickly but the beast's speed was incredible. She managed to deflect one claw with her sword, but the other ripped across her shoulder and chest. Flying backwards she used the momentum of the strike, spinning in the air and rolling across the ground. It felt like a bull had struck her, but she had no time to inspect her wound. She had to hope that her elven chain mail had kept the razor sharp claws away from her flesh.

Evryn ripped his mind from the fear that was controlling his body, lifting his mighty axe just as the demon hound leaped at King Kromm. His ears still rang, but his king needed him. Bellowing a war cry he lunged toward the leaping hound, bringing his axe down as hard as he could. The blade was sharp and well made. It had seen him through many battles, yet it felt as if his blade had struck a flying rock. The beast's momentum and iron-like hide caused his axe to rebound with such incredible force that the warrior was thrown to his back.

Kromm dove to the side, the demon hound landing where he had been. He came up quick, slashing his blade out with one hand as the beast attacked relentlessly with teeth and claw. Kromm used his prodigious strength and huge blade to swat the demon's paws away, but the hound kept coming and Kromm was forced backwards.

Meanwhile, Tyn had also finally broken away from the fear that had imprisoned him, pressing his mind into blackness. Shaking, sweating, and gritting his teeth, he fought off the evil beasts' spell. It felt like he was walking through a windstorm and that once he broke the spell, the oppressive wind had just disappeared.

He ran forward to help his king, but he never made it. Out of the corner of his eye he caught sight of third beast as it bounded from the brush behind them. He hadn't heard it at all. It was the creature's smell that caused him to turn just in time to see his death before him. His last sensory impression was the smell of burnt hair and rotting flesh as he felt the demon's claws tear at his chest. He was soon relieved of his pain as the world went black around him just as the beast's jaws closed over his head.

Allindrian spun and danced, trying to evade the deadly claws. She moved backwards using her silver blade to deflect the blows. Her magical blade cut the beast many times, but it seemed to have little effect. But the demon was bleeding. Her magic bolts had struck home and she could see several holes in the demon's hide bubble with black blood. Its paws sustained numerous shallow cuts as well and black blood was splattering against her every time it attacked. Yet it kept up the attack, and the pain in her shoulder began to slow her down. She couldn't tell for sure, but she may have broken something. She needed to take the offensive to win this fight, but it was all she could do to defend herself. Then she thought of an idea.

"Ul anthar Luminos!" she yelled, shooting her left fist forward. Instantly a bright ball of light rocketed from her hand, hitting the demon in the face. The light was harmless, but it flared so brightly that the hound stopped, dropping its head low to shield its eyes. That's when Allindrian ran forward, jumping high and through the light. She came down sword first on top of the demon's back. The sharp spines on its back cut into her hamstrings as she straddled the beast, but her sword managed to slide through the demon's ribs, sinking to the hilt in the beast's muscled body. Her elven blade hummed with joy as it sought the demon's death.

Roaring violently, the beast bucked its powerful body, tossing Allindrian into the air. Yet she managed to hold onto her blade as black blood erupted from the creature's deadly wound. The beast threw her four paces away and she landed hard in a patch of grass.

Kromm, engaged in his own struggle, ducked under one swipe of a claw, while moving quickly to his left to narrowly avoid the second. The demon's speed was astonishing and Kromm felt the power of each blow as it skimmed by him. Then, to his dread, a second beast joined its comrade. The newcomer growled, and bared its fangs, dripping blood and spittle that stained the ground. Kromm backed up slowly as the beasts circled him, toying with their prey.

"So it ends like this," Kromm growled, ready to fight to the death. But as soon as he contemplated his own death, he thought of his family, and his kingdom. He couldn't die here. Refusing to accept that possibility, he felt a surge of power and determination rise up in him, fueled by anger so intense it nearly consumed him. Just the thought of his wife and son being without him caused his sword arm to shake with uncontrolled rage. These feelings erupted within him, invigorating his tired muscles with renewed strength. He stood up straighter, his eyes glowing from the surge of energy now coursing through his body.

The demons growled, hesitating, sensing the change in their prey. Kromm, flexing his muscles, roared with a fury he couldn't control. The ground shook and the demons froze as the power of his anger hit them in a blast of sound. His body coursed with so much adrenaline that he felt as if he would burst into flames. He threw himself toward one beast, swinging his sword down with intense fury. The hound attempted to deflect the sword with its claws. This time Kromm struck the strongest blow, and his sword powered through the demon's strike cutting through skin and flesh. Kromm then reversed the strike, bringing his blade across the demon's head. The beast howled as Kromm's blade sliced across its eyes.

Then, the second demon hound struck him from the side. It felt as if he had been struck by a dragon's tail, forcing the wind from his lungs as he landed on his back with the demon on top of him. Kromm felt the crushing weight of the hound as the beast tore its back legs into Kromm's thighs. His greaves and thigh plates protected him somewhat but they were not enough. Its claws raked his legs, creating deep valleys of bleeding flesh down his legs.

The king roared in defiance and pain, releasing his sword and bringing both hands up to catch the descending jaws of the creature. It was like catching a rock thrown from a giant. Both hands closed on the demon's throat as he fought with all his strength to fend off the black fangs that hungered for his flesh.

The demon's eyes flared with uncertainty as it struggled against the man's surprising strength. But Kromm knew it was useless. The beast was too strong. Bleeding profusely from his shredded legs, he felt the beast's front claws puncture his armor on his shoulders. Images of his wife and son flashed before his eyes.

Allindrian, struggling to get up, gasped as she tried to regain her breathe. Her shoulder pounded and she could barely hold onto her sword. She switched hands with her blade looking up to see the wounded demon slowly walk towards her. She could not believe the creature was still alive. That blow should've killed it. But the beast had learned a lesson. The hound was slowly advancing on her now, obviously wary of the dangerous half-elf.

Allindrian had no idea how the rest of the group was faring, and she did not risk a glance to find out. The hound was so quick that one glance would be all it needed to end the fight. Gripping her sword tightly with her left hand she focused on her training, concentrating on the dance and the movements that had kept her alive for so many years.

Then the demon attacked. Her agility kept her moving left and right, narrowly avoiding the deadly claws. Yet one claw finally caught her, slicing deep into the flesh of her thigh. As blood poured from the deadly wound, she stumbled to her knee. The beast charged forward, sensing the end of the fight.

It was ironic, but her injury saved her life. The hound was as tall as a bull, so when it charged forward its snapping jaws just missed her head as she dropped to her knee. Spinning her blade with her left hand she rammed the razor sharp point up through the demon's neck. The silver tip burst from the demon's skull, killing it instantly. The huge creature landed heavily on Allindrian's legs as she tried in vain to leap free, pinning her under its enormous weight.

Kromm's forearms trembled with the strain of keeping the beast's jaws from his face. No other man could have held the beast at bay for so long. The demon's red eyes narrowed, whether in confusion, or anger, the king could not tell. But he felt his arms weaken as the loss of blood began to take its toll. He knew his death was imminent. As he felt his weary arms began to let go, he closed his eyes, waiting for the moment when blackness would engulf him. But it didn't come. Instead, he felt the demon hound jerk several times and then the weight was gone.

The king's eyes slowly opened. There, to his left, he saw two of the beasts. They seemed to be focused elsewhere, toward the tree line, toward two glowing warriors in silver armor. *Maybe I did die* he thought. It seemed he was looking at an illusion.

Kromm tried to stand but his legs gave out on him. He looked down and all he saw was blood. Gritting his teeth he somehow found the strength to stand. He picked up his sword on wobbly legs and slowly stood up to his full height.

He wasn't dreaming; nor was he dead. There, over twenty paces away, were two cavaliers, surrounded by God Light, moving rapidly toward the beasts. Both were carrying bows, and in a blink of an eye, one arrow after another flew across the meadow, slamming into the demons.

Kromm could see that the one hound he had cut across the eyes was having trouble seeing. It was shaking its head from side to side, vainly trying to focus. One eye was completely destroyed and the other was filling with black blood. As several of the magical arrows slammed into it, the blinded beast roared in fury as they penetrated its tough hide. The second demon roared, charging the two cavaliers even as the arrows were hammering into it.

The king took advantage of the situation to glance around for Allindrian. He saw her across the clearing struggling under the body of a dead hound. Clenching his jaw in stubborn determination he found the strength to move. He pushed the fog of pain away, stepping one foot after another. The short distance to her seemed endless, as if it would take an eternity to cover. As he ambled towards her he left a trail of blood behind him. Crimson streaked the grass as it brushed against the mangled and torn flesh of his legs. His vision swam, but again he shook it off, forcing one leg in front of the other. He growled in defiance, willing the dizziness away, forcing the blackness of unconsciousness back with mental hammer blows as he slowly made his way to her.

Straddling the beast's head he wrapped his arms around it in a bear hug. He didn't need to tell Allindrian what he was doing. He lifted with all his remaining strength. She only needed a few inches and he gave her that. She slid out from under the demon and Kromm dropped the beast's massive head to the ground. There was a loud thump as its head hit the grass, followed by a second thump as Kromm's body hit the ground behind it.

Jonas's heart pounded as he watched the enraged demon hound run at him with incredible speed. His arrows were hitting their mark but he couldn't tell if they were doing much damage. The beast did not slow and he only had seconds before the hound would smash into him.

At the last moment Jonas dropped his bow and quickly drew one of his blades, which took on a blue glow as the demon was nearly upon him. He channeled Shyann's energy into his other fist, forming a glowing ball of blue flame. When the beast was just five paces away he screamed and hurled the ball of flame forward, simultaneously diving to the side. Azure flames erupted, creating a loud whoosh as the fire sucked in the air around them. The demon howled as the God Fire seared its head, but still it did not stop its charge. As Jonas jumped to the side, the beast's momentum carried it past him. Jonas then used his sideways movement to roll out of the way, and come to his feet, this time holding both glowing blades before him.

Several arrows flew from the brush nearby, hitting the hound in its flank as it attempted to shake off the burning pain from Jonas's fire. The arrows, unfortunately, were not magical, and they bounced harmlessly off the beast's tough hide.

Jonas calmed his beating heart, found his center, and transformed his mind into the state of Ty'erm. As the familiar iron wall dropped over his consciousness, he then charged the distracted beast. At least that was how he would describe the feeling. When he entered Ty'erm, all of his superfluous emotions disappeared, as if a wall were formed around them. There was no fear, no worry, just pure concentration. Totally focused on the task at hand, his instincts took over, his body moving with practiced precision, unhampered by the thought of death.

Both blades struck true, slicing deep wounds across the hound's muscled chest. The hound roared in pain, swinging its clawed arm in a deadly sweep so quickly that Jonas could not avoid the attack. The deadly claws raked the side of his helm, the tremendous force of the blow lifting him into the air, spinning him in a full circle and throwing him onto the grassy ground. He rolled, quickly regaining his footing, and trying to get his blades up to fend off any new attacks. His jaw ached but his helm had saved him again. The demon's claws had not penetrated his magical armor.

Jonas, suddenly hearing Fil's roar, shook off his dizziness. "No!" Jonas screamed as he saw Fil charging from the brush. The demon pivoted toward this new attacker, shooting towards Fil with lightning speed. Fil was so surprised by the beast's speed that he barely had time to lift his spear to meet the charge.

The tip of his spear penetrated just under the demon's eye, but there was nothing there but bone, and the razor sharp point snapped off under the force of the impact. Fil's arm jerked violently, his spear torn from his hands. Then he felt the full weight of the hound smash into him, using its huge bony head like a battering ram. Fil heard the cracking of his ribs as he was tossed into the air and launched backwards. He landed hard, tumbling several times, as searing pain erupted in his side. But along with the pain, he also suddenly had trouble breathing, every intake of air accompanied by excruciating pain. It was a familiar feeling, one he had experienced recently when an ogre had broken several of his ribs at the battle of the Lindsor Bridge. But this was worse. Any attempt to breathe was a struggle, as if an anvil were sitting on his chest.

Taleen's light flared brightly as she fired another arrow into the injured hound. The beast had finally cleared the blood from its only good eye and its head jerked, bird-like, toward her, finally able to see the cause of its pain. Four arrows protruded from the demon's hide but they did not seem to cause it much damage; they only made it angrier. Instantly the hound used its powerful hind legs, launching itself toward her. Taleen drew her sword as the beast shot forward with cat-like speed. She dove to the side as the demon hound lunged toward her, its front paws raised and its claws splayed wide and fully extended. One paw clipped her leg, cutting her across the back of her unprotected calf.

She rolled, coming up quickly and using her sword to deflect the striking claws. Her magical blade cut into the demon's legs as the beast sought to get in close and rip her apart.

The hound stopped for a moment, roaring loudly. The sound was deafening, the magical onslaught striking Taleen like a hurricane wind. Her ears pounded and she ground her teeth in pain, the horrible sound shaking her to the bones. Doubling over she struggled to concentrate enough to pray to Bandris for help.

She had almost shaken off the magical attack when she felt the weight of the demon hound crash into her. She felt something in her arm break as she flew onto her back, the demon hound landing on top of her, its crushing weight forcing the air from her lungs.

Jonas, hearing Taleen scream, tore his eyes from Fil to his fellow cavalier. He trembled with fear for her as he watched the other demon hound land on top of her. He quickly glanced back to Fil seeing that Kilius, Jangar, and Myrell had emerged from the brush and were engaging the hound as Fil squirmed in pain on the ground.

Returning his gaze to Taleen, he was filled with foreboding as her screams echoed in the clearing. He could not reach her quickly, nor could he use his God Fire as he would burn her along with the beast, so he brought forth his cognivant power, gathering the energy around him. He could see the energy in his mind's eye collect and swirl in a whirlwind just in front of him. After a few seconds he threw the power across the clearing, focusing its impact on the beast's thick side. It was like an invisible wall shooting across the clearing, and as it neared the beast Jonas concentrated all the energy to a spot on the beast's side, a spot about as large as a warrior's shield. The force of the strike slammed into the hound, breaking its ribs, lifting it into the air and launching it against the rock face twenty paces away.

Jonas was already running towards Taleen when the demon, unbelievably, regained its footing. Reaching her, he looked down, blanching at what he saw. Though her armor had protected her vital mid-section, she was bleeding from numerous deep lacerations on her arms and legs. But it was the wound on her neck that terrified him. Taleen's eyes, wide with shock and fear, stared beseechingly at Jonas as she frantically tried to cover the puncture wounds with her hands, a futile effort, as her blood continued to pulse through her fingertips.

"No!" Jonas cried, bending down to heal her life threatening wound. But he did not have the time, the roar of the hound alerting him that the beast was nearly on him.

Shaking with fear for Taleen and fury toward the demon hound, he had no time to think; his only concern was to kill the demon and to protect Taleen. His anger and fear coalesced in a hurricane of power. His scream echoed for miles as his body flexed tightly, every muscle tightening, bringing forth his cognivant force like a cracking whip. He drew such massive amounts of energy into the strike that the demon hound didn't know what hit it.

Instantly the force of the strike struck the demon from all directions and its body caved in like a smashed clay pot. There was a loud cracking noise as the demon's body was crushed, leaving nothing but an amalgam of broken body parts in an emulsion of black blood.

Jonas's head reeled with pain from the use of such immense power, rendering him almost unconscious. But he could not let that happen or Taleen would die. He forced the pain away, the sight of her damaged body giving him renewed strength. He was near collapse, but her moans and the sound of her struggling to breath gave him enough energy to push away the blackness that was fighting to overwhelm him. He had to stay conscious, he had to help Taleen.

While Jonas was struggling to maintain consciousness, Jangar and Kilius were engaged in a desperate struggle with the last demon. Jangar brought his blade down hard on the hound's head as it swiped at Kilius who was frantically trying to deflect the blows. His blade hit hard but did little damage. The demon kicked out with its back leg so fast that Jangar could not react in time, the sharp claws slicing through his cheap armor and ripping three deep cuts across his chest. The impact of the blow sent him sprawling backwards.

Kilius continued to swing his sword from left to right but the demon hound easily swatted it away, and before Kilius could bring the blade back to defend himself, the beast reared up on its hind legs, bringing both front paws down toward his face. Kilius jumped backwards away from the deadly claws, but not quickly enough. He felt the creature's claws pierce the flesh in his face, ripping long deep cuts all the way down to his chest. His poorly made armor did little to protect him and he screamed in pain, falling backwards into the grass.

Myrell struggled to get to her feet as she watched her brother fall away from the demon. She had taken a claw to the leg and the painful wound was bleeding badly.

"Kilius!" she screamed as she saw him howling in pain on the ground.

The demon, momentarily distracted from its prey, jerked its head in her direction. She stood, holding her sword defensively, a pitifully feeble posture for such a formidable foe, but it was all she could do. The demon growled, slowly moving towards her.

Just then a tremendous roar came from the brush to their right. As Myrell turned toward the sound, she saw a rock the size of her head flying through the air and crashing into the demon. There was a sick crack as the rock struck the beast in its hind leg. The power of the throw spun the beast so that it was facing the brush from which the rock had come. A large form then came crashing through the brush charging the injured hound. Myrell's eyes widened in surprise as she recognized Hagar the ogrillion. He must have been following them at a distance the entire time.

Hagar barreled through the brush rushing the wounded hound with no hesitation. The demon hound tried to lift its body onto its hind legs to meet the charge with teeth and claw, but its back leg was broken and it didn't respond. Hagar gave a tremendous roar as he kicked out his large foot. The hound's front claw and Hagar's foot came together with a crack. Bones broke and flesh was torn, but it was hard to tell who was injured more.

Hagar then came in quick with both fists, crashing them down on the demon's head. The force of the blows slammed the demon's head down into the dirt. Frantically, the hound swiped its claws out toward the powerful ogrillion. One claw slashed deeply into Hagar's calf causing the ogrillion to fall down on his knee.

Myrell, taking advantage of Hagar's sudden appearance, stumbled towards her brother, finding him rolling on the ground in severe pain. "Kilius! What can I do?" she cried, reaching down and pulling his hands away from the bleeding wounds. His face and chest was covered in blood and she could clearly see two deep cuts running down his cheeks and continuing to the top of his chest. It looked as if Kilius's chin had deflected the claws from ripping his throat out, but his wounds were severe and bleeding profusely.

"I can't stop the bleeding," moaned Kilius.

Myrell tore her cloak off her back, pushing it into his chest hoping to stop the flow of blood. She glanced to her left and saw Jangar lying on his side, in a pool of his own blood, staring back at her with lifeless eyes. His chest was torn open and blood still dripped from the mortal wound. She kept up the pressure on her brother's chest, glancing back at the demon and Hagar.

The demon lunged forward with tremendous speed for an animal with one useless leg, clamping its huge jaws on Hagar's leg and shaking its head from side to side. Though Hagar was larger than the animal, the powerful beast was able to toss the injured ogrillion several paces away.

Hagar roared in pain, his calf mangled beyond recognition. The demon hound rushed at him again but Hagar kicked out with his one good leg, connecting solidly with its jaw. The crack of its jaw breaking echoed off the mountain's walls, as its head snapped violently to the side, blood and teeth flying from its mouth. But still it kept coming. Hagar scooted back quickly, but the beast caught him with its front claws, raking deeply into his flesh, climbing the ogrillian's body like a cat clawing up a tree.

As the hound went for Hagar's throat, the ogrillion punched the beast in the face with all his strength, breaking several bones in his hand, but wounding the demon as well. The bones in its snout had been crushed, and it had now lost most of its front teeth, but it had been created by powerful magic, and still it came at the ogrillion. The demon hound ripped its front claws across Hagar's chest, as it attempted to reach his throat. Hagar grabbed its jaws with both hands, barely managing to hold the heavy head at bay. Shaking its head from side to side the demon tried to bite through Hagar's grip.

Hagar roared with the effort, and continued to hang on firmly. The ogrillion's immense strength was beginning to pay off, and slowly he began to pull the hound's jaw further apart. But the claws of the demon continued to rake Hagar's chest and the blood from his wounds bathed them both in crimson. Still, Hagar held on. He strained, pulling harder, forcing its jaws farther and farther apart, until finally he heard the snapping of tendons and bone, and with one great heave Hagar ripped the beast's jaws completely open until they were just flapping useless in his hands. Yet, despite the horrendous wound, its front claws continued to shred Hagar's flesh.

"No!" Myrell screamed, as she witnessed Hagar's desperate struggle with the demon. He was being torn to pieces and she could do nothing. She couldn't leave her brother who was now starting to lose consciousness. Besides, what could she do against such a beast? Myrell frantically looked around for help, knowing that if it didn't come soon her brother would die.

Hagar's mind began to cloud over, and he felt himself weaken as he struggled to fight off the demon's deadly claws. He had to make one last attempt to destroy the beast before he completely lost consciousness. Digging deeply into his last reserves of strength, he grabbed the demon's lifeless upper jaw with one hand, punching his other massive fist into the demon's open mouth. He felt something crush inside the demon's mouth, as the hound tried frantically to pull away. Hagar grabbed onto something wet and fleshy inside its mouth and held it firm. He had grasped the creature's wet fleshy tongue, and with his last roar of effort, ripped it violently from its mouth, black blood spraying from the deadly wound. Within moments the ogrillion had lost consciousness, collapsing back onto the bloodied ground.

Myrell stared helplessly at the two fallen combatants, both lying motionless. Hagar's right hand hung to the side, his fist still clutching the demon's bloody tongue. The ogrillion had saved their lives and she could do nothing to help him. Her brother lay at her feet bleeding to death and she could do nothing for him other than try to minimize the loss of blood. She had never felt so helpless and overcome with fear and frustration.

Jonas, now leaning anxiously by Taleen, quickly clamped his hands on her bleeding neck. Blood covered her hands, face, and chest. She looked at Jonas, eyes wide with shock as she felt her life blood draining from her body.

Jonas frantically called upon Shyann's power, channeling the healing energy into her. His heart pounded with fear as he searched out her wounds, hoping he wasn't too late. Though the wounds on her neck were not deep, they had nonetheless punctured her arteries. With her slit throat bleeding so rapidly and profusely, that she was unable to pray and heal herself. Jonas mended them, frantically looking elsewhere for other wounds. He found more cuts and lacerations on her legs and arms, healing them as well. She had several broken ribs and her sternum was cracked. He also fixed those injuries. Sweating with fear, his heart raced as he focused intently on her wounds, so intently in fact that several minutes passed before he noticed that her heart was no longer beating.

Eyes wide with fear, he saw Taleen staring back at him, her own eyes blank and sightless, seeing nothing.

"No!" Jonas screamed. "Shyann, please help me!"

He sent healing magic into her body again, finding her heart. It was not beating; the loss of blood had been too much. He pushed Shyann's energy into Taleen's heart, trying to get it beating. He continued trying, again and again, but nothing was working, even his powers could not bring back the dead. He could heal her wounds, but not replace her blood or her inner light. Jonas cried in anguish as he fought to restart her heart. He struggled on and on, for how long he did not know, finally giving in to utter fatigue and exhaustion as he finally gave up, slumping over her still body as he wept in despair.

High on a rock ledge Gullanin stared at the scene below. Things had been developing well until the cavaliers' arrival. They had managed to kill the Hounds of Gould but their losses were great. He could see that the king and the Blade Singer were wounded and that one of the cavaliers was dead. Other warriors had also been killed but he was not worried about them. Now was his time to strike.

Dandronis and his men heard the commotion of battle before they saw it. The knowledge that their king may be fighting for his life spurred them forward. They ran into the clearing, fanning out with bows, spears, and swords held tightly.

Dandronis stood next to Durgen, both warriors quickly scanning the area. It was a chaotic scene and it took a moment to take it all in. There was one huge beast nearby lying on top of another beast that appeared to be an ogre. Next to their bodies was a dead human and several that were injured. One was a young woman yelling for help as she tried to aid another wounded man.

Beyond them another dead beast lay still, destroyed beyond recognition. A young warrior in shining silver armor stood up from the grass next to it. His helm was off and he turned toward the newcomers, making eye contact with Dandronis. The man's eyes were red and there was no mistaking the tears streaking down his face. But he was no longer crying, his face was hard and cold, void of emotion.

There was movement behind the young warrior, and Dandronis saw the Blade Singer and another warrior run towards the man is silver armor. He recognized the other warrior. It was Evryn the axe man. But where was the king?

"Search for the king and see to the wounded!" Dandronis yelled to the men near him.

"De warrior be a cavalier," Durgen the dwarf stated matter-of-factly. Dandronis looked again, realizing the dwarf was right. The warrior's armor was brightly polished and devoid of blood or dirt. He wore a blue cloak, shimmering with silver thread, that despite the recent battle was clean and unmarred. Shyann's mark sparkled back at them from across the glade and he noticed her mark on his forehead for the first time.

"Let's get some answers, good dwarf," Dandronis replied, quickly heading toward the cavalier.

Jonas turned toward Allindrian as she quickly approached him. She was bleeding and her right arm hung useless at her side. Next to her was a burly warrior carrying a large axe.

Allindrian's eyes glanced down to Taleen and back to Jonas's face. She did not need to say anything, nor did he. They both understood the loss. And there were no words that could give comfort or explain such a tragedy.

"Jonas," she said, "My heart swells with joy in seeing you but the king needs you now. My magical healing is not enough; he will die shortly without your help."

"Where is he?" Jonas asked, his voice cold and weary.

"Near the other dead demon. Follow us," she replied, turning on her heels.

They hastened to the king's body which was lying behind the dead demon hound, his sword still clenched in his fist. Jonas could clearly see deep wounds on the king's legs, and there was so much blood. But miraculously the cuts seemed partially closed, and the blood was beginning to coagulate, no longer pouring from the wounds. It seemed strange to Jonas that they had stopped bleeding so quickly, but the amount of blood around the king still worried him that it might be too late.

Quickly kneeling by his body, he laid his hands on the king's giant chest. Again, he summoned Shyann's power, which instantly flooded from his body into the Tarsinian king. He felt the king's heart beat softly, but steadily, and so he sought out the man's wounds, sealing up the cuts in his legs and arms and staunching the blood flow. He neutralized any incipient infection, and repaired damaged tissue and broken bones.

In the process of healing the king Jonas sensed something deep in the man's spirit. He had never felt the likes of it before. It was as if there was a separate force within him watching over the king. He couldn't find the source of the energy nor did he know what it was. Its presence was very subtle, as if it were hiding and waiting for when it was needed. Jonas finally finished, releasing the energy and opening his eyes. He swayed slightly as dizziness overtook him.

Allindrian was there to catch him and it took a few moments for it to pass. His head throbbed with pain and he felt utterly exhausted. The loss of Taleen had wounded his spirit, and his physical injuries, along with the use of his cognivant abilities, had wounded his body. He would need to rest, and soon.

Standing on wobbly legs he noticed two more newcomers. One was a stout dwarf who wore magnificent plate armor. The dwarf stood just above his waist but his heavily muscled legs and arms made him look as fearsome as any warrior. The other was a tall warrior wearing the armor of a Tarsinian Knight. His head was mostly shaved and he was looking at Jonas with a worried expression.

"Will he live, Cavalier?" Dandronis asked with concern.

"He will not!" a voice erupted from behind them.

They all turned quickly, staring in surprise at an aged man wearing gray robes and holding a polished black staff. His pallid skin was stretched tightly over his gaunt face. His thin gray hair was scraggily and un-kempt, but his eyes glared with power.

"Silvesta!" Gullanin yelled, angling the tip of his staff at the prone body of the king.

The unexpected sight of the wizard appearing out of thin air temporarily froze the warriors with uncertainty. Even Allindrian, tired as she was, did not quickly react to the evil wizard's spell.

A bolt of lightning shot from the tip of the staff seeking the king's body. The warriors stared in horror, the scene before them unfolding in slow motion, their eyes glued to the sizzling bolt shooting towards the helpless body of the king, everyone's eyes, that is, except for the dwarf's.

Durgen leaped in front of the king's body holding his axe out before him. The bolt struck the weapon with a violent flash, the impact sending the dwarf flying backwards, somersaulting over the king.

Durgen's action instantly unfroze everyone. Dandronis jumped away from the flashing bolt while Jonas dropped to his knees, calling forth his God Fire. Though he was exhausted, the image of Taleen's sightless eyes gave him the strength to bring forth the flame. With both hands raised, he shot forth the magic in a fiery blue cone.

Allindrian and Evryn dove backwards away from the bolt as Jonas's fire struck the wizard. At least it struck where the wizard had been. Jonas saw the wizard disappear just as his flames came into contact with him. Letting the flames subside, they all turned to look at the dwarf who was struggling to get up.

"Errr, that stung, it did," Durgen muttered, hefting his son's axe up to inspect it. His hair and clothing were slightly singed, and smoke drifted from his axe.

"That bolt should've killed you. How did you survive?" Allindrian asked, moving toward the short warrior.

"This axe," Durgen replied, lifting it up before him, "was made by me own hands for me son who now sits next to Moradin himself. It was blessed by our clerics with the ability to absorb magic."

"You saved our king, Trader Durgen. We are grateful for it, as I'm sure he will be when he awakes," said Dandronis.

Jonas's mind drifted to Taleen as the warriors spoke, and he found himself walking away from the scene. He was utterly weary, and his head pounded inside his skull. His sadness was complete and it drained his body of any energy that still existed. But he had one more thing to do before he could let total exhaustion claim him, and so he stumbled on shaking legs toward the tree line. He had to check on Fil and the rest of his companions before he took that rest.

Allindrian, Durgen, Evryn, and Dandronis watched the cavalier walk away.

"He has suffered much," Allindrian said softly, answering their questioning stares. She turned back to the warriors as more Tarsinian soldiers approached Dandronis awaiting their orders. "Dandronis, are you in charge?"

"Yes, the men elected me to lead," he said flatly.

"Have your men gather wood and light three large fires in a perimeter. We need warmth and food and a place to rest and see to our wounds," Allindrian ordered.

"Very well, Blade Singer, it shall be done," he replied, turning to his men and giving the orders.

Jonas moved as fast as he tired muscles could carry him towards Myrell, who, with the help of two Tarsinian warriors, was trying frantically to stanch the flow of blood from her brother's wounds. They immediately stepped back as Jonas approached. Myrell grabbed his arm and looked at him pleadingly. Blood covered her arms up to her elbows and her eyes were red from crying.

"Jonas, please help Kilius! Can you save him?"

"I have little energy left but I will try to stop the bleeding," Jonas replied calmly, kneeling next to the unconscious young man. He laid his hands on Kilius's chest, breathing deeply, searching for Shyann's energy. He found it but the link was tenuous, his tired mind having difficulty focusing. He thought of Kiln's training, breathing deeply again, calming his mind and searching for Ty'erm. He was finally able to find it and immediately he felt the surge of power flow from his hands into Kilius. The young warrior was weak but his heart still beat, just barely. Jonas closed the wounds, sealing the torn veins and blood vessels. It only took a few moments and when he was done he opened his eyes, noticing that Kilius was sleeping and no longer moaning.

"Is he going to be okay, Jonas?" Myrell asked anxiously.

"Yes, he will be fine. He will be weak for some time from loss of blood, but rest and food will help." Jonas stood up on shaky legs, motioning for the two Tarsinian warriors to help Kilius. "Men of Tarsis, see to this man. Myrell, go with them and help where you may. I will check on Fil."

"Yes, sir," replied the men in unison.

Myrell reached out, touching Jonas's arm as he moved towards Fil. Jonas turned at her touch, his face showing signs of exhaustion but devoid of emotion.

"Thank you, Jonas, again," she said. Jonas nodded his head, turning to leave, but she held his arm firmly forcing him to turn back again. "And, I'm sorry, Jonas, about Taleen."

Jonas looked at her, sharing a silent moment. He didn't say anything, afraid that he would break down completely. He simply nodded his head again and turned to leave. This time Myrell let him go.

Fil was lying motionless but moaning in obvious pain. As Jonas knelt near his friend, Fil smiled through clenched teeth.

"That thing…hit…harder than that …ogre," Fil stammered softly.

"Shhhh, don't strain yourself. How do you feel?" Jonas asked.

"I can feel several ribs move, so I know they are broken. Other than that I'm not sure. I hurt all over. It hurts just to talk," Fil stammered in pain.

"Then don't talk. I need to rest for a moment before I see to your wounds."

Fil nodded his head and looked at Jonas with concern, despite the pain he felt. "Jonas, did Taleen survive the fight?"

Jonas didn't say anything. He just shook his head slowly.

Fil reached up and grabbed Jonas's hand. "I'm sorry," he said, gritting his teeth as fresh pain lanced through his body.

Jonas grabbed the leather water pouch strapped to Fil's pack and poured some water into his mouth. Fil drank slowly, closing his eyes in pleasure as the cool water dripped down his parched throat. Then Jonas took a long pull from the pouch, gulping down the refreshing liquid. "I think I'm ready, Fil. I am too tired to do much, but I should be able to alleviate some of your pain. Once I rest I can heal you further."

Fil nodded his head gratefully.

Jonas put his hands on Fil's body, searching for Shyann's power one last time. He coaxed it forth again, sending it into Fil and healing his more serious wounds. A couple of his ribs were snapped and the sharp edges had torn into Fil's flesh, causing internal bleeding and trauma. He mended the bones while seeking to repair any bleeding tissue. Fil had several more broken bones and all Jonas had the energy to do was weakly put them back together. He could not firmly fuse them which would mean that Fil would have to limit his movement and rest until Jonas regained his strength to heal him properly. Jonas faltered, losing concentration and almost falling on top of Fil. He caught himself with his right hand, opening his eyes to see Fil looking back at him.

"Thank you, Jonas. The pain has subsided," Fil said, slowly standing and lifting Jonas with him. Fil flinched slightly, his wounds still aching, but he was able to stand on his own. "Are you going to be okay?" Fil asked.

Jonas stared at his friend, too tired to stand anymore and too exhausted to speak more than a few words.

"I must rest, Fil. I can barely stand. We will talk, later," and with his last words Jonas leaned into Fil, letting himself go and succumbing to merciful unconsciousness. Fil was able to catch his friend, slowly lowering him to the grass covered ground where he could now find the rest that his body and mind both desperately needed.

Six

Preparations For War

King Baylin stood on his balcony looking out over his great city. It was early morning and the city was just coming awake. He could see smoke from fires rising from the stone chimneys and the peddlers were already out setting up their goods for sale in the city streets. The young king sniffed the cool fall air, taking in the clean and invigorating smell. It was late fall and the winter snows were soon to arrive.

Every morning the king went out on his balcony and looked at the city of Finarth. It was what he did to prepare himself for his day to come, for the many duties and hardships that his position required. It reminded him daily of what he was working so hard to protect. His city, his people, all were in danger, and it was his duty and desire to protect them and keep them safe.

Every day was filled with preparations for the siege that they all knew would occur. The questions were many. Would Malbeck arrive during the winter? Or wait out the snows in Tarsis and come in spring? Would he take the time to crush and burn every town and village from Tarsis to Finarth? Would he try to take Cuthaine? Surely Cuthaine's Free Legion would slow him down. The Free Legion warriors were well known for their skill and courage, and they would surely deliver a sting to Malbeck's army. Scouts were being sent out continuously for information, but either way he had to make sure that his city would be prepared.

A call to arms had gone out weeks ago requesting all able bodied men to prepare themselves to defend their land. Men and boys alike were arriving by the thousands and erecting make-shift camps outside the city walls. Some were returning warriors who had been on leave to tend to their farms; others were retired veterans, while some were just farmers, men and boys alike who came to defend their homes. The king was doing all he could to bring in food and supplies for these men, preparing for a certain drawn out siege. He was emptying the royal coffers and buying up wheat and salted meats and storing them for the battle to come. Necessities like water, blankets, medical supplies, as well as weapons were being bought and collected in copious amounts and stored for safekeeping. The population of Finarth was growing rapidly, as more warriors and refugees came in from the outlying areas to be protected by their liege. It was a responsibility that weighed heavily on the new king, but one that he carried fiercely on his powerful shoulders.

The king had changed over the last few months. The injuries that he had suffered under the knife of the Dykreel cleric had a lasting effect on the young and untried monarch. He had lost his joy for life and it had been replaced with cold hard determination. His eyes no longer sparkled when he looked upon a young child, a beautiful woman, or even a piece of art. He simply could not enjoy them anymore; neither physically, nor mentally. Never again would he lie with a woman. His royal line, the Gavinsteal name, would be no more, destroyed with one quick swipe of the dark cleric's knife. Now his moods were almost constantly dark, and he thrived on a rage that never seemed to leave him. He did not sleep much. His was often plagued with nightmares that were filled with images of pain, rage, and revenge. But he took one positive thing from his experience; he no longer felt any fear. He would face Malbeck and his army unhindered by the fear of death. Death was no longer something to fear.

King Baylin ran his hands through his long hair, sighing heavily. He had a lot to do today, as he did every day since his father's death. He spun on his heel, moving through the large double doors, pushing aside the long white silk curtains draping the doorway. His room was spacious but sparsely furnished. The bed was unmade and covered in heavy blankets and furs to protect him from the cold winter air. A large fire was burning brightly in the stone fireplace and he could feel its warmth as he walked by it to the arched entry into the anteroom. As expected, Persinius, his servant, waited there for him ready to perform his morning duties.

"Good morning, my King, your breakfast is ready," the young man said, standing and indicating the table sitting next to a big window overlooking the courtyard below.

Persinius was young, twenty six, but he had served the Gavinsteal royal family since he was thirteen. In fact he had been trained to do so by his father, who had served the family his entire life. The young man was handsome, almost feminine in appearance. He was of medium height and build and he moved with a grace typical of someone raised to cater to royalty.

"Thank you, Persinius. I will be in need of my armor shortly. Please see to it. Also, find Alerion and bring him to me," he ordered as he sat down to eat.

"Yes, my King," replied the young man, bowing and walking from the room.

***

Kiln walked through the make-shift roads and paths crisscrossing the hastily built huts and tents that covered the fields in front of Finarth. Dagrinal and Graggis accompanied him as they surveyed the living conditions of the refugees who were pouring into Finarth in a steady flow. Graggis and Dagrinal were of equal height, both taller than Kiln, but that is where the similarities ended. Where Dagrinal was lithe and sinewy, Graggis was thick and heavily laden with dense muscle. There were few men who looked as powerful as Graggis, and still few more who could actually match him in strength. Both men were Finarthian knights, officers who had earned their station, and reputation. Dagrinal was the finest swordsman in the order, next to Master Borrum, the weapons master for the knights. Both men were an integral part in helping prepare Finarth for war.

They had worked hard to provide decent conditions for the refugees. Huge amounts of timber were cut down and brought to the area to be used for shelter and fires. They built latrines for the thousands of people that had come to Finarth's gate for protection, and Kiln had ordered that they begin training the young men in basic formation fighting.

Every morning and evening the men of fighting age met in the fields to be trained by the experienced officers. The number of refugees was growing daily and it was becoming more and more difficult to provide adequate living conditions for them. But the advancing army of Malbeck was bringing the people together under a common goal, that of survival.

"Dagrinal, how many more came in last night?" asked Kiln, greeting men and women alike with a smile and a nod as they prepared for their day.

"Just over a thousand, Commander."

"And how many are capable of fighting?"

"Three hundred or so," Dagrinal answered.

As they made their way past the various tents and cook fires, many of the refugees greeted the three men with smiles, nods, and hellos. Kiln's presence alone seemed to remove the tension from the air. Word had spread quickly among the ranks and the refugees that Kiln, the legend, was back in Finarth, and taking command of the army. His name was whispered around the fires at night as if he were a ghost come back to defend them. His very presence attracted people from all around, some eager to fight under him, others just wanting to see him, all acutely aware that Kiln was a key player in the city's defense.

"Any men arriving with weapons of their own?" Kiln asked the two officers, stopping briefly to greet an aging woman stirring her morning meal of oats over a cook fire.

"Fifty swords were counted, forty bows, and thirty spears," Graggis answered, scanning an inventory scroll.

"Not many," Kiln sighed. "How goes the training?" he asked, stopping to focus on his two officers.

Graggis shrugged a bit dejectedly, "Not well, Commander...they..."

"Are doing their best," interjected Dagrinal. "Many of the men arriving have only seen fifteen winters, some are well beyond that, and even fewer have any military experience. But they are determined and willing, and that is all we can ask."

"They are scared, Commander," added Graggis. "The thought of Malbeck and his Banthras arriving at the gates of Finarth is beyond their imaginations, but, as Dagrinal said, they are willing, and they are working hard."

"Good, I would like to observe the training this evening," Kiln said.

"Very well," replied Dagrinal.

***

Alerion walked briskly over the polished stones leading to the king's room. Persinius had found him in Finarth's library going over ancient scrolls and writings from long dead kings and wizards, hoping to find some clue to the meaning of the riddle that the pit fiend had given him.

Months ago Alerion had brought forth Ixtofin, a pit fiend, from his home plane in the Abyss, demanding answers to his questions. He got them, but one was in the form of a riddle, a riddle that was the key to defeating Malbeck, at least that is what the demon had said.

"An Ishmian with the blood of Finarth in his veins," Alerion whispered to himself, moving through the familiar passageway. He had not yet found the answers he sought, but he had found some clues.

As he reached the king's door the two knights standing guard stepped aside without question.

"The king is expecting you, Sir," announced one of the guards.

"Very good," Alerion replied, stepping through the door that had been opened by the other guard.

He entered the king's anteroom and saw King Baylin standing near a big window wearing his royal armor. He was just strapping his father's sword to his belt when Alerion entered.

"My Lord, you requested my presence?" Alerion asked.

"Yes, Alerion, how goes your search? Have you solved the riddle?" the king asked, pouring himself a cup of tea. "Tea?" he gestured with the jug.

"Yes, my Lord. That would be nice." Alerion stepped forward to take the cup from the king. "I have not yet solved the riddle, but I have found some interesting information."

"Please tell me what you have found, my friend." Baylin sat down in a soft chair, motioning for Alerion to do the same. The wizard sat next to the king, taking a sip of the warm tea. It had been sweetened with honey and it warmed his stomach.

"I have found writings of some interest," the wizard began. "I have been perusing diaries and writings that are thousands of years old that go back before King Ullis Gavinsteal was even born, before the first great war with Malbeck. But what caught my interest was a journal entry from King Ullis Gavinsteal himself, from when he was just sixteen winters." Alerion paused, sipping the fragrant tea. It smelled of orange and mint. "The entry spoke of a female interest that he had, a young girl from Mynos. She was the daughter of an emissary from King Rhinehorn."

"And what is the importance of the entry?" the king asked.

"I do not know yet, my King, but if for some reason the young king had relations with this female, before he was king, that..."

"There may have been a child conceived that we do not know about," added the king.

"Exactly, my King, and this child's line, if there is one, would carry the blood of Finarth. But I cannot find any further mention of her. So I will need to travel to Mynos to see if there is any mention of this forgotten piece of history."

"It seems unlikely. It was so long ago, and reaching Mynos will take many weeks of travel. But you must investigate all possible explanations. Leave at once, Alerion. We must find the answer to this riddle."

"As you wish, but I will not be gone so long. I have another means of travel that will get me there much faster."

"Very well. Now Alerion, what type of magical assistance can we expect when Malbeck arrives?" asked the king seriously.

"My King, I have sent messages to Shyval requesting battle wizards. They know of the dangers of not confronting Malbeck. I believe they will help."

The king was leery of Shyval, the dwelling of wizards, located far to the east over the Tundren Mountains. The tower of Shyval sat on the end of a peninsula overlooking Milnos Bay, a giant tower whose size eclipsed the mouth of the bay. It was said that it had been made by wizards, for no ordinary human, not even a dwarf, could have made a structure as large and magnificent. Hundreds of the most powerful wizards of Kraawn lived and studied there, paying no homage to any kingdom. Wizards had always made the king feel uneasy, but he had to hope that help would arrive from Shyval. They would need more than just steel to combat the Dark One.

"Very good, may Ulren guide you in your search. Report back to me as soon as you find something," the king said, dismissing the wizard.

"I will, my King," replied Alerion as he stood up and walked from the room.

***

King Baylin Gavinsteal rode his chestnut mare to the edge of the training grounds. Ten knights of Finarth accompanied him, all wearing the gleaming armor made specifically for them. The king cantered next to Commander Kiln and Fourth Lance Dagrinal. Both sat tall on their warhorses giving them a commanding view of the training. There were several hundred untrained men and boys in the field moving through maneuvers and practicing signals.

"Commander Kiln, how goes the training?" the king asked.

"Slow, my King. But the new recruits are willing and eager to learn."

"Will they be ready?" the king asked.

"They will respond to signals and flags, and maneuver accordingly, but that is all I can say. Let us hope they have heart, for that is something that I cannot teach them," Kiln replied, cringing while observing a line of spearmen. "Excuse me, my King," Kiln said, nudging his horse forward.

Kiln rode to the line where Captain Lathrin was hastily trying to get a group of spearmen in line. Lathrin was a Third Lance in the Finarthian order, leader of his own modrig, or five hundred men. But when leading men from the regular army he was of captain rank. The long lances were entangled and the men were tripping over one another.

"Get in formation!" yelled the captain as Kiln came up beside them. Lathrin looked at Kiln apologetically. "I'm sorry, Commander. They keep getting their lances entangled when they march or turn."

"Do not fret, Lathrin. They are just farmers, and frightened ones at that." Kiln, dismounted from his horse and walked forward, standing in front of the line of men. The men had just gotten their lances untangled and were frantically getting in line when Kiln stepped up to several of them.

One was just a boy, maybe sixteen, and the man to his right was a few years older, while the man to his left was pushing fifty winters. Kiln swept his steel eyes over them as they stood up straight, trying to act like the soldiers they were not. They avoided his stare, except for the youngest, who was looking right at him with wide eyes. Kiln stopped and stared back. The boy's face was round and dirty, covered with freckles. His hair was reddish brown and his eyes were as blue and piercing as a lightning bolt.

"What is your name, boy?" Kiln asked.

The boy was just about to respond when the older man next to him spoke up. "I'm sorry, my Lord, he doesn't mean to stare. It's just that my boy has heard much about you and speaks of you often, but we have never seen you."

"Are you Commander Kiln?" the boy asked quickly, interrupting his father.

"I am," Kiln said with a slight smile.

"I knew it!" the boy said, elbowing the older boy next to him.

Kiln looked at the other boy and saw the resemblance. He was the spitting image of his younger brother, but maybe three or four years older.

"Be quiet, Kye, you are embarrassing us," the older brother muttered through tight lips.

Kiln looked at the two young boys for a moment before returning his gaze to their father. "What is your name?" he asked.

"My name is William Gastros and these are my sons, Kye, and Sylos."

"Have you any military experience, William?"

"No, my Lord, most of us haven't, but we will fight hard. We just want to do our part."

"I do not doubt that. You have courage for being here." Kiln directed his gaze to the dirty piece of cloth that William had wrapped around his head to keep the sweat from his eyes. "May I borrow that strip of cloth?"

"This?" the farmer said, pointing at the head band.

"Yes."

"It is dirty and sweaty, my Lord," the farmer said, pulling it off.

"It will do," replied Kiln, taking the cloth and squatting at the man's feet. "Now, position the lance next to your right foot, and keep it as straight as you can."

The man did so as the others watched intently. Captain Lathrin rode forward to get a better look. Kiln took the cloth, wrapping it around the shaft and the man's leg, tying it tight, lashing the wooden shaft to his right ankle. Kiln stood up, stepping to the side.

"Now, march forward, William," Kiln ordered.

The farmer looked at Kiln uneasily as everyone stared at him. He took several steps forward and the lance easily moved with him. The tip stayed high while the bottom portion was secured to his leg. "Now turn right," Kiln instructed. William turned right, somewhat gracefully, taking a few more steps before stopping and smiling broadly at Kiln. "Very good," added Kiln, moving towards Captain Lathrin and mounting his horse.

"Have everyone do the same," he ordered. "Use whatever you can find."

"Yes, Commander!" replied the captain, turning his horse sideways and speaking to Kiln under his breath. "But, sir, this will only work in marching. I'm afraid it will be of little use in combat."

"You are right, Captain, but it will give them confidence, something they desperately need at the moment."

"It will be done!" the captain replied, seeing the logic in his words.

"Good work, Captain. I will leave you to your task." Kiln turned his horse around and galloped toward the castle. There was still more work to be done, there always was.

***

Alerion stood before the great mirror preparing for the spell. The mirror was a magnificent artifact, one given to him by Durthilliam, a council member at Shyval. Every great court wizard had a similar mirror, magically enabling the wizards to travel to Shyval, which was over a month away, in just a few moments. Alerion did not have the power to teleport such great distances, but he could enact the magic in the mirror to create a very powerful teleportation spell, creating a link to a replica of the mirror in Shyval. Despite the great distance to Shyval, he could arrive within moments using the mirror. Once there he could travel to Mynos by boat in a day. He had to hope that somewhere in the records at Mynos there would be a clue to help unravel the riddle.

He spoke the words of the spell slowly and accurately as he looked into the mirror. He saw himself in the mirror until he finished the last word of the spell. Suddenly his image rippled as if the surface of the mirror was water, then it quickly faded to black. He was in complete darkness, but his eyes were still open.

Then, in just a few blinks, light came flaring back at him and he found himself looking into the mirror again, but it wasn't his mirror, but another just like it. And he was no longer standing in his room, but in a much larger room with high ceilings and smooth ivory colored walls draped with great tapestries. The room itself was rounded, with no sharp points or angles anywhere to be seen.

Alerion had been in this room before. The wizards at Shyval called it the Room of Arrival, for it was where the court wizards would arrive when using the mirrors. It was the highest point on the giant tower and there were four round openings leading outside to look out over the battlements and the water that surrounded the tower. To the west was the Sardast Straits, to the north the city of Tiarg, and the east and south faced Milnos Bay and the lands of Mynos.

"Welcome, Alerion, it has been a long time," came a voice from behind him. Alerion recognized the voice, turning to face the wizard with a warm smile.

"Tuathone, it is good to see you as well. You have aged little since I saw you last."

Tuathone was one of the leaders of the council and she had been at Shyval for a long time, over two hundred years. She was a powerful wizard whose magic had kept her alive beyond the life span of a normal human.

But she did, indeed, look ancient, and she took Alerion's comment for what it was, a jest towards the obvious. They had joked about her age many times and she knew there was no malice in his words. Her long gray hair was pulled back and tied with a silk ribbon into a bundle. Her robes were stark white, contrasting sharply with the sky blue strip of cloth that draped her neck and hung down to her waist. It was a mark of her high rank at Shyval.

Shyval has no allegiance to any kingdom in the lands, but it did have its own order. The council's job was to rule the tower

158

and control the vast amounts of power that the wizards controlled there. Wizards came to Shyval at young ages to learn the ways of magic. They signed a pact in doing so, that they would live at Shyval and never use what they learned for personal gain or power. Many agreed to this contract, for the knowledge and power they had access to here was beyond what most wizards could access and maintain on their own. It became their base for learning the laws of magic. But many rulers of Kraawn often jockeyed for access to this power, and the ruling council was needed to make the decisions necessary to maintain their neutrality.

"What brings you here, Alerion, you have the look of urgency about you," asked Tuathone, dismissing Alerion's previous comment with a smile and wave of her hand.

"You are very perceptive, counselor. I wish to speak with the council and then travel to Mynos immediately."

"Sounds important, my friend, but I cannot gather the council on such short notice. Councilman MyGathin is away and he will not return until tomorrow. May I suggest that you go to Mynos first and I will assemble the council for when you return?"

"That will do," replied Alerion.

"Come," motioned Tuathone, "Let us eat a warm meal while I send a messenger to Mynos to inform them of your arrival. I will have a boat prepared for you immediately." The wizard turned and ambled toward a set of stairs.

"Your generosity is appreciated," replied Alerion, as he followed her down the stairs.

***

Three large fires burned brightly in the mountain clearing. King Kromm, still unconscious, was surrounded by his men who were eating their food and seeing to their wounded. The Blade Singer was warming her hands by one of the other fires as Durgen the dwarf and Dandronis were discussing the day's events next to her. The third fire was occupied by Myrell who was nursing Fil's and Kilius's wounds. Jonas was lying next to them, sleeping soundly within the warmth of several wool blankets.

Myrell had insisted that they build the fire by Hagar's body. The ogrillian was alive, but barely. His heart beat slowly and faintly, but he had not recovered consciousness. They had very little material available to bind his wounds, nor were any of the men courageous enough to get anywhere near the beast regardless of his apparent vulnerability. Myrell had taken on the task herself as Fil and Kilius were still too tired to help.

It had taken her several hours and their own wool cloaks, but she had managed to stop most of the bleeding. The wounds were severe; the ogrillian's flesh was ripped and torn, exposing bone in many places. She did not know if the beast would survive, but she owed him much. He had saved their lives.

"Blade Singer, tell me 'bout de Hallows," requested Durgen. Allindrian turned to face the two men who were now sipping soup made with salted beef, potatoes, and onions, almost the last of their supplies.

"The Hallows is a place of darkness, Master Trader. Everything there thrives on death and nothing of light lives there," she replied, taking a bowl of soup from a Tarsinian warrior.

"Then why do we go there, Blade Singer? What is the advantage?" asked Dandronis.

"It is only great need that drives the undertaking. The queen and prince must be reached quickly. We believe them to be in Cuthaine," she replied.

"But what good will come from it if we die in the Hallows? Death sounds imminent in that horrible place," Dandronis countered.

"It will be dangerous, but I know the dangers of the Hallows and the path we seek. We can make it through alive. And if Jonas travels with us then we will have a greater chance."

Dandronis looked over at the other fire to the still form of the cavalier before looking back at Allindrian.

"What do you know of him? He seems so young to be a cavalier."

160

"He is young, Dandronis. His village was destroyed by boargs led by a Banthra. They were after him, but they failed to kill him. Airos, the cavalier, was sent there to protect him. He died, but he killed the Banthra in the process and Jonas survived. Jonas was only fifteen at the time and he escaped with his friend, Fil, the other young man at the fire with the girl," she replied, glancing toward them. Dandronis and the dwarf both followed her gaze.

"I knew of Airos. He was a great warrior and friend to the dwarves," Durgen interjected.

"Yes he was, Master Trader. I was traveling with a Tarsinian caravan at the time and we met Jonas and Fil on the road to Finarth. I do not feel at liberty to tell you his entire story, nor do I even know it all, but I knew even then he was on his way to becoming the first chosen cavalier when I met him, and it would appear, by the looks of it, that he has succeeded," she replied.

"Chosen?" asked Dandronis.

"Yes, men and women who become cavaliers usually try to attain the honor through the process of testing and training that can only be found at a kulam, but Jonas did neither. He was...chosen...by Shyann herself to become her warrior. At least that is what I am assuming. I have not been able to speak with him since he started his training as a Tarsinian knight almost four years ago, training that obviously was interrupted by some outside force for he does not wear the armor of a knight, but instead dons the metal of a cavalier. I can only assume that Shyann has had her hand in the boy's growth, and that connection has also attracted her enemies for the Forsworn have surely been hunting the boy."

"I see," responded Dandronis thoughtfully.

"Will the cavalier be travelin' wit us to de Hallows?" the dwarf asked bluntly.

"I do not know, Master Trader. His road is Shyann's road, and I do not know the path she has set for him. We will find out after he has rested."

***

161

Jonas awoke early the next morning. His head still ached and his body and soul felt drained. The only reason he slept at all was because he was so physically exhausted from the use of magic and his cognivant abilities. But the real drain came from the oppressive feeling resulting from Taleen's death. He looked at his hands as he sat up from his blankets, and noticed that her blood was still caked under his fingernails. He couldn't believe that she was gone. He was angry at himself, and at Shyann. Why couldn't she give him the power to save her? Why did he live while Taleen died? It wasn't fair that everyone he loved seemed to die around him.

Loved...he had never openly admitted it to himself, but he had loved her, or at least loved what he thought they could have had. She was an incredible woman who had devoted her life to helping people and battling those who wished to do harm. And now she was dead.

Jonas rubbed his tired eyes and glanced over to the nearby rock face. Her body was wrapped in several blankets. He didn't want to have to see her again, but he had a duty to perform. She needed to be buried, and he would perform that task today.

Jonas stood up next to the dying fire. The sun was just beginning to rise over the mountain peaks and its light was slowly creeping into the clearing. Many of the men were still sleeping in the dawn light but Jonas could see a few starting their morning tasks.

Myrell was asleep next to her brother. Kilius looked better. His cheeks were showing a more rosy hue, in contrast to the pallor of sickness. Jonas would need to take another look at him now that he was rested. Fil was just to their left, sleeping soundly.

But first he needed some food. When they had left their horses they had taken small packs with them, each filled with essential rations, wool sleeping blankets, tinder boxes, and a few other supplies. Jonas found his pack and quickly consumed some salted ham and a big chunk of cheese, washing it down with cold mountain water. He was still exhausted, but the food revived him somewhat.

Jonas stretched his back and buckled on his sword belt. Then he turned and walked the fifteen paces to Taleen's body. He looked down at her inert form and images of her began to dance through his head. He saw her when they had first met, fighting the Greever, and when they traveled to Annure. He could picture her face when Tulari, his steed, had arrived just outside of Finarth. Images of her fighting at the Lindsor Bridge dominated his visions. They didn't know each other for long, but they had formed a bond of friendship forged through combat and a common purpose. She had helped him understand what it meant to be a cavalier.

He could not stop the tears that began to cascade down his face. As he slowly wiped them away he decided he would bury her here, in the clearing. It was a beautiful place and a fitting spot for someone as magnificent as she.

"Can I help carry her?" a voice whispered behind him.

Jonas, turning around, saw a tall warrior with a shaved head.

"My name is Dandronis, of the king's men. I am sorry for your loss, Cavalier," he said sincerely.

"Yes," Jonas replied, wiping away the tears from his red eyes, "I could use your help in moving her body. I'd like to bury her over there, next to the rock face," Jonas replied, indicating the spot he had chosen.

Dandronis nodded his head in agreement. "It is a fitting spot for a cavalier."

Jonas dug a shallow grave and covered her body with the many rocks that littered the area. He took her sword and rammed it into the ground at the base of her cairn. Then he draped her holy symbol, a silver chain with a pendant embossed with Bandris's mark, over the crosspiece of the blade.

"May Bandris guide you," was all he could say. He had already said his goodbye to her during the many hours it had taken him to construct the grave. All of the men looked upon the scene with sorrow. They wanted to help but they knew that Jonas needed to prepare her resting place on his own. For some reason, Jonas didn't mind that Dandronis gathered rocks for him, laying them nearby so he could arrange them as he wished. The man seemed solemn himself, like he could empathize with Jonas's pain, and the simple task of gathering the stones seemed therapeutic for the tough warrior.

When Jonas was done he closed his eyes, praying to Shyann, asking her to protect her and telling her what a magnificent person she was. His eyes were closed but he still saw something flash, and felt a vibration in the ground around him.

"Ummm...Cavalier," he heard Dandronis say in amazement.

Opening his eyes he saw that her cairn had melted into a stone sarcophagus. It looked like a roughly hewn stone coffin submerged into the ground, looking like it had been there for hundreds, if not thousands, of years. Her sword and religious symbol had turned to stone, as well, and was embedded into the stone sarcophagus, the top of which was engraved with the mark of Bandris, the double bladed battle axe. Jonas was speechless.

"What happened?" he stammered to Dandronis.

"While you were praying there was a single bright flash. It was strange because there was no noise. After the light subsided the cairn looked as you see it. She has been honored it would seem," Dandronis finished, his voice clearly impressed. "I wish I could have met her."

The men standing nearby, seeing the bright flash of light, came over and surrounded them, staring in awe at Taleen's cairn. No one spoke. They looked upon the beautiful sarcophagus in amazement. It looked so out of place in the mountain setting, and yet at the same time it seemed as if it had been there for a very long time, as if it were part of the surrounding rock structures.

The men said a few prayers for Taleen, and then departed to bury the rest of the dead, leaving Jonas to his thoughts.

Myrell stood near Hagar's body, anxiously watching his shallow breathing. He had still not awakened, and his heartbeat had become fainter, a slow rhythm she could barely feel when she laid her hand on his blood splattered chest. The dark wool cloth that was wrapped around his terrible wounds glistened with the wetness of his blood.

"How is he?"

Myrell turned to see Jonas approach. His red eyes were rimmed with dark circles. Myrell knew he was exhausted. The fight had obviously drained him mentally and physically.

"He lives. Jonas, did you see what he did?"

"Part of it."

"He saved us. He killed that beast. Is there something you can do?" she asked pleadingly.

"I will try, Myrell. He deserves that, but he is so big and I am still so tired. I cannot risk losing consciousness again as we must leave this place soon."

"I understand."

Jonas moved next to Hagar. His body was so large that he could easily place his hands on the beast's shoulders without bending over. Jonas took a deep breath and began to pray to Shyann. Her warm energy flooded his body and Jonas pushed it into Hagar. It was like a slow moving river, and Jonas directed the flow into the ogrillion, moving the healing magic to the most serious wounds.

In his weakened state Jonas could not sustain the healing for long. He quickly found the sources of bleeding and healed those first. Hagar's body was so massive that that task alone strained him to the edge of his current abilities. Quickly he shut off the flow, releasing his hands from Hagar's still form.

Jonas sighed heavily, taking a deep breath of cold mountain air before opening his eyes. He was dizzy and very tired, but he felt good about helping the beast, even if it was a minimal attempt.

"Will he be okay?" Myrell asked.

"I do not know, Myrell. I could only stop the bleeding. If he is strong enough, he may survive. It is all I can do," Jonas said sadly, his eyes wandering over to Taleen's cairn. He turned and walked away without another word.

The day was spent hunting and gathering food as they waited for King Kromm to awake. After some warm food, Jonas had completed the healing of Fil and Kilius. They were now up and about with only a bit of soreness and scarring left behind. He had also taken a look at Allindrian, healing her beyond what her own meager healing magic could do, fixing her shoulder completely, which was the most serious of her injuries.

Jonas then laid his hands on the king to look for any further injuries or signs of early infections. He sent Shyann's power into him a second time, scouring his body, concentrating on finding the injuries he may have missed the first time.

Kromm's heart was beating strong and there was no evident infection. Jonas sent more energy into the king's wounds, finishing the job that he did not have the energy to do the previous night. After a few moments he lifted his hands, opening his eyes to many eager faces.

All the warriors were standing around him, including the Blade Singer. They were all looking at him with apparent concern.

"He will be fine," Jonas said as he stood up. "He should awaken shortly."

"Thank you, Cavalier," Dandronis said, relief evident in his voice.

Jonas nodded, and walked away, deep in his own thoughts. He had better be worth it, Jonas thought, the anger at losing Taleen on this mission overwhelming his thoughts. Fil, who had been there watching, turned and followed Jonas as the rest of the men and women watched them leave.

Fil caught up with Jonas as he settled down on a large rock overlooking a sea of green trees, some still capped with a dusting of white snow. Fil sat next to him and they both stared at the wondrous sight in silence.

Finally Fil spoke, out of concern for his friend. "Are you going to be okay, Jonas?"

After a few moments Jonas glanced at Fil with a look of utter despair. "I don't know. I'm so tired, Fil. Why does everyone I care about die?"

"I'm still alive," Fil replied in jest. His smile disappeared quickly, seeing Jonas's look. "I'm sorry, Jonas. It was the wrong thing to say. I'm not trying to make light of Taleen's death. I just don't have any answers for you."

Jonas drew one of his sabers, holding the glinting blade sideways on his lap. "What good is this if it cannot protect the ones I love? What good is my commitment to Shyann if she cannot protect the ones I love? Our cause seems so hopeless, my friend." Jonas slid the blade back into its scabbard. "How can we compete with evil that thrives on so much death?"

Fil looked out at the beautiful scenery and thought about Jonas's questions. "Jonas, look at this place. It is beautiful. There is no way that chaos is supposed to rule this land. The land fights the stain of darkness every day. We are part of that fight. Taleen was part of that fight. I think that is the real difference between good and evil. The defenders of order and light work together, but the minions of darkness fight and jockey for power. I believe that to be their ultimate demise. They may win occasionally, but they cannot, and will not, win the war."

"I wish I could believe that. I am beginning to lose my faith, Fil," Jonas said sadly.

Fil patted Jonas on the leg, smiling brightly, trying in vain to lighten Jonas's dark mood. "Good, then you are human like the rest of us," Fil said. "Join the crowd, my friend. It is a rare man who does not falter occasionally. You will regain your confidence in yourself, and in Shyann," he replied, getting up from the rock. "Don't be too hard on yourself. We all know the risks, but we chose this fight because it is the right thing to do. Taleen chose that fight as well," he added, leaving Jonas to the silence and his own thoughts.

The fire was dancing wildly as Durgen the dwarf added another massive log to the hot flames. Sitting around the fire and sharing a meal of freshly cooked venison were Jonas, Kilius, Myrell, Allindrian, Dandronis, and King Kromm, now awake and famished.

Hagar had not yet regained consciousness and his still form rested within reach of the firelight. Myrell took comfort in seeing his huge chest slowly move up and down. He was not out of danger, but at least he was still alive.

Kromm stuffed a huge piece of dripping deer meat into his mouth, washing it down with cold mountain water. He was famished, his body begging for nourishment. His wounds were completely healed; all that remained were pink scars. But they had left him tired and sore and he needed nourishment to complete his journey back to health.

The others ate heartily as well, many also feeling the drain of their wounds on their strength. Kilius and Fil were healing well, and they would be ready to travel by morning. They had just started discussing the morning plans as they began to consume their hot meal.

"Cavalier, I thank you again for coming to our aid, and my healing. I owe you my life," the king said after draining his cup. "I'm afraid I would have bled out if you had not arrived in time."

Jonas had been eating silently, deep in thought, but the king's statement forced him to acknowledge the huge man.

"You owe me nothing. It was my mission," Jonas replied flatly.

"Can you tell me why Shyann has sent you on such a long journey to reach me?" he asked.

"I do not know. All I know is that you play a vital role in the destruction of Malbeck." Jonas paused, and then added, "Let us hope that you were worth the cost." He continued eating, ripping a piece of deer meat from the bone, ignoring the stares of the others around the fire who had stopped eating and were now looking at Jonas with wide eyes. Even Fil could not believe that he had been so blunt with the king. Durgen chuckled softly, drinking from his mug. Allindrian looked away, dropping her head sadly, feeling the young man's pain and knowing how out of character his remark was. Dandronis looked as if he were going to drop his food and leap over Durgen to get at the cavalier for being so disrespectful to his king. But he held himself in check, glancing at

King Kromm, half expecting the huge warrior to go after him himself.

The king stared hard at the young cavalier. His brilliant blue eyes shone with anger, his body tensing, but it was brief, and he quickly resumed his normal demeanor. Jonas didn't even look at the king, unaware of his remark, lost in thought, as he continued to eat his meal.

"Jonas, I am sorry for the loss of the cavalier, but…"

"Her name is, was, Taleen," Jonas interrupted, looking up for the first time.

The king paused again, taken aback by his unseemly behavior. It was not often that people spoke to him in such a way, and if they did, it usually did not end well for them.

"Cavalier, you are young and inexperienced, and because of that I will forgive your rudeness…"

"Inexperienced! That is one thing I am not!" Jonas snapped at the king. "I have fought giants! Killed a Banthra! I have slain evil clerics of the Forsworn and demons sent to kill me. During all of this chaos people that I've come to love and trust have died, and for what?" Jonas was now on his feet and everyone was staring at him in shock. He was breathing heavily, his eyes wide with an anger that failed to mask his deep despair.

"Sit down, boy!" the king bellowed, standing up abruptly, his huge frame looming over Jonas. His voice was abnormally powerful and everyone at the fire leaned away from the strength of it. Even Jonas stepped back. There was something in the king's voice that held no room for argument. The very ground shook with the power of it. All the men at the other fires jumped like scared rabbits as the king's voice shattered the silent night. "You are a cavalier and that means something! Now start acting like one! We have all suffered! My men have died trying to protect me! My entire city burns as we speak. My people's bodies rot as the night feeders desecrate their corpses! My wife and my son are gone! They are somewhere far away and are most likely being hunted just as I am!"

Jonas's tense body suddenly relaxed, his intense anger evaporating as he dropped back down to his seat on the log, staring at the ground in silence.

"I know your sorrow, Cavalier," continued the king, his voice softening, "but do not assume that you are the only one who has reason for grief. Look around you. Everyone hurts; death is following us, as it has followed you. You are indeed young to have done all that you said, and I'm sure you are a great warrior worthy of your status, but do not mock our pain again. It belittles you for doing so. Do I make myself clear?"

Jonas stared at the ground for a few moments, everyone staring at him in anticipation. The silence was tense while the king waited for an answer. Finally Jonas slowly lifted his head, looking at the king. His eyes were red and rimmed with tears. "I am sorry, to you all. I do not know what has overcome me. I have not been myself," he said softly, wiping away a lone tear. "My sorrow sits on my heart like a demon's fist, and it squeezes the hope from it. It hurts."

"You are human," said Durgen. "It is in your nature to be guided by your emotions, but I know your pain, young cavalier. I lost my only son days ago. This axe is all I have left of him." The burly dwarf patted the beautiful weapon. "And this blade will drink the blood of chaos until I die and see me boy again in the halls of Moradin.

"I am sorry for your loss, Durgen. I truly am." Jonas directed his gaze at the king who was looking at him intently, the anger he earlier expressed no longer evident. "King Kromm, I hope you will forgive my behavior, and my weakness. It seems my experience in battle does not carry over to my experience in life. I'm sorry for my poor judgment and the disrespect I have shown to you all."

The king nodded his head. "You are forgiven, Jonas."

"Now that we have that out of the way, we need to speak of tomorrow," interjected Allindrian. "Jonas, tomorrow we are entering the Hallows Road in hopes of getting to Cuthaine quickly. Will you be accompanying us?"

Everyone looked at Jonas hopefully, remembering Allindrian's words earlier about their chance of success improving greatly if he accompanied them.

"I do not know the Hallows Road. What is it?" he asked.

"It is a place of darkness, where predators lurk around every gnarled tree. The realm is perpetually dark and permeated with evil, and those of light run a great risk entering this dark realm, for the beasts of the Hallows can sense them."

"Where is this road?" asked Fil, speaking up for the first time.

"It is hard to explain. Think of the universe as an onion. Every layer is a world that is similar and different from the layer before, or after it. This world that you know is just one layer, with one set of rules. The Hallows Road is a thin layer that lies between our plane and the Abyss. And things there are...different."

"Why do you want to enter such a place?" Jonas asked the question that Fil, Myrell, and Kilius were posing in their own minds.

"Time in the Hallows is different than time here. If we travel through the Hallows then we can get to Cuthaine, where we believe my wife and son are, in a matter of days rather than weeks," the king answered firmly.

"But how do you know where to go, and how do we enter the Hallows?" Fil asked again before Jonas could ask the same question.

"I have traveled the Hallows before," Allindrian said, "and I know the way, but it will not be without risk. On my own, I was able to circumvent the dangers there. But with a group this size, that may not be possible. That means we may have to fight. Some of us will likely perish in that dark place; but that number will be considerably less if you are with us, Jonas."

"I see. King Kromm, my mission is to get you to Finarth in all haste. I do not know why but I know time is of the essence. Do we even know that your wife and son are in danger?"

"I will not leave without them. We leave for the Hallows first thing in the morning. The question is…will you be traveling with us?" the king asked.

Jonas looked at Fil, Myrell, and Kilius, before looking back at the king. "I will be by your side," Jonas replied resolutely. "But I cannot speak for my companions; their paths are their own to choose."

"I have already chosen," Fil said without hesitation. "My spear is yours, King Kromm."

Kilius looked at Myrell, trying to guess her decision, which was easy, for she immediately gave him an affirmative nod. "My sister and I go where Jonas goes," Kilius said firmly.

"Very good," replied the king, smiling. "We are grateful for your swords."

"Let us get some sleep," suggested Allindrian, "we will move at first light."

***

"What word do we have from our scouts?" asked Kiln to the group of men sitting around the large wooden table in the king's audience hall. King Baylin was surrounded by General Gandarin, General Kuarin, General Ruthalis, Lieutenant Dagrinal, Lieutenant Graggis, and Captain Lathrin.

"Commander, no scouts have returned," replied General Ruthalis. His handsome face could not mask his disappointment. The men around him felt the same. They were blind without information about Malbeck's whereabouts.

Kiln ran his hand through his hair, sighing in frustration. He was worried. They had sent out scouts continuously for the last six weeks and none of the men had returned.

Where was Malbeck? They had to find out. They had to know if he was laying low for the winter and gathering strength or marching south from Tarsis. What were his plans? How much time did they have? The questions rolled around in his head constantly, making it difficult for the commander to sleep.

"What of our emissaries? Have we heard from the dwarves or elves yet?" asked the king.

The question brought Kiln from his thoughts. Kiln looked at King Baylin, who seemed to have aged ten years since the battle at the Lindsor Bridge. He appeared tired and his eyes were swollen and red from lack of sleep. We are a sorry bunch, thought Kiln, feeling immense empathy for the king.

"Sire, we have not yet heard from our emissaries. The road is long and full of dangers. I'm sure that news from them will arrive soon," replied Kiln.

"Can we not contact the elves and dwarves magically, Sire? What of Alerion?" asked Dagrinal.

The king shook his head. "Alerion is in Mynos as we speak. He is busy with research on how to kill Malbeck. When he returns we will see if that can be done, but for now I place more value on trying to decipher the riddle."

They had all been briefed on the riddle, and most of them held little faith that the answer to Malbeck's death could be found in a riddle given to them by a demon. They held little trust in magic since they did not understand it.

"What of the training?" asked the king.

"It goes as well as it can. Our numbers are increasing, which is good, but that poses other problems." Kiln paused. "Captain Lathrin, can you elaborate?"

"Yes, sir. The people are frightened, Sire. They have left their homes and they worry that their farms will be destroyed by the coming army. There are many good stout people flowing into Finarth, but with them comes the filth. Thieves and brigands are taking advantage of the situation, robbing and killing the refugees as they come in."

"We are even having problems within the camps. Fighting and brawling is common, as well as thievery," added Graggis.

"What have you done to correct the problems?" King Baylin asked, addressing Kiln.

"Sire, I have doubled the patrols at night, which has helped, but as our numbers increase so do our problems. Food and water are in short supply. Waste removal will soon be a big concern."

"It is important that the people of Finarth feel safe. We must keep up their morale. Triple the patrols. Do whatever is necessary to put an end to these problems. This lawlessness and disorder will eat away at their courage and fortitude. Their resolve will blow away like the wind when Malbeck's forces arrive," added the king sternly.

"I understand, my King, but we are stretched thin. The losses at the Lindsor Bridge have hampered us greatly. Between our daily patrols, our training, and now our constant dealings with the thousands of refugees, well, we just don't have the manpower," Kiln replied wearily.

The king, rubbing his eyes in frustration, looked at his equally frustrated commanders. He knew that they had been working hard and they were pushing their men to their limits. He couldn't ask more from them. And yet he had to. He pursed his lips in frustration as he spoke.

"You've all worked hard. I know you will not fail me, but we must put a stop to these bandits. Do what you must. Tomorrow I want ideas," he demanded.

"Very well, Sire. We will find a solution," Kiln said with renewed determination.

"You are dismissed," said the king, standing up from the table. He had more work to do with his scribes. Vast amount of paperwork had to be perused as they had to figure out the daily problems of rationing and supplies, and how they were going to pay for everything.

The others got up as well, following the king from the chamber. Kiln stayed back, motioning for Dagrinal and Graggis to do the same. He busied himself with the maps and paper work on the table as the king and the other officers walked the long hallway to the main door leaving the audience chamber.

Dagrinal and Graggis looked at Kiln expectantly.

"You have an idea?" Dagrinal asked.

"I do," Kiln replied with a sly smile.

***

Kiln pulled the hood of his cloak down low to shadow his face. The air was cold and he wrapped the edges of his dirt brown cloak around his arms to fight off the chill. His transformation was perfect. He looked like a refugee coming in from the distant Finarthian lands. He walked with slumped shoulders as if he had journeyed a great distance. His clothes were worn and dirty and he led an oxen pulled cart filled with the belongings typical of a corn farmer. The old cloak covered his armor and his long sword was strapped to his back hidden under the cloak. All he had to do was throw the hood back and draw the weapon concealed behind his head.

Next to him rode Dagrinal on a tired old mule. He too wore a heavy travel cloak that had seen better days, but he also carried a little more baggage. Stuffed into the cloak were a handful of little round pillows to give him more girth and to add an ample bosom to his tall frame. His cloak was pulled around his face but he purposefully let several strands of long blonde hair hang loose across his large chest. The wig would not hide his identity in the open sun, but under the shadows of his hood it did the job. He looked like a big woman, but a woman nonetheless. It was not uncommon to find a farmer's wife with the same girth.

Riding a wagon behind them was Graggis, also disguised as a burly farmer. He wore a creased straw hat and his clothes were made of dirty and threadbare wool. But hidden under it was his gleaming plate mail, and resting under the blanket on his seat was his formidable battle axe. His eyes scanned the forests under the brim of his hat.

The wagon was covered with the flaps drawn. To a bandit it would look like an easy target, but they did not know that in the wagon were five other knights who were armed with sword and crossbow. They were picked for their skills and their discretion, for Kiln did not want others to know what their plan was in case there were spies, which was a common resource used by thieves. Many bands bent on thievery used spies in cities to report the coming and going of trade caravans moving expensive goods and supplies from city to city.

The others were not so sure of Kiln's plan. It was a risk, thought Kiln, as he scanned the road and the shadowed forest. The snows had started to fall and there was a thin dusting of white that gave the landscape a quiet solitude. The snow was beautiful, but thankfully not too deep, making the travel bearable. They had tried several different roads over the last few days and had yet to meet any bandits. But Kiln knew the brigands would be out looking for food and supplies to get them through the winter. The wagons would be a temptation they could not ignore.

That was Kiln's plan, to attract the thieves. From the accounts of survivors of attacks, there were several large groups roaming the lands around Finarth. They needed to end the thievery, and they needed more good men to fight. Kiln hoped to solve both problems together.

Kiln believed that most men were good, or at least wanted to be good, and that few desired the hard road of a brigand, but in many cases that mantle was thrust upon them by circumstances not of their making. He had known several such men, men who eventually came to work for him at his homestead deep in the Tundrens. Many were men who had lost their farms to drought or their families to sickness or war. There were many men who could not get work and resorted to stealing to fill their stomachs. There were countless stories of men, and women, who were generally good, but in Kiln's mind, too weak to fight off the tantalizing pull of crime when the alternative was starvation and despair. Some were good men who needed to feel the strong pull of hope again. Kiln gave the men at his ranch that chance, and now they took care of his home while he was away. He had turned them into proud men, and now he planned something similar, on a larger, more dangerous scale.

He reached under his cloak, feeling his long dagger. They were more than ready to deal with any threat, but he hoped it wouldn't come to that.

Kiln's eyes narrowed as they came around a corner. In the road, no more than a stone's throw away, were four men standing casually. From the distance Kiln could see that they were covered in travel worn clothes and heavy wool cloaks. They held no weapons, but he could see swords dangling from their belts.

"Stay alert, more are sure to be in the woods," Kiln whispered to Dagrinal, who slowly eased back on his mule's reins, positioning himself just behind Kiln. He did not want to be too close to the men when they stopped for he feared they would see his true identity.

Kiln slowed, stopping five paces away from the men. He kept up the act, his fidgeting eyes giving him the appearance of a scared farmer.

Several of the men were just past middle age, but even the younger ones looked tired and thin. Their skin was pulled tight to their bones but their scraggly beards helped mask their hungry look. Kiln could tell that the winter was hard for them. More than likely they had a camp somewhere with women and children and the meager rations they took from travelers did little to curb their hunger.

One man was older, and his beard was more gray than brown. He stood tall and firm with his legs out wide and his arms crossed. Kiln noted that his sword and belt was an old cavalry issued weapon from when Kiln had been commander twenty years ago. Either this man was an old soldier or he had stolen the weapon. Kiln believed it to be the former considering his casual and confident stance.

"Evening, farmer, my name is Gaal and today is not your lucky day," announced the man calmly, just as more men emerged from the brush. They too wore old wool clothing, and their breath emerged as clouds in the cold air. They were undisciplined and clearly not experienced, but there were enough of them to make them feel confident. Kiln glanced left and right, counting over twenty men as they surrounded the wagon and cart. He didn't say a word, which seemed to unnerve Gaal a bit. But he quickly masked his unease by announcing loudly, "I hope that you have plenty of supplies in those carts for your life will depend on it."

Kiln counted six bows in the crowd surrounding them, and most of the others had old pitted swords or woodsman's axes. It was a sorry looking lot, but they did outnumber them two to one. Still, Kiln hoped it wouldn't come to a fight. Now was the time to unfurl his plan.

"Let's just kill them!" yelled a skinny man to Gaal's left. The man's shrill voice grated on Kiln's nerves and his shifty eyes gave Kiln the gut feeling that he could not be trusted.

"I would not try that if I were you," Kiln replied softly from under his hood, as he slowly drifted forward.

The casual calm advance of the farmer further unnerved the bandit leader, and his eyes darted left and right with uncertainty. Usually the farmers became frightened and pleaded for mercy. But this man was not afraid, and he was advancing on them even though he was surrounded.

"Don't come any closer or you will soon look like a pin cushion," threatened the man.

Sure enough, the closest bowmen, who already had their arrows nocked, drew back on their long bows. The sound of the tension on the wood as the bows were slowly drawn back seemed to echo in the tense silence.

Kiln stopped several paces away from the men. "As I said, I would not do that if I were you."

"Kill him, Gaal," whispered the skinny bandit again.

"Shut your mouth, Waylin," barked Gaal, keeping his eyes on Kiln. "What is your name, farmer?"

Here was Kiln's opening, and he hoped it would work. Kiln reached up, pulling back his hood revealing his face. "My name is Kiln, and I believe you have heard of me."

Gaal took a step back, looking into Kiln's steady gray eyes. The men near the leader looked at him nervously, their eyes darting back and forth.

"Yeah, and I'm the king!" laughed Waylin. The others near him laughed as well, taking his lead.

But Gaal stood still, staring at Kiln.

"This man is crazy and I'm done talking," said Waylin, stepping forward suddenly, trying to skewer Kiln with his long sword.

Kiln, expecting the move, side stepped the sword while drawing his concealed blade. His body was a blur as he spun, his polished sword leading the maneuver, glowing momentarily just before it sliced through the man's throat. The move was so fast that no one even registered it.

Kiln quickly stepped back; his bloody sword held low as Waylin's body hit the ground, followed a few seconds later by his head landing nearby. "I *am* Kiln!" he yelled loudly.

As he spoke, he spun quickly, addressing the bowmen, hoping that none would release their arrows. Just as he spun he heard the unmistakable sound of a bow string being released. Kiln dodged to the side while whipping his blade in a protective arc. The archers were close and he only had the blink of an eye to catch the blur of the arrow and angle his blade towards it. He just caught the end of the arrow, but it was enough to deflect it to the ground. The sound of his blade hitting wood was quickly followed by another twang and a grunt.

Kiln glanced up, seeing an archer fall to the ground with a crossbow bolt protruding from his neck.

"Hold! Lay down your arms and no harm will come to you!" Kiln demanded again.

Dagrinal had jumped from the saddle, drawing forth his long sword that was hidden on the mule's side. Simultaneously he tossed back his hood, throwing the wig on the ground.

Graggis dropped the crossbow he had fired, hefting his mighty axe from under the blanket. He jumped from the wagon and landed firmly on his feet, the bandits near him scattering from his dangerous presence. They were deer surrounded by wolves, and they knew it.

The knights in the back of the wagon poured from the opening, flanking both sides of the wagon and cart. They each carried loaded crossbows and they were also armed with sword and dagger. Their armor gleamed like the snow in the sun's rays.

"I am Kiln, commander of the armies of Finarth! Lay down your weapons!" he demanded again. "There need be no more bloodshed!"

Kiln ripped off his traveling cloak revealing his magnificent plate mail beneath, the Finarthian symbol proudly resting in the middle of his armored chest.

Dagrinal and Graggis followed his lead and the bandits backed up slowly, unsure of what to do against such splendid opponents. Few of them were warriors and very few of them wore any armor at all. They all looked to Gaal, their leader, for support.

"Do as he says, lower your weapons!" bellowed Gaal. The men did as he ordered and Gaal stepped toward Kiln slowly.

"Is it really you? Are you Kiln?" asked the bewildered leader.

"I am," replied Kiln, looking into the man's eyes. Kiln saw recognition there. The sword the man carried, the knowing stare, he must have fought under Kiln many years ago.

"I recognize you. I only saw you a few times those many years back, but I could never forget your eyes. You are he, you are Kiln. Why are you here? What is the meaning of this deception?" the man asked, as his men looked around with apprehension.

"Deception? It is not I who have been reduced to stealing from my own people, people that I swore to protect many years ago."

Gaal's eyes narrowed in anger but he held his sword. He knew that any action on his part would mean his certain death. "It is not that simple, sir. I was injured in service and cast out to fend for myself. My wife and boy died of the scratch fever when it swept through here years ago. I could not run the farm on my own and after the crop failure two seasons ago I had all but exhausted my money and food. I did not want this, but it was all I could do, it is all *we* could do," added Gaal, using his hand to encompass the rest of the men around them. "But you did not answer my question, why are you here disguised as farmers?"

"We came for you, to find you. I have a proposition for you."

Gaal hesitated for a moment before speaking. "I'm listening."

"How many men do you command?" asked Kiln.

"We have two hundred men who are spread between two different camps, and half that many more are women and children. Why do you ask? I will not give you their whereabouts," he said firmly.

"You have been raiding the refugees as they come to Finarth. That we cannot have. Besides that, we need more men, strong men, to help fight when Malbeck and his armies arrive!" stated Kiln loud enough for all to hear. Kiln saw Gaal's eyes widen at Malbeck's name.

"So it's true? We have heard rumors that Tarsis was destroyed. Does he march his army here?" Gaal asked.

"Yes. We are bringing in all able bodied men, but we need more. We need you," Kiln stated flatly.

"And why would we do that? What is in it for us?"

"I will pardon you of all crimes. You and all that follow you will be given food and shelter. You will gain your honor back. What is a man without that?" Kiln asked.

He could see that his words had hit home with the brigand. And he hoped that it had with most of the others as well.

"But what happens after the war, if any of us survive?" asked Gaal sarcastically.

"If any wish a commission in the army then it will be granted. If not, then each man can leave with ten gold pieces."

"Why would we trust you?" asked a heavy set man to Kiln's right. He was carrying a large woodsman's axe and wearing old leather armor that was too tight for his round belly. "The word of an oath breaker means nothing to me."

"Hold your tongue or I shall cut it out," snarled Dagrinal, advancing toward the man.

Kiln, impressed with the man's courage, showed no anger toward him. After all, he was right, and Kiln was well aware that few knew the entire story.

"Stay your blade, Dagrinal," Kiln ordered, stepping towards the man. "What is your name?"

"Toban," he replied, locking eyes with Kiln.

"Toban, you are right. I broke my oath many years ago. But know this!" Kiln said, raising his voice so all could hear. "You do not know the whole story, and what you have heard whispered in taverns is not the truth of it! The dead king, Uthrayne Gavinsteal, and I had a disagreement, that is all, and the circumstances required that I leave his service! That is all you need know!"

Kiln turned to address all of the men.

"The way I see it is that you have two choices! One, take my word and join us to combat a great evil! An evil that will find you regardless of the choice you make! In doing so you will receive full pardons and walk away with honor and gold! Two, stay here as a thief and struggle to live off the meager belongings that you steal from your own people! But know this, if Malbeck doesn't kill you, I will personally hunt you down and kill you as a criminal."

Kiln paused to let it all sink in. "So, what say you?" Kiln asked them all, turning to face Toban. "You have courage, Toban. You spoke your mind when few would. I could use a man like you. What say you?" he asked again.

All but three joined that day. Kiln spent another week searching for brigands, and he was able to gather a hundred more bandits, not including Gaal's group. All in all it was a success. The roads were safer and the very threats to the refugees' safety were now their allies.

Seven
The Hallows

The party moved at a swift pace. Time was of the essence. They had to reach the gateway to the Hallows as quickly as possible. The sooner they made it through the Hallows, the sooner the king would be with his queen and their son. At least that is what they hoped. Jonas knew that the only way he was going to get the king to go to Finarth was to find his family and reunite them as quickly as they could.

They had a brief argument before they left, but were forced to settle it quickly. There was no time to quarrel. Hagar was still unconscious and he seemed no better. Myrell did not want to leave him, but they had no choice. Besides, many of the men did not want to waste more time over an ogrillion, a beast that by their reckoning would just as soon rip them apart. They had not witnessed Hagar killing the demon hound. If Jonas had not confirmed that the ogrillion was not a threat, they may have killed him while he was unconscious, simply to bury any fears they had of the beast waking up and attacking them. Jonas, exhausted and still weak, did not think it wise to push his energy and attempt to heal a beast so large, not when so much was at stake. They would likely be facing more challenges in the Hallows and he would need his strength to survive them.

"Myrell, I understand your feelings but I think Hagar will survive. His heart is strong and I think he can pull through," Jonas reasoned with her.

"But Jonas, we can't just leave him here, unconscious and bleeding. What will happen when he awakes and finds he is alone? I can't bear that thought, not after what he has done for us."

The rest of the party was waiting impatiently, adjusting their gear and glancing at them anxiously. They wanted to get moving. Nobody knew what had happened to the wizard that had attacked them, nor whether more of Malbeck's minions were in pursuit. It was time to get on the trail.

"I cannot risk further weakening myself. Hagar will survive, I can feel it. Now we must go, Myrell," Jonas pleaded.

Myrell looked at the others. They returned her gaze with eyes that could not hide their anxiety. She watched the king pacing back and forth, flexing his jaw muscles tensely. He, more than anyone, was anxious to leave, and she knew it wouldn't be long before he ordered everyone to move out, whether she was ready or not.

It was time to go and she knew it. "Very well," she said with a resigned sigh. Myrell turned to Hagar, brushing her hand lightly over his bloody shoulder. "Thank you, Hagar." She wanted to say more but the right words could not be found. Finally she turned away in frustration, and marched down the trail. The rest of the party quickly followed her.

Allindrian led the group and Jonas brought up the rear. The group was small, consisting of fifteen Tarsinian warriors, Dandronis, Evryn, Durgen the dwarf, and the king. This allowed them to move fairly quickly over the rock strewn mountain paths. Myrell, Kilius, and Fil stayed near Jonas at the rear of the column. Their eyes darted from tree to rock as they moved at a jog, hoping to make it to the gateway without more of the trouble that seemed to plague them.

After several hours of hard travel they finally stopped at a small crystal clear pool centered in a little clearing at the base of a tall rock cliff. From the top of the cliff a powerful waterfall dropped the expanse, crashing into the pool with a roar and sprays of icy water. It was a beautiful sight, but they did not have time to take in the scenery.

The warriors drained their water skins, refilling them as Allindrian and the king gazed into a deep section of the pool at the far end of the waterfall. Everyone replenished their energy by ripping into pieces of day old venison. Jonas joined the Blade Singer and the king, refreshing himself with a long pull from his water skin.

"Are we near the gate, Allindrian?" Jonas asked.

"We are, it is there," she said, pointing into the deep water.

Jonas peered into the clear depths, and saw two large stone pillars rise from the bottom of the pool. It was obvious that someone, or something, had placed them there, a seemingly impossible feat since they were in the middle of nowhere

"We have to enter the water?" Jonas asked incredulously.

"Yes, I will open the gate and then we each must enter the water and stand between the pillars. The magic will do the rest," she said.

"And our armor?" asked the king.

"Keep it on. You will sink to the bottom but have no fear, you will not drown. The magic will work and you will be transported to the Hallows," she said, catching the worried expressions of the two warriors.

"Who put the gate here?" Jonas asked.

"I do not know," Allindrian admitted. "We elves have long memories and yet we do not know how the gates came to be. There are others placed throughout the realms that go to different planes of existence. It is thought by some humans that the gods placed them here; others think it was an ancient people advanced beyond our imagination. We do not know."

"Let us begin," Kromm interjected impatiently. "How much time do you need to open the gate?"

"Just a few moments," she said calmly.

It did not take long to get everyone through the gate. And Allindrian was right; although a bit strange, the process was simple and smooth. Jonas was the last to arrive. The hardest part was leaping into the deep pool wearing his full armor. He quickly sank to the bottom of the pool and, keeping his eyes open, stepped between the pillars. He felt a wave of power flow over him. His body tingled briefly and then everything went black.

185

He awoke, shivering, to the sounds of Myrell's voice. His body felt chilled to the bone.

"Jonas, open your eyes," she said softly.

He was lying on his back as he opened his eyes. Myrell was looking down at him. The rest of the men had all experienced the same sensations and were now busy taking in their new surroundings. He realized that he was still holding his breath, so he exhaled in relief, and took a deep breath of air as he looked more closely around him.

He almost choked. The air was not only bitter cold, but it felt strange and foul in his mouth and lungs. It was as if he could taste it, an unpleasant, almost evil taste that stank of death and oozed despair. Jonas was struggling with the weight of it and he could see that everyone was feeling the same discomfort.

"It will pass. Your body will get used to it," promised Allindrian, drawing her sword. The gesture was casual, but the meaning was obvious; they were not in a safe place.

"I'm not sure I want to," spat Fil, trying to get the nasty taste from his mouth.

Jonas stood up straight, and looked around him. They were in a forest, a very dark forest, but it didn't have the healthy earthy feeling that you get in most lush forests. This forest was dark, really dark. The darkness was more than just blackness; it seemed alive. The trees and brush all had a spindly look to them and they were covered in thorns and a blackish moss clung to everything. A dense mist covered the ground, floating around them menacingly. It was dark, but there was a faint bluish light emanating from above, bringing a subtle eerie glow to everything around them. It was not a pleasant place, and Jonas immediately wanted to leave.

"Blade Singer, where do we go?" asked the king, stepping up to them with his giant sword held easily in his right hand.

Jonas was impressed with the man's stature. It wasn't just his incredible size and strength, it was also his aura that gave Jonas pause. He radiated power and charisma, and for the first time Jonas realized that this man was the type of man that moved worlds, the type of man that men followed without question. He had seen that charisma before in Kiln. They were both men who did not need magic to inspire. Jonas felt the pull of his personality, and he suddenly felt small and embarrassed under his gaze. He had not noticed the man's power before as he had been too distraught over the death of Taleen, his mind unable to focus on much else. He scarcely paid the king any attention. Now, he realized he had acted like an arrogant child and he could hardly believe that he had spoken to the king as he did. He would make amends somehow, that he promised himself.

"Follow me," Allindrian said. "Stay close to one another and do not wander off. If you do, you will most certainly get lost and perish. Keep your weapons drawn and do not say a word unless I tell you to."

Everyone drew their weapons, but the usually comforting noise of steel scraping on steel did little to strengthen their resolve. Jonas could feel the mist and the oppression of the place drain the courage from their bones.

"Blade Singer, what matter of beasts we be fearin' from this place?" asked Durgen, his son's axe held easily in one hand and his shield strapped to his back.

"Many, Master Trader. Many strange creatures live in the trees and brush, and we must try to avoid them at all cost. But we should fear the trysts the most. Though blind they can hunt by sound, and they exist in large numbers. The beasts resemble humans, but with extraordinarily long arms and very short legs. And their faces are more mouth and teeth than anything, with two pronounced ears on the top of their heads giving them excellent hearing. They are strong and fast, and where there is one you will surely find more."

"They sound pleasant," Fil remarked wryly.

"Make no mistake," Allindrian continued. "This may be the most dangerous and frightening thing you have all ever done. It is very possible we may not all make it through, but if you follow my lead, we have a chance."

"How long do we have to stay in this place?" asked the king. He spat on the ground, trying to get the taste of the place out of his mouth.

"Two and a half days to reach the gate that will take us to Cuthaine," she answered.

"Then let us start," he said impatiently.

The mist and the lack of sunlight slowed their progress. With no sun or real source of light, they could only just see a small distance in front of them. Jonas gazed through the cracks in the canopy of trees, and finally came to the conclusion that the bluish glow was coming from some horizon that never seemed to change. It was like a moon had set, staying in one spot, bringing its nightly glow to everything. It was eerie how the lighting and surroundings never changed, and Jonas wondered how Allindrian could find her way through the maze of trees and brush.

Jonas's thoughts were interrupted by a sudden piercing scream from in front of him. He sprinted forward, both blades in his hands. The blades glowed faintly, matching the subtle bluish light from the strange horizon.

The party had stopped and he saw several men trying to calm a comrade on the ground who was clearly struggling against some unseen threat. He was screaming and rolling around on the forest floor as three warriors tried to subdue him.

Allindrian and the king ran from the front of the group, pushing their way to the downed man.

"Silence him," hissed Allindrian, her eyes darting into the shadowed darkness.

Jonas was concerned as he had never seen Allindrian lose her composure. She appeared worried and tense, her eyes darting anxiously from the screaming man to the black forest surrounding them. Jonas remembered her warning about making noise. The last thing he wanted to do was attract a group of trysts. He joined Allindrian in scanning the woods around them, half expecting an army of the blind beasts to attack.

Three men had secured the struggling man while a fourth clamped his hand over his mouth. There were a few moments of muffled sound before the squirming man bit his hand, filling the Hallows again with his anguished cries.

"What is wrong with him?" whispered Fil.

Many of the men were now taking Jonas's lead, facing the forest, expecting the noise to bring the trysts down upon them. They had formed a circle around the screaming man and more than one had nocked an arrow.

Then Kromm took action and pounced on the man, pinning his arms down with his heavy legs.

"Sorry about this," he said, bringing his fist down hard on the side of the warrior's head. There was a thud and then he went limp. After a few seconds the warrior's limbs began to twitch slightly, as if he were having a seizure, but luckily he was no longer making noise.

There was a pall of silence as everyone's eyes darted from tree to shrub. The mist continued to drift lazily around them adding to the nervous tension that was thick as butter.

"Flip him over," ordered Allindrian, anxiety evident in her voice.

The king turned him over and stood up, while Allindrian knelt down and slowly pulled back the man's cloak near the base of his skull.

"I was afraid of this," she said, standing up and looking at the king. "A soul worm," she announced, pointing down to the back of the man's neck. "It must have dropped from the trees above and burrowed into his skin."

Sticking out of the warrior's flesh was a green worm about as thick as a man's thumb. One end had dug into the man's flesh while the other end wiggled around slowly. It was a sickening sight.

"What is a soul worm?" the king asked. "Can we remove it?"

"No. The worm has already eaten into his spine, permeating it with numerous tiny tendrils. The worm severs the

189

spinal cord, then patches the connection to the host's brain, keeping him alive, but unable to function, so it can continue to feed. If we kill the worm or remove it, he will die."

"What is it feeding on?" asked Myrell shakily

"The worm is feeding on his soul, on his life force, so to speak. There is nothing we can do."

"Can I heal him?" asked Jonas, sheathing his blades.

"No. You could probably heal the spinal cord but not the damage to his soul. He might live but he would be a useless shell of himself."

"In Bandris's name, I can't sit here while his soul is sucked from him. Is there nothing we can do?" the king asked in frustration.

"Yes," she replied. "You can kill him."

"What!" exclaimed Dandronis.

"If you kill him the worm will leave, for what is left of the man's energy will disperse to the Ru'Ach and it will have nothing to feed on. He is suffering now, as you can see," Allindrian added, gesturing to the convulsing man, "and his pain will disperse as well."

Everyone was silent as the king digested her words.

"But you must hurry. The man's screams very likely attracted the trysts. We must get moving," she added quickly.

The king sighed, with sorrow and frustration, stabbed his sword into the ground, and drew forth his knife. Everyone looked away, in respect for the king's choice and for the man who was to die. No one wanted to watch the killing stroke. Killing an enemy was one thing, but killing your own comrade while he lay on the ground unconscious was difficult to stomach. But it had to be done, and everyone knew it.

After a few moments, the king stood up. "It is done," he said softly, despair dripping from every syllable. "Let us go, I long to leave this evil place."

As he spoke, a sudden shrill screech filled the Hallows. The sound, though distant, was terrifying.

"We are found," Allindrian hissed. "Follow me, and stay together." Without another word she darted off into the mist and everyone followed with weapons drawn. There was no need for silence. They had been discovered. Everyone ran as fast as they could to stay on Allindrian's heels, crashing through the thorny brush, frantically trying to elude their pursuers.

Another screech erupted into the night. This time it was much closer. The beasts were fast and it was obvious that they would not outrun them. Despite the chilling coldness, Jonas began to sweat as he ran the unseen trail that Allindrian miraculously followed. He kept Fil and Myrell in his sight as they followed the rest of the men, fleeing through the brush after Allindrian.

Suddenly Jonas found himself, with the others, at the edge of a clearing, the first they had seen since they entered the Hallows. Mist floated around the clearing so they could not see the ground, but in the center of the forest opening was a rise of rock and dirt sprouting a black spindly tree as big around as a person. The tree's branches reached out in different directions resembling the long skeletal arms of a demon.

"Follow me!" Allindrian yelled. "Step where I step! The ground is littered with deep pits of black water that will pull you down to your death. They are to close. We cannot outrun them, we must fight! The high ground of that rise," Allindrian pointed to the tree, "will give us a better chance."

More screeches came from just behind them.

"Go! Now!" Jonas yelled. "I will hold them off!"

Allindrian was about to say something in protest, but she caught herself, realizing that she was the only one who could lead them to the hill and the tree. Only she could see the correct path. The mist in the clearing covered the swampy waters like a white blanket. If anyone stepped into those waters they would not be coming back out. The water, black as a demon's heart, would suck them into its depths, the magic of the place pulling them in and feeding on their energy. Only she could get them safely to the hill.

Allindrian gave Jonas a quick good luck nod before advancing into the mist, the men slowly and cautiously following behind her.

Jonas turned to face the forest, holding both blades low. He saw two of the men step up next to him. One was Fil and the other was Evryn the axe man. Then he noticed Durgen the dwarf step from behind the large form of the axe man.

"Can't have all the glory," the dwarf growled, un-slinging his shield and hefting his silver axe.

Jonas had no time to argue with any of them. As more screeches came from the forest it was apparent that the trysts would be on them in a matter of seconds.

Closing his eyes, Jonas concentrated on Shyann's power, bringing it forth deep within him. He brought the God Fire into his chest and slowly sent it into his arms, channeling it into both swords. Blue flames erupted from his blades and he opened his eyes just in time to see the brush part in front of them, a hairless gray form bursting from the gap.

The tryst was a bit taller than a dwarf, with long spindly arms and two powerful back legs. Its gray hairless body looked almost opaque. Jonas could see the beast's blue veins under its ghostly skin. The tryst's hands were tipped with three long fingers capped with white claws that looked like large eagle talons.

But it was the tryst's head that was the most terrifying. The animal had no eyes at all. Its entire face was a huge gaping mouth filled with white razor sharp teeth. Two twitching deer-like ears protruded from the top of its skull, and Jonas could just make out two holes positioned under the ears that must have been its nose.

As the tryst came at them, it opened its mouth, screeching loudly. But Jonas cut the piercing sound short with a burst of flames. Lifting his blades, he sent two massive jets of fire into the forest. Moving his blades left and right, he directed the fire into the brush blanketing the area with flames.

They heard screams of pain as Jonas continued to direct the flames into the forest. Evryn, Fil, and Durgen had flanked him, prepared for any trysts that made it through the God Fire. But none did.

Finally the awful screams died out and Jonas let the power subside, the fire disappearing as quickly as it had come. The brush in front of them had been obliterated, and the unusual thing was that most of the flames had extinguished themselves when the source of the fire stopped. The wood here was not normal, as it didn't burn as wood should. But then nothing in this place was normal. At least five trysts had been caught in the flames and their bodies were blackened and burning, adding a putrid stench to the already foul air.

But they didn't have time to admire Jonas's work, for another handful of the creatures leaped from the brush at them. They moved quickly, charging them fearlessly. It was hard to believe that they could not see, for they seemed to know exactly where the group was standing.

Fil jabbed his spear forward at a charging tryst, impaling it through its gaping maw. The animal bit down hard, snapping the spear off before it jerked a few times and fell to the ground convulsing in death.

Two more came from the brush at Durgen, and another two came at Jonas. Evryn, standing next to Durgen, engaged the tryst to the dwarf's left. One beast jumped from the ground at the dwarf, who lifted his shield high, using his powerful legs to push forward, smashing the beast in the side and launching it far to his left where it crashed into the tryst next to it.

Evryn was there to cleave a crease in one of the tryst's skulls, but the other one rolled away quickly, springing right back at him like an enraged cat. He tried to yank his axe blade from the skull of the tryst he had killed, but he could not free the weapon in time. The tryst hit him hard in the chest, plummeting them both backwards into the mist.

Jonas brought his glowing blade down over the long arm of one of the trysts, severing it at the elbow, while simultaneously lunging forward with his other sword and skewering a second beast through the chest. That one fell dead, but the first beast shot its large mouth forward with a vicious snarl. Its mouth was big enough to engulf Jonas's entire head, and he had no doubt that its teeth could easily slice through muscle and bone.

Jonas swayed backwards away from the dangerous mouth, pivoting his body to the side. The tryst had just missed him, and instead found Fil's sword crashing into its skull. It fell dead at their feet, and Fil yanked his blade from the grisly mess, smiling briefly at Jonas.

Durgen had seen Evryn go down but he couldn't see a thing in the fog. But he didn't have any time to worry about the warrior as another tryst had emerged from the mist to his left. The dwarf growled, engaging the creature and dispatching it with several powerful swings of his deadly axe.

Jonas glanced behind him seeing that Allindrian and the men were now climbing from the mist up onto the hill.

"Time to go, Dwarf!" Jonas yelled.

Durgen heard the cavalier and looked around for Evryn. He could hear some struggling nearby and then suddenly a tryst flew from the mist, landing in the smoldering brush at the edge of the clearing. Evryn stood up from the fog making eye contact with the dwarf, and gave him a quick smile. Blood dripped from several puncture wounds in his shoulder but his armor had protected most of his body from the deadly bite. He also had several deep cuts across his face, probably from the tryst's sharp claws.

They all regrouped, facing the forest with their backs to the clearing. They could hear more commotion in the forest and they knew that more trysts were soon to arrive.

"How do we get across the swamp without Allindrian?" asked Fil worriedly, glancing back over the mist covered bog. Jonas held his blades toward the brush, searching his brain for a way across the swamp.

"Let's take our chances with the fog. More of those damned beasts are coming, and from the sounds of it, a LOT more," Evryn said.

"No," Jonas replied. He had come up with a plan. "I will part the fog and you will guide yourselves to the hill."

"What if the trysts come before you can get across?" asked Fil.

"Then I will deal with that problem when it arises! We are out of time!" Jonas said, closing his eyes and seeking out his cognivant powers. The energy of the Hallows felt different, and it took a few more seconds to concentrate on the swirling power of the place. But he managed to grab the energy around them and use his mind to push it through the mist toward the hill.

His head began to pound with the effort, but still he concentrated on his task. It was much harder work to control the energy of the Hallows. Everything seemed wrong, out of place, and fragmented. But he gritted his teeth, focusing on using the energy to part the mist. And it was working. He kept pushing and concentrating and finally he created invisible walls that the fog could not penetrate, forming an opening in the mist about ten paces wide all the way to the hill. Now they could see the ground and the brackish holes of dark water.

"Go!" Jonas yelled through gritted teeth. Durgen ran forward, leaping from dry spot to dry spot, making his way toward the hill.

The men on the hill were cheering them on and the bowmen faced them with arrows nocked and ready.

Fil looked back towards the brush and heard more trysts nearing. They had to go, and now.

"Damn it, Fil, Go!" Jonas yelled. His head pounded and his face was contorted in pain as he fought to hold the cleared path.

Fil hesitated no longer. He ran past Jonas, carefully finding a path through the swampy ground.

Evryn was just about to follow Fil when the brush behind Jonas shook and two trysts emerged. Wasting no time they barreled toward them. Evryn didn't hesitate; acting out of instinct he ran forward to protect Jonas's back. He gripped his axe at the end of the handle, stepping into a powerful throw. The weapon somersaulted the short distance, slamming into the chest of one of the trysts and nearly cutting the beast in two. Then, maintaining his forward momentum, he drew his long hunting knife, and dove right into the second tryst with his two powerful arms extended in front of him. His weapon was pitiful against such a creature, but he knew he could at least stop the beast from ripping into Jonas's back.

They crashed into each other and tumbled across the mist covered ground. Evryn fought to subdue the beast so he could stab it with his knife, but it was like trying to hold back an angry lion. Clawed hands raked his body and more than one found openings in his armor. He saw the beast lunge forward with its powerful jaws and he did the only thing he could do. He lifted his arm to protect his face.

The Tryst clamped onto Evryn's arm and bit down hard. The power of its jaw was incredible. He felt sharp teeth slice easily through his flesh and heard the sound of his bones being crushed as if they were dried twigs. Shaking its head viciously, the beast continued to cut and tear into Evryn's arm. And unfortunately it was the arm that was holding his knife. Screaming in pain, Evryn punched the animal with his free hand, but it did little damage. Finally the tryst jerked its head hard, taking Evryn's arm off just below the shoulder.

Evryn's screams caused Jonas to glance backwards. He could only hold the mist back for a few more moments and it was going to be now or never. Jonas blanched at what he saw. A tryst lifted its huge head from the mist and Jonas clearly saw Vern's arm dangling from it.

Then he saw Evryn jump from the mist with a second smaller dagger in his only hand. "Go!" he screamed. Blood sprayed into the air from his mortal wound, but it didn't stop him from plunging the dagger into the thing's neck as they crashed together, tumbling into the dense fog again.

Another beast emerged from the brush, attracted by Evryn's blood, and dove into the fog with an eager howl. Jonas heard more chilling screams followed by more screeches as a handful of trysts emerged from the brush to join their feeding comrades.

Jonas knew it was time to go. He sprinted towards the hill, leaping and dodging steaming pits of black water. As he dispersed the cognivant energy behind him, the dense fog drifted in, quickly closing off the path.

He ran up the hill, climbing over several large rocks to get to the plateau where everyone waited for him. They had formed a perimeter and everyone was looking fearfully down into the fog.

"Nice work, Cavalier. But what of Evryn?" asked the king, gripping his hand and helping him up the last rock.

"I'm sorry, Sire. He died trying to protect my back," Jonas replied, clearly in pain. His head throbbed and he stumbled forward on shaky legs.

"Are you hurt?" asked the king, catching Jonas in his strong arms and holding him upright.

"I am fine. My powers...there is a...side...effect," Jonas muttered, doing his best to shake off the pain in his head, finally standing up straighter.

More screeches snapped their attention to the mist and the forest around them.

"We cannot run! Therefore we fight! We must kill them all or die in this dark place! Prepare yourselves!" Allindrian shouted.

Everyone readied their weapons, gazing out into the dense fog. Jonas drank from his water skin, breathing deeply, trying to lessen the ache in his skull. Using his cognivant powers within the Hallows seemed to exponentially increase the side effects, causing him more pain than normal. He sought the place within himself to calm his mind; he sought Ty'erm, and gradually he found it.

As his breathing slowed and he concentrated on the pounding of his heart, the ache in his head gradually began to recede. He opened his eyes, releasing his breath slowly. The headache was still there, but it had lessened significantly. He had pushed it away, burying it deeper in his mind.

Jonas sheathed his blades, unslinging his bow that was strapped to his back. Nocking an arrow he looked into the mist for a target.

The screeching was getting louder and ghostly shapes flitted in and out of their vision as the trysts traversed through the dangerous mist toward them. Occasionally they would hear a splash and a sucking sound followed by a quick shriek. But more and more trysts emerged from the brush, moving into the fog with little fear. They had tasted blood, and they wanted more.

"Jonas, stay here!" the king roared so all could hear, "I will take the west side! Allindrian, you take the south side! We must hold the circle!"

Everyone found their positions with Fil, Kilius, and Myrell flanking Jonas. He could see that Myrell was frightened. Her wide eyes and shaking sword arm betrayed her. Jonas reached out and touched her hand reassuringly. "Myrell, stay behind me. If any get through our defenses then strike them with your sword. You understand?"

She nodded her head, but said not a word, her eyes wide with fright. Jonas could feel her fear. He wanted to tell her that it was going to be okay and that he would not let anything happen to her, but he couldn't. Taleen had died right next to him and she was a cavalier. What chance did a farm girl who was a novice sword wielder have against these beasts?

"Go ahead, move back," he said softly. She smiled nervously, stepping back behind them.

Kilius moved closer to Jonas, filling in the gap and doing his best to protect his sister. Neither of them wanted to see Myrell succumb to those horrific jaws.

"We hold them here! Harness your fear, and release it with every strike! Let them feel the power of our steel!" The king yelled in encouragement, his powerful and confident voice lifting Jonas's spirits.

Suddenly the fighting began.

Trysts scurried from the mist with abandon, shrieking and howling, quickly scampering up the steep hill from all sides. Their powerful long arms and short muscular legs allowed them to easily climb the rocky hill.

They were met with walls of arrows as the men with bows fired into the howling beasts. Many died instantly, flying back into the mist, but there were too many of them, and it didn't take long for the men to drop their bows, drawing their blades as the trysts advanced.

Jonas's first arrow took a howling tryst in its open mouth, propelling it back into the mist. He fired his arrows with speed and precision and not one beast got close to them.

"Time to die!" Durgen roared like a madman, swiping his axe through the throat of a tryst as it pulled itself up the rock face at the dwarf's feet. The beast fell back into another one and Durgen kicked a third in the face as it, too, reached for the edge of the rock. His metal shod boot smashed through its teeth, the force of the kick throwing the tryst off the rock as if it had been fired from a catapult.

As more and more trysts scampered up the hill, more bowmen were forced to drop their bows for close combat weapons. Fil and Jonas worked their blades left and right, cutting and jabbing at any creature that moved toward them. There were so many of them, at least fifty, much more than Jonas had originally thought. For every one they killed it seemed two more took its place.

One tryst lunged forward, managing to clamp its long arm onto Kilius's ankle as the young man battled another beast. Kilius was jerked from his feet, landing hard on the ground, the back of his head slamming into the dirt.

"No!" Myrell screamed behind them.

Jonas glanced nervously to his right, hearing Myrell's scream. He cursed silently as he saw the young man go down. Instantly he called for his God Light and his body flared brightly, his light blanketing the entire clearing. The trysts had no eyes so the light did nothing, and since they were not inherently evil, just animals in a strange place who wanted to feed, the light did not harm them as it would creatures of a truly evil nature.

But the light did have an effect on the men. As the light bathed them their fear gave way to increased strength and confidence. Their swords and axes suddenly seemed lighter and they moved more fluidly, their senses alert and their hearts pounding with new hope.

Myrell, too, felt the power of Jonas's light, and the fear that had paralyzed her disappeared like morning dew in the hot sun. She jumped forward, skewering the tryst that had attacked her brother. The animal was just about to clamp its jaws on Kilius's exposed leg when its plan was foiled by Myrell's sharp steel. The beast screeched, jerking its head sideways and yanking the blade from her hand as it fell over dead.

Kilius struggled to get up as another tryst tried to jump on him. He met the animal with a straight kick to its chest, launching the beast backwards. Then he quickly scrambled to his feet. He had no time to thank his sister as two more trysts emerged from the mist below him.

On the other side of the circle Allindrian fought brilliantly. Her silver sword was a blur as it spun and danced from one tryst to another. The sound of her blade hummed in the clearing and its music gave strength to the men who fought nearby.

Several men had gone down as the beasts swarmed toward them. Their circle tightened and shrank as the small group of warriors closed the gaps where their comrades had fallen.

Trysts were piling up near the king's feet as he cut them down like grain in a field of wheat. The king swung his great sword with one hand and completely cut a tryst in half, at the same time catching movement in his peripheral vision. Turning quickly, he saw a tryst fly at him, its great mouth open, ready to tear his face off. Kromm had no time to bring his sword to bear, so he simply shot his giant arm forward, catching the beast in the neck with his massive hand. In an incredible feat of strength, Kromm held the beast several feet off the ground, continuing to tighten his grip on the ferocious animal. The tryst howled, snapping its huge jaws down again and again as it struggled in the giant man's iron grip. It managed to rake its deadly claws over the king's arm and several found flesh under his metal forearm guards. Lines of crimson appeared as the sharp claws tore at his flesh.

Kromm, ignoring the pain, squeezed harder, simultaneously ramming his blade into the body of another creature. His forearm rippled and his hand turned white as the pressure pushed blood from his fingers into his engorged muscles. It didn't have a chance. Its neck finally snapped and Kromm flung the beast into several other advancing trysts as if it were nothing more than a dead bird.

Jonas and the circle of warriors closed further as several more of their men succumbed to the relentless attacks of the trysts. Their comrades watched in horror as they were dragged down the hill screaming and crying for help. But they could do nothing as they were all battling to stay alive themselves. The screams of the dying men didn't last long as the trysts quickly ripped into them, howling into the night with Tarsinian blood dripping from their terrible jaws.

Jonas had a quick reprieve from the fight as he whipped his razor sharp blade across the neck of a tryst. He had relinquished his light in order to save his energy, and the oppressive darkness of the place again descended on them. He wanted to bring it forth again, but decided against it. He may need all his strength later.

Dandronis, meanwhile, was struggling to hold back two of the creatures. They seemed to sense the movement of his sword arm and they both darted in as an opening presented itself. He was tiring and his arm was beginning to feel heavy. Parrying one of the tryst's attacks, he sliced a deep cut across the beast's arm. The animal shrieked in pain, but the move cost Dandronis, as his right foot slipped on a loose rock and he stumbled to his knee. The trysts were on him immediately.

One raked its claws across his shoulder, but luckily his dwarven armor protected him. He swatted the other with the flat of his blade, hastily trying to regain his footing. The tryst took the flat of the blade on its upraised arm, but it did little damage, and the creature dove forward with its razor sharp teeth leading the way. The tryst hit Dandronis in the chest, but he dove backwards, rolling with the beast and coming up on top of the scrambling creature.

The tryst used all four legs to cut into Dandronis, but again his armor saved him and he only received a few cuts. The tryst, however, didn't fare so well. Dandronis had dropped his sword but as he rolled with the beast he had drawn his hunting knife and as he came up on top of the animal he slammed the long blade into the side of its head. It shook briefly in its death throes before lying still under the bleeding warrior.

But just as Dandronis withdrew the knife he felt the weight of the other beast on his back. Pain shot through him as sharp teeth closed over the side of his head. He cried out, feeling the long needle sharp teeth clamp down on the side of his face. Then, miraculously, he felt the teeth withdraw and the weight lifted from his back just as quickly as it had arrived.

Dandronis was hoisted up by one hand. He turned to see his king standing by him holding a bloody sword. He smiled his thanks, reaching down for his sword that was lying on the ground. Then he noticed the blood. It started to pour down the side of his face and under his armor. It felt thick and wet, but he felt no pain. Luckily there were no more trysts coming at them. He tried using the end of his cloak to wipe away some of the blood. But there was a lot of it, and as he tried to stem the flow his head grew light as it drained from his body.

"Let me help you," the king said while he scanned the mist for more attackers. With no enemies near them, he ripped a piece of cloth from his cloak and held it firmly to Dandronis's wounds.

Jonas and Allindrian were not so lucky. A score of trysts came howling up the hill for one last charge. There were few men left and Jonas wanted to end the fight quickly. He decided to bring forth his magic one last time. The power began to emerge deep within him, and as he built up the strength of it, he held it in check until the trysts were just a few paces away. Then, releasing it through one blade, he shot blue God Fire forward, engulfing the creatures as they tried to get at the tired defenders. They died quickly in the hot fire, and when Jonas finally extinguished the flames an eerie silence engulfed them.

Jonas glanced to his left and right, seeing the remaining survivors standing among the dead, their bloody weapons held before them. Exhausted and breathing heavily, they scanned the mist with eyes still alert for danger. Jonas was relieved to see that Durgen had survived. The burly dwarf stepped up to him, his axe and shield smeared with blood. Despite the fact that he, too, was splattered with crimson, he looked as if he had come through the battle relatively unscathed. His long flowing beard, now matted with blood, did little to mask the smile under his unruly hair.

"Nice work, Cavalier, but you took away the sport."

"I'm sure there will be more, Trader Durgen," Jonas replied, as he glanced at Fil, Kilius, and Myrell to make sure they were okay. They had suffered some cuts and bruises, but otherwise they were fine.

"Cavalier, we need you!" shouted the king from the other side of the hill.

Jonas ran to him, jumping over several dead trysts and Tarsinian men to get there. He found the king kneeling over Dandronis.

Jonas knelt next to them and examined the wounded warrior. Puncture wounds surrounded the side of his head in a large semicircle. It was obvious that a tryst had bitten the warrior, but luckily, for whatever reason, was not able to finish the job.

Dandronis was conscious, but he was rapidly losing blood.

"Am I to die?" Dandronis asked softly.

" No," Jonas replied simply, laying his hands on the warrior. Instantly the heat of the healing magic answered his call and he sent it into the warrior searching for the deep wounds. Jonas quickly sealed the cuts and fused his damaged blood vessels. The flow of blood abruptly stopped, and Dandronis opened his tired eyes.

"I'm glad I don't have to die in this place," he said with a little more strength.

Jonas opened his eyes, removing his hands from the warrior. He was tired and the use of his powers combined with the oppressive feeling of the place seemed to suck the remaining energy from him. He stood up, looking around at his surroundings. Many were dead, but he counted six survivors as well as Fil, Myrell, Durgen, Allindrian, Dandronis, and the king. The ground was littered with at least fifty trysts. Jonas spent a few moments healing any other warriors that had any serious wounds, including the king, who was bleeding badly from the lacerations on his arm. Luckily his forearm guard had protected most of his arm, but the beast's nasty claws still managed to find some exposed flesh.

"We have to go, and now," Allindrian said, moving next to Jonas. Her face and clothes were splattered with blood but her eyes shone with fire. "More trysts may be coming. Or worse, the battle may have attracted something else, something bigger."

"Then let us go," replied the king, hefting Dandronis to his feet.

They hastily collected the water, bows and arrows, and food from their dead comrades, and were off down the hill and through the mist covered swamp in a matter of moments. They were all exhausted, but the need for survival kept them moving.

The day dragged on as Allindrian guided them through the dark. Was it night? No one could tell in the Hallows. The bluish light did not change. The landscape was filled with more wicked looking trees, and the brush was covered with moss and thorns. The mist didn't relent either, and it continued to coldly caress their tired legs as they pushed further into the Hallows. They were forced to take a few quick breaks for water and quick rations, but other than that they didn't stop for many hours.

Finally Allindrian halted in a small clearing and they set up camp for a quick rest. The group settled down under a canopy of black twisted branches. Dark moss hung from the trees like rotten skin on a corpse. The wood was too wet for a fire so they ate cold venison and chunks of cheese. The cold clean water tasted good.

It seemed to wash away some of the slime of the place as it poured down their throats.

Everyone seemed lost in their own thoughts in the unnerving silence. They had lost a lot of men, friends and comrades alike. And their surroundings didn't bolster their confidence much. It was deathly silent. There were no birds, crickets, wind, nothing. The forest was completely still and it seemed to leech their very will to speak.

Finally, the king looked up at the men around him. "We will make it," he said, as if reading the doubt in their minds.

Durgen grunted, slapping his axe blade as if survival was a forgone conclusion. "Sur'en we will, me blade has not yet bathed in enough blood."

"That was a difficult fight, but I will lead us from this place," Allindrian added firmly.

Jonas was thinking of Taleen and was paying little attention. He could almost hear her voice, and the absence of her presence suffocated his heart. It came and went but he just couldn't shake the melancholy feeling of her loss, especially in these dismal surroundings which amplified his sorrow. It was hard for him to choke back his anger at himself and the world for her death.

"Jonas, are you okay?" The distant sound of the king's voice dragged Jonas from his thoughts.

Jonas glanced up from the forest ground, seeing that everyone was staring at him with worried expressions. The king's blue eyes looked at him intently, and they were filled with concern.

"Are you okay? I was speaking to you," the king said.

"I'm sorry, Sire. I was lost in thought and I'm very tired."

"I understand. I was asking about your powers. How did you part that mist? I have never seen a cavalier with that skill."

"What I did was not Shyann's magic," he replied with a pause. "I am also a cognivant."

The king made no attempt to hide his surprise. "A cognivant? You are a rare man indeed. I have only met two in my life."

"And I none," said Dandronis. "And I thank you for your healing. I'm afraid I would have bled to death if not for you."

Jonas nodded his head in acknowledgement.

"We need a few hours of sleep. I will take the first watch. I do not think that I need to mention how important it is that the watch not fall asleep in this place," Allindrian warned.

"Wake me in an hour. I will take second watch," the king said, leaning back and sprawling out on the ground. It didn't take long before everyone was asleep, the fighting and physical exertion acting like heavy weights on their eyelids.

Allindrian sat calmly on a dark moss covered log, alert, and sharpening a small hunter's knife she wore in her boot.

They had all taken their turns at watch and everyone was able to get a few hours of sleep. It was disheartening to awaken in the same setting as the one in which they had fallen asleep. Nothing had changed, the air was still cool and oppressive and their surroundings were ominous and filled with shadows. But their rest had not been interrupted and they were all thankful for that.

The king was wiping a cloth over his blade while the rest of the group prepared for their day's travels. Jonas, feeling much better from his rest, approached the king.

"Sire, I would again like to apologize to you."

The king looked up, polishing the handle one last time before putting the cloth away. "No need, your apology was accepted. These are hard times, young warrior, and our emotions are running high. Do not fret it."

"Nonetheless, I'm sorry for my outburst. It was spoken from pain and anger and you did not deserve to be the target."

The king stood up from the black rock he was sitting on and faced Jonas. He was a good head taller and much broader in the shoulders and Jonas had to look up at him. He seemed so small standing next to this giant of a man.

"I understand the outburst and I empathize with your loss...with your losses," the king corrected himself as he gently rested his giant hand on Jonas's shoulder. "I would like to thank you. You saved us back there. Your presence makes our chances for survival much greater, which puts me closer to my family, and for that I am extremely grateful."

"It is my duty, it is what Shyann has asked of me," Jonas said simply.

"And yet she picked *you* for a reason, which is why I thank you." The king paused for a second before continuing. "Jonas, do you really not know why I am needed at Finarth?"

"I do not, but I assume it is to help destroy Malbeck. What else could it be?"

"I do not know. But I also do not know what one man can do to help when he has no kingdom anymore, no people to lead, nor an army to add to the Finarthian ranks. What you see here is all that I know I have left…a handful of Tarsinian warriors." The men were now up, readying their equipment and watching their conversation with quick glances. "In what way are we to aid the army of Finarth against the might of Malbeck?"

"Don't ye forget to add Durgen the dwarf to your numbers."

"And a Blade Singer," added Allindrian, crossing her arms over her chest.

Jonas looked at the king, seeing the pain of loss in his face. It was hard for him to imagine what it would feel like to have lost your entire city, and to have your army and your people scattered across the lands being hunted by minions of the Forsworn. Not to mention your remaining family being alone in a strange city, more than likely being hunted by the same evil that was hunting them. It was a harrowing thought and it made Jonas's losses seem smaller in comparison.

"A wise warrior once told me to never underestimate the power of one," Jonas said, thinking back to a conversation by a fire under a bright moon.

"A wise sentiment and I know it holds value, but it is hard to feel its truth in these hard times. Who was this wise warrior?" asked the king.

"Kiln, commander of the Finarthian forces."

The king's smile disappeared. "Kiln? You know him? And he leads the Finarthian forces again?"

"I do, and he does."

The king's surprise was replaced by a smile as he clapped the cavalier on the shoulder. "That is good news. You are full of surprises, young cavalier. I would like to hear this story, but let's save it for another time where we can enjoy our surroundings with good drink and cheer. We should be on our way, I long to leave this horrible place."

"And I as well," mumbled Dandronis, gazing into the forest apprehensively.

"Blade Singer, lead the way," the king said, sheathing his blade on his back.

They traveled as fast as Allindrian could guide them through the difficult terrain. Staying in a tight group, everyone remained on the alert, constantly scanning the underbrush and trees for possible attacks. They were tense, knowing that another confrontation could be disastrous. Every shadow held the possibility of death. That reality, along with physical exhaustion, was taking its toll on the men. The Hallows had a way of sucking anything positive from anyone desperate or foolish enough to enter, and a solemn feeling hung on everyone like a heavy coat.

They traveled for most of the day, or night, whatever it was, luckily without mishap. Suddenly Allindrian raised her hand, quietly signaling them to stop. Everyone did and they stood tense with weapons drawn looking intently at the Blade Singer.

She craned her head slowly to the side as if she were trying to hear something. Nobody moved as she turned to face the men, putting her finger slowly to her mouth, making the obvious signal to be silent.

Raz, a young Tarsinian warrior, stood behind the giant form of his king and he did not notice Allindrian's gesture. He was looking out towards the thick foliage flanking them, his eyes darting nervously from shrub to tree, searching the forest for an attacker.

"What does she see?" he whispered more to himself than to anyone, stepping further towards the trees to get a better look at his surroundings.

Suddenly, faster than a striking snake, a tree limb shot from above, hitting the warrior in the chest. The sharp point of the scraggly limb punched through his armored chest, erupting out his back with an explosion of blood and gore. He was then lifted off the ground and up into the unseen canopy of the tree. Then all the branches from the two massive trees on either side moved down hungrily, freezing in the air above the group. It happened so quickly that by the time everyone blinked, the warrior was gone and the only thing left of him was his sword and a patch of wet scarlet on the ground.

"Don't move!" screamed Allindrian at once.

Instantly a black branch jerked several paces toward her, freezing an arm's length from her.

Everyone was in shock from the attack and they were just getting ready to react when Allindrian's voice had made them freeze. Two, however, did not.

Kilius, who was closest to the slain warrior, reacted on instinct. He jumped away from the branches hoping to distance himself from the attacker, whatever it might be.

"Do not move! It hunts on movement! Stay still!" Allindrian yelled again, keeping her body totally still.

"No!" screamed Myrell as Kilius moved away from the hovering branches.

A veteran warrior named Palick also reacted. He ran forward under the branches, attacking the trunk of the tree with his drawn sword.

Everything was a blur as the branches reacted to the movement, shooting down with incredible speed. One branch bolted towards Kilius as he leaped away. Kilius frantically dodged the sharp point of the descending branch, swiping his blade across the attacking limb. His sword did no damage that anyone could see.

"Kilius, stop moving!" Jonas roared. It was all he could do to not help the youth, but it was obvious that the creature was attacking anything that moved, and there were plenty of limbs above them to take care of them all.

Palick's movement doomed him. He attacked with a scream, hitting the trunk with his sword. The blade bounced off the trunk, barely breaking through the protective skin, or bark, whatever it was. But he didn't have time for a second strike. Two wicked looking limbs came down quickly from above, punching through his back. They lifted his screaming form into the air and then each limb pulled outwards completely ripping him in two. His mangled body fell to the ground near them with a sick wet thud.

Palick's final scream seemed to get through to Kilius and he finally stopped moving. A thick limb covered with sharp spikes shot down towards the young man just as he froze. Kilius used all his mental strength to stay still as the limb short towards him like a ballista bolt. He closed his eyes half expecting the limb to shatter his body.

"No!" Myrell screamed again as the branch descended.

Then it just stopped. Kilius slowly opened his eyes to see the limb no more than a hand's span from his face. Then, as fast as it descended, it shot back up, hovering above them. His eyes were wide with fright and his breathing came in anxious gasps, his arms held wide and visibly shaking.

"Blade Singer, what manner of beast is this?" The king whispered slowly, trying to keep the movement of his mouth very slow.

"It is an eecap, a stationary monster that hunts prey by movement. I think there are two of them. Once it kills its victim then it uses vines to suck the blood from the flesh."

As if the eecap were listening, suddenly a bunch of black vines snaked down the trunk moving across the ground towards Palick's body. They stopped before it and the ends of the vines, like snakes, lifted up off the ground and shot forward like a striking adder.

"The vines sense, or smell, the blood," Allindrian explained.

The vines were digging into Palick's flesh. They began to convulse and undulate as their comrade's blood was quickly drained from his body.

"How do we kill it?" asked Fil in disgust.

"I do not know," she said flatly. "They are very rare and I have never fought one."

Just then the body of Raz fell from the canopy above, landing with a thud at their feet. The young warrior's body, sucked dry of its fluids, resembled a skeleton wrapped with white skin.

Jonas looked up at the limbs and for the first time noticed that they were not limbs at all. They were arms, many of them, and they looked just like the many branches that they had seen in the strange trees all around them. But the ends were capped with sharp black spikes. In fact, pointed spikes covered all of the limbs and more than a handful were as long as a man's arm.

And the thing was fast. If they tried to flee there was no way they could outrun the deadly barrage of spikes that would come for them. Jonas glanced at the eecap's trunk, noticing that it was a bit different than the other trees. It rippled slightly and it shuddered as the blood from its victims poured into it.

"What do we do?" asked Kilius slowly, the shock from his near death experience straining his voice.

"Cavalier, what about your fire?" asked the king.

The same idea had come to Jonas and it seemed like the only attack that might harm the monster, but that was the problem, it *might* harm the monster.

"I was thinking of that as well. If we run, we will die. That thing is too fast. I do not think that our weapons will do much damage either," Jonas said, slowly looking up at the branches hovering menacingly above them.

One twitched, descending towards Jonas and halting only an arm's length away. The movement was so quick that they barely registered it, but it was obvious that it had sensed Jonas somehow. Maybe he had spoken too quickly. Jonas stopped talking regardless, staring at the branch and the glistening black spike. His heart was pounding and he could feel his hands start to shake.

He closed his eyes, calming his mind, and slowing his heart rate in order to enter the state of Ty'erm. After a few moments he opened his eyes feeling more alert, calm, and ready to deal with the situation.

"Jonas, if your fire doesn't work then you will be torn to pieces. There has to be another way," pleaded Myrell.

Everyone was silent for what seemed like an eternity. They were trying to think of a way out of their predicament that didn't end with someone dying.

"I can think of no other way," Jonas finally replied.

"Nor I," stated Durgen.

"Jonas, can you discharge your fire as an explosion all around you?" asked Allindrian.

"I don't know, maybe. I've never done it before."

"But that will burn us all to ash," Dandronis said, stating the obvious.

"Not if we are protected by a sphere of energy," Allindrian said, posing the statement as a question and looking directly at Jonas.

Jonas caught on to Allindrian's idea, but his confidence began to slip away as he realized what she was asking of him.

"Jonas, can you hold a cognivant shield and release your God Fire at the same time?" Fil asked, unable to hide the fear in his voice.

It took Jonas a few moments before he answered.

"I do not know. Allindrian, you are asking me to try something that I've never done. And the result of failure will be all our deaths. I don't know if I can do that," he said as fear began to creep back into his heart.

"Jonas, if we move, we die. I can think of no other solution. You must try," said the king. His voice was calm and filled with a confidence that Jonas did not feel.

Jonas breathed deeply, forcing the fear from his mind. He concentrated on Ty'erm again, keeping his center and tucking his emotions away so as not to hamper his actions. He could not let any doubt enter his mind if he was going to attempt this.

"If I do this then I must get everyone's approval. I will not risk any of your lives without it. So what say you?" Jonas asked the group.

Although Fil and Myrell were both reluctant, everyone voiced their approval. There seemed to be no other way.

"You can do it, Jonas," Fil added.

"We trust you," Myrell said, her voice tight with anxiety.

So Jonas closed his eyes, taking several deep slow breaths. The first thing he did was concentrate on the energy surrounding him. The task would be difficult even in their own plane of existence, but in the Hallows, in this warped and twisted place, it could likely be impossible. But they were all correct, he had to try. There were no other options available to them.

The swirling energy didn't have any patterns here. Jonas was forced to expend more of his own energy to harness it, which took more time. But he focused every ounce of his will on forming an invisible shield over him. Once he had created it he opened his eyes, letting out a long breath. Creating the weave of the shield was what took most of the time and energy, but once it was built, holding it intact required much less of his power and concentration.

"I'm going to move forward now to get closer to the tree and distance myself from you. Don't worry, I am protected," he said calmly, so they would all know what he was doing.

He then quickly ran forward, and as he did so the spikes came crashing down. Even though they were expecting it, the movement almost caused the rest of them to jump. They exhaled a sigh of relief as the spikes smacked against an invisible barrier just above Jonas. As he came to a standstill, the branches moved back up to their resting positions.

Now came the difficult part. Jonas released the energy above him, reaching out for more. His mind was a giant vacuum drawing in all the available energy around them. He had to create a large shield to cover them all and it took him a while to gather enough to weave the protective barrier.

Jonas's head was pounding fiercely, but he pushed the pain away, hiding it deep in his subconscious, all the while finishing the last touches of the shield. He didn't bother telling them that he couldn't include himself under the shield or he would not be able to release the flames. He had to hope that the fire would be enough to protect him.

He held the shield and his eyes squinted with exertion as the pain escaped from the hiding place like an explosion. He struggled fiercely to hammer the pain away and hold the shield. His body was shaking and Myrell moaned with fear as a branch inched toward the movement. Then it stopped suddenly as Jonas again gained control of his mind and body.

Now he prayed to Shyann. He sent his call out and instantly felt that familiar tingle deep in his body. The link to her was tenuous though, as he had to concentrate on the shield and call forth her power at the same time. He was struggling with the new sensation, but eventually he powered through the difficulty, finding the center of her power. The God Fire started in his belly, slowly boiling outward, filling his chest, his limbs, and finally his head. It felt as if the blood inside him was simmering, rising to a boil as the God Fire reached its pinnacle of power.

He purposely kept it controlled, however, bringing more and more power up from his center to fill his body. He knew he would only have one shot at this, and he had to make sure he released enough power to kill the eecaps. The effort took a terrible toll on his mind and body as he tried desperately to contain the power and maintain the shield at the same time.

Everyone in the circle was watching in tense amazement as Jonas struggled with the task. It was painful to watch, for every little movement that Jonas made caused a nearby branch to twitch or convulse in hunger.

He knew he couldn't move, but his body wanted to drop to its knees and release the power. Fighting back that urge he screamed inside his head. He had to release the power or it would consume him. The last thing he heard before he exploded in God Fire was Allindrian's soft words.

"You can do it, Jonas," she whispered. Her words floated towards him, giving him strength. They held up his quivering body just as he let his power explode in a rush of blue flame.

They all closed their eyes as the intense energy engulfed them. The furnace of his God Fire roared around them but they felt very little of its heat. They kept their eyes closed in fear that the magical flames would sear them, and because of that they did not witness the awesome display of power. But they certainly heard, and felt it. It sounded like a hurricane and the heat inside their protective circle slowly increased as the flames continued to coalesce around them.

Jonas stood tall as the hot flames erupted from his body, burning everything around them. The massive explosion created a sphere of fire that shot well past the canopy of branches far into the starless night. He didn't think of the branches seeking his blood, but only of the sphere that protected his friends. He focused on that one thing only as his fire reached the pinnacle of its power.

Then, as fast as it had erupted, the flames were sucked back down, disappearing into his body. He fell to the ground unconscious.

If he had been awake he would have seen his comrades struggling to get up, some of their clothing singed and smoking, standing in a protected circle surrounded by a charred and decimated forest extending farther than any of them could see.

The two smoldering eecaps were skeletons of their former selves. Nearly all of the limbs were gone; all that remained were burnt and blackened trunks rising over thirty paces into the air. They stood in the center of a wide open hole that had been created in the midst of black and twisted trees.

Everyone ran to Jonas as he lay unconscious on the ground. Their exposed skin and clothes had suffered minor burns from the heat but other than that they were fine. Fil was first at his side, quickly checking to make sure he was still alive.

"His heart beats," Fil said through a sigh of relief.

"In Bandris's name I have never felt anything like that," said Kye, one of the Tarsinian warriors who had traveled with Dandronis when they fled the burning city of Tarsis.

"Nor I," added an amazed Dandronis.

"We must move now!" Allindrian interrupted, her steady eyes penetrating the darkness of their surroundings. "That explosion will surely bring more predators down upon us."

"But Jonas is unconscious, maybe injured; we must see to his wounds," Myrell said heatedly.

"He did not save us just so we can be killed by trysts," Allindrian replied calmly.

"I will carry him," announced Kromm. He reached down and lifted Jonas as if he was just a child. "Tie his arms around my neck and I will hold his legs."

They did as he ordered while Durgen, Dandronis, and Allindrian circled them, guarding their backs. It only took a few moments and finally the king grabbed Jonas's legs, lifting him off the ground. Jonas hung limply on the king's broad back.

"Get us out of here," ordered the king.

Allindrian ran with all speed as the king followed her with long powerful strides. It didn't take long before they heard the unmistakable screeching of the trysts. They were still a ways away but the frightening and familiar sound felt like it was tapping them on the shoulders. Their previous battle with the creatures was still a terrifying memory, and they wanted nothing more to do with them, especially now that they were reduced in numbers.

So they ran on in desperate silence. Fil, behind the king, was amazed at the man's strength and endurance. He seemed not to tire, and even with Jonas's weight on his back his gait was strong and fluid. They kept up the pace for minutes, then hours, and though everyone was feeling increasingly fatigued as the day (or night) wore on, they dared not slow down. The screeching seemed to follow them for some time, but as they ran they seemed to be creating more distance from their pursuers. They knew the trysts could move with lightning speed, but perhaps it was not a pace they could maintain over time. Yet they pushed on, energized by fear, and continued their dangerous flight through the Hallows, trying to keep as silent as possible. They ran on and on until the adrenaline of their flight was exhausted, making them more keenly aware of their tired and sore bodies. Finally, the sound of the hungry trysts disappeared altogether, and Allindrian slowed their pace.

She motioned silently for everyone to stop. The king turned to face them and Fil looked at him in astonishment. He was breathing hard but his eyes still sparkled and his back was straight and strong. Fil was bent over, breathing heavily, and all he wanted to do was lie down and rest.

The others were just as exhausted. Myrell fell to the ground, physically spent and nearly unconscious.

"We'll rest here for a few hours. I'll take first watch," Allindrian stated.

"Someone help me with Jonas," the king said.

Fil and Dandronis moved to help him remove Jonas from his shoulders. They laid him down gently on the forest floor. The ground was covered with the strange black moss and it was comfortable enough. They were in a small clearing surrounded by the same strange trees and shrubs they had encountered when they first entered the Hallows. Nothing was different, and that alone unnerved them.

King Kromm knelt next to Jonas, checking to make sure his heart still beat.

"How is he?" Myrell asked with concern, moving next to him. She gently laid her hand on his forehead, absently touching the raised scar.

"His heartbeat is weak, but he is alive," the king said.

"We need to keep him warm. He feels cold," she said, softly stroking Jonas's cheek.

The king removed his cloak and placed it over Jonas's still form. Fil removed his sleeping roll from his pack and draped

Jonas with it, then looked down at his sleeping form, relieved to see the movement of his chest as Jonas slowly breathed in the cold air.

"He saved us," Myrell said.

"I have never seen anything like that. His power was overwhelming. I cannot believe that it didn't consume him," the king said in wonder.

"I think it almost did," replied Fil.

"Aye, and us," muttered the dwarf, stroking his singed and smoke blackened face.

They were a sorry looking group. Most of their armor, except Jonas's, was marred or blackened in some way. It would take many hours of polishing to restore it back to its original state. Their clothes, hair, and skin had suffered minor burns, but they had nothing to help alleviate the pain. Luckily they were all so tired that they felt very little of the discomfort. It was more of an inconvenience as they tried to get a few hours of sleep.

Myrell lay down next to Jonas, laying her head on his chest and falling asleep in moments. It did not take long for the others to find sleep, for their eyelids felt like lead and their bodies begged for a quick reprieve from the constant running and fighting. Allindrian stayed awake and alert, as did King Kromm.

"You should rest, Sire. You do not know when you will get another chance," Allindrian said. Kromm sat on the ground with his legs crossed before him, staring at Jonas.

"I will be okay. I do not need much sleep, I never have," he replied absently. The king appeared to be preoccupied by his own thoughts as he continued staring at the young cavalier.

"What are you thinking?" Allindrian asked.

He looked up at her. "I was just thinking how young Jonas is, and how much he has been through. He had no time to be a boy. I'm surprised at how much it saddens me."

"I imagine you were not so young when you first bloodied your blade," Allindrian replied.

"You are right; I was seventeen, younger than Jonas, but I am a king, he is not."

"No, he isn't, he is a cavalier. There are those that must carry the heavy weight of responsibility, for only a few can. You are one of those men, as is Jonas."

"I understand that, but it saddens me just the same," the king said, his blue eyes looking up at Allindrian. "He saved us today, and he may die tomorrow and he has never experienced all that life has to offer. There are so many things that he has missed and he may never enjoy. When I look at him now I see my own son, and I don't like to think about how their fates may mirror each other," he said bitterly.

The anger and frustration were there, deep in his gaze, pinpoints of boiling blue fire ready to explode.

"We will find your son and queen. And I do not think that it will be so easy to kill Jonas," Allindrian said with a slight smile.

The king's smile finally pushed through his darker emotions. "I think you are right. The boy has skill and power that I have never seen in one so young."

"He is special, a warrior with an unbreakable heart, a young man who cannot be corrupted," she added, and then seemed to get lost in her own thoughts.

Kromm looked at her for a few moments. "You care for him, don't you?"

Allindrian looked over at the king, the question startling her from her reverie. "Of course, as I said he is a special man."

"That is not what I mean."

Allindrian blushed for a moment before gaining her composure. It was a flash of emotion but the king caught it just before she returned to her stoic self.

"He is young, and human," she said matter-of-factly, but she did not deny it.

"He is still a man, and you are still a woman, even if you are half-elf. All people have needs and emotions, is there a reason why you deny yours?" the king asked softly.

"I am a Blade Singer, and he a cavalier. There are too many factors to consider for me to entertain those emotions. It would not work."

"The reasons you state seem to be reasons enough to entertain those emotions, for life is precarious for warriors like us. But I will mention it no more, and I did not desire to make you feel uncomfortable."

Kromm glanced back down at the boy thoughtfully as Allindrian turned her vigilant gaze to their surroundings. After a few moments of silence the king looked back at the Blade Singer.

"Thank you for being here, Allindrian. Your presence has saved us more than once, and I do not take that lightly."

"As I said, those of us that can, do. With skill and power comes responsibility. That is what makes us different than the evil that hunts us."

"Nonetheless, I thank you."

Allindrian smiled, nodding her head in acknowledgement.

"Get some sleep, Sire. I will keep watch."

"How much further to the gate?" he asked, lying down on the soft dirt.

"No more than half a day."

"Very good, wake me for the second watch." His tired eyes closed and sleep quickly overtook him.

Jonas slowly opened his hazy eyes, taking a few moments to orient himself. He was lying on his side in dirt and grass and the first thing his eyes focused on was a large piece of stone, shaped into a perfect rectangle, rising from the earth like it had been there a long while. The stone was familiar to him, and as his eyes gazed past it to the mountain rock face and forest surroundings, he realized that he was lying in the very same meadow where Taleen had died. In fact it was Taleen's cairn that he was looking at.

"I'm sorry, Jonas," a familiar voice said from behind him.

Jonas slowly stood, shaking the grogginess from his mind. He was dreaming again, but his head still ached and his body felt like it had been stomped on by an army of ogres. He turned to face Shyann, who was standing tall a few paces behind him wearing her silver armor. Even though he had seen her wearing it before, the splendor of it caused a sharp intake of breath. She did not have her helm on so her raven black hair cascaded down her armored shoulder plates covering most of her chest. Her features were earthy and

220

tanned, the appearance you might expect from a farmer's wife. But she was no mere peasant, her full lips were the color of ripe cherries and her angular chin and cheekbones gave her demeanor a look of power and confidence. A shimmering blue cape was fluttering in the breeze behind her and a long sword rested comfortably at her hip. The whole scene was bathed in bright sunlight and Jonas breathed in the sweet smell of cherry blossoms.

"Why did she have to die?" Jonas asked bluntly as Shyann took a step closer to him. She moved with liquid grace and Jonas's heart caught in his throat as she stepped to within an arm's length of him.

"We all die, but few can say they died for a cause," replied Shyann with a comforting smile.

"But what did she die for? Did her death change anything? Why couldn't you help her?" Jonas asked, looking into her eyes. They were stars filled with the warmth of goodness and Jonas fell into them immediately.

"Jonas, she died for what she believed in, and in doing so pushed the cause of good further along. Every single action that she took in life helped others, and that in turn has been a catalyst for good in the world. She helped change the world for the better, Jonas," Shyann whispered softly, her melodic voice drifting around Jonas, drawing the fear and anger from him.

"But you could have stopped her death. Why did you let her die?" Jonas asked, almost pleading.

"Jonas," Shyann began. "I am not what you think. I am not a god in the sense that you imagine. I cannot control all things. I could not save Taleen because I did not have the power to do so." Shyann paused as she turned and looked out over the snowcapped trees, the peaks of the Tundrens poking through the layers of clouds beyond them. "The world is so much more than you know, so much more than I knew as a farmer, and even now, much of it is still a mystery to me. But know this. There are many worlds such as yours, all unique in their own way. But one thing they have in common is the struggle between light and dark. Ulren has had many names over more years than you can imagine, and his presence has been known in memories of ancient peoples across many worlds."

"What of the Forsworn?"

"They too have had many names, and have impacted different people in many realms. Jonas," Shyann said, turning back towards him. "I do not know the answers to all the questions that plague you. There are many things

that elude even me. I am but one player in a very serious game. I am a warrior for Ulren, as you are a warrior for me, and yet I have never met him as you and I speak now. There have been times in our world, and other worlds, where darkness has reigned, and other times where it was pushed back into the holes and shadows from which it came."

"But why would Ulren and the other gods allow evil to rule?" Jonas asked, slowly trying to grasp all that Shyann was saying, and failing miserably.

"Ulren was not strong enough," Shyann whispered.

"How is that possible? I don't understand."

"Jonas, I cannot answer all these questions now. But know that I am sorry that I could not stop Taleen's death." Then she reached out, gently touching his face. "I am sorry for the pain it caused you," she said, grazing his face with her fingers. At her touch, there was an instant flash of light that exploded in his mind and he was momentarily blinded.

When he opened his eyes he found himself standing on a tall hillock looking out at an expanse of rolling hills covered with golden grasses undulating in the evening breeze. There were patches of snow dotting the hills but its cold embrace was losing the battle against the fast approaching warmth of spring. The sun was setting and the last remnants of its fiery light touched the tips of the tall grass.

He was still dreaming, he could feel the lack of connection to his surroundings. It was like he was there, but not physically. He was gazing at the scenery in its ethereal form, yet he could still feel the breeze and smell the clean cold air.

"Turn around, Jonas," Shyann whispered next to him.

He did so and what he saw made his heart pound.

Before him was an army that expanded across the plains as far as the eye could see. Pinpoints of flame were springing up all over the hills as fires were being built and evening meals prepared.

"They are not men, Jonas," replied Shyann, reading his thoughts clearly.

Jonas, squinting his eyes, tried to get a closer look, but he could not, they were simply too far away. At their distance they looked like dark forms and shadows moving around tiny points of flame. "What you see is Malbeck's army."

Jonas looked at her, awed by the scene in front of them. And then the sounds of the army assaulted him. His ears were bombarded by the screeching and howling of beasts, the deep guttural voices of orcs, ogres, and other dark creatures that inhabited the lands of Kraawn.

"It is so big. Where are we?" he asked, looking around.

"We are just south of Tarsis. The snows are slowly subsiding and Malbeck has begun his march to Finarth," she replied.

"How long do they have?"

"Several months at least, depending on how long it takes Malbeck to destroy Cuthaine and the other villages and towns unfortunate enough to be in his path."

Jonas shook his head in wonder. "How will we fight that? There are so many," he asked in stunned amazement.

"Strength is in the heart, my young cavalier, not in numbers. Just look at yourself. What you did in the Hallows defied all possibilities. It was your mind and your heart that gave you the strength to hold that shield and release my fire." She continued to speak in her soft voice, turning to face him again. "Now, once you reach Cuthaine you must make haste and depart immediately as dark forces lurk there as well. Stay with King Kromm and his family and get them to Finarth safely and quickly."

"What happens after that?"

"You will know when the time is right," she answered, reaching out with both hands to cup his face. Jonas closed his eyes at her touch and her warmth flooded his soul. She gently touched her lips to his forehead and the same warm light exploded in his mind and then...

...he awoke to find himself lying on his back, draped with a cloak and a warm wool blanket. Nestled by his side was Myrell, sleeping soundly, her face snuggled up against his shoulder. Her body was warm and it surprised him how good her touch felt.

He felt refreshed and his head no longer hurt. He glanced around him seeing the remaining members of their group sleeping soundly, tightly huddled in the middle of a small clearing. They were still in the Hallows, that much was obvious from the gnarly skeletal branches floating above them and the thorny dark foliage surrounding them like hungry demons.

"Good to have you back."

Jonas flicked his gaze to his right, pushing himself up on one elbow. King Kromm sat on a log with his right hand resting on the hilt of his great sword. The other end was sunk into the soft moss covered dirt. Even in this dark place and covered with black soot and burns, he looked like a king of legend.

"I guess it worked," Jonas replied. "I remember the roaring of the flames and that is about it."

"It was incredible. You destroyed a sizable section of the forest, including those creatures. You saved us, again, and again I thank you," Kromm said, standing to his full height.

"Thank me by getting to Finarth safely, and quickly," Jonas responded.

"Done," Kromm said. "Now let's get moving so I can make good on that promise."

After the group's quick rest they made it to the gate without any further conflicts. It was similar in appearance to the gate they had entered earlier, though luckily this one was not under water. Two large stone columns rested in a clearing surrounded by the same dense black trees and foliage. The columns appeared ancient, gray fingers reaching up from the ground, frozen in time, their rough surfaces mottled with black moss and patches of white.

Allindrian stepped up to the columns whispering several words of power under her breath. Suddenly the clearing thrummed with magic and everyone could feel it vibrate deep inside them.

Eager to leave the Hallows they each quickly stepped between the pillars, disappearing in a blue flash.

Eight

The Shadow of Night

Kiln was restless. None of his scouts had returned and the problems and difficulties in managing the refugees and preparing the city for siege seemed insurmountable. He slammed the ledger shut, gazing out his window into the dark night.

The royal coffers were running dry and they still did not have enough supplies to last through a long drawn out siege. They needed more coin, more food, more weapons, and more trained soldiers. More importantly they needed information. They needed to know Malbeck's location, how large of an army he led, whether or not they had cavalry. They needed to know *something*, anything to give them an idea of what they would be facing.

He sighed heavily, scratching the back of his neck as he arched his tired back. It was late; he had been up all night perusing books and charts. He stood up and walked to the slow burning fire, placing several large logs onto the red embers. The flames jumped up immediately, chasing the chill from his body. Warming his hands by the fire he lost himself in the dancing orange and yellow flames.

His room was small but cozy. The bed was large and comfortable, the goose down mattress fully capable of draining the tired tension from his body, which it had done on many occasions. There were chairs and a desk covered with books, charts, maps, and ledgers. The large fireplace occupied one wall. The thick solid oak mantel was supported by two columns carved in the shape of two beautiful women, elegantly posed in wispy gowns that clung to their bodies. Above it was a burgundy tapestry that bore the Finarthian mark, a fist within a rising sun, embroidered in gold.

There were two doors in the room, a heavy oak door that led to the hallway outside, and an oak door that opened to a small balcony three stories above one of the four courtyards in the king's inner castle. The small window in the room looked out to the balcony and beyond to the outer wall of the inner castle. Kiln could see the glow of torches in the distance as knights vigilantly walked the castle wall.

Kiln's silver plate armor hung on a wooden rack off to the side of the bed. The king's own metal smith had spent a month crafting the suit for him and it was magnificent. His sword belt with his sheathed blade hung from the rack within an arm's reach of his bed.

Kiln withdrew his hands from the warmth of the fire and rubbed his tired eyes. He would do no one any good if he didn't get some sleep, so he decided to retire for the night. But before his working mind would allow his body to rest he needed to meditate, to calm his body and mind so that sleep would come to him more quickly.

So he moved to the foot of his bed and took three deep breaths, attempting to slow his breathing and his heart rate. On the third breath he put his hands down to the cold stone floor lifting his body easily into a handstand. Kiln was beyond fifty winters but his body was as strong and flexible as someone much younger. He balanced perfectly for a few moments, breathing slowly, before lowering himself into the position of Ty'erm. His head met the floor softly as he settled his knees on the back of his bent elbows.

Ty'erm was the position of power, taught to him by a Sharneen chief many years ago after he had left the service of Finarth. For two years he lived with the fearsome nomadic warriors far to the east, and he had developed a relationship with one of the many tribal chiefs. Kiln taught them formation fighting techniques, while they in return taught him many secret combat skills, from sword fighting to hand to hand combat. But the most important tool that was taught to him was how to achieve Ty'erm, the state of mind that enabled him to focus on the world around him in a different manner. The position of power enabled one to meditate and focus one's energy in a way that allowed the person to experience the mental state of Ty'erm. It was how Kiln learned to control his body in a way that he didn't think possible. Once the position was mastered, entering the mental state of Ty'erm could be done in mere moments, without assuming the position. In that meditative state Kiln was able to hear and see things he would otherwise not notice. His senses became sharpened and he was able to react on instinct, not emotion. It was an invaluable technique that had helped keep him alive for over twenty years.

Kiln was already exhausted so it only took him a few moments to enter the state of Ty'erm. His breathing and heart rate slowed quickly and his mind seemed to fold in on itself. Everything was quiet and still as his mind found its focus, its center, and then he began to sweep all the tension and worries away until he was left with a feeling of peace and surrounded by an aura of contentment.

Opening his eyes, he lifted his body back into a handstand, holding the position perfectly still for a few more deep breaths before flipping his legs under him and standing up straight with his eyes still closed. Now that he was calm and relaxed, he would be able to sleep soundly without focusing on all the problems that had been hounding him for weeks. He moved softly over to the table, blowing out the candles and blanketing the room in shadow. He took off his cotton shirt, leaving on his comfortable black cotton breeches as he climbed into his soft down bed.

Kiln lay on his back, breathing deeply, and drifted off to sleep.

***

Alerion the wizard sat at a large table made of thick oak. Across the table were various scattered old tomes bound in leather so old and dried that it seemed they would crumble and fall apart when opened. But they hadn't, and Alerion had spent the better part of the day carefully going through books and parchments, looking for anything that might help solve the riddle.

An IshMian with the blood of Finarth flowing through his veins, Alerion whispered the riddle over and over again inside his head. There had to be something here that would give him a clue as to the meaning of the riddle.

He glanced up, rubbing his tired eyes. The room was large and filled with tall book shelves lined with tome after tome of ancient works. He could tell the sun was beginning to set for its rays of light had moved slowly down the north book shelf as it penetrated the large window behind him. Besides Alerion, the room was empty except for the aging "watcher", as they called him. His job was to organize, care for, and "watch" the many valuable pieces of literature and tomes of knowledge in Mynos. His name was Xerandus, and he had been guarding the books for most of his lifetime, which was quite extensive as his long gray beard and wrinkled visage suggested.

Xerandus looked up from a scroll he was reading to make sure everything was as it should be. He was very meticulous and he did not like anyone touching his works without his permission, even a powerful court wizard. He glanced at Alerion momentarily before looking back at his work.

"Xerandus, I cannot find anything in the ambassador's family tree. Do you perhaps have anything of his personal writings, or writings from his daughters?" asked Alerion.

Alerion had been looking for information pertaining to an ambassador of Mynos who had lived over a thousand years ago. His name was Catarus Milfis, and he had traveled to Finarth with his daughter. This event had become the subject of Alerion's research. It was this daughter, whose name was Larrea, who may have had a secret relationship with King Ullis Gavinsteal when he was just a boy, a relationship that no one knew about, but had been mentioned in his own personal journal. If this liaison had brought forth a child, then there may be another royal blood line in existence today. There were a lot of maybes in this possibility, but it was worth investigating.

Xerandus looked up from his scroll and stood up slowly. He used a crooked cane to support his bent body as he walked.

"Let me check for you, Master Wizard," replied the old watcher as he slowly made his way to a tall book shelf on the far side of the room. The wall was as high as eight men and books lined the shelves that rose to the ceiling. A ladder mounted on rolling tracks reached to the top.

Alerion eyed the old man curiously, wondering how he would be able to climb the ladder, if he indeed needed to. The answer to his question came quickly, however, as Xerandus stopped in front of the shelf and whispered several soft words into the staff that he carried. The staff glowed instantly and a small whirling form appeared in front of the watcher. The glowing form was made of a swirling translucent mist, but it didn't seem to take on any particular shape. It spun and danced around the old man for a few moments before it shot up the book shelf to one of the top rows.

"You are a wizard, Xerandus, I did not know," Alerion said in surprise.

The old watcher looked at Alerion, shaking his head slowly. "I am no wizard. The staff is called the *watcher staff*. It has the power to call forth a small wind elemental. I have used the staff for fifty years and it serves me well to maintain the tomes and books for the royal family."

"I see," Alerion said just as the little elemental brought several books down from the top shelf. The books floated and danced in the air as the elemental quickly moved them to Alerion's table, gently setting them down. "Thank you, Xerandus," added Alerion.

Xerandus nodded his head in acknowledgement and whispered several more words. The little elemental flew towards the old man, disappearing into the top of the staff.

"One of the tomes before you contains the writings from Ambassador Milfis himself. The other is from his wife, who died at an early age giving birth to their youngest child. That is all that we have in our records. I hope it will help," he said as he slowly ambled back to his desk and scroll.

"Again, thank you for your help," replied Alerion as he eagerly dove into the books, hoping that there would be some insight, some speck of knowledge to help enlighten him.

***

Delvin stood quietly still, bored out of his mind. His post was important, and in fact it was only the most veteran knights who were given such a post, but it was tedious nonetheless. His job was to stand guard outside of the Commander General's door. Sometimes he guarded the king's room, or those of the other important generals or high ranking officials. There was always someone to watch, and it was nearly every night.

He yawned, trying to shake the sleepiness from his mind. He disliked the task, but he was still a Finarthian knight, and a knight would not fall asleep at his post. He glanced down the dark hallway seeing the same thing that he always did...nothing.

The passage to his left led to stairs that went up to the king's own personal chambers. There would be two more guards there, probably struggling against the same monotony that he was fighting.

To his right was another passage that led to an anteroom. That room always housed several more guards, who were probably sleeping now, thought Delvin. From that room was a flight of stairs that went down to more hallways and more rooms that would be set aside for more of the royal family and their guests.

There were two metal wall sconces flanking his position and each was now lit, casting a faint glow against the cold stone that formed the passageways. The light only illuminated a few paces out in the hallway, leaving the ends of the corridor as dark as night.

Delvin leaned back against the wall, setting the back of his head on the cold stone. He looked up at the ceiling of the passageway and let his mind drift to Cora, his girlfriend. He

230

missed her. It had been over a week since he had caressed her soft skin and stroked her glossy black hair. All the knights had been constantly busy trying to prepare the city for the siege that was sure to come, and he had had little time to spend with her. He smiled openly as he pictured her milky white skin, and oh how he missed her fragrance of rosemary and lavender. It always bewildered him how women managed to have such pleasing aromas.

As he shook the pleasant thought from his mind he lowered his head back down from the wall, barely catching a flash of movement in front of him. His eyes caught the blur of a dark form before everything went black.

Uthgil slowly slid his blade from the dead guard. The assassin had moved forward like a wraith, quickly ramming his knife under the guard's chin and into his brain. The man died instantly, falling forward into Uthgil's arms. He was heavy, but the sturdy assassin managed to maneuver the guard's lifeless body to the ground without a sound.

Three other guards lay dead in the anteroom and Uthgil wanted to quickly perform his task and get out before the bodies were found. The castle was busy and more alert than it normally would have been, but Uthgil was a hunter and the night was his home. It had not been overly difficult to get into the inner sanctum of the royal castle.

The door would be locked and the Sharneen didn't even bother to check it. He pulled back a dark sleeve withdrawing a slender metal pick from a leather sheath at his wrist. There were other various tools there but he only needed one.

After a few seconds Uthgil heard the familiar subtle click of the lock disengaging.

But so did Kiln.

Kiln's eyes bolted open and he held his body still, listening for any other sounds that were out of place. He had been sleeping, but in his calm state of mind he could still hear and sense his surroundings. It was something that he had learned to do a long time ago.

There was no further sound, but then his eyes flicked toward movement by the door. In fact it was the door. Kiln noticed a thin sliver of light penetrate the darkness of his room from outside as the door slowly opened. The hallway was mostly shadow, lit only by a few sconces, so the light that entered Kiln's room was not bright, but it was enough.

His eyes glanced to his sword hanging on his armor no more than an arm's length away.

Uthgil held his small crossbow in his right hand as he silently floated through the tiny gap in the door like a nightly breeze. Both of the darts loaded into his crossbow were poisoned; he would take no chances with this one.

Uthgil quickly located the man's bed, aiming the crossbow at the still form lying there.

Kiln slowly gripped the edge of his thick fur blanket keeping his cold gaze on the assassin entering his room. He slowed his breathing, focusing on the man's movements. The killer lifted something, aiming it at Kiln. Suddenly Kiln was a blur, hefting the blanket and whipping it out in front of him as he leaped from the bed towards his sword.

Uthgil reacted on instinct to the movement. He fired his crossbow, shuffling quickly to his left, toward the balcony, and spinning the weapon he fired the second bolt.

Both bolts slammed into the thick blanket getting caught up in its folds. Kiln dropped the blanket, gripped his blade and in one smooth movement drew the weapon and reversed his direction. Quickly he rolled backwards over the bed, coming up with his glowing weapon in front of him.

Uthgil recognized the man's speed and grace and felt as if he were looking at himself in a mirror. Finally, a challenge he thought, dropping his crossbow and drawing his two deadly blades from their sheaths at his thighs.

Kiln's sword emanated a bright green light and the room lit up in a jade-like glow. The man before him was small and shrouded all in black. Even his head was hooded in black, and a black cloth covered his mouth and nose. The only thing that Kiln

232

could see was the man's eyes, and they were eyes he recognized, oval in shape and slanted at the corners with cold black pupils. The man standing before him was a Sharneen assassin.

Kiln knew this killer probably had a plethora of weapons to use against him, some probably poisoned, and he did not want to give the assassin time to use them, so he attacked without hesitation.

He spun his sword left and right, attacking and lunging at the intruder hoping that his relentless pressure would catch the warrior off guard. It didn't. The Sharneen met his attacks with his two short swords and his perfect balance and movement kept him out of harm's way.

The two warriors danced and spun across the room, their blades continuously connecting, the loud clanging of steel on steel echoing in the still night. Neither gained an advantage as they fought furiously for an opening. They were both experts and their skills mirrored each other. Each movement and attack was met by a counter and followed by another attack and counter. They seemed to know what the other was going to do ahead of time, as if their weapons were attracted to each other, clashing in a deadly dance, neither opponent doing harm to the other.

Kiln's bare torso was glistening with sweat as he pushed his skills to the limit. This man that threatened him was a master swordsman, and probably much younger than he, for his movements had that grace that one expected from the young who had been well trained. Yet he fought like a veteran, recognizing every attack and strike that Kiln directed at him.

Uthgil's blood pulsed with adrenaline as he realized that the confrontation of his life had finally arrived, that the warrior that represented the ultimate challenge was standing in front of him.

But he also realized that the sound of their battle was echoing down the hallways and help was sure to arrive soon. He had to either end this fight quickly, something he was not sure was possible, or flee and hope to meet him again.

He could try again to kill him with poison, but now that he had tasted the man's skill, he would not sully his chance to fight him again evenly, blade to blade, by using poison. He didn't have to use poison; he had other options.

Uthgil had made up his mind. He spun away from the swordsman toward the door to the balcony, bringing his right blade up and catching it under his arm pit. Faster than the eye could follow he continued his free hand's movement across the bandolier on his chest, gripped a throwing dart, and flung the bolt side armed at the fast approaching swordsman.

Kiln caught the movement as he closed the distance that was purposefully created by the Sharneen warrior. He was so close, but in the state of Ty'erm, everything seemed slower and his movements were more precise, so he was able to redirect his attack, stepping aside and swiping his blade across his body, the entire time focusing on the small dart flying at him. Kiln's blade hit the dart with a clang, sending it banging against the stone wall. So focused was he on the first dart, that he missed the second one. A small bolt hit him in the shoulder, spinning him to the side. Though the dart was tiny and it only entered his flesh a few inches, he immediately knew that it was coated with poison. It stung fiercely and Kiln gritted his teeth, looking up to see the Sharneen pick up his crossbow and flee out the door to the balcony.

Uthgil had prepared for his escape prior to his attack and it took him mere moments to set it up. Strapped to his dark leather belt was a thin black rope rolled up perfectly in a small bundle. The rope was very thin, and would have been too thin to hold his weight. But it had been enchanted and it would actually hold twice that. Not only was it much stronger than its appearance, but with a mere magic word the end would take the shape of a hook, stronger than metal and capable of returning back to its rope-like shape and suppleness with another magic word. It had cost him a fortune to have a wizard make it, but it had saved his life many times and was well worth the cost.

"Talvar," Uthgil whispered to the rope, pulling the end free from the belt after sheathing his twin blades. Immediately the tip formed a strong hook and Uthgil placed it on the rail. Then he threw the rope over the edge, looked back as Kiln stumbled through the balcony door, and bounded over the rail with the rope held tightly in his gloved hands.

Normally the rope would have burned his hands as he slid down, but not this rope. His gloves had been made with the rope and their magic partnered each other. The magical gloves not only protected his hands, but they created an unnatural friction, which slowed the assassin's descent to a controllable pace.

Uthgil landed lightly on his feet in seconds, whispered the triggering word to release the hook, and caught the rope as it fell from above him. He wrapped up the rope, shoved it into his tunic, and raced off into the night, disappearing into the shadows like breath in the wind.

Kiln stumbled through the balcony door, falling to his knees. His vision swam as he reached up, yanking the dart from his shoulder. He shook his head, trying to push away the blackness that was encroaching on his mind. He tried to move forward but his body wouldn't cooperate. *Am I dying*, Kiln thought, as he struggled to stand. His mind was drifting like a rudderless ship and he couldn't seem to remember what had happened, or why he was on the floor. Then he found himself lying on his stomach, where he finally succumbed to the blackness.

Jormell was standing at his post outside Captain Lathrin's barracks when he had heard the commotion. He turned his head toward the courtyard where he heard the noise. Listening intently, he wondered if his tired mind was playing tricks on him.

Jormell was young, just over twenty winters, and he had recently earned the honor of knighthood. His round face still had the pimpled skin of youth, but it lit up like the sun when he smiled.

Then he heard it again. The sound was unmistakable, steel on steel as blades met in combat, and it was coming from the courtyard.

He hesitated, wondering what he should do. If he went to investigate the sound then he would be leaving his post, but if he didn't, then whoever was in trouble might end up dead. He knew he should raise the alarm, but maybe he should tell the standing officer first.

He ran into the barracks and went directly to Fourth Lance Dagrinal, who was sleeping near the main door. Third Lance Lathrin did not sleep in the barracks and the officer in charge was Dagrinal. It was dark, but enough ambient light from the moon shown through the windows to guide him to the lieutenant's bed.

"Sir!" Jormell hissed, shaking the sleeping form.

Dagrinal was a light sleeper and he bolted up immediately at the disturbance. Jormell jumped back, startled by his sudden reaction. "Fourth Lance, something is happening in the courtyard."

"What? What do you mean, Jormell?" asked Dagrinal, now alert and wide eyed.

"It sounds like fighting, sir, coming from the courtyard!"

"Why didn't you sound the alarm?" cried Dagrinal, leaping from his bed and grabbing his sword that was leaning against the wall.

"I'm sorry, sir. I thought to inform you first before I woke the entire compound."

"Are you sure its fighting?" Dagrinal drew his sword from its scabbard.

"Yes, sir, the sound is unmistakable."

"Then sound the alarm!" Dagrinal yelled, running toward the door. The sound of the alarm horn bellowing in the night followed Dagrinal as he leaped out into the darkness and ran toward the courtyard.

Uthgil heard the horn, swearing softly under his breath. He had to get to the south wall where he had placed his rope to scale the inner wall. Once over the inner wall of the king's compound he could easily disappear into the dark city streets of Finarth. But he had to move fast, for the grounds would soon be swarming with knights.

The moon was bright and it pierced the darkness like a cat's eye. But the shadows of the barrack and stable walls provided enough cover for him to move quickly, unnoticed.

Uthgil's mind drifted back to his fight with the warrior as he moved from shadow to shadow. It seemed that the man's reputation had been well earned. His quickness and skill sent a shiver down Uthgil's spine as he thought about their brief encounter. Where most men sought ecstasy in the pleasures of the flesh, Uthgil found it in combat, and the recent skirmish with this battle legend left him excited and eager for more. He would face him again and then they would know who was best.

The Sharneen smiled at the thought of his victory. He was still smiling as he rounded the corner of a large stable, when he suddenly came face to face with a warrior running at him with a long sword held easily at his side. The man was tall and lean, wearing only gray leggings. He wasn't even wearing his boots, and it was probably his shoe-less feet that enabled him to get so close to the assassin without being heard. The warrior's features were dark and shadowed and his muscled chest was covered in thick black hair.

The assassin's smile disappeared as he cursed himself for being so careless. It was not like him to make such stupid mistakes, and it unnerved him that the warrior general had that effect on him, allowing his mind to drift with thoughts of their next encounter when, instead, he should have been paying attention to his surroundings and his escape.

Uthgil had to get through this man quickly or risk being surrounded by more men as they flooded out of the barracks. He launched himself forward so quickly that the warrior barely had time to register surprise, let alone the attack.

But Dagrinal was a seasoned warrior, one of the best swordsmen in Finarth, and his quick reactions saved his life. He whipped his sword out frantically, jumping back from the man in black. The assassin's onslaught was ruthless, however, and Dagrinal's breath caught in his throat as he frantically tried to counter his attacker's moves. The Sharneen fought with two identical short swords, using them independently of each other, as if each had a mind of its own. Pivoting and lunging, his blades sought openings in Dagrinal's defenses. The Finarthian warrior was skilled, exceptionally so, but Uthgil fought with all his talent, and the necessity of ending the fight quickly fueled every strike and move. Dagrinal attempted an offensive move by flicking his sword toward the assassin's neck. Uthgil spun by the sword in a blur, slashing the bladed guard that covered his hand across the warrior's thigh.

Each of Uthgil's knives had a unique design. The long blade curved back and over the assassin's fist, shooting back another six inches beyond the pommel, protecting his fingers from attack and giving him another weapon. He could punch or use the second blade with deadly effect as he had just done.

Dagrinal flinched, pulling his injured leg back from the deadly fighter and fending off a second and third attack from the warrior. The cut was deep and Dagrinal could feel his blood drench his leg.

But he had no time to worry about his wound for the assassin came at him again. Twice more the dark warrior's blades slipped in and cut Dagrinal. The wounds were shallow, but they bled heavily, and the cut on his thigh was beginning to take its toll as Dagrinal stumbled back, trying to create some space between him and the assassin, as he heard behind him the distant pounding of booted feet. His men must have been awakened by the alarm. But would they get to him in time? Dagrinal had never fought anyone this skilled, except perhaps Master Borum, and the helpless feeling of being outmatched was not something to which he was accustomed. The feeling unnerved him and his heart beat with an uncharacteristic fear. This was not a practice yard. This fight was for real.

Uthgil cringed as he too heard the sounds of approaching men. There was no more time. He had to finish this swordsman, and quickly, as he was the only thing standing in the way of his escape. But the man was evidently less vulnerable than he had anticipated, and it was taking longer than normal to dispatch him.

So instead of pressing the attack, he spun his blades into their resting places at his thighs, and for the second time that night, reached up to his chest, grabbed a dart, and flung it at the warrior.

Dagrinal stopped his retreat as the warrior changed tactics. He was bleeding from several wounds and he was starting to feel lightheaded. But he didn't have a second to worry about that as the warrior sheathed his blades and flicked his hand in a casual motion. It all happened so quickly that Dagrinal barely registered the movement before a sharp pain bit him in the chest.

Instantly his chest flared with fire and he dropped his sword to the ground. He reached up, gripping the dart in his chest, barely having the strength to pull the poisoned weapon from his flesh. An intense pain gripped his heart in a deadly embrace. His eyes opened wide in surprise and disbelief as his breathing rapidly became hindered, and then ceased altogether as his heart simply stopped beating. Then he fell, face first to the ground, as the blanket of death enshrouded him.

***

"I will crush him!" stormed Graggis as the enraged man slammed his fist into the stone wall. His eyes were red and fresh tears streaked his face as he fought for control of his emotions. Dagrinal, his friend, was dead, killed by a poisoned dart, and the fearsome pain of the loss was almost unbearable.

They were in Kiln's room and the general was lying in his bed. He had just awoken from his poisoned sleep, leaving his mind groggy and his body weak.

The king was there, as was Androg, high priest to Ulren, who was inspecting the warrior general's wound in his shoulder. Sitting at the table, in thought, was Gandarin, a second rank general and confidant to King Baylin. Gandarin's face was covered with a thick beard and bushy mustache and the heavy set man was wearing nothing but a night robe and cotton breeches. They were all similarly outfitted due to the suddenness of the late night attack.

The king's eyes were also wet with tears over the loss of Dagrinal. He wiped his eyes in frustration, turning to Graggis. "We will find the assassin, Graggis," he said, his tone bitter and dripping with anger. "Kiln, how do you feel?" he asked, turning his gaze to the warrior.

"I feel fine, a bit weak from the poison, but I will live," he said softly. He too was obviously feeling the loss of Dagrinal.

Androg then spoke up. "The dart in his shoulder was coated with a sleeping poison called Nurag," he said, obviously puzzled. "Why would the assassin use sleeping poison on Commander Kiln and fatal poison on Dagrinal? It makes no sense if Commander Kiln was the target."

"The assassin was very skilled," said Gandarin. "He defeated Dagrinal and yet..."

"He did not defeat him!" Graggis yelled, interrupting Gandarin. "He murdered him with poison, like a coward!"

"I meant no disrespect, Graggis," replied Gandarin, standing and placing his hand on the warrior's muscled shoulder. "Dagrinal was a great man and he deserved a better death."

"Graggis, Gandarin is right. Dagrinal's wounds suggest that he faced a better swordsman, regardless of how difficult that may be to accept," the king said kindly.

Graggis collapsed tiredly into a chair, his energy drained by the sorrow and frustration of his friend's death. He dropped his head into his hands.

"He was the best I've ever faced," Kiln said thoughtfully. "I think he wanted me to live so he could face me again. I could see it in his eyes."

"But someone paid him to kill you. You think he gave that up because you represent a challenge?" asked Gandarin.

Kiln directed his gaze toward the burly general. "I do, Gandarin. Men like him live to test their skills. And he was Sharneen. They, more than any other race I know of, deem combat as the truest test of courage and greatness. He came in to kill me, but he left with a new goal. He wants to face me on even terms. He wants to find out who is the better."

"Is that feeling reciprocated?" asked the king.

"Yes, I will face him, and I will kill him," replied Kiln coldly.

The king looked at Kiln for a few moments before directing his gaze to Gandarin. "Gandarin, continue to patrol the city and double the guards in the inner castle. Kiln needs his rest, let us leave him to it," he ordered, moving to the door.

"Yes, sir," Gandarin replied.

The king stopped, turning towards Graggis. "We will find him, Graggis, and he will face justice, one way or another," he said firmly. His gaze flicked to Kiln for a moment, then he turned, moving into the shadows of the hallway.

***

Alerion was exhausted. His tired eyes hurt from reading late into the night by candlelight. He leaned back in the solid wood chair, stretching his back before returning to the tome in front of him. He had been reading a diary written by the wife of an Ambassador from Mynos more than a thousand years ago. The pages were stiff and brittle and he had to use the utmost care in turning them. In some spots the ink had faded and blown away with the passage of time.

He had found an interesting entry, one that further suggested a liaison between the young prince, Ullis Gavinsteal, and the Ambassador's daughter. The entry spoke of a day when Ambassador Milfis returned from Finarth and his daughter Larrea spoke to her mother about the young Finarthian prince. The entry was brief, simply mentioning that her daughter talked of the prince continuously for some time. But that was it, nothing more.

Alerion got to the end of the book, gently shutting it. It was very late and Xerandus had left with instructions to Alerion to leave the tomes on the table. Alerion stood up, gripping his staff. There was only one more thing to do and he had been hoping he wouldn't need to do it, but the lack of information and the pressure of time had now made the decision for him. Time was of the essence, so much so that he did not have time to get proper permission from the Mynosian king.

Alerion stood, walking from the library towards the cemetery.

It was easy to find. He had seen it when he came in from the docks. The cemetery was located just inside the outer wall of the city and it was surrounded by a ten foot stone wall with only one entrance, an iron gate locked at this time of the night. The entire stone wall was lined with cherry trees that were just starting to bud as the warmer spring breeze blew in off the Algard coast. Thick green shrubs also lined the wall, offering plenty of shadows in which Alerion could work his spells.

He would need several this night, one to get him in, and one to conjure Larrea's spirit, the latter being the more difficult. Alerion stood next to a large cherry tree at the base of the stone wall. He looked around and saw no one. It was late, very late, and the only people he might see this time of night would either be the house guard, or common city thieves, neither of which he relished meeting just now.

He drew a feather from one of his pouches, holding it in the palm of his hand just before his face, and whispered several words of power. He then dropped the feather, which fell to the ground like a rock. As the feather fell, his body simultaneously rose from the ground, light as the feather. Using his mind to control his body, he moved up and over the wall, landing softly on the other side. Then he spoke another word of power that cancelled the spell.

The night was black as pitch, and dark clouds had moved in from the sea, shrouding the ambient light of the moon and stars. He would need some light, so he casually whispered a simple word. The tip of his staff slowly began to glow, until, after a few seconds, a bluish-white light shone brightly, penetrating the oppressive darkness.

He knew not where the ambassador and his family had been buried, but he guessed it would be toward the mausoleum, and so he walked briskly toward the center of the cemetery where he guessed the structure would be located.

It didn't take him long to find it. The mausoleum was a large square building made of heavy stone, and each corner was supported by a giant column of white rock. It was expertly built and the walls were graced with numerous fine carvings representing many figures which Alerion recognized as guardians of the dead. Verdant vines had made the building their home, covering the pillars and walls with a lovely mesh of green that was beginning to show the buds of a fragrant white flower.

Alerion walked up to the only entrance, a square opening with steps leading down to where the many coffins would be lined up along the interior walls. Only the important people in Mynos would be buried here, so it would be the most likely spot where Alerion would find the ambassador's family. At least that is what he hoped.

Without pausing, he walked confidently down the steps, his bright staff pushing back the thick darkness. At the bottom of the stairs were two branches that led to long hallways lined with coffins that had been stacked onto the many stone shelves. The air was thick with the mustiness of age and mildew, yet not overly unpleasant as one might expect from a room filled with rotting corpses.

Alerion took his time moving from one coffin to another, his staff held before him, his eyes scanning the writing etched into each stone sarcophagus. It took some time for Alerion to examine the many coffins lining the walls. Dust and cobwebs covered everything, and Alerion had to frequently wipe away the dust and grime to read the writing.

He found nothing down the first hallway so he made his way to the second and began his search anew. Finally his persistence paid off. He found the ambassador's sarcophagus, flanked by that of his wife's, but Alerion cursed under his breath when he realized that there was no coffin marked with Larrea's name.

"What am I missing?" he whispered to himself, standing back from the coffins. He thought for a moment. Then it came to him. She may have married, and if so, would be lying near her husband and their children, if they had any. So he continued his search looking carefully at each dusty coffin. He only had to move a few paces down the hallway before he came across a coffin that bore the name, Larrea Penurrien. It might not be her, but more likely than not it was; at any rate he had to try.

The spell to conjure a spirit was much different than the one needed to conjure a great demon. Most spirits cannot cause harm, nor do they desire to, so a symbolic prison does not need to be drawn. In order to perform the spell, one needed something from the person, something like hair or a fragment of bone.

The large stone sarcophagus was too heavy for Alerion to lift. But he was a powerful wizard and he rarely relied on the strength of his physical body. He leaned his staff against the wall so the light bathed the area, then he calmed his breathing and closed his eyes in concentration. The spell was not difficult, but it did require some mental concentration. So once his breathing had slowed he focused on the heavy stone lid, and, picturing it in his mind, he whispered the words to the spell. He then felt the air around him shudder with power as he drew energy from the earth.

The elves called this form of magic Telsirium, a special form of magic where the wizard doesn't just draw magic directly from the Ru'Ach, but from the energy of all the things around him. The energy could be more quickly accessed this way, and extremely powerful in short bursts. But it had its drawbacks. If you took too much energy it might kill the surrounding plants and animals. Also, the amount of energy that you drew upon was limited, in comparison to when energy was taken directly from the Ru'Ach, the river of energy that made up the universe. Energy from the Ru'Ach was infinite, and the amount that could be taken was directly correlated to how much energy the wizard could physically and mentally handle. There had been more than one wizard who had burned himself to ash trying to channel too much energy from the Ru'Ach.

Alerion opened his eyes, using his hands to manipulate the energy around him, pantomiming moving the sarcophagus so that, without touching it, the lid slowly slid to the side, exposing a sliver of blackness which gradually enlarged as the lid continued to move. Alerion hoped that no one was around to hear the grating sound of stone on stone.

The gap in the coffin was now large enough, so Alerion stopped the movement of the lid. As he approached the coffin he felt a wave of thick moist air wash over him, carrying with it the odor of rotting leaves. But it could have been worse Alerion thought, bringing the light from the staff closer to the opening.

Inside he could clearly see a dusty skeleton covered in a rotting piece of silk that at some point was probably a beautiful gown. Pieces of dried skin and flesh clung to her bones like dried, flakey paper. The sparkle of jewelry that lay on her neck and wrists still managed to glitter through the musty dust of her resting place. He reached in, gently withdrawing a small piece of hair still clinging to her skull. The hair was brittle, breaking easily, but it mattered not, all he needed was a small amount, and the few strands of hair would be enough.

Alerion moved away from the coffin, leaning the staff against the wall again. Then he reached into a pouch at his side and took out a small candle. It was a conjuring candle, so difficult to create that only an expert alchemist could do so. Alerion was such, for his talents leaned in that direction.

He set the candle down on the ground, lighting it with a quick word. Then he sat on his knees before the candle and concentrated on the spell. This spell was not as difficult as the spell needed to conjure a demon, as he had done recently with Ixtofin, the pit fiend that he had called from the fiery lower planes. He calmed his heart and breathing and recalled the words of the spell. They appeared in his mind as they always did. Alerion's constant studying and preparation enabled him to bring forth the words to his spells quickly, but once the spells were cast, he would have to go back to his book and relearn them. It was like the words themselves disappeared from his mind when the magic was released. That is why a wizard's spell book was so valuable; it was the key to all their magic.

Alerion opened his eyes, and began to recite the spell. The words flowed from his mouth smoothly and after a few moments he neared the final word, the word that released the magic of the spell. As he spoke that word, he dropped the lone hair on the open flame of the candle.

Instantly the flame flared with a white light and from the candle came a shimmering mist. The room instantly grew cold and Alerion could see his breath in the cold night air. The temperature dropped significantly, as it always did when conjuring spirits. Slowly the mist took shape and floating in the air before him was the translucent form of a woman wearing a blue gown of silk. She was still beautiful for one who looked to have lived fifty winters, probably the age at which she had died. Though her form was somewhat blurred, it was still obvious to Alerion that she had once been a stunning women.

"Larrea? Larrea Milfis?" Alerion asked.

The spirit looked around and then focused on Alerion, as if she were trying to figure out her surroundings before looking at the stranger in front of her.

"Long ago, I can barely remember," the spirit women whispered softly.

"But you were Ambassador Milfis's daughter, Larrea?" Alerion asked again.

"Yes, I was, and am still. Why am I here? Where have I been?" I am confused," she said softly. She resembled a lost child looking around at her strange surroundings.

"You have been in the Ru'Ach. I have called your energy back, for I need your help," Alerion said gently.

"Please, will you send me back? It feels wrong to be here," she said, glancing furtively at her surroundings as if something might jump from the shadows and attack her.

"I will, you have my word. I will send you back to the Ru'Ach where you may rest once again. I need to ask you a question, one that is important to the survival of the living."

"Who are you?" Larrea asked.

"I am Alerion, court wizard to King Baylin Gavinsteal of Finarth."

Her form fluttered for a moment as if Alerion's words had hit a nerve. He hoped that they had, that they would bring back some old memories.

"Finarth, I remember, so long ago. My first love," Larrea's voice drifted off as she thought back to long dead memories.

"Did you conceive a child with the young Ullis Gavinsteal?" Alerion asked directly.

The spirit looked back at Alerion, staring at him for a moment before speaking. "Yes, I loved him. But we were young, it was not meant to be."

Alerion's heart quickened at this news. "What happened to the baby?" he gently prodded.

The tone in the spirit's voice seemed to change, becoming sad and distant. "I had to give her up. I was not allowed to keep her. We were too young and the child was conceived out of wedlock."

"Did the young prince know of the child?"

"No," the spirit said simply.

"Where did the child go?"

"My daughter," the spirit continued softly, her voice now filled with sorrow, "was sent to Tarsis to be raised by my cousin who was married to the youngest Tarsinian prince."

"Do you know what happened to your daughter?"

"Her name was Tamralyn," she whispered, her voice growing more distant.

"Do you know what happened to her?" Alerion asked again.

"She married just before I died."

"Who did she marry?" Alerion asked.

"A commoner, I can't remember his name, it was so long ago," her voice trailed off. "Can you send me back now?"

"Yes, and thank you, Larrea," Alerion added, reciting the words of power that ended the spell. Her form fluttered as he blew out the flame of the candle, sending her energy back to the Ru'Ach where it would join with the energy of all things.

Alerion stood up, moving to Larrea's coffin again. He was just about to start the spell to close the lid when he caught a glimpse of movement and a flash of light in his peripheral vision.

He turned to face three men as they emerged from the base of the stairs. They each held flaming torches and Alerion could see several weapons glitter in the flame's light.

The man in the lead wore a dark cloak and a hood that covered his face. He was holding a pitted long sword in his right hand. Their clothing was ragged and they had the overall appearance of thieves that were not very good at their profession. One of the other thieves carried a small hand axe while the other carried a long hunting knife. The one on the left was thick with more fat than muscle. The man on the right was young, very thin, and his eyes betrayed his youth as they darted about nervously.

Great, thieves, that is all I need thought Alerion, grabbing his staff and turning towards the trio.

"I told you I saw a light," whispered the boy on the right. His thin face sprouted patches of newly grown hair, obviously too young to grow a decent beard.

"Yes you did, Kip, nice job," the lead man said before addressing Alerion who was standing calmly before them. "Nice night for a walk, eh?"

"Indeed," Alerion said calmly. "Now be on your way. I do not want trouble, nor do you."

"I'll tell you what we want. We want your valuables. And since you have that coffin open, we'll take a look in there as well," the leader said.

"Are you brave or stupid?" Alerion asked.

The man was somewhat taken aback by the question. "What are you talking about?" he asked.

"Well, you are threatening a court wizard to the King of Finarth. So you are either very brave or very stupid. Which is it?"

"Lots of people could make that staff light up like that, it does not mean you are a court wizard," the man replied, as if to convince himself.

"True," Alerion replied, "but could lots of people do this?" he asked, launching into a spell.

He dug deep for the Telsirium magic again. It was a great form of magic when you needed power quickly. Whispering a few words, he sucked in the energy around him. With a few flicks of his staff he shut the coffin lid and slammed the two thieves flanking the leader against the stone wall.

He used just enough energy to launch them into the wall without doing any serious damage. They hit hard, tumbling to the ground, dropping their weapons in the process.

The leader backed up slowly, his nervous eyes darting to his men and back to Alerion. Alerion pulled back the edges of his cloak revealing his tunic and the glittering symbol of Finarth, the fist in the sun.

"Now, do not make me kill you. If you have any brains at all you will recognize the mark on my chest as the Finarthian royal insignia, and you will deduce that the amount of magic I just used is but a pittance of what I can call upon. So, if you wish to live out your meager lives as leeches of society, stealing from your own people, then you best leave now. If not, I would like nothing better than to fry you to a crisp so that you may join the rest of the corpses around you. What say you?"

The trio needed no other prompting. The lead warrior turned and ran, while his two men grabbed their weapons and frantically regained their footing, following him out into the dark night.

Alerion smiled and followed the thieves. He had some answers, but he still needed more.

Nine

Cuthaine

Gullanin advanced toward two huge Gould-Irin Orcs. The beasts were standing before a large black tent, the entrance being an extended vestibule draped with more heavy black cloth. The wizard was in a foul mood and the orcs stepped aside quickly as he neared them. Speaking a quick word and motioning with his staff, the heavy fabric that draped the opening flew open with unseen force. He continued walking without breaking stride, the sharp end of his black cane biting into the thick red carpet that covered the expansive floor of the tent.

Gullanin did not relish this meeting. Things had not gone well for him and the Hounds of Gould. Everything had been progressing as planned. The hounds had the king of Tarsis in their deadly jaws, ready for the kill, when the cavaliers had arrived. The female warrior had been killed in the struggle before the hounds were dispatched by the other cavalier and the ogrillion.

An ogrillion? It made no sense. Why would an ogrillion show up and help defend the humans? Gullanin was frustrated, he had even tried to kill the king himself, but that blasted dwarf had got in the way at the last moment. Every time he was close to fulfilling his lord's plans, something got in the way, and Malbeck would not be pleased.

Gullanin walked the ten paces of the vestibule, stopping at a large oak door. The structure was quite impressive, but what was more impressive was that the entire tent was torn down and rebuilt after each day of marching. Tarsis had been destroyed and now Malbeck's army was moving south, heading for Cuthaine before advancing into Finarthian lands. It would take many months to get to Finarth. Their progress was slow as the ground was still covered with patches of snow. But as they progressed, the days would get longer and warmer, and the snows would melt away into spring, making the long trek more bearable.

Gullanin was just about to tap the door with his staff when a commanding voice came from within. "Enter, Gullanin." The door swung silently open.

The interior of the tent was dark, really dark, except for a reddish glow emanating from the center. Gullanin's eyes were drawn to a strange orb floating in the middle of the room. It was shaped like an egg, but it was the size of an orc's head and it glowed with an eerie red light. Tendrils of dancing orange and red light buzzed about the egg shaped sphere, casting flickering shadows about the interior of the large tent.

The tent was basically empty, except for a giant throne positioned in the middle. The throne was constructed of bones, but not just any bones, for they were huge and obviously those of a dragon. The back of the throne had two leathery wings fanning out in both directions, their black and withered skin clinging to their skeletal frames, and appearing as if they had sat in the hot desert sun for a month. The throne's feet were also made from the bones of a dragon, the claws splayed out wide, easily supporting the massive structure. In fact, it looked like the skeletal dried up form of a dragon.

Malbeck was not sitting in the throne. He was standing before the glowing orb, gripping a young woman in one hand, and holding her up a full pace from the floor. She was dead, for her body hung lifeless from his powerful arm and blood ran from her severed throat down her body. Then Gullanin noticed that Malbeck had dripped her blood over the orb, which pulsed several times as it drew the blood into its translucent body.

Malbeck tossed the girl aside as if she were an old shirt, moving with long strides to his throne. The demonoid was incredibly strong. Gullanin was fully aware of how easily he had held the girl in the air with one arm, and how effortlessly he had tossed her useless body across the room with just a flick of his muscular arm.

Gullanin glanced at the girl. She must have been no older than eighteen winters. Her body was beautiful, marred only by the splattered blood and lifeless eyes that stared back at him

Malbeck, the Dark One, was impressive. His body was tall, straight, and covered with tight muscle. His pale, almost bluish skin contrasted sharply with his tight black dragon skin breeches. His torso was always bare, except for the crisscrossed leather harness cinched tight across his bulging chest. He also wore a long black cape that matched the darkness of his hair. But it was his eyes that always gave Gullanin a chill. They were pure white, and it looked as if he were looking at nothing and everything at the same time.

"Do you like my orb?" Malbeck asked as he sat down in his dragon bone throne. The demonoid's deep voice resonated with power, and as he spoke, the tips of his sharp teeth could be seen beyond his bluish-black lips.

"It is beautiful, my Lord. I have never seen anything like it." Gullanin spoke softly, his eyes glancing to the orb and back to the ground in front of him. He always kept his head bowed when speaking to his lord, to show respect and submission. Besides, it was too difficult to make eye contact with Malbeck. His eyes seemed to suck the life force from him.

"Do you know what it is, my faithful servant?"

"I'm sorry, my Lord, I do not."

"It is the egg of a Blood Dragon," Malbeck said proudly.

Gullanin was momentarily shocked. Blood Dragons were beasts that inhabited the lower planes and they were very rare. You could live a thousand lifetimes and never have seen one. They were uncommon even on their own plane of existence, and as far as Gullanin knew, they had never existed on the material plane. Black as a bottomless pit, their powerful bodies were covered in veins of fiery orange and red, similar to what Gullanin saw on the surface of the egg. They were creatures of magic whose hearts beat with the energy gained from the devoured blood of their victims. They were also called Demon Dragons, *a fitting name* thought Gullanin as he glanced again at the floating egg. "I have heard of them, my Lord, but have never seen one. They are said to be very powerful."

"Indeed, they are. Power that will be mine in good time," he whispered softly, catching Gullanin looking again at the lifeless body of the girl. "You wonder why I killed the girl?"

"Is it to feed the egg?" Gullanin asked, reasoning that much on his own.

"It is. I need the blood of a hundred strong souls to speed up the hatching of the egg. Young virgins offer the most sustenance for the egg, but strong warriors will do as well. It is unfortunate that these humans succumb to their earthly desires so quickly. I am having difficulty finding so many untouched women," Malbeck hissed angrily.

"I'm sure there will be more at Cuthaine. If not, surely the Free Legion warriors will suffice. And we will kill many of them," Gullanin said, shuffling uncomfortably in front of the demonoid.

"I'm sure you are right," whispered Malbeck, sitting up straighter in his throne. "Now, tell me of your failure, I can smell it on you and it sullies my presence with its weakness."

"I'm sorry, my Lord, but the king escaped. Two cavaliers arrived just as the hounds were about to finish them all. But one of the cavaliers was killed," he added, hoping the news would mollify Malbeck somewhat.

"Which one?" Malbeck asked impatiently.

"The female, cavalier to Bandris," Gullanin whispered softly, knowing that was not what Malbeck wanted to hear.

"Continue," Malbeck ordered, his voice strained with fury.

"All the Gould-Irin Orcs were slain, along with the hounds. But their party is now reduced to Jonas, the young cavalier, the Blade Singer, an unknown dwarf, and a handful of Tarsinian warriors. It is only a matter of time, my Lord. I will find them again and kill them. This time I will not fail you."

"Where have they gone?" Malbeck asked after a long pause.

"Into the Hallows."

"Why would Shyann send the two cavaliers to protect the king?" Malbeck whispered to himself. "Find them!" Malbeck said to Gullanin. "There is something I am missing. I want them dead. Take more Gould-Irin. Do whatever is necessary to kill them. Now leave me before I decide not to give you a second chance!" Malbeck waved his hand impatiently in dismissal.

Gullanin pivoted on his cane, striding from the Dark One's tent without another word, eager to leave his angry presence.

***

The small, tired, battle scarred party stood on a hill facing the distant city of Cuthaine. All that remained of the group were the king, Allindrian, Jonas, Kilius, Fil, Myrell, Durgen, and Dandronis. They had materialized from the gate in the middle of a stand of trees less than half a day's travel from where they stood. They were dirty and covered in sweat, blood, and soot, but the sight of the city gave them new hope. Especially King Kromm, for somewhere below, in the city, he believed he would find his family.

"What if they are not there?" Allindrian asked.

The king turned his gaze from the city to Allindrian. "They are there, I can feel it."

Jonas was the only one of the group who looked refreshed. His armor and clothing were immaculate, the stark contrast with the others making them look like beggars. Jonas looked down at the city, wondering if the king was right. He had a task, and that task was to get the king to Finarth as quickly as he could. If Kromm didn't find his wife and son there, would the king leave with him? He guessed not, and he couldn't blame him. Nor could he tell the king why it was so important to get him to Finarth, for he did not know.

"Sire, what can you tell me about Cuthaine?" Jonas asked.

"Cuthaine is a free city that was founded by a warrior named LeeOntis many years ago. These lands are wild, filled with raiding nomads, tribal wars, and brigands looking for easy prey. LeeOntis carved a place for himself with his sword. Cuthaine separates my kingdom with the kingdom of Finarth. To the west are the Tundren Mountains, home of many violent barbarian tribes. Luckily for us, the Hallows took us past their lands. To the east are the Nomad Lands, rightly named as several nomadic tribes live there. Cuthaine is surrounded by potential enemies but LeeOntis was able to build the city and his kingdom through war and diplomacy. He attracted lots of followers over many years. I do not know much about his family and history but after hundreds of years the city has grown to what you see now. But now it is governed by a ruling council elected by the people. They are protected by the Free Legion, skilled warriors who have honed their skills from centuries of fighting and protecting the small kingdom from the wilds of the lands. Their army is small, but it is said that their infantry is the best."

"Do you know any of the council members?" Durgen asked.

"I have met with the council, although only a few times," the king replied.

"That may be useful," Allindrian added.

"Let us banter no more. I long to find my wife and son," the kind said, ending the conversation.

And with that they followed the monarch down the hill towards the city.

The group made their way to the gate. To their surprise it was closed. They could see men milling about on the battlements above them and five soldiers stood at guard before the large wood and steel gate.

The soldiers came to attention immediately when they saw the companions approach. They appeared tense and each had a hand on their weapons. Jonas noticed that the warriors on the walls now held crossbows aimed down at them. The soldiers of the Free Legion were heavily armored in plate mail, metal thigh guards, greaves, and helms. Each carried an infantry sword and a long thick spear. Every one of them wore a red sash cinched tight around their waists, the mark of the Free Legion.

Jonas wondered why they were all so tense. He had heard that Cuthaine was a free city where all were welcome, but that certainly did not seem to be the case here now. He judged it would not be long before they found out why.

"Halt!" one of the guards commanded, striding purposefully toward them. He was followed closely by four other warriors who stopped just before the haggard party, fanning out to face them, their faces tense and alert. The leader was tall and thin, with a long mustache below his hooked and pointed nose. His eyes were bright and intense. Jonas observed him as he quickly looked each of them over, finally settling his gaze on Jonas. "Cavalier," the man stammered briefly before regaining his composure, "I am sorry, I did not see you at first. My apologies," he said with a deep bow.

The rest of the men relaxed a bit, holding their spears more casually. The guard did not recognize the others. The king's armor was so dirty and black from their fight in the Hallows that the Cuthanian soldiers probably did not see the Tarsinain symbol embossed on his chest plate. Allindrian stood in the back with her hooded cloak pulled tightly around her so they did not see her for who she really was. Jonas stood out like a beacon, as he always did.

"No need to apologize; you are just doing your job. What is your name, sir?" Jonas asked.

"Captain Hadrick."

"Sir, standing before you is King Kromm of Tarsis and his companions. We desire entrance into your fine city," Jonas said.

The warrior directed his gaze to Kromm and after a few moments his eyes lit up with recognition. Turning, he addressed his men hastily. "Open the gate, quickly." Then he turned back to King Kromm, bowing deeply again. "I am sorry, King Kromm. I did not recognize you. We have all heard about Tarsis and I am glad to see you alive."

"Captain, thank you for your words but I need to meet with the council. Time is of the essence," Kromm said.

"Very well, Your Highness, please follow me," the captain said, turning and walking toward the gate that was now being opened.

"Captain Hadrick," the king continued, "Why is the gate locked, and why are travelers being met by soldiers with hands on their swords?"

"I'm sorry, Sire. But things have gotten bad here at Cuthaine. We have to be cautious with who now enters," he replied.

"Things?" questioned Allindrian.

The captain looked at her for a moment before responding. He still could not see her face well, nor any indication that she was a Blade Singer. "Yes, dark things. Followers of the Forsworn," he said, making the four pointed star gesture over his chest. "Blackhearts have been crawling out from their dark holes. People have disappeared. Murder, rape, theft, and all kinds of crime have been increasing. Two of the council members have been murdered in their homes. Young girls have gone missing all over the kingdom. The city is not safe anymore and we are doing what we can to rectify it, but we have not met with much success."

"I see," Allindrian replied, glancing at Jonas.

Jonas, hearing the captain's words, was just as concerned as Allindrian. They had to find the king's family and then he had to get them safely out of the city and to Finarth. They had to do all of this in a city that was now crawling with Blackhearts, as the people here called the followers of the dark gods. Jonas could not afford wasting time here. It was the unknown that was giving him pause. What would they find in Cuthaine?

They followed the captain through the gate and were met by ten more armed Free Legion warriors. A burly bushy haired warrior approached the captain and the king.

"Thank you, Captain Hadrick, I will take them from here," announced the big man in a deep strong voice. His green eyes went to King Kromm, and he bowed slightly. "King Kromm, it is good to see you alive. I am General Kurraris. We actually met five years ago."

"I remember, it is good to see you again," the king said, shaking the general's hand in the warrior's grip.

The general turned towards Jonas and offered his hand in greeting. "Cavalier, you are most welcome here. Are you here to help us rid the city of our vermin?"

"I'm sorry, General, my mission is directly related to the king, but while we are here I will certainly help where I may."

"I understand. I'm sorry, King Kromm," the general said, redirecting his gaze towards Kromm. "But we must not stay here. It is not safe. I will escort you to the inner palace where you can get cleaned up and refresh yourself. I have sent runners to alert the council. You may meet them within the hour." The general turned and signaled for his men to move out.

Jonas noticed that the Free Legion soldiers had fanned out expertly, continuously looking out towards the quiet shops, homes, and roof tops as if they were expecting attacks.

The city was more or less a ghost town. There were a few people about, and some of the shops were open, but not many, a stark contrast to the normal bustle of the city.

"Is the city always this quiet?" Fil asked, walking behind the general.

"No," the warrior replied without looking back, his eyes ever vigilant. "The mornings see more activity than what you see now, but all in all the town's normal activities have all but disappeared. Bad things have been happening, and the people are frightened. So they mostly lock themselves in their homes, especially at this time of the day, when the sun is getting ready to set."

Sure enough, as they moved deeper into the city the sun's rays were slowly disappearing over the tall towers of the inner palace. The west side of the buildings was still lit by the setting sun, but dark shadows were growing and reaching out at them from the expanding darkness.

And just as darkness began to fall, Jonas felt a slight tingle, both on his chest and his forehead, a subtle warning that evil was near. It was nothing alarming, just a warm buzz nudging him, letting him know not to relax his guard. He felt the presence of the Forsworn around him and his hands absently went to the hilts of his blades. But they were not yet needed as the general brought them through another guarded gate and into the inner palace.

The large building before them was beautiful, built of huge square stones and covered with green vines and foliage that had taken over the entire front façade. Ornate bushes and trees, pruned into topiaries, covered the grounds. The sculpted trees and shrubs gave a rich and formal appearance to the palace grounds, and the entire building was surrounded by a white stone wall that was at least five paces high. There was a large fountain positioned before a series of flat steps that led to a set of heavy oak doors. The fountain was magnificent. Five massive stones, each easily the size of several men, and each one a different height, jutted from the ground. Round river rocks of various sizes surrounded the base of the stones and water boiled from various holes along the tops, cascading down and disappearing into the river rock. Jonas wondered how the water was continuously pumped through the structure, but the thought was fleeting as he again concentrated on his surroundings, knowing that they were in a dangerous place.

General Kurraris and his guards escorted the group past the fountain, up the stairs and through the doors. They did not stop once, moving with direct purpose, but once inside the palace doors they seemed to relax a little.

The room they entered was large and crowned with tall vaulted ceilings. Iron braziers burned brightly in the corners of the room, ready to fend off the darkness brought about by the setting sun. A pair of ornately carved stone stairs rose from opposite ends of the room to a hallway above. There were two doors on the main level, plus a set of large double doors in front of them, flanked by two large pillars rising to the tall ceiling.

"King Kromm," the general said, turning to face the Tarsinian king, "I will have one of my men show you and your companions to the bath house. I will have food and drink sent there while I inform the council of your presence. Is there anything else you desire?"

"Yes, General," the king said, glancing at the Free Legion warriors around them, "now that we are away from prying eyes, I will tell you that I am here looking for my wife, Queen Sorana, and my son, Prince Riker. They may have arrived with my court wizard, Addalis, who I believe has a cousin here. Have you seen them?"

"I'm sorry, Your Highness, but I have not. What is the name of the wizard's cousin?" General Kurraris asked with concern, hoping to be of some service.

"Geardon Embley, I believe he runs a gaming house here," the king replied.

General Kurraris's eyes lit up with recognition. "Indeed he does. His place is called The Oasis, and it is the most popular gaming house in the city. It is one of the few places that is still operating and doing well."

"I need to go there," Kromm said with urgency.

"Do you wish to forgo the meeting with the council?" the general asked.

"Yes. The bath can wait as well."

"Very well, but may I suggest a quick refreshment and some hot water to wipe your faces clean. It will only take a few moments. If they are with Mr. Embley then they are very safe, and a few more moments will not hurt."

"Very well," Kromm replied reluctantly.

The general was true to his word, hot water and towels, dried meats and cheese, and a cold sweet white wine was brought to them within a few moments. The servants hurried in, setting the trays and bowls down on a side table, and then quickly departed.

They washed the grime from their faces and hands with the hot water and towels that had been provided. It didn't take long before the towels and the water were black with the residues of dirt and blood that had covered them. They quickly consumed the food, drank the wine, and departed through the palace doors, feeling a bit refreshed and slightly more presentable.

The general decided to escort them personally, along with the ten Free Legion warriors. It was now completely dark and the city streets swarmed with shadows. The only light available was from the torches carried by the guards flanking them and the occasional candle light flickering from inside the windows of nearby homes.

As they made their way toward The Oasis, they passed a few people with hooded faces, who, once they saw the warriors, averted their gazes, and moved hastily away. Jonas saw an occasional Free Legion patrol, but otherwise the streets were empty. He still felt the slight warning, the presence of evil, and he remained constantly alert. He had learned at Annure, when they had been attacked by assassins who had served Nazreen, that he could not detect all dangers, and that some attacks could elude him. He could only truly detect something of pure evil. Men who had not fully crossed over into the service of darkness, but still had an evil purpose, such as thieves, or other brigands, might not be detected. Detecting evil was not an exact science, as the nature of evil is not always so black and white. So he had to be vigilant, as he knew the others were.

They turned, moving down a dark alley, the guards holding forth their torches as they peered into the darkness for any possible threats. The alley was lined with tall stone walls and as they neared the end of it they could clearly see two large braziers burning, casting an orange glow over a single metal door. The narrow alley was a dead end and with its tall walls, was an ideal location for an ambush. Jonas didn't like it, and he was constantly scanning the roof tops and walls for any concealed attackers.

"We are probably safe here, although it doesn't feel like it," the general said, trying to reassure them, seeing the group's worried expressions and their hands gripping their weapons.

"Why do you say that?" the king asked, obviously uneasy.

"Mr. Embley's guards are concealed in secret locations along these walls. If you look closely you can see the arrow slits," the general said, indicating a few of the locations.

Sure enough, at closer inspection, Jonas could make out cross patterns every three paces or so. He couldn't see anything beyond the slits but he took the general's word in the matter and assumed that someone was there, lurking in the darkness, probably holding a loaded crossbow as they spoke.

"At any sign of trouble, his guards can rush from that metal door and fire arrows all along the corridor if need be. In normal times these defenses were just designed to keep out ruffians and to protect his patrons from thieves hoping to steal the winnings from an unsuspecting client. But now his security has been expanded, as there are now darker things about than just common thieves."

When they reached the door General Kurraris knocked on it with his large fist. The sound echoed in the confines of the corridor and seconds later a small metal window slid open at eye level. Jonas could not see inside the opening, only an orange and reddish light behind a pair of dark beady eyes.

"Who wishes to enter?" demanded a deep voice.

"General Kurraris, and guests to see Mr. Embley."

"Very good, General," the voice responded quickly.

Instantly, several bolts and latches were withdrawn and the heavy steel door swung open on silent hinges. Standing before them was a huge man wearing black leather armor with matching leather breeches. Flanking him were two more men, equally as large, outfitted similarly. Each one carried a giant two handed sword strapped to their backs.

The guard stepped to the side and motioned for them to enter. Everyone, excluding the Free Legion escorts who had remained in the alley for the general's return, fanned out into the anteroom, taking in their surroundings with military precision. The room was large and made of stone, but the wall in front of them was covered with a thick crimson cloth. Two large braziers illuminated the room and Jonas could now clearly see the three guards.

They were not men at all, but half-orcs. Jonas had never seen a half-orc before, but their heritage was obvious. A mane of thick dark hair extended all the way down to the top of their broad backs. But it was trimmed and nicely kept, framing, basically, a human face. But they were larger, with a more animal-like appearance, Jonas thought, trying to think of a better description. But that was it. They were basically big humans with a wild look to them. Their bony foreheads were dominated by thick and pronounced brow ridges, beneath which peered dark beady eyes that appeared small in comparison to their large heads. Their noses were human-like, but with wider nostrils. Their mouths, however, were much larger than those of their human counterparts, and their animal-like canines could be seen when they spoke, though their teeth were much smaller than their orc cousins, which enabled them to pronounce words more clearly. Their bodies were tall and thick, covered with coarse black hair and dense muscle. Each half-orc was about as tall as Kromm, nearly a full head taller than a large man.

The guard shut the heavy door behind them, engaging the locks while a second guard addressed them. They could be triplets, thought Jonas; all three looked so much alike.

"General, you are always most welcome here," the half-orc said in a slow baritone voice, turning his gaze to the rest of the companions. "May I have the names of your companions so I may inform Mr. Embley?"

It was strange, but the guards were very polite and well spoken, which seemed in contrast to their heritage and size. Jonas did not detect any evil in them, so their hearts were obviously not corrupted by their orc blood.

The king stepped toward the large guard before General Kurraris could respond. "My name is King Kromm of Tarsis and I wish to see Mr. Embley," he said. "I am in the company of Jonas, cavalier to Shyann, Allindrian, Blade Singer to the elves, Durgen, Master Trader from Dwarf Mount, and these warriors from Finarth and Tarsis. I believe we warrant a meeting, so will you please escort me to see Mr. Embley?"

Jonas saw the guard's eyes light up momentarily at the mention of their names, then reverting quickly back to his normal stoic expression.

"Very good, if you will please leave your weapons here and follow me," he replied calmly.

Kromm smiled, but Jonas saw his fists clench impatiently. He could tell that all the formalities were driving the king crazy. He just wanted to find his wife and son, and Jonas could understand his frustration.

"We will not leave our weapons. We have been running from enemies and fighting for our lives over the last few weeks, and I will not relinquish the items that have so far kept us alive," Kromm replied, taking a step closer to the big half-orc. The king's eyes were intense and Jonas was afraid that he was going to strike the guard.

"I'm sorry, Sire, but no one is allowed entrance while in possession of their weapons. That is how..."

"Sir, what is your name?" Jonas interjected, stepping forward to face the guard, simultaneously laying a gentle hand on the king's massive bicep.

"Toklish, sir," the half-orc replied. Jonas was impressed with the guard. He did not seem fazed at all by the esteemed guests facing him. He was just doing his job and he was doing it well, and without bias.

"Toklish, I am a cavalier and you know that my weapons cannot be used to cause harm. Nor can I give them up in the chance that they might fall into the hands of the very evil that I am sworn to fight. I know you are just following the rules, but do you really think that Mr. Embley would ask the King of Tarsis, a cavalier, and a Blade Singer to disarm themselves? In fact, our presence will increase the safety of your patrons; surely you know this to be true. Let us pass, for Shyann's mission is urgent and requires that we see Mr. Embley immediately." Jonas finished, hoping that mentioning Shyann would encourage a quick and peaceful solution.

Toklish looked at Jonas for a moment before returning his gaze to the king. "Please forgive me, Sire. I am just trying to do my job," he said, directing his gaze at Jonas again. "You are quite right, Cavalier. I believe that Mr. Embley would make an exception in your cases. You may enter." The half-orc stepped aside, gesturing to the other half-orc guard standing in the corner of the room.

Jonas noticed that the other guard was holding a chain connected to some pulley system. Immediately the guard pulled the light chain and the heavy crimson curtain slowly opened, revealing a spacious hall filled with hundreds of people playing countless games. The place was spacious with tall ceilings. It had the opulence of a king's hall. Everywhere Jonas looked he saw something ornate. The walls were covered with gold tapestries lined in maroon, with the same color thread weaving beautiful designs throughout the cloth. The furniture was hand carved and every polished surface glistened in the glow of the braziers that lined the walls. Jonas could see flights of stairs on both sides of the room, constructed of hand carved ebony and leading to landings with railings of ornately crafted iron. He could just make out doors along the landings that probably led to private rooms or other game rooms. But the strangest part about the entire scene was that they couldn't hear anything. They could clearly see hundreds of people laughing and talking but no sound came their way.

"If you will follow me," Toklish said, walking into the gaming hall. Fil glanced back at Jonas who shrugged his shoulders and followed the guard. As soon as he stepped through the entrance into the gaming hall, a cacophony of sounds assaulted him. People were laughing and talking, with the voices of the game keepers intermixed in the din that echoed around him. There must have been a spell cast in the anteroom to keep out the noise, allowing the guards to interact with potential guests, and creating an impressive ambience. The effect was successful thought Jonas; it gave him the sense that the place was something special, something unique, which by the looks of it, it was.

The others felt it too, and they were looking about the place with eyes wide and mouths slightly agape. The place was amazing. Magical light shone from floating orbs and richly adorned furniture filled the spacious room. It was decadence at its finest. Jonas had never seen anything like it, and it was hard for him to focus on any one thing as the sights and sounds came at him from all directions. Serving women wearing low cut, tight dresses, moved about in all directions. There were several bars about; each one crowded with patrons who were eagerly vying for the attention of the scantily clad females whose job it was to keep the guests imbued with the intoxicating spirits that lined the many shelves behind them. Guards wearing the same black leather armor and black breeches with knee high boots stood at all corners of the room, watching the guests carefully. Most of the guards were human, but Jonas did catch one that might have been half-elf and one that was most definitely a dwarf.

"Sir, may I suggest that your warriors stay here and refresh themselves while I take you and your most esteemed guests to see Mr. Embley?" Toklish said smoothly.

"Very well. Dandronis, stay here with everyone. Jonas, Allindrian, General Kurraris, and Durgen, will you please accompany me," Kromm said, eager to get on with it.

"As you wish, my King."

"King Kromm, I be a bit parched, and would prefer a decent mug of ale," the dwarf said bluntly, looking around the gaming house with a sparkle in his eye.

"Do as you wish, Master Durgen. Now Toklish, please take us to see your boss," Kromm said impatiently.

"I have business to attend to, Sire, but I will leave five guards outside the establishment in case you need them. You can find me at the inner palace if you need anything else," the general said.

Kromm nodded his thanks to the general. "Thank you, Kurraris. Your help is appreciated." The general bowed slightly, turned, and walked towards the entrance. Kromm turned toward Toklish again. "Lead on," he said.

Toklish motioned toward a tall dark haired woman wearing a tight black dress. Jonas had noticed her earlier as she stood nearby, casually inspecting the new arrivals. In fact, everyone had noticed them. It was not often that a large group of dirty warriors patronized the gaming house, along with a cavalier in polished sparkling armor. They were the cause of many stares and much interest. But most simply looked at them curiously, and then went back to their games and drinks.

The raven haired lady walked toward them with a slow sensual gait that was hard to ignore. Her form fitting dress was made from some thin shiny material, which revealed the shape of her breasts and the curve of her hips, assets that did not go unnoticed by anyone. She smiled broadly as Toklish introduced her.

"Ravenna, please take care of the king's guests," the half-orc ordered.

"My pleasure, Toklish," she replied with a dazzling smile. "If you will follow me, I will take you someplace private where you can relax and wait for the king." Ravenna stepped to the side, motioning for the group to follow. Jonas was amazed at how sensual just that simple movement was. He glanced at Myrell, noticing that she was staring at him with a curious expression. He smiled sheepishly as she shook her head sardonically.

"Men," Myrell whispered under her breath, moving past Ravenna without giving her a second look.

Fil looked at Jonas with an upraised eyebrow and a mischievous smile, and then he, Dandronis, and Durgen, followed the lovely hostess through the crowd.

"Follow me please," Toklish said to the other guests, making his way to a flight of stairs. The two guards at the base of the stairs immediately parted for the group. Kromm and the others followed Toklish up the stairs and down the hall, coming to a set of black double doors made of solid wood and lacquered to a shiny brilliance. Just as they neared the doors, they burst open and Queen Sorana ran towards Kromm.

The movement was so sudden that Toklish, more quickly than Jonas would have thought possible, leaped in front of Kromm and had a dagger in his hand before the king could get past the surprise at seeing his wife.

Toklish, quickly assessing that she was no threat, stepped briskly aside, sheathing his knife. Sorana jumped into Kromm's outstretched arms, crying openly and kissing the big man furiously.

"My King, I knew you'd come for me," she said sobbing. Riker, his son, came from the door as well, joining his mother and father in an emotional embrace.

"Ah, King Kromm, please come inside," a man said, appearing in the doorway. The man was short and round, and he was wearing a ridiculous silk robe, lined in gold thread and the color of a ripe plumb. His jet black hair was slicked back tightly over his ears, but his smile was genuine as he eagerly motioned for everyone to enter. "Toklish, please stand guard."

Everyone hurried into the room as the man introduced himself to the group.

"I am Geardon Embley. Welcome to The Oasis. I have never had the pleasure of having such esteemed guests in my humble home. I am honored," he said with a slight bow. They all introduced themselves to the proprietor as the king and his family talked.

"How did you get away?" Kromm asked, still holding his emotional wife.

"Addalis sent us here through a dimensional door. I was so worried for you, Father," Riker said, wiping a few tears from his eyes.

"I told you, son, it would take more than a few orcs to bring me down. Where is that crafty wizard anyway?" Kromm asked.

"Here, my Lord," Addalis replied with a happy smile as he walked through an arched entryway in front of them.

The king moved towards him, hugging him fiercely. "My friend, it is so good to see you. Thank you. You saved them and I owe you much."

"It is my duty, and my pleasure," Addalis said as the king released him. "But how did you get here so quickly. We arrived just last night. You could not possibly have traveled that distance in a half day."

"Allindrian led us through the Hallows," the king said quietly.

"What? You traveled the Hallows Road?" asked the astonished wizard.

"We did. We lost most of our group, but Allindrian and Jonas saw us through."

Addalis looked to Jonas for the first time. He smiled, walking toward him to shake hands. "Cavalier," he said, gripping Jonas's hand, "it is good to meet you. Your presence is most welcome, and greatly needed it would seem."

"Come, everyone, let us move into a more comfortable room where we can talk and refresh ourselves," Geardon said, leading them all through the archway that Addalis had come from.

***

Ravenna was easy to follow as it was not difficult at all to keep their eyes focused on the swaying of her hips as she led the way. The only one that seemed impervious to her feminine charms was Durgen, as he was spending more time staring at the gaming tables and the mugs of ale being heartily consumed all around him. Myrell had rolled her eyes in annoyance at the gawking men, and excused herself to find a wash basin and a place to clean up.

The hostess had led them to a roped off alcove along an outer wall where they were all invited to sit down on some comfortable couches. The couches, which surrounded a large low table made from black polished wood, were adorned with numerous soft velvety pillows. Candles flickered on every wall from black iron sconces, illuminating the room with a soft glow.

"I hope this is comfortable enough for you. Can I bring you all some refreshments?" Ravenna asked smoothly. Her every word, her every syllable, dripped with sensuality.

Durgen, who seemed amazingly oblivious to her beauty, spoke first. "A pitcher of yer best mead, dwarven if you have it. If not, Tarsinian Black will do."

"Very good. And you, gentlemen?"

"Some honey mead please," Fil said.

"A mug of wheat ale will suffice," Dandronis ordered.

"I'll have the same," Kilius added.

"I will be back shortly with your drinks and a plate of smoked meats and cheeses," she said with a sensuous smile before turning gracefully and disappearing into the throng of people.

"Wow," was all Fil could say.

Dandronis chuckled at Fil. "This place is truly amazing; I have never seen the likes," he said.

"Nor I," said Fil, looking around in complete amazement of their magnificent surroundings.

"In Ulren's name I've never been out of the Tundrens, let alone in a place like this," Kilius said, equally amazed at what he saw.

"So, boy, tell me 'bout yer friend, de cavalier," Durgen said, seeking a comfortable place on the couch. The pillows were too big and the couch too high, making it difficult for the dwarf to find a suitable spot.

"I'm no boy, Trader Durgen," Fil answered, a bit defensively.

"Bah! You're a boy in human terms, but to a dwarf yer not but a baby fresh from yer mother's womb," he said, finally stuffing enough pillows behind him to form a comfortable seat.

"How old are you, Fil?" Dandronis asked.

"Nineteen…almost twenty," he added quickly.

"And Jonas is the same age?" Dandronis asked.

"Yes."

"So young to have so much power," Dandronis continued, just as Ravenna returned with the drinks. Just behind her was a male servant carrying a plate of succulent meats and a variety of soft cheeses. The young man set the plate on the table and quickly departed.

"Here you are, gentlemen. Is there anything else I can get you?" she asked, her dark eyes looking each of them over before resting on Fil.

Durgen didn't respond as he was already gulping down the thick dwarven mead.

"We are fine, thank you, Ravenna," Dandronis replied.

"And you, young warrior?" Ravenna said seductively, her eyes lingering on Fil again.

"Uh...I...am good," Fill stammered.

"Very well," she said with a mischievous smile before turning and joining the mass of people in the main hall.

"Boy, I be thinking you could move onto manhood with that raven haired lass," Durgen said loudly, followed by a powerful belch.

"I think you might be right, but it would cost him," Dandronis agreed, smiling as he took a long pull from his mug.

Fil didn't know what to say, so he too took a long draught from his mug. The honey mead was delicious; cold and refreshing with just a hint of sweetness.

"Back to de cavalier, tell me what you know of him," the dwarf asked again.

"We grew up together in a small town deep in the Tundrens. He was a cripple with limbs so twisted that he could barely walk. Four years ago a cavalier came to our town to warn us that boargs, led by a Banthra, were about to attack."

"Why would boargs attack a small town? And a Banthra? Really? Did you see it?" Dandronis asked in astonishment.

"I don't know why they attacked. But they killed everyone, except for Jonas and me. We were hidden. The cavalier and the Banthra killed each other. And yes, I saw the demon knight, and I saw another at Finarth when Lord Moredin attacked. And I hope to never see another again. Their very presence grows ice on your bones if you know what I mean. Jonas killed that one, along with three clerics of the Forsworn, although he had Taleen's help." Fil took another long drink of his mead.

"Methinks Shyann had a say in your survival. Keep goin', boy," Durgen muttered.

"Well, we hid out in the mountains, and that is when Shyann healed him and gave him a God Mark on his chest," Fil continued, looking at his companions who were now clearly interested in his story. "From there we went to Finarth and trained as knights."

"But Jonas is no knight, how did he become a cavalier?" Dandronis asked, stuffing some meat and cheese into his mouth.

"He was being hunted by the Forsworn. A demon attacked the barracks, killing nearly half of the apprentices. Something had to be done, so he was secretly removed from Finarth and sent to train with Kiln, the swordsman, far away in the mountains. I do not know the details of that story, but he stayed with Kiln for two years, and during that time his cavalier powers slowly surfaced." Fil paused to eat some meat and cheese and wash it down with his mead.

"Kiln, eh," Durgen grumbled.

"I have heard many stories of Kiln, but I did not know he was still alive. I would relish the chance to fight with him," Dandronis said.

"You just may get yer chance, Dandronis," the dwarf replied.

"He is incredible," Fil said. "I saw him fight at the battle at the Lindsor Bridge. He defeated an ogre in a few heartbeats. I have never seen such fluid movements, except from Jonas and Allindrian."

"I had heard he was an oath breaker, is that not true?" Kilius asked, tearing his eyes away from the scenes around him and rejoining the conversation.

"I have not heard the whole story, but Jonas has indicated that there is more to that tale than what we've heard," Fil answered.

"There usually is," added Dandronis.

They paused their conversation temporarily so they could resume stuffing their faces with the savory meats and cheeses.

"It's strange that Shyann would pick such a young man to be her warrior," Dandronis said, chewing thoughtfully.

"Maybe, but if you knew Jonas, you would not think so," Fil said, a little defensively.

"Why that be?" Durgen asked.

"Jonas is an astounding person. When he was a cripple he was ridiculed by nearly the entire town, yet he persevered, bearing the abuse, and I never once saw him show any anger towards anyone. His has a kind heart, an incredible sense of honor, and is utterly incorruptible. You can trust him with your life. He would die protecting a complete stranger. He is a friend, a friend you would die for," Fil said emotionally.

"It sounds like Shyann indeed picked well," Dandronis said.

"She did," Fil agreed.

"Enough serious talk. Let us eat, drink, and talk of women and glory," Durgen bellowed loudly, pounding his empty mug on the table. "More ale!"

Dandronis, Fil, and Kilius smiled, following suit and emptying their cups with long deep swallows.

***

The room they had left was warm and decadent, but the room they now entered made the latter look like a dirty brothel. Spacious and open, the large circular room was furnished with two large softly cushioned couches placed in the middle, around which brightly flickering sconces cast an illuminating glow. The tall walls were covered with thick tapestries, and large pillars were placed around the perimeter. The tables flanking the couches overflowed with several bottles of wine, plates of exotic fruits, and a variety of meats and cheeses. It was splendid, warm and comfortable. Geardon Embley's Oasis was obviously turning quite a profit.

They talked for over an hour, each telling their stories. Jonas listened absently as he thought about Taleen. He missed her dearly and this was the first time since her death that he really had the time to think about what she had meant to him. He had been running and fighting ever since she had been killed, and now, as he sat on the soft couch in peace and comfort, he was able to really think about her. They had only known each other for a short period of time, but Jonas had come to rely on her blade and her support, and he missed her council. She was a rock for him, helping and guiding him through the difficult and tumultuous events of the past year.

"Jonas…Jonas," Addalis said, "Are you okay?"

Jonas's attention snapped back to the present, and he quickly wiped a lone tear from his eye before it could fall from the weight of his sorrow. Everyone was looking at him with concern.

"Yes, I'm fine. I was just thinking," Jonas reassured them. "I'm sorry, Addalis, what were you saying?"

"I was saying that I have never met a cognivant. I would like to talk with you about that skill someday, when it seems more fitting."

"I would like that, although I know very little about it myself. I am still learning about the power and its limitations."

"From the story that Kromm just told, it sounds as if you have mastered it well. I have heard of creatures such as you faced in the Hallows, but I have never met anyone who faced them, let alone defeated them. It is an incredible story."

"Addalis, my cousin, they have traveled long and fought hard. I bet they would like to rest. Come, I have rooms for you all," Geardon said, clapping his hands loudly. Two black garbed warriors quickly materialized from another archway. "King Kromm and Queen Sorana, you will stay in my personal chambers. And there will be no discussion about it," he said quickly as the queen was getting ready to decline. "A bath is already drawn and servants await your orders. Rabalis here will take you to my chambers. Prince Riker, you can stay here on the couch," he finished, seeing the boy's uncertain look. "Unless, of course, you would like your own room."

"No thank you, I want him near me," Kromm said.

"Thank you, Geardon. You are most gracious," the queen said.

Kromm hugged his boy one more time. "I'll see you in the morning." Then the king and queen followed Rabalis from the room to their chambers.

"Calvin, please take the Blade Singer to her room," Geardon ordered. "Unfortunately I am short on rooms and you will be staying with your other female companion. But the room is spacious with two large and comfortable beds."

"It will be perfect. Believe me, Mr. Embley, it will be a huge upgrade compared to what we've been sleeping on. Thank you," Allindrian said.

"You're welcome. Calvin, put Jonas in room six next door," Geardon continued. "Ravenna has already placed all your other companions in rooms. They are probably enjoying a warm bath as we speak. Now, is there anything else you need before you take your rest?"

"We are very content, sir," replied Allindrian. "You have been most gracious."

"If you will please follow me, I will take you to your rooms," Calvin said with a slight bow.

Geardon was true to his word. Fil and Kilius were already in a room as were Durgen and Dandronis. He put Myrell and Allindrian in their room and Jonas was given his own suite that was generally reserved for the high stakes gamblers. It was not terribly big, but it was very comfortable, furnished with high quality furniture and a big soft bed. Sitting in the corner was a copper basin filled with steaming hot water infused with the tantalizing fragrance of exotic oils. The welcome sight of the bath made him aware of how sweaty and dirty he was, despite the immaculate condition of his armor.

Jonas poured himself a glass of cold water from a pitcher and took off all his armor and clothes. There was a tall mirror on the wall and he took a close look at himself as he stood before it. His God Mark had continued to grow and there was now no spot on his torso that was not covered with the symbol. Branches from the oak tree had expanded over his strong shoulders and stretched down his muscled arms. He wondered how much more it would expand. His hair was longer now, no longer stubble but a short growth of wavy dirty blonde hair fell just above his eyes. He looked at the scar on his forehead and was genuinely amazed at the mark. The lines were perfect and the scar was smooth, not bumpy and rough like you might expect from a burn. He remembered that day vividly. He had almost died from the wounds he received from the demon that had once been Prince Nelstrom, and he probably would have if Taleen had not healed him immediately. Again he thought of the fallen cavalier and his heart felt heavy with grief. He tried to think of Fil's words, attempting to come to grips with her death and focus on what Fil had said, that every action she had taken her entire life furthered the cause of good, and that she knew the risks of her position. Still, it gave him little comfort.

As he continued trying to make sense of her death, Jonas came to a realization. What made them different from evil was that they cared about life, not just their own life, but life in general. But it was this emotion, this desire to protect life, which made it more difficult to combat this evil, because they had so much to lose. The spark of life that they possessed, this inner light, so to speak, gave them hopes and dreams, but the desire to keep this light lit hampered their ability to fight evil. It was ironic really, and quite simple, but Jonas had never thought about it in that way. To truly fight evil, you had to be prepared to die, and you had to be prepared to have loved ones die around you, especially if they had also taken the oath to fight against the forces of darkness. Taleen had taken that oath, and so had Jonas. For some reason this thought did make him feel a little better.

Jonas turned away from the mirror, and slowly lowered himself into the tub of steaming hot water, his tired body relishing the soothing feeling as the intense heat drew the tension from his muscles. He reached for a clean cloth and a bar of soap sitting on a side table next to the basin. He lathered himself up and used the cloth to scrub his body clean. The soap foamed up quickly and before long there was a layer of suds covering the warm water. He leaned back in the tub, sighing heavily, and closed his eyes.

His mind drifted around as he thought of everything that had happened to him. His body was relaxed, and the warm water submerged his anxious thoughts, which sank like stones to a place deep within himself. Within a few moments he drifted off to sleep, which was why he did not notice Myrell slowly open the door and move towards him.

She was wearing a long flowing white gown that clung to her body as she walked into the room. She, too, had bathed, and her long brown hair, now washed and clean, glistened in the soft candlelight. Her tanned and flawless skin was now devoid of the dust and sweat that had covered their bodies the last few weeks.

"Jonas," she whispered, kneeling by the tub.

Jonas thought he was dreaming. There was a part of his mind that had heard his name. The voice was familiar, and the gentle whisper stroked his mind, making him feel at ease.

Then he felt a soft wet pressure on his lips. His tired mind drifted with the possibilities as his mouth slowly opened to accept the kiss. Her touch was light and searching, and Jonas slowly opened his eyes as his mind drifted back to reality.

Instantly he scooted back in the tub, splashing water over the edge. Myrell was on her knees by the side of the tub, her face close to his own, and her mouth slightly open and glistening with moisture.

"Jonas. It is just me," she said softly.

"What...what are you doing here," Jonas stammered, very much aware of his nudity, though, luckily the thick suds managed very well to hide his body.

"Well, I should've thought that was obvious," she replied with a mischievous smile.

Jonas was acutely aware of her beauty. His eyes were drawn to the thin white fabric that clung to her body, the transparent fabric revealing much more than it concealed.

She reached up, touching his face softly. Her fingers slowly traced the outline of his jaw as she gazed into his eyes. "Jonas, I cannot stop thinking of you. I was lying in bed and you kept appearing in my mind. Then it came to me. I, or you, may die tonight, or tomorrow, and I would never know what it was like to lie in your arms, to feel your strong body against mine. I want that Jonas, more than anything I have ever wanted."

Myrell leaned in and softly kissed his cheek. The touch of her gentle lips sent a tingle down his spine and an overwhelming feeling of warmth spread through his body as blood rushed to his extremities, bringing a flush to his face.

Her kiss slowly moved across to the tip of his nose. Her breath was warm and her mouth tasted of sweet wine. Her soft hair, infused with the tantalizing aroma of some exotic fruit, gently brushed his bare neck.

Jonas had never before experienced such a strong pleasurable feeling. He was so overcome by it that he could barely restrain himself from grabbing her and pulling her into the water. Then her lips again found his and that simple touch broke down the wall that was holding back his passion. His mouth opened eagerly to accept her kiss, and he reached up and grabbed the back of her head, pushing her face tighter to his, their mouths opening further as they both succumbed to their passion. His whole body ached for her, and their kisses lost all control, becoming desperate and animalistic, born of a desire that neither could control.

Finally, Myrell broke the kiss, leaving Jonas panting. She stood up quickly, reached up to the top of her gown and unfastened the two buttons that secured it, allowing the light garment to slowly fall to her feet.

Jonas's eyes widened as he gazed at her, taking in her beauty. His eyes wandered from her lovely face to the rest of her body, lingering over her smooth skin and her shapely limbs, toned and muscled from physical labor. The soft candlelight silhouetted her sensuous body, filling him with a sense of wonder. He wanted to savor and prolong the moment, but his body couldn't wait.

He locked eyes with her again and she smiled, slowly stepping into the warm water with him. As their lips again found each other, they quickly succumbed to the pent up passion that claimed their bodies. They lost themselves in the spiraling sensations of pleasure, that, for a brief moment in time, allowed them to forget all else.

***

Gullanin stood in front of a huge roaring bon fire built of man sized logs, and standing behind him were another fifty Gould-Irin Orcs, outfitted for war and eagerly waiting for the chance to spill blood. They were nearly eight feet tall and their bulging muscles rippled over heavy bone. They all bore thick black plate mail that they wore like a repugnant, impenetrable second skin. Their weapons were crude slashing blades and heavy war axes. Neither spears nor bows would be needed where they were going.

Malbeck stood before him holding the Spear of Gould high in his right hand while he finished the last few phrases of his spell. Normally a dimensional door spell could only move a few people magically from one spot to another, but this spell was being cast by Malbeck himself, and was supported by the Shan Cemar, the ancient elven book that held the true words of magic. Long ago the elves were the first to harness the power of the Ru'Ach, therefore their ancient language holds an affinity to that power, a link stronger than any other language. These words, long ago hidden but now found, would be transporting much more than just a few bodies through this door.

An elaborate plan had been set forth as soon as Gullanin had returned from his failed trip. He had teleported himself into Cuthaine and schemed with the Blackhearts hiding out in the city. Even in the best of times, Blackhearts were always around, lurking in cities, hiding in the shadows, and waiting for victims and hoping to perform tasks that would make the Forsworn reward them with riches and power. But the news of Malbeck's rise and the destruction of Tarsis were helping spread darkness everywhere in Kraawn, and now the Blackhearts were getting bolder. There were more and more followers of the Forsworn roaming the streets of

Cuthaine, and they were more than eager to be a part of Malbeck's plan.

The powerful wizard spent two days there, meeting with several dark priests in the city. After they had developed their plan, Gullanin had teleported back to Malbeck's army, where he had prepared the fifty Gould-Irin Orcs, thus initiating the final stages of the plan. The king of Tarsis and the meddling cavalier would die tonight!

The tip of the Spear of Gould crackled with energy as Malbeck finished the last part of the spell. Gullanin felt the hair on his arms rise as the energy in the clearing grew and grew until a swirling vortex spun before the orcs. Then the vortex opened and a black door expanded, the entrance darker than night with not a speck of light penetrating it.

Gullanin took his cue, motioning for the huge orcs to enter the door. The Gould-Irin ran through the opening without the slightest hesitation, and their heavy footfalls could be felt on the grassy ground. Gullanin brought up the rear, walking through the dimension door without a glance back.

Malbeck whispered behind him, "Don't fail me again," as the magical portal closed with a flash.

Ten
Oasis

Jonas bolted up in bed, the familiar tingle on his chest waking him instantly. His hand unconsciously went to his God Mark as the grogginess of sleep vanished. Strangely, his palm rested on plate mail and Jonas noticed that he was miraculously wearing his armor and outfitted for war, just as he had been when he was warned of the treachery in King Uthrayne Gavinsteal's tent the night the king had been murdered by Prince Nelstrom.

Jonas jumped out of a bed. Myrell, who was sleeping beside him, her arm draped over his body, woke with a start.

"What is it?" she said in alarm, sitting up in bed with Jonas's light cotton shirt clinging to her body.

"Get up! We are in danger! Go to your room and gather your gear and weapons!" Jonas said urgently. Myrell wore an expression of confusion as she looked at Jonas who was fully dressed for war. "Now!" he yelled.

Without another word she leaped from the bed with the blanket wrapped around her and ran to the door with Jonas right on her heels. They entered the hall above the gaming room and Myrell ran to her room, which was just to the left, while Jonas went to the railing and looked down at the huge gaming hall half expecting a demon to burst from the floor in a shower of flames.

It was late in the night, but the large room was still occupied with many hopeful gamblers. The Oasis guards stood calmly, but alert in their places, and Jonas didn't see anything amiss. But he knew something was coming. Warnings from

Shyann had so far been accurate, and they had saved his life several times already.

Immediately he moved down the hall and banged on Fil and Kilius's door. It took a few moments, but finally Fil opened the locked door wearing his long underpants and shirt. His eyes were still half shut, but they bolted open quickly when he saw Jonas standing at the doorway wearing his gleaming plate mail and horned helm.

"Jonas, what is it?" Fil asked as he looked warily down the hall.

"I have been warned. Hurry, wake everyone. We need to move. I will go and get the king. Meet me at Mr. Embley's as soon as you are dressed."

"I'll be there," Fil replied quickly, shutting the door to get dressed.

Jonas raced down the long hall towards the door of Mr. Embley's suite. Toklish was still there standing guard before the entrance.

"Toklish, we are in danger, open the door and alert your guards," Jonas commanded, reaching for the door.

Toklish hesitated for a second, unsure of what to do, but still he remained standing in front of the door, blocking Jonas with his massive body.

"Toklish," Jonas said again. "I am a cavalier. Shyann has warned me that danger is near. Stand aside or I shall use her power to move you aside."

Finally, the big half-orc hesitated no longer, and he stepped away from the door. Jonas understood his pause. He had probably never met a cavalier, let alone seen one run to his boss's door in the middle of the night with warnings of danger and commands to open his door. Nonetheless, he could wait no longer, so he was glad that he had finally moved.

"I'm sorry, Cavalier. What sort of threat do we face?" the huge warrior asked calmly, drawing his giant blade from his back.

"I don't know, but get the customers out of here, and set your guards at all likely entrance points. Be ready for anything," Jonas said hurriedly, opening the suite door and rushing inside.

Jonas ran into the formal living room and found Prince Riker sleeping soundly on the central couch. He shook the boy roughly and the young prince awoke with a jolt.

"Prince, get up and get dressed! We are in danger!" Jonas yelled, already moving toward Mr. Embley's personal chamber.

Jonas ran down the short hallway and as he neared the big solid wood door a sudden pain in his chest caused him to stumble.

"They're here," he whispered, relinquishing all caution and calling on his God Light. His body lit up brightly, but he kept it slightly subdued. He wanted his light to wash away fear and wake everyone quickly without blinding them.

He burst through the door, his white light eradicating the darkness that covered the king and queen who were already up. The queen wore a light flowing gown, while the king was stark naked, his body tense and ready to fight whoever came through the door.

"What is the..." the king began to yell before he noticed it was Jonas.

"King Kromm! We are in danger! Dress quickly, we must leave now! Meet me out front!" Jonas said urgently as he raced back out the door and into Mr. Embley's living room. Riker was just strapping on his armor and sword belt when Addalis, already dressed, and Mr. Embley, wearing only a night shirt and pants, emerged from another door.

"Cavalier, what is it?" Addalis asked, unable to mask the fear in his voice.

"Danger, something is coming," Jonas replied, his white light illuminating the room and its occupants. Addalis stood up straighter and the prince actually growled as he cinched his belt tight, standing tall and waiting for orders. "Mr. Embley, do you have a secret way to leave this place?"

"In the kitchen, down the stairs, a secret tunnel takes you out of the compound," he said quickly.

Suddenly screams erupted from inside the gaming hall causing everyone to jump at the sudden shrill noise. The echoing sounds of battle followed, and in a matter of seconds it sounded like an army was fighting just outside the suite door.

"Prepare yourself!" Jonas said, drawing both blades.

Allindrian ran from her door as Myrell frantically got dressed inside. The ranger always slept dressed, so it had only taken her an instant to arm herself with her blade and bow. She ran to the railing and saw Toklish and other guards escorting many frightened gamers from the tables towards the main entrance. Some of the customers scowled in disappointment at the interruption of their winning streaks, but it only took a small show of muscle to encourage their rapid departure.

Jonas had warned everyone that danger was near, lurking in the shadows, and now they knew it to be true; there could be no doubt as Jonas's sudden warnings in the past had all proven to be accurate. Allindrian drew an arrow from her quiver on her back, nocking it quickly and scanning the grounds below. What sort of threat would they be facing? It could be anything, demon or beast, assassin or wizard, she knew not. But it would be formidable and innately evil, for the cavalier had a knack for attracting powerful enemies.

Then she saw it; a dimensional door opening in the middle of the gaming floor. She had been scanning the entrance, and would not have noticed it but for the loud roar which was followed closely by a swarm of Gould-Irin Orcs who poured from the magical door, scattering tables and chairs and cutting into anyone near them with their heavy cleaving blades.

Allindrian reacted immediately, firing arrow after arrow into the horde of orcs. She focused on the entrance of the magical portal as the orcs stacked up there momentarily, slowed by the tight confines of the door, before they swarmed into the room. They were easy targets and every arrow hit its mark.

Jonas burst from the suite door to find Allindrian at the rail firing arrows into the gaming room below. Fil and Kilius raced from their room with weapons and gear in hand to join Allindrian, followed by Durgen and Dandronis whose room was next to theirs.

"Who attacks?" Jonas asked, moving to the railing and looking down.

"Orcs," she said, still moving in a blur as shaft after shaft found their targets.

"They look much bigger than the orcs we fought at the Lindsor Bridge," Jonas said, gazing down at the powerful beasts.

"They are, a different breed, the same that we fought in the mountains," Allindrian replied, never slowing the hail of arrows.

Myrell ran from the room behind them, hastily shouldering her pack. She carried her bow in one hand and joined her comrades at the rail.

"Look!" Fil yelled over the fighting.

Their eyes followed Fil's hand and they saw a flood of black masked warriors attacking the patrons and guards as they tried to get them out the front door. Trapped between orcs and the black masked warriors, they were being ruthlessly cut down.

The unarmed gamers fell quickly, dying on the gaming floor where just moments earlier they had been laughing, drinking, and enjoying the many games The Oasis had to offer. The scene was utter chaos as Blackhearts and orcs massacred anyone who was near.

The new attackers wore dark clothes and masks, similar in appearance to the men who had attacked Jonas, Kiln, and Taleen, at Annure. Most carried curved swords or axes but a few held short deadly crossbows, the latter of which were now aimed towards them.

"Get back!" yelled Jonas as five or six of the warriors fired their crossbows directly at them, hoping to take down Allindrian and stop her deadly rain of arrows. Everyone jerked back from the railing as the bolts flew at them.

One hit Jonas in the chest but it ricocheted off his magical armor. He was unsure if anyone else was hit, but Allindrian quickly returned to the railing to fire at the men as they were forced to reload their weapons. One, two, three arrows flew from her bow faster than it took the others to regain their footing.

Myrell nocked an arrow to her bow and joined the Blade Singer at the railing just as King Kromm, his wife and son, Addalis, and Geardon ran from the suite's door to join them.

"What is happening?" stormed the king.

Jonas moved away from the edge of the railing before he spoke. "Orcs and assassins are attacking! We need to get to the escape tunnel!" he yelled over the din of battle.

The king's eyes narrowed and his big hand tightened on the handle of his sword. "Geardon, which way to the tunnel?" he asked.

"Down the flight of stairs, take a right and go through the double doors. Stay to the right, move through the kitchen and go through the last door on the left. It is a dry storage area. There is a shelving unit in the back that slides from right to left. Behind it are stairs that lead to old catacombs under the city," Geardon replied quickly as he looked out over his gaming room. His face sunk in despair as he saw his patrons being slaughtered and his loyal guards die trying to protect them.

"Very well. Jonas," the king replied, "you and I will lead while Durgen and Allindrian bring up the rear."

"King, get down!" yelled Geardon as he pushed the big warrior aside. Just in time, as a crackling bolt of lightning shot from below and took Geardon in the chest. The area erupted in crackling energy and the fat proprietor flew back from the power of the bolt and slammed into the wall behind them. He landed in a heap of burnt flesh as everyone around him scattered.

Geardon had managed to push Kromm out of harm's way, though the king still felt the sizzling heat as he crashed into the wall. The heat from the bolt had singed both his arms, but it did little to slow him down.

As Kromm gazed at the gaping hole of blackened flesh in the center of Geardon's chest, his anger and despair threatened to boil over. He got to his feet, shielding his wife and child as he crouched low. Everyone else did the same, staying away from the railing and the direction of that devastating lightning bolt.

"They have a wizard." Addalis stated the obvious as he clenched his jaw, overcome by emotion as he stared at what was left of his cousin.

"We have to move! We are easy targets up here!" yelled Allindrian.

"Go, I will shield us from the wizard!" yelled Addalis, as he stood and began his spell.

Kromm turned to Jonas. "Let's go!" he yelled as he moved forward toward the stairs. They crouched as they ran, staying as close to the wall as possible, maintaining their distance from the railing in hopes of staying clear of arrows or spells. Kromm and Jonas led them to the top of the stairs while Dandronis and Durgen brought up the rear.

Addalis recited the words to his spell, finishing it off by punching his right hand forward. Instantly a tendril of white energy shot from his hand, forming a shield of translucent light about two paces high and three paces wide. Addalis moved quickly toward his companions who were now at the base of the stairs. As he moved his hand that gripped the tendril, the shield followed and conformed to whatever space they were in. He couldn't hold the shield for very long, but it was powerful enough to keep out most things, including spells.

As they moved quickly down the stairs Jonas noticed that Toklish had gathered the remaining guards to form a perimeter around the base of the stairs. Many of the guards were dead and the gaming floor was littered with the corpses of The Oasis patrons. The half-orc guard must have realized that it was useless to try and protect the customers, so he quickly reformed the men and provided a protective barrier around the base of the stairs, hoping to give his boss and the king time to escape. The brave guard may have just saved their lives.

Jonas silently thanked the warrior as they made it to the landing of the stairs without conflict. The guards were hard pressed, many falling to their deaths, and the rest being pushed back by the powerful orcs. Jonas could tell that it would only be a moment before the guards crumbled altogether and the orcs and assassins would rush in to overwhelm them.

Another lightning bolt flashed brightly and flew at them from the opposite set of stairs. The sizzling bolt crashed into Addalis's shield, knocking the wizard backward into Durgen.

"I have ya, Wizard," growled the dwarf, holding his battle axe in one hand and the dazed wizard in the other.

"I have never felt that kind of power. My shield can't withstand much more," the wizard gasped as he managed to stand up on his own.

"Jonas, get the king out of here! I'll cover the kitchen door," Allindrian yelled as she replaced her bow with her silver sword. She wore a quiver of arrows on her back and there was a sleeve made for her bow. Even when it was strung she could attach the bow to her quiver quickly if she had to. She could fight with her sword in one hand and her bow in the other, but in the confines of the hallways she thought it best to sheath the elven bow.

Jonas glanced back to the guards and saw that Toklish and his two brothers were all that remained. The space was so tight that the large half-orcs could block it with their broad bodies and gigantic swords. Just as Jonas looked their way, one brother was dropped by a sword to the neck, causing the other two to stumble backwards towards them. The dam of resistance was about to break, and they had to get moving or they would be crushed.

"Let's go!" Jonas yelled, racing to his right with everyone close on his heels.

Gullanin stood at the top of the opposite stairway looking at the scene below. His lightning bolts had been thwarted by the young wizard, but he knew Addalis could not withstand his power much longer. His Gould-Irin would overrun them and there was nothing they could do. Besides, Gullanin knew about their escape route, and they were running right into his trap. The wizard laughed loudly, lifting his staff again. "Let's see how strong that shield is!" he yelled, sending another powerful bolt towards the wizard.

A third bolt slammed into Addalis's shield just as Toklish and his brother fell to the orc blades. The Tarsinian wizard flew back into Allindrian as Jonas and the rest of the group ran through the door behind them. The wizard's shield fluttered but did not disappear. Addalis gritted his teeth in determination and stood up straight before the rush of enemies. He lifted his magical shield in front of them just as the orcs slammed into them. The power of the orcs, reinforced by numerous Blackhearts, pushed Addalis and Allindrian backwards through the kitchen door. The orcs were pushing and striking the translucent shield with their powerful fists and weapons, but they couldn't break through the magical wall. They roared furiously as they hammered the shield, causing Addalis and Allindrian to slide backwards further. They had entered a narrow hallway that led to the kitchens and the shield that Addalis still held conformed to the stone passageway. The enemy could not get around it.

"Allindrian, Go! I will hold them off!" Addalis yelled, his shield fluttering again.

"No, I will not leave you!" she screamed as the angry orcs continued to crash into the weakening shield. Their roars and howls were deafening in the tight confines of the hallway.

"You will do the king no good if you die in this hall. You know this to be true! I can buy you some time, but not much. Now go!" he yelled frantically, mustering all his strength to keep the shield up.

Allindrian knew in her heart that the wizard was right. Even with her many skills she would be overrun in the tight confines of the hallway. It was useless, but Addalis could hold them off a bit longer. The Blade Singer gripped the wizard's arms tightly and whispered into his ear, "Good luck...and thank you," she added as she turned and disappeared down the hallway and into the kitchen.

Jonas led them all into the dry storage room and just as Geardon had promised there was a shelf in the back that slid to the right. A flight of stairs covered in dust led down into the dark depths below the city. Jonas called forth his God Light and jumped down the stairs into the catacombs with his companions just behind him.

His light easily filled the dark passageway and the group moved double time. Jonas led with swords drawn while the king brought up the rear. The tunnel was narrow and they had to run two abreast through shallow murky water. If it came to fighting then only one sword could be wielded at a time in the tight confines of the underground passage.

Jonas came to a spot in the corridor that split in two directions, one straight ahead, and the other to the right. "Which way?" he asked frantically, knowing that no one knew the path.

"Geardon didn't say," Myrell said, her voice shaking with fright.

"I say we continue straight," replied the queen as she looked down the right passageway. "He would have given more detailed directions if we were to veer off the straight path."

"I agree," said Fil.

"Good enough for me," muttered Jonas as he led them forward, his God Light shining brightly in the passage.

Addalis, meanwhile, was losing ground. The orcs had pushed him a good three paces and as he glanced backwards he saw that he would soon be entering the main kitchen. At that point the room would be too big and the shield could not block the beasts. They would swarm around him, kill him, and then rush off toward the rest.

He growled in frustration and from the strain of holding the shield, which was about to falter. He yelled in defiance and looked down, gritting his teeth as he tried to find the last bit of strength to keep the shield up, for what purpose he did not know, as death seemed inevitable.

But what he saw at his feet gave him hope. He was standing on a metal grate. Addalis reasoned that it was probably used to drain away the water when the kitchen was cleaned, likely emptying into the sewer or some sort of drainage system. The large grate was almost the length of the hallway, and it would likely be heavy. He was slowly being forced past it as the screaming horde of orcs continued to push on the weakening shield. He only had a few seconds.

He had no other choice. He took his left hand, which wore one of his magical rings, and brought it to his lips. The ring was a Telsirium storage device. Addalis was not proficient in the use of Telsirium magic, earth magic, so it was not as easy for him to collect the energy from the objects around him. Telsirium experts could quickly draw energy from their surroundings and manipulate it into a variety of spells. Addalis could not, at least not very well. But what he could do was slowly collect the energy in his ring, storing it for when it was needed. And he needed it now. He quickly whispered a word, triggering the ring's power, and instantly felt the connection to the magic stored there. There wasn't much, but it would be enough.

Pulling the energy from the ring, he wrapped it around the grate, easily lifting it and sliding it forward. It only took a second. Then he looked up just as the magic from his shield unraveled.

He screamed as he quickly leaped forward, tucking in his arms and dropping blindly into the dark hole, barely missing the heavy edge of an orc blade as it zipped by his head. As he fell he heard the orcs howl above him, their booted feet sounding like a herd of Tarsinian cattle. The sounds faded quickly as he hit the ground hard, falling face first into a pool of dirty water. He rolled to his side as a wave of dizziness overwhelmed him. His head pounded and he tried to fight off the blackness that was creeping in from all directions, but it was to no avail, and with a final sigh Addalis lost the battle to stay conscious.

It wasn't long before they heard the howling and roars of the orcs moving in fast behind them. It was difficult to assess the distance, for sounds traveled quickly down the narrow corridor. It sounded as if the hoard of orcs were right on their heels. Jonas glanced back, his God Light revealing the worried expressions of his companions.

"They are gaining on us!" yelled King Kromm who was bringing up the rear of the party. "Move, Jonas! Faster!"

Just as Jonas was about to turn and run as the king had suggested, he caught sight of Allindrian bounding down the dark hallway towards them, her long strides eating up the distance as if the tunnel were fully lit and not blanketed with mud and water. She reached them quickly; her eyes uncharacteristically filled with worry.

"Where is Addalis?" the king asked urgently.

"I don't think he made it, Sire, but I cannot be sure," Allindrian replied. "But we must move. They are not far behind."

The king growled in frustration turning his fierce eyes towards Jonas. "Get us out of here, Cavalier."

Without a word Jonas turned and ran down the dark passageway, his God Light covering the shadowy stone walls with a bright glow. They ran for several hundred paces before Jonas's chest again burned with warning. Another enemy must be close.

Jonas, heeding the warning, slowed cautiously, on the lookout for this new danger. Half expecting to see some powerful enemy rushing at them, he was surprised to see a slowly moving band of figures lurching toward them. As they approached, he realized why they were approaching slowly. They were already dead. Incredibly, a group of rotting corpses was marching inexorably toward them. The queen and the others bumped into Jonas as he stopped abruptly at the sight.

"What is it?" the queen asked. The corridor had widened a little, but not much, and only two could stand abreast in the tunnel with weapons drawn. "In Ulren's name, what are they?" she asked again, her voice cracking with fear.

"The dead, it is a trap," Jonas said, stating the obvious as the endless stream of corpses made their way towards them. Most of the hoard of men and women looked like walking skeletons draped in putrid flesh. Some, however, resembled their more human counterparts, except for their pasty and bloated skin.

Whatever clothing they wore hung on them like rags, their hair hanging in similar fashion, stringy, and in some cases ripped off in patches or even completely gone. They were only twenty paces away, but they kept advancing from the darkness in a horrific jerky gait.

Jonas felt a soft hand on his arm and looked over to see Myrell. Her face, white with fear, looked at him with absolute horror. "Jonas, what are we to do?"

"We fight! We have no other choice!" Durgen growled, pushing past them to stand in front of the corpses who were slowly closing the distance. They could smell them now, their rotting stench wafted towards them almost making them retch, the tight confines and lack of air amplifying the odor.

As they prepared to do battle with the corpses, they were suddenly accosted by the din of howls from close behind them, so close that they could hear the pounding of booted feet as the orcs pursued them down the dark corridor.

"Prepare yourselves!" yelled the king behind them. "Dandronis and Fil, stay behind me! Durgen and Jonas, take the front, and Allindrian, fill any gaps if either are to fall! Kilius and Riker, stay in the middle with Myrell and Sorana! Jonas?"

"Yes?" Jonas asked, glancing back at the king.

"Make a hole through these abominations. I will hold off the orcs. If we stay in this tunnel then we will die. We need an exit!"

And with that the king turned to face the advancing orcs, spreading his large muscular arms so wide they totally encompassed the width of the tunnel. His huge biceps bulged and the veins in his arms pulsed as blood pounded through his giant frame. Holding his large sword in one hand, he yelled defiantly as loud as he could, his booming voice echoing down the corridor.

"Durgen, get out of the way!" yelled Jonas, as he called on his God Fire. The magic answered his call, and he felt the power rise from within him. Durgen jumped back behind Jonas, remembering the damage he had caused in the Hallows, just as a corpse reached out toward the dwarf. Jonas pointed both swords toward the walking dead, one blade tip just touching the closest undead when he released his God Fire.

The undead near Jonas's swords were engulfed in blue flames, so searing and powerful that they blew through the decomposing bodies, instantly converting them to ash. The corpses behind the undead in the front also erupted in flames, turning to ash as the force of the God Fire launched twenty paces down the tunnel destroying anything that it touched. The heat and power from the fire created a wind tunnel that blew all the ash and remains down the dark corridor.

Everyone covered their eyes and ducked behind Jonas to avoid the intense heat as the flames created a swath of destruction. The roaring flames continued for several moments more before they disappeared, leaving behind a corridor filled with the falling ashes of the burnt corpses.

"Let's move!" Jonas yelled, leading them forward cautiously as they made their way through the ash and charred remains of the undead. But they had only gone a handful of paces before they saw more of the creatures moving towards them from the dark corridor.

"Can you use your fire again?" Myrell asked.

"I can, but I best not. I need to conserve my energy. Durgen," Jonas said, turning toward the dwarf, "get your axe ready."

"Aye," replied the taciturn dwarf as he and Jonas stepped forward to face more of the undead.

Luckily for Kromm, Jonas's light was powerful enough to shed light in both directions. The orcs appeared in Jonas's light so quickly that Kromm only had a few moments before they were on him. He was ready for them though, and he roared like a man possessed, his great magical sword sweeping left and right, cutting through orc armor and flesh. Any unfortunate Gould-Irin that managed to escape his dangerous blade had to face the powerful force of his fists and feet. The corridor quickly became a scene of chaos as the group fought for their lives.

The fighting was fierce on both sides as Durgen and Jonas slowly pushed their way through the walking dead. Though slow, and possessing no weapons other than their hands and teeth, they were not hampered by feeling fear or pain, and their advance was relentless. But Jonas and Durgen were also relentless, cutting into the macabre hoard with continuous steady strokes. It wasn't long before they had developed a rhythm together, his swords swinging high, slicing through necks and chopping off arms, while Durgen's axe cut into knees and legs, dropping the corpses to the ground where Myrell, Riker, and Allindrian would finish them off by dismembering them completely as they stepped over the bodies. They had to work quickly as the undead did not stop, regardless of losing an arm or leg. The only way to put them out of commission was to make their movements impossible.

The problem became apparent quickly. There were so many of them that the sheer weight of their numbers began to push into the two warriors, slowing them down drastically. It was taking them too long to cut them to pieces, and as soon as one was completely dispatched, there were three more pushing into them. Kilius and Riker used their blades to further dismember any undead who continued to writhe and wiggle on the ground at their feet, but they never really completely died.

Kromm was facing the same problem. Orc weapons continued to pound away at the giant warrior. As the king dropped one beast to the ground, two more took its place.

Finally an orc weapon broke through his defenses and sliced across his shoulder guard. The power of the blow was tremendous, but hitting Kromm was like striking a boulder. His armor deflected the blow and he returned the strike with a lightning quick jab to its jaw, just as he yanked his blade from the chest of another. The orc's head snapped back and the stunned beast barely had time to refocus before Kromm's magical blade took its head off, easily cutting through flesh, armor, and bone. But more orcs reached out for him and he was forced to retreat, hastily changing the momentum of his blade from left to right, taking off two orc arms at the elbows. Covered in the blood of battle, he roared his defiance as he dug deep for more energy to continue his reckless onslaught.

Jonas desperately prayed to Shyann for more strength as he felt his arms tire. Bodies were piled up around them and they had to step over the still moving body parts as they slowly advanced. But as Jonas prayed, he began to feel Shyann's strength infuse him. The fatigue that gripped him evaporated and his heart pumped fresh re-energized blood throughout his body.

"Durgen, take rest! Allindrian move up!" Jonas yelled over the chaos of the fighting.

Durgen was a dwarf, tough as the rock in which they lived, but he was also smart, and it made no sense to waste his energy when there were others to share the burden. Besides, there was no glory in killing the walking dead. So he swung his axe through the neck of a nearby corpse and jumped back just as Allindrian scooted forward with a downward chop of her sword, relieving the decapitated corpse of one of its arms. She was still fresh, and her movements were quick and devastating.

Jonas and Allindrian worked side by side, their sword work was precision at its best. There was no need to parry or dodge; they simply swung their magical blades in rhythmic slashes, the sound of Allindrian's blade singing joyously in the tunnel.

Kromm must have killed twenty orcs before he was finally cut. One orc, out of frustration, threw his heavy sword at Kromm's face. Kromm just got his hand up in time to take the full brunt of the sword's impact. It was just his bad luck that the bladed side of the heavy sword struck the underside of his wrist, cutting through his leather guard and slicing flesh. The power of the throw also knocked his head back causing him to stumble, giving another orc enough time to swing its sword across Kromm's plated thigh. The thick steel blade hit Kromm's leg hard, nearly taking his leg out from under him. Luckily his armor was dwarven made and it stopped the sharp edge from cutting through flesh. The strike, however, bruised his leg severely, and the force of the impact caused Kromm to stumble back even further.

Dandronis was standing behind King Kromm just as the monarch stumbled to the right. The sturdy warrior reacted quickly, lunging forward and taking the attacking orc in the gut just under its steel chest plate. But the Gould-Irin's momentum carried him forward and he tripped over Kromm's leg, falling towards Dandronis. The Tarsinian warrior jumped back, swinging his sword across the back of the orc's neck, killing it instantly. Kromm regained his position by pushing off the stone wall with his right hand, launching forward and shoulder striking another charging orc. Normally an attack such as this would have little effect on a Gould-Irin, but Kromm was not built like a normal man, he was equally their size and strength. Consequently, the beast flew backwards into its comrades giving Kromm enough time to get his blade up, reforming their defensive wall of steel.

"Jonas, there must be a cleric or dark wizard before us somewhere!" Allindrian yelled over the sounds of battle. "Someone raised these dead!"

"I had thought of that!" Jonas yelled back, whipping both blades across the neck of a large walking corpse attired in old rusty armor. He must have been a warrior at some point, long dead, and now brought from his resting place and forced to take part in this abhorrent deed. The warrior's head flew off easily, but the big corpse continued on, reaching for Jonas's throat. Jonas kicked out with his right leg, striking it in the chest. It did little damage but it knocked the beast back far enough where he could now maneuver his blue glowing swords left and right, slicing off both its arms.

"Jonas, look to your right!" Queen Sorana yelled from behind him. Jonas glanced in that direction and saw another passageway a pace ahead of them. It was narrow and pitch black and Jonas had been too busy keeping the undead away from them to notice it.

"Do you see it, Allindrian?" Jonas yelled through deep breaths as they neared the narrow passage.

"I do, should we take it?"

"It can't be worse than here!" Jonas yelled. "Allindrian, lead them through! I will stay here with Durgen to hold them off!

Kromm, attired in the blood and grime of battle, continued to fight furiously and did not hear the exchange of words behind him. He had suffered several cuts, and though Fil and Dandronis joined in the fight where they could, mostly they just stood behind the giant warrior waiting for an orc to slip through. But few did. Kromm was unstoppable.

"My Lord, there is a tunnel to your right! We are slipping through it!" Fil yelled, hoping the king would hear him over his battle frenzy. "Jonas and Durgen are holding the gap while we slip through!"

Just then the dark corridor beyond the mass of orcs was illuminated by an orange ball of fire. The bright ball of fire, appearing small in the distance, rapidly enlarged as it neared them. Kromm was distracted by several orcs but Dandronis clearly saw the danger the fireball presented.

"My King, move!" he yelled. Dandronis's instinct was to duck to avoid the flying ball of fire, but if he did that, the ball would likely strike the others behind him, so he did the only other thing he could. He shoulder charged the king, sending the startled warrior crashing into the stone wall and out of the direct path of the fireball. Luckily for everyone behind Dandronis, the ball of fire hit the orc's head in front of him, exploding in orange flame, and releasing a tremendous amount of energy, the brunt of which was taken by Dandronis and the nearby orcs.

Luckily, Myrell, Queen Sorana, and Riker had just slipped through the narrow opening after Allindrian. But Dandronis was blown from his feet and he flew backwards with tremendous force, crashing into Durgen who was still trying to keep the undead at bay.

The rest of the group, however, was caught in the fiery inferno that exploded around them, slamming them all to the ground in a tangle of limbs and searing fire. The power of the blast sent Fil crashing into the stone wall, knocking the wind from his lungs as flames painfully seared his flesh before disappearing just as fast as it had arrived.

Everyone had fallen to the ground, badly burned. Even Jonas's armor did not fully protect him from the powerful blast. Over a score of orcs had taken most of the brunt of the fireball spell, since it had struck one in the back of the head, sending most of its power backwards into the rest of the beasts. Whoever had cast the spell did not care about killing their own; they simply wanted to destroy the fleeing party. The flames had also caught several of the undead in the sudden inferno, blowing them backwards and tumbling them to the ground.

Jonas managed to rouse himself first, and rushed over to Dandronis, who was sprawled inertly near the king. One look told him that there was nothing he could do. The warrior's right arm was missing as well as part of his left foot. Dandronis's armor had melted and fused into his flesh.

The man was clearly dead, so Jonas ran forward to help up the struggling dwarf, who had landed near the slowly advancing undead. Though nearly all of Durgen's beard had burnt off, and he was covered with burns and soot, he seemed relatively unhurt.

"Let's go! Everyone in the tunnel! I'll hold them off!" Jonas yelled, directing everyone up and through the tunnel. The orcs had suffered as much injury as they had, maybe even more, but they were already getting up and preparing for their attack again. "Let's go, hurry!" Jonas yelled, helping Fil and Kilius through the tunnel, both of them badly burned and dazed.

The king and Jonas were the only two left in the blackened tunnel. King Kromm was a mess, blood, soot, and sweat coating his massive body. His face and arms had been severely singed, yet his eyes still glowed with the adrenaline of battle. He seemed to show no signs of pain or exhaustion.

"Get in the tunnel, I will hold them off for a moment and catch up with you!" Jonas yelled.

"Don't do anything stupid, Cavalier!" the king ordered, glancing over at the still form of Dandronis. The King's eyes smoldered with fury and then in a blink he slid past Jonas, disappearing in the dark side tunnel.

Jonas glanced left and right, seeing his enemies close in. The undead were nearly on him when they just stopped and stood still, staring at nothing. The orcs that hadn't died in the explosion stood less than five paces away, snarling and gripping their weapons in their huge fists.

But for some reason they too were not advancing. Jonas did not want to wait around and find out why they were not attacking, so he quickly turned around to flee through the narrow corridor, only to run into a stone wall. The side corridor was nowhere to be found. In its place stood a smooth stone wall, as if the corridor had never existed.

"It's a simple spell really, one that even a novice wizard can learn," Gullanin said, walking through the orcs who had parted for him as if he were a god. Jonas glanced to his left, toward the undead, hoping to see some way of escape, but the undead had stepped aside as well and three dark robed men were drifting towards him. They all wore hooded black cloaks and carried dark staffs.

The cloaked man in the middle was taller than the rest, and as he neared Jonas he lifted his hood from his face revealing a thin visage of pasty white skin. The man's eyes were sunken and black and his shoulder length hair hung from his cruel face in scraggly patches.

"There is no escape, Cavalier," hissed the dark cleric as he raised his staff before him.

Jonas quickly threw up a cognivant shield, hoping that it would deflect whatever the cleric was throwing his way, but the move was just a ruse and as Jonas raised the shield, Gullanin, who was behind him and the shield, launched a powerful spell. A translucent magical fist shot from the end of Gullanin's staff, crashing into Jonas's unprotected back. The fist, as large as Jonas's torso, and propelled by the power of Gullanin's spell, might as well have been connected to a frost giant.

Jonas was slammed against the rock wall, snapping his head back into the stone. Though his helm protected his head from cracking, the force of the blow severely dazed him, as well as leaving him gasping for breath as it knocked the wind out of him.

Gullanin then directed the disembodied fist toward Jonas again just as he was slumping to the floor. This time the fist was open, and it grabbed Jonas firmly, lifting him roughly into the air and slamming him again against the hard stone wall. The impact caused Jonas's vision to swim, and all he could hear were distant voices as he felt his body being lifted off the ground, before all went black.

Eleven
The Ties that Bind

Kromm stumbled down the dark corridor. The ground was still wet and muddy; he could feel it slosh against his boots. He used his hands as guides, brushing them along the narrow rock wall. He glanced back a couple times, expecting Jonas's light to shatter the darkness at any moment, but it didn't, and that worried him.

He was just getting ready to turn back when he saw a sphere of light just ahead of him, a bright floating ball that illuminated the area before him exposing Allindrian and the rest of the group. The Blade Singer was facing him with her sword drawn and the rest of the group stood behind her looking disheveled and worried.

The bright light enabled Kromm to move faster now that he could see the ground in front of him. Quickly he ran to them and Queen Sorana jumped into his arms.

"Thank Ulren you're okay," she whispered, her voice breaking with emotion.

"Where is Jonas?" Fil asked anxiously.

"I don't know. He said he would be right behind me. Allindrian, since you can see in the dark can you leave your light here and run and check on his whereabouts? I did not hear anything behind me and that worries me."

"Yes. The sphere will not move with you, so you will have to stay here. Hopefully I will just be a moment," she said, sprinting into the black corridor.

"What happened, my Lord?" Myrell asked fearfully.

"Jonas said he'd hold the opening. He should have been right behind me," the king said as he grabbed his son and hugged him tight.

Allindrian materialized in front of them from the darkness just a few moments later. Her expression was grave and so were her words. "King Kromm, there is no longer an opening. It is sealed off by stone."

"What! How can that be?" he said.

"Smells of wizard to me," Durgen mumbled.

"What do we do? We can't just leave him!" Myrell exclaimed.

"There be nothin' we can do," Durgen said, his voice flat with resignation.

"What do you mean? How can you say that when he saved your skin more than once!" yelled Fil incredulously.

"We must go find him!" Myrell added forcefully.

"Durgen's right," Allindrian whispered, as if she didn't want to believe it.

"How can you say that? He would never leave you, never!" Fil stormed.

"Fil, we cannot go back," Allindrian reasoned. "It is sealed shut; therefore we have no other choice but to go forward. I did not say that we would leave him, but we can no longer reach him. We have no idea where he is or what happened to him. We must get the king out of here, and now. You know that is what Jonas would want. It is his...it is OUR mission."

"I will not leave without him," Fil said adamantly.

"Nor I, boy, rest assured I will not leave this city until we find him. But now is not da time," Durgen replied.

"Jonas's mission was to get Kromm to safety. You know he would tell you to go on and succeed in that mission if he were here. We fulfill that task first, and then we find Jonas," Allindrian said firmly.

"Jonas is a cavalier," Kromm added. "He will not be so easily taken. I agree with Allindrian. Let us worry about getting out of here alive so we can look for Jonas later." The king's tone made it clear that this was an order, not a suggestion. "Allindrian, lead the way."

And with that, Allindrian moved quickly down the passageway with her sphere of light floating above their heads. They hadn't gone far before they came to a point where they could no longer go forward. The tunnel ended in a "T" with a path to the left and a path to the right, each looking equally ominous.

"Which way do you think?" Allindrian asked.

"Matters not," Durgen said.

"Left," Riker said behind them.

"Why?" Kromm asked.

"The water flows in that direction, maybe it will lead us out of the city," the young prince reasoned.

Sure enough the brown murky water had carved a small trench down the tunnel, slowly trickling to the left.

"Good work, Boy," Kromm said. "It is left then."

Allindrian smiled at Riker as she moved off to the left. They progressed silently for another hundred paces until they came to a spot in the tunnel where the ceiling disappeared, rising fifteen paces up to a metal grate. Allindrian sent the sphere up and everyone's gaze followed the light. Sure enough, there was a metal grate above them and embedded into the wall were metal rungs obviously used as a ladder.

"Up or straight?" asked Fil.

Just then they heard a familiar howling behind them, accompanied by the pounding of the orcs' booted feet, the sound growing louder as they drew nearer.

"They have found us!" Kilius said.

"Up we go! I will go first to make sure I can move the grate! Durgen and Allindrian, you bring up the rear," the king ordered. "Sorana and Myrell, follow me up and stay close. Riker come up behind them."

"Yes, Father," the boy said, his face white with fear but his stance set and rigid with determination.

The king quickly climbed up the fifteen paces with Allindrian's magical sphere lighting the way. He reached the grate and looked through the narrow slits. He could see the moon illuminating the edges of buildings and figured they must be somewhere in the city. Reaching up with one hand he gripped the iron grate firmly. It was heavy, but no match for Kromm's strength. He grunted and lifted with all his might. The old rusty grate held for a moment before succumbing to his power, breaking away from its position with a crack. Then, with one powerful shove, he flung the grate forward, completely exposing the drain hole.

"Follow me, and hurry!" Kromm yelled down as he reached up and pulled himself through the hole into the cool night air. A quick inspection showed that they were on the side of some street somewhere in the middle of the city. Tall stone buildings rose all around him, but no one was in sight. Kromm reached down, easily lifting Sorana and Myrell from the hole. Riker was just behind them and he quickly scrambled out, eager to leave the confines of the tunnels.

"Allindrian, move it!" Kromm yelled into the sewer.

Allindrian looked up just as the noise of the charging orcs became deafening. "Climb on up, Dwarf, I'll be right behind you!" she said.

***

Jonas awoke slowly, his head heavy with aching pain. His eyes fluttered open and his vision slowly shook away the grogginess, revealing a dark room lit with several braziers, their fiery orange light subtly conquering the darkness of the room.

It took Jonas a second to remember what had happened and to fully take in his surroundings. He had been knocked unconscious by the wizard, whose powerful spell had slammed him against the hard stone wall several times. That would certainly explain the pounding pain in his head.

As Jonas regained his senses, he looked around, gradually realizing the severity of his predicament. He was naked and strapped down to a flat cold stone surface of some sort. His consciousness came with a price, as his wrists and ankles instantly flared with pain when he tried to move. He looked at the straps that bound him, straps that were made from black leather embossed with Dykreel's mark, the barbed halo. Blood covered his wrists and ankles and he finally realized why. The underside of the straps had sharp hooks, that when strapped down would embed into the flesh of the victim, causing severe pain and keeping the victim from moving. Jonas gritted his teeth, slowly moving his head to get a better look at the room.

He was in a large square room made of a gray stone and surrounded by dark shadows. The high ceiling meant the meager light from the braziers could not penetrate the darkness above him. Jonas could see that one of the walls was covered with a thick red curtain the color of congealed blood. There was a door he could see, made from oak and iron, but it was closed at the moment. As his eyes adjusted to the dark room he noticed carvings in the walls and ceilings that chilled his blood. The mark of Dykreel was expertly carved into the rough stone on every wall, and the menacing symbol seemed to suck any remaining shred of confidence from him. He suddenly felt cold and his body shook, causing more pain to lance through his wrists and ankles. The warm trickle of blood oozed from the leather straps as the barbs dug into his flesh.

Instinctively, he prayed to Shyann, hoping to gain some of her power and strength, something he was in dire need of, for his mind and body ached with weariness and pain. Exhausted and weak, his mind reached for her power, but he found nothing. Beginning to panic, he searched for her presence within him, but she was not there. The magical link to her was nowhere to be found. Searching again, he looked within himself, trying to grasp a thread of her anywhere, something he could hold onto and draw strength from, but it was not there. He was alone.

He panicked, jerking hard against his restraints, screaming as the barbs bit in deeper and new blood poured from his wrists and ankles. A sound to his right interrupted his screams and he jerked his head toward the door where he saw two men in dark robes emerge through the opening. Their hoods were pulled back and Jonas could clearly see their faces as they neared him. One looked familiar, and Jonas realized that it was the same dark cleric who took part in capturing him in the underground corridor. His pale skin, stretched tight on his thin face, was almost translucent, a web of blue veins clearly visible underneath. His greasy black hair hung from his scalp like wet seaweed might from a water troll. The man's companion was thicker in the face and his hair was shaved short near the scalp. Both of his ears were pierced numerous times with barbed loops, Dykreel's mark. He smiled as he neared Jonas, revealing yellow teeth covered in brown spots and pitted like an old worn sword.

"Cavalier, please keep trying to escape, for your screams are music to my ears," the tall thin cleric whispered as he moved to stand next to Jonas.

Jonas stopped thrashing about. His eyes narrowed in anger as he glared at the cleric. Furiously he began reaching deep within himself for his cognivant powers. He would make these two pay. Maybe he couldn't access Shyann's power, for whatever reason, but he could surely use his innate abilities, and he would pay them back by wrapping them in energy and slamming them against the stone wall.

But as he reached out for the energy around him, a powerful force slammed into him. It felt like an ogre's hammer had just hit his head, and he screamed in pain a second time.

"Does it hurt, IshMian?" the larger short haired cleric hissed. "You see, we know all about you," the cleric continued, tapping Jonas's forehead. "You cannot see it, but we have placed Dykreel's mark on your forehead, so that when you try to use your powers you are denied. It interrupts your energy field, wrapping your brain in Dykreel's fire, causing the terrible pain that you just experienced. I wish you could see it. It is most beautiful. The black metal barbs of the loop are embedded into your skin, fastening it securely to your head, right over your disgusting God Mark. Oh don't worry, you are still God Marked, but by the master of torments. You are part of the Forsworn now, my young Cavalier."

"Never!" Jonas hissed through the pain still pounding in his head.

The tall thin cleric laughed. "As if you have a choice, Cavalier," he said, spitting out the last word like it was a foul taste in his mouth. "You are in a Dykreel temple, strapped down to his altar where you are completely shielded from your precious goddess. She cannot find you here, and you cannot help yourself."

"My friends will find me," Jonas said quietly, trying to gain some confidence in the fact that he knew they were out there somewhere.

"Oh no, they will not. They are running for their lives as we speak. They do not know your whereabouts. Besides, they will be dead within the hour. There is no escape," the heavier cleric gloated.

"So, Cavalier, are you ready to be broken?" the thin cleric snickered, lifting a heavy hammer into view.

Jonas said nothing. He closed his eyes and tried to think of something, anything to take him away from this place, to take him away from the pain that was sure to come. It was then that he thought of Taleen. He remembered when she had told them about the tests that cavalier candidates had to take, and he remembered the one where they were tortured for five days by their own priests. He could not believe that she had gone through that, and passed the test. And this was why. This was the purpose of that trial. It was to prepare them for what would happen if they were ever captured. Somehow Jonas took strength from this thought. If Taleen could withstand such a test, then so could he. He pictured her face in his mind, and concentrated on every detail, hoping that it would somehow make him feel better. Then he opened his eyes, fully prepared to face the two clerics.

Yet, as he prepared to face his impending ordeal, it suddenly dawned on him how utterly alone he was. Lying here in this dark room, whose very walls seemed to ooze with the pain and suffering of the many victims before him, he felt as if the cold stone altar was slowly and inexorably draining his confidence and resolve.

They were right; his friends were not going to rescue him in time. They might not even be alive, and even if they were they had no idea where he was being held prisoner. He didn't know his whereabouts himself. Jonas again closed his eyes in resignation, waiting for the pain to come.

***

"What should we do, Father?" Riker asked frantically, as the howls of the orcs down in the tunnel grew increasingly louder. "They are almost upon us!"

Just then Durgen pulled himself up through the opening with a grunt. Allindrian soon followed, coming up through the opening effortlessly.

"Let us find our way to the inner palace and the Free Legion. We need their swords!" shouted the king.

"What about Jonas?" Fil asked in frustration.

"I told you. We find safety first, and then we launch a search for Jonas. I will not have my wife and son at the mercy of orc blades. Besides, we will do no good running around in the dark looking for him."

"Which way to the palace?" Queen Sorana asked as she looked around at the strange buildings.

"I know the way," Allindrian said, glancing to her left down a dark street.

Suddenly the noise from the orcs drowned out their conversation. Kromm looked down into the hole. "Here they come," he said, reaching over and picking up the heavy grate, dropping it with a bang over the opening. "Allindrian, lead the way."

They ran after Allindrian who led them quickly down the dark street. Every once in a while they caught the movement of someone inside a window hastily closing their shutters or blowing out candles. It was as if they knew what was happening on the streets, and they wanted no part of it.

They kept to the edges of the dirt street where the shadows were thickest next to the buildings. Nervous and alert, they carried their weapons in hand as their eyes darted from shadow to shadow, always expecting an attack.

Their fears were soon realized as they came to an intersection with roads veering to the left and right. Allindrian hesitated for a second, scanning the roads for enemies. There was no sign of anyone so she turned right, toward what they hoped was the inner palace, but they had only gone twenty paces when arrows suddenly began to rain down upon them from the rooftops.

Kromm immediately surged forward in front of his wife, while several arrows struck him in the chest. Two were deflected by his dwarven armor but a third penetrated the muscle on his forearm, skewering it like a kabob. Another arrow pierced Allindrian's thigh while yet another struck Myrell in the throat. The young farm girl tried to scream, but all that came out was a gurgling sound as her eyes widened in shock. She stumbled to her knees with both hands on her throat, blood splattering from her mouth and between her fingers, and then she fell over, landing with a thud on her stomach.

"Run! Move quickly!" Kromm yelled, leading everyone rapidly down the street, hoping to find some cover. As he ran he snapped off the barbed end of the shaft, yanking the arrow out with a grunt.

Kilius screamed in anguish as he saw his sister fall. He ran over to her still body lying in the dirt road. Arrows flew down around him as he tried to heft her body over his shoulder. One arrow took him in the hip, penetrating his poorly made chain mail, and a second arrow clipped his calf. He grunted in pain, dropping his dead sister to the ground.

Allindrian, rapidly assessing the situation, took immediate action. The pain in her thigh, though severe, was not life threatening as no major arteries had been damaged. She snapped off the feathered end so it wouldn't snag on anything and quickly leaped into action, sprinting toward Kilius, while Durgen and the rest of the group followed the king and ran as fast as they could down the street in the opposite direction, hoping to evade the deadly onslaught of arrows. As she ran, she fired arrow after arrow at the black garbed archers above, a true reflection of her incredible skill. The wound in her leg slowed her some, but did little to hamper the speed of her bow arm, nor her accuracy. Her hands were a blur as her elven vision found its targets as they bobbed up and down on the rooftops. Each arrow disappeared into the darkness, striking its mark, unhindered by the fact that she was simultaneously running at full speed toward Kilius, who was now moaning in pain and sorrow over the body of his sister.

The Blade Singer skidded to a stop at Kilius's side, still firing her deadly shafts toward the roof tops. The onslaught of arrows from above stopped momentarily as the remaining archers took cover from the deadly ranger.

"Kilius! We have to move! Can you walk?" Allindrian had stopped firing, and was scanning the roof tops for anyone daring enough to show their head.

Kilius looked up from his sister's body, tears streaking down his dirty face. In the brief moment when their eyes met, Allindrian saw a change come over the young man. The sadness in his eyes, the humanity, seemed to dissolve, replaced with a cold and piercing glare of hate.

"Yes, I can walk," he said, reaching down and yanking the arrow from his calf with no acknowledgement of the pain. Then he broke off the feathered end to the one in his hip, and staggered to his feet. Allindrian caught him momentarily before he regained his balance on his injured leg. "Let's go," he muttered, urging Allindrian forward.

They ran as hard as their injuries would allow, all the while Allindrian was scanning the rooftops for more archers. They had either disappeared or were too scared to show themselves. It was then that they heard the howling of the orcs behind them, followed closely by the sound of combat ahead.

They hurried on, coming around a bend in the street and seeing why the archers were no longer peppering them with arrows. The archers had moved farther down the rooftops so they could take part in the fight that was progressing in front of them.

Kromm, Durgen, Sorana, and Riker were fighting furiously against a mob of Blackhearts, but they were not alone. Forty Free Legion warriors were attacking the Blackhearts from behind, and cutting them down with practiced precision. Their shields were up in a neat row and sharp spear tips moved in and out from the shield wall, killing the enemy with ease.

Allindrian and Kilius moved up behind them, but the fighting there had slowed down as the Blackhearts that remained were frantically trying to defend themselves against the Free Legion warriors. Consequently there were only a few of them that pressed the king and his group. Any that did were immediately cut down by Kromm and Durgen who made an unstoppable duo.

Kilius dropped to his knee to take the weight off his injured leg while Allindrian kept her eyes on the rooftops. She was limping now from the pain in her leg but she could still move and fight. The wound was mostly superficial, and the pain was nothing more than a discomfort. A few archers remained above, but it didn't take her long to dispatch them with shots that could only be described as impossible.

The pounding of heavy boots brought Allindrian's attention from the rooftops to the orcs that were now running toward them.

"King! The orcs!" Allindrian yelled as Kromm and Durgen pivoted toward the beasts. Just then Captain Hadrick, the man they had met at the gate the day before, hacked his way through the remaining Blackhearts to get to them. All but a few of the Blackhearts were dead, and the Free Legion warriors moved their formation forward.

"Good to see you, Captain," Kromm said as he held his bloody sword before him.

"And you, King of Tarsis," the captain replied sternly. "Men, form up! There is orc blood to be shed!"

The Free Legion warriors all wore plate mail and carried large heavy shields and short jabbing spears. Sheathed at their sides were short infantry swords with heavy blades made for hacking. The men were grim faced and moved with a confidence only seen in warriors accustomed to winning.

Fil glanced behind him and saw a discarded spear lying next to a dead Free Legion soldier. He smiled and picked it up. "Now this feels good," he said, moving toward the middle of the line to stand next to Kromm.

The orcs were almost upon them and their sheer size was alarming, even though Fil had seen them before in the tunnels. Armed with large swords made of dark steal and wearing thick dark plate mail painted with Gould's white eye, they ran with no hint of exhaustion or fear.

"I have never seen orcs that big," muttered Captain Hadrick. The man had blood splattered across his chest plate and he carried a wide metal shield and a stout spear.

"They are a different breed, much stronger and faster," Kromm replied, widening his stance as he faced the rapidly approaching Gould-Irin orcs.

"Father, let me fight next to you," Riker urged, moving to the king's side.

"No! Stay back with your mother! I need you to protect her in case any get through. Do not question me on this!" he said fiercely, leaving no room for argument and lifting his sword in his iron grip.

Riker nodded his head obediently and moved back behind the line. He had seen his father like this before, an impending battle melting away the kind gentle father and replacing him with the fierce warrior of legend. There would be no arguing with him, and his orders were followed without question.

Kromm planted his feet into the ground and lifted his sword in his right hand. "Stay clear of me! Keep your formations tight to the left and right. I will hold the center!"

Captain Hadrick glanced at the huge sword the king carried so easily in his hand and understood why. "Tight formations left and right! The king holds the center!" the captain shouted as the Free Legion warriors brought up their heavy shields, angling their spears outward. The maneuver was beautiful to behold as the shields came up in unison, clashing together once as they butted up against each other.

Yet the orcs did not falter once, and within moments they came crashing into the shields and spears. Many of the fearsome beasts were lanced, but they continued their momentum forward, bringing their heavy swords down upon the Free Legion warriors even as they died. Veterans of many battles, the tough soldiers had never fought an enemy so devoid of fear and pain. Handfuls of orcs and soldiers died as the two lines came together.

Kromm did not need a shield to stop the two orcs that came at him. Growling like a beast he brought his blade down and across them both. Power and strength surged through his body and he focused it all on that one strike. His magical blade cut through armor and orc, nearly cutting the first orc in half and then cleaving into the neck of the second. The orcs behind their dead brethren stumbled over the two bodies and Kromm and Durgen were there to finish them off.

Allindrian and Kilius stayed in the back with the queen. Allindrian continued to watch the rooftops with an arrow nocked and ready. Their wounds were still bleeding and soon they would need attention, but for now the threat of enemy arrows and swords kept them on their feet and ready to fight. Riker and Queen Sorana stood next to the Blade Singer, watching the fight before them with weapons drawn and nervous eyes searching the darkness around them.

The fighting was intense as the two formidable groups sought to gain advantage. At first the heavy Free Legion shields did their job, holding most of the orcs back as the giant beasts did all they could to punch gaps in the line. Some, even though fatally wounded by the legions spears, managed to grab their shields, ripping them from the warriors' arms even as they fell dying. Others merely used their immense size to push through the shields, showering the Free Legion warriors with blow after blow from their heavy cutting blades. A quarter of the orcs had been killed, but nearly that many soldiers had suffered the same fate, and it didn't take long for their formation to crumble under the powerful onslaught of the Gould-Irin. The fighting became more chaotic as the wall fell apart and the warriors drew their close formation swords.

Kromm continued to swing his heavy blade with incredible speed and accuracy, cutting into the orcs as they came at him. Durgen fought next to him, his short stature enabling him to stay clear of Kromm's sword, all the while using his axe with deadly efficiency.

One orc attempted to bring his sword down on top of Durgen's head, forcing the dwarf to dodge to the side just as another orc kicked at him. But Durgen managed to spin around the booted foot, taking only a glancing blow to the shoulder, and used his forward momentum to come in fast toward the orc's other leg, his silver axe arcing through the air in the middle of the spin. The razor sharp blade took the orc on the side of the knee, nearly severing its leg. Howling, the orc dropped to the ground as the first attacker again attempted to dispose of the dwarf with another downward chop of its sword. Durgen brought up the handle of his axe to stop the devastating blow, angling his axe at the last second. As he blocked the sword he simultaneously used the beast's strength and weight of the blade against him by causing the weapon to slide down the haft of his axe as he pivoted to the side. The orc stumbled forward, bringing its ugly head close to Durgen. The powerful dwarf then reversed the momentum of his axe and brought the blade up and across the orc's face, slicing through its open mouth. The orc shrieked in pain as it fell backwards, its jaw flapping open, the muscle and skin completely slit all the way to its ears. Durgen roared defiantly as he swung his blade down onto the chest of the downed orc, completely disabling the mortally wounded beast.

Gullanin's invisibility spell worked well to hide his appearance, but it did nothing to stop any sounds that he made, which was why he was extra cautious as he moved from the darkness behind the fighting king. The Blade Singer was just in front of him and she had her attention focused on the rooftops, but he knew that her elven senses could pick up the slightest noise, which was why he was extra careful as he slowly emerged from the darkness behind her. The queen and the prince were next to her and Gullanin could clearly see the tall form of the king fighting like a berserker just beyond them. He was wary of the Blade Singer. She was dangerous and powerful and he knew that he had to hit her first before he could focus his attention on the king.

Then something happened that worked to his advantage. Two daring archers emerged from the rooftop to his right, shooting arrows down toward the ranger. One arrow hit the queen in the side. The other flew at Allindrian, but missed, hitting only ground as the Blade Singer danced quickly out of the way. Even Gullanin was impressed with her skill. She moved so quickly that he barely saw her fire two arrows toward the attackers. Both hit their marks and the Blackhearts tumbled off the roof landing on the ground with a thud.

But Gullanin wasted no time marveling at her speed. He dropped the invisibility spell, jabbed the base of his staff into the ground, and simultaneously called upon his Telsirium magic. The staff, acting as a conduit for the energy, drew up the earth magic all around him, and sent it flying at Allindrian as an invisible wall of force. Gullanin was a master at Telsirium magic, and the wall he thrust at her was enough energy to flatten the Free Legion warriors behind her.

Allindrian spun towards the movement behind her just catching a glimpse of the wizard before the invisible wall hit her. The power of the strike was so intense that she was blasted from her feet and thrown up and back with enough force to send her flying over the top of the fighters. She landed in a crumpled heap more than thirty paces away.

Kilius, though wounded, made a feeble attempt at attacking Gullanin, but he was brushed aside with a second surge of Telsirium magic. A gentle flick of Gullanin's staff sent the young villager flying to the left, crashing hard against a stone wall before he fell to the ground, his head hitting the cobblestone walkway with a sickening crack.

The queen was lying on the ground, moaning in pain. The arrow had pierced her side and the bloody barbed point had emerged from her back a good hand span in length. The intense pain had immobilized her. Riker had run to her side as she had fallen, and his strong hands held her close.

"Mother, are you okay?" he yelled just as Kilius was blasted from his feet. Riker's eyes went wide as he lowered his mother softly back down and turned to face the approaching wizard.

"Hello, Prince, it is so nice to finally meet you," Gullanin snickered. Riker said nothing; he simply stood up in front of his mother, holding his sword protectively before him. Gullanin looked down at the queen who was struggling, despite her pain, to get up to face the wizard.

"Leave him be, I beg of you, it is not him that you want," the queen moaned, finally getting to her knees behind her son.

Gullanin drew forth more Telsirium magic from around him and stored it in his staff. "That is true, Queen, it is your husband that I want, but I don't think the prince here will stand aside while I kill his father. Isn't that right, Prince?"

Riker narrowed his eyes in fury and lunged at the wizard, his sword whistling toward his head.

"Noooo!" the queen yelled.

Gullanin gestured with his staff, again releasing the magic stored there. Gullanin's staff had many powers, one of them being the ability to store spells in the form of energy. This time the energy was released in the form of an arcing lightning bolt that struck the prince in the chest, flinging him backwards with enough force to cave in his armor. He hit the stone wall of a building twenty paces away, landing with a bone crushing thud as arcs of crackling energy buzzed briefly across his armor.

The queen was crying hysterically as she crawled slowly towards her boy, the pain all but vanishing at the sight of her only son crumpled on the ground.

In some part of the king's brain he heard his wife cry. His mind was focused on the combat in front of him, but her cry of torment reached deep within him, yanking his focus from the orcs to what was happening behind him.

He ripped his sword from the heart of a dead orc, disengaging from the fight. Durgen, also hearing the scream and sensing the situation, jumped into the gap to hold the orcs back, giving the king the time he needed to see to his wife.

Kromm spun around and ran forward several paces, frantically taking in the scene. His eyes searched for her but instead fell upon an aged withered man that looked frail enough to blow away in a gentle breeze. The man held a staff and wore an evil grin, and that was enough to surmise the newcomer's intent.

But before the king could act, a sizzling bolt of lightning erupted from the wizard's staff and slammed into his chest. It felt like searing fire shooting through his body. He staggered backwards, dropping to his knees. He was in more pain than he had ever felt. Every muscle and joint sizzled with the energy of the electrical attack and he felt as if he were burning from the inside out. Screaming in agony as smoke rose from his body, he fell forward, catching himself with one hand at the last moment. Through his pain, he again heard the faint cries of his wife. He closed his eyes, his screams turning into a roar of fury as he desperately searched for the inner strength to push away the pain that was hammering his body.

"I can see why my master wants you dead. You are stronger than I thought. That bolt should have killed you," Gullanin said as he moved closer to the injured king. "But you will not live through another," he said, as he began another spell.

"Nor shall you!" a voice roared from behind him. Gullanin pivoted quickly, just as another lightning bolt shot towards him from the darkness. The wizard was so surprised by the attack that he didn't even have time to put up a proper shield. Luckily for him, his staff was a conduit of energy and therefore it absorbed much of the power of the bolt as it struck him from the darkness.

Fiery pain shot through Gullanin's body and he tasted smoke on his tongue. He stumbled to his knees, convulsing as the energy shot through him. He tried to speak to bring forth a spell but his mouth was locked shut as the magic rocked his body.

Addalis stepped from the darkness, wet and covered in grime, limping slightly on his right leg. But his eyes blazed with fury as he stepped closer to the downed wizard.

Gullanin looked up as Addalis whispered the words to another spell, raising his right hand at the same time. Gullanin was struggling with the pain, but he was finally able to pull himself to his feet and recite the words of a quick spell. He had used up most of the energy stored in his staff and he didn't have time to bring forth more, so he simply spoke the words necessary to trigger the release of the remaining energy in his staff, pushing it all forward, and hoping it would be enough to at least interrupt the wizard's spell casting.

Two magical bolts shot from Addalis's hand as a weak wall of force hit him in the stomach. It was enough to push him backwards and knock the wind from his lungs, disrupting the spell before he could send more of the bolts at the evil wizard. The two magical missiles, shaped like glowing crossbow bolts, struck Gullanin in the chest. He grunted in pain, but Gullanin was an ancient wizard whose power was strong, strong enough to counter the magic from the missiles. He had been wounded, but it would not be enough to stop him.

Addalis had keeled over from the attack and was gasping to get his breath back. As Gullanin slowly stood up, Addalis reached for the magical throwing daggers at his waist. The evil wizard smiled wickedly at Addalis, fully confident in his ability to deal with the threat.

But then it was Addalis's turn to smile as he saw the giant form of Kromm stand up behind the wizard, smoke rising from his burnt body, his huge sword already screaming in a deadly arc towards the wizard's neck. Gullanin's smug expression disappeared instantly as Kromm's blade separated his head from his shoulders. Gullanin's wizened body fell to the ground, and

Kromm stumbled forward to his knees as the strength he had brought forth to kill the wizard vanished, and the pain from the lightning bolt again consumed his body.

Addalis rushed to Kromm's side as the king struggled against the pain. His body was badly burned and his mouth tasted like a combination of metal and charcoal.

"My King, take this," Addalis said, producing a healing potion. It was the last one that Addalis had, and he had been saving it for just such a moment.

"No," the king said through clenched jaws, "give...it...to Sorana."

As if on cue the cries of Queen Sorana directed their gaze to a building on their right. There, the queen was kneeling over the still body of her son. Kromm growled, a combination of anger and pain as he tried to stand.

"Help me up," he ordered, his voice strained with fear. Addalis allowed the king to use his body as a crutch and they both hobbled over to the prince's inert form. Kromm quickly dropped to his boy's side while Addalis, not needing an order, uncapped the healing potion.

"Does he live?" Addalis asked fearfully.

"Yes," Sorana said, weeping. "But I know not the extent of his injuries. His pulse is weak and I cannot wake him."

"Give him the potion," the king ordered frantically, as he cradled his son's head.

Addalis gently opened the boy's mouth and poured the small amount of fluid into it. The magical elixir seeped down his throat and they all waited for any sign that it had done something.

The sound of booted feet turned the king's gaze from his boy to a group of fifty armored Free Legion warriors running up behind them from a side street. The group, led by General Kurraris, immediately sent his men to reinforce the struggling warriors who were still fighting the orcs, while he and several other men ran towards Kromm.

"King Kromm, are you okay?" he asked, his worried eyes gazing over Kromm's body, still smoking from his burns.

"No, but I want my boy healed first. Do you have a healer?"

"Yes, I will see to it," the general said, motioning for the two men with him to take the boy. "What happened?" the Free Legion commander asked.

"Later, General, my wife needs medical help. And I need it as well," Kromm said, his voice obviously strained.

"I'm sorry. I will see to it," General Kurraris said as the two Free Legion warriors carried the young prince off. "Altair!" the general yelled to a young warrior at the rear of their force. "Bring men, and get the king and queen to a healer!"

***

The heavy hammer came down with a crack, connecting solidly to Jonas's knee. Jonas did not notice it before, but there were spaces under each knee and elbow, and his limbs were cinched down tight with black leather straps on either side of the space. He was completely immobilized, but as the hammer descended, his instincts took over and he screamed, trying to jerk his leg out of the way. But the straps would allow no movement as the hammer struck his kneecap.

As the pain exploded in his leg, he realized the purpose of the spaces. The hammer shattered his knee, forcing the joint backwards, hyper extending it and driving bone and flesh backwards into the space under the joint.

Jonas screamed again, desperately seeking Shyann as the excruciating pain pulsed rhythmically through his knee, matching the rapid beats of his heart. Yet still she eluded him as he pleaded for her help deep within his heart. Where was she? Why wouldn't she help him? He screamed the questions in his head.

"I can make the pain go away, Cavalier. Just denounce your goddess and pay homage to Dykreel. It is as simple as that," the thinner cleric whispered in Jonas's ear. "The Forsworn will make

321

all your dreams come true. Submit to them and you shall know true power!" The cleric's whisper had grown to a shout.

"Never," Jonas grunted through the pain.

"Very well, Raykin, do the other leg," he ordered.

"As you wish, Dakar," Raykin replied as he moved to the other side of the table, an evil smile contorting his face. Jonas opened his eyes through the cloud of pain and saw the blood covered hammer descend a second time.

Again Jonas jerked, instinctively trying to move his leg, but the magical straps held him tight and the hammer struck his other knee, again smashing bone, tendons, and muscle. His screams reached a crescendo of anguish. He thought that he could not feel any worse pain, but he was wrong. Fresh waves of it racked his body and he continued screaming, louder than he thought possible, tears streaming down his face, his body shaking in agony. He searched for his center as he fought to control the pain, but his mind was scattered and fragmented, and the only thing he could concentrate on were the spheres of fire pulsing at each knee cap.

The last thing he heard before he lost consciousness was a gentle whisper in his ear, "Submit...and it will all...go...away."

***

The king and his family had all been taken to a temple dedicated to Ulren. Falstis, a heavyset priest, tended to the royal family while other lower ranking priests cared for the injured Free Legion warriors that were brought in after the battle in the streets.

With the help of General Kurraris's men they had finally defeated the orcs and what was left of the Blackhearts, but it had been at great cost, and the powerful Gould-Irin had killed many of the brave warriors.

Kromm and Sorana stood above their son who was still lying unconscious in a makeshift cot in the middle of the temple. Allindrian, too, lay motionless nearby and her condition looked no better. Many of the benches and seats were being used as beds and resting places for the injured while the priests went from man to man to tend to their wounds. The low ranking acolytes did not have the power to heal, but they did have some knowledge of medicine, a subject taught to all priests when they came into the fold. The magic granted by Ulren to his followers was given later as they proved their loyalty and faith and the quality of their hearts became apparent.

Falstis had sent healing magic into the young prince immediately before seeing to the king. Kromm had been adamant about that. The large priest had told Kromm that if it hadn't been for the healing draught he had taken earlier, that his son probably would have died. The power of the wizard's strike had caved in his armor and crushed his sternum, breaking numerous ribs, several of which had punctured his lungs. The young prince would have suffocated in his own blood if the healing potion had not stopped the bleeding. But he could not explain why the lightning bolt had not cooked him from the inside out. There were no signs of burns or damage from the bolt.

"You say he was hit with lightning and the force of the bolt flung him fifteen paces?" Falstis asked incredulously.

"Yes, will he live?" Queen Sorana asked desperately.

"He will, but that bolt should have killed him. It almost killed you," Falstis said, turning to King Kromm, "and yet I see no signs of burns on your son. The only damage I see was caused by the impact. I don't understand it."

"I care not how it happened, just that it did," Kromm said with gratitude.

High priest Falstis spent the next hour using his magic on Queen Sorana and Allindrian, while another high ranking priest used Ulren's power to heal Kromm's damaged body. With a little rest and some food and water, they would be fully healed before the morning.

King Kromm and his wife sat by Riker's side for over an hour before Falstis was able to return. "How is he doing?" the high priest asked as he approached them. High priest Falstis was characteristically a jolly looking fellow. But now, however, his chubby cheeks were flushed and he was sweating profusely in the cool evening air. Many men had needed his care, and there were still others waiting for help. The constant work was taking its toll on the heavy man. He was obviously exhausted, but he smiled nonetheless as he neared the king and queen.

"His breathing seems strong," Kromm said. "I thank you, Falstis, for helping us, we are most grateful."

"Think nothing of it, it is my duty and my pleasure."

"Lord Kromm." Allindrian's voice came from behind him and they all turned to see the Blade Singer walk towards them. Her healing had taken well and she was moving with the same grace as she always had.

"Yes, Blade Singer," Kromm replied.

"We need to talk. Fil is very agitated and I'm afraid he will go after Jonas on his own, and I agree with him. We cannot delay any longer. We must find a way to locate him. I fear that if he has not returned by now he may already be in their hands."

"You are quite right. Where is Fil?" Kromm asked.

"Outside in the courtyard with Durgen and Addalis."

Kromm turned to his wife, kissing her and holding her at arm's length. "You will stay here with Riker. I have to go after Jonas," he said, kissing her again on the forehead.

The queen did not argue for she knew it was his duty and the right thing to do. "Come back safe, and bring Jonas with you, we owe him much," she said, pulling him in for one last embrace before the giant man turned and walked toward the courtyard with Allindrian just behind him.

Kromm walked through the open door and into a small square courtyard paved with red stones and surrounded by a stone wall about waist high. In the middle of the courtyard was a statue of Ulren surrounded by stone benches. Bare cherry trees lined the walls and the entire area was tranquil and quiet.

Durgen was sitting on one of the benches with his hand resting casually on his axe while Fil paced, clearly agitated. Addalis was sitting on another bench carefully reading pages from his spell book. The group looked tired and ragged, but their expressions told Kromm that they were all ready.

"King Kromm, thank Ulren you are well!" Fil said, hurriedly approaching the monarch. "But we must go after Jonas. I fear he is in great danger."

"How's yer boy?" Durgen asked, standing up from the bench.

"He will live," Kromm replied with a forced smile. "Where is Kilius?" the king asked as he looked around for him.

"He did not make it," Allindrian replied. "His neck snapped when the wizard flung him against the wall".

The king shook his head sadly. "And Myrell was killed as well?"

"Yes, an arrow struck her in the throat."

"I lost Dandronis in the catacombs. He gave his life for me. He saved me from that fireball," Kromm said, more to himself than anyone else. "So much death, I am sickened by it all," he continued softly. "And we do not want to add Jonas to the list of lost warriors. We must find him!" the king said more forcefully. "What do you suggest?"

There was a pause as everyone tried to come up with some ideas. It was no easy feat. How would they find Jonas in this vast city? Was he captured? If so, where would they take him? Was he dead? Everyone wanted to find him, but no one knew how to accomplish that goal.

"I have an idea," Addalis announced thoughtfully.

"What is it?" Fil asked eagerly, desperate to find his friend.

"I have a spell of location, but…"

"But what?" Fil interrupted.

"But it will not work unless I have something of his, something that was close to him or his body. Does anyone have something that belonged to him?"

There was a pall of silence following Addalis's question, as nobody could think of such an object that Jonas might have left behind. As they digested the grim reality of the situation, their expressions went from hopeful to sad resignation.

Then Allindrian spoke up. "I might know of something," she said hesitantly.

"What is it?" Fil demanded.

"Well, last night, Myrell spent the night with Jonas, and in the morning, when she rushed into the room, she was wearing his shirt."

"That would do," Addalis said hopefully. "I don't like the idea of taking a shirt off of a dead woman, but..."

"She would have it no other way. Where is her body?" Fil asked.

"The orcs and Blackhearts have all been taken outside to be burned, but the Free Legion warriors that fell were taken to the funeral grounds to be buried with honor. I made sure she was among them, as well as Kilius," Allindrian replied.

"Then let's go, we have no time to spare," Kromm said, turning to leave the courtyard with his companions eagerly following.

They found the funeral grounds easily enough as Captain Hadrick had led them there personally. He had been helping bury his fallen men and he was more than happy to bring them to the bodies of their comrades. The grounds of the cemetery consisted of a long expanse of cut grass lined with hundreds of stone markers, each etched with the name of one of the fallen. There were at least thirty bodies lined up for burial, each wrapped with a heavy wool cloth. There were many men about, as well as priests, each going about their duties, preparing the dead for burial. It was still dark, but torches stuck into the ground at various intervals lit the area so the men could work into the night digging the graves. It was tough work, but the Free Legion warriors considered it an honor to give their comrades and friends a decent burial.

Captain Hadrick quickly took them to Myrell's body, and they all turned around to give the dead respect as Allindrian removed Jonas's shirt from her cold form. The Blade Singer did not enjoy the task, but she knew it had to be done, and she knew that Myrell would understand. It was obvious to the ranger that the young village girl had cared for Jonas, and it would help settle her spirit knowing that she had helped in Jonas's rescue.

Allindrian, kneeling at Myrell's side, gently closed her wide staring eyes, settling the wool blanket back over her face. She then whispered the ancient elven burial blessing, "Kuthware ulnos tai amos ruathos." *May you find peace in the Ru'Ach.* Allindrian stood and turned to the others. "I have it. Let us go."

They moved quickly back to the courtyard where Addalis could prepare the spell. He closed his eyes, concentrating on the words as he held Jonas's shirt in both hands. As the magical words appeared in his mind, he focused intently on the correct pronunciation of each word and the proper syntax of the phrase. When he fully felt prepared, he opened his eyes and began to recite the spell. Since the spell was fairly short, it took only a few moments to finish. With a slight raise of his voice and a flick of his wrists, he sent the shirt into the air and enacted the magic. Instantly the shirt burst into a green flame, quickly shrinking and coalescing into a small sphere of floating green fire about the size of a closed fist. Addalis smiled and turned to his companions. "Are you ready?"

Their response was a hefting of axe and bow and the ringing of steel as blades were drawn from their scabbards.

***

Jonas woke up to a sharp sting in his chest. His vision was blurred and it took him a few seconds to orient himself. Standing over him were the two priests and Dakar, the leader, was putting pressure on his chest with both hands. Again he was hit by the pain in his chest, and was horrified to see that the Dykreel cleric was using a small blade to slice open the skin on his chest all the way to the bone. Jonas screamed, his muscles straining against the straps that held him securely to the table. How long had he been unconscious? He had no idea. The pain from his crushed legs had sent his mind away to hide, but now, the pain, as his chest was slowly being sliced open, jerked him back to the awful reality he was facing. He cried out again in agony, in fury, and in utter frustration.

"How does it feel?" Dakar whispered. Jonas could not respond, nor did he care to. It was all he could do to stay conscious as the cleric continued slicing an X shape into his chest. And then, using his bare fingers, he reached into the cuts and began to pull up on the flesh and skin. Jonas screamed again in agony as more pain than he could possibly imagine flooded through his body. Dakar was pulling the flaps of the incisions up, using the sharp edge of the knife to cut away any flesh that was still attached to the bones on his chest. He was being flayed open as he lay helplessly on Dykreel's altar. His vision swam and he hoped that consciousness would leave him and end the agony.

Raykin, the larger of the two clerics, approached Jonas and lifted something over his chest. Jonas's mind was retreating again, but he struggled hard to stay awake, to try and get a look at what was happening to him. Would they now kill him? What was he holding? Jonas squinted, just catching the shape of a black loop of barbed wire about as big around as a skull, being lowered onto his chest.

Just as he was about to lose consciousness, his entire body again convulsed in pain, and he was horrified to see a black barbed halo resting on his flayed open chest. The loop glowed softly red, and as Jonas watched, eyes wide with disbelief, the barbs of the wire elongated, burrowing into his flesh and bones like black worms. More pain assaulted his body as he felt the black cursed steel bind around his ribs, melting into his flesh and bones as the vile symbol of Dykreel became embedded in his body. "Shyann, help me!" he screamed, though he knew she could not hear him.

"Oh, she can't help you now, no one can," Raykin said, beginning to fold the flaps of skin back over the symbol.

Jonas's mind reeled as dark emotions raced through him, hunting down his *self* and forcing it to retreat. There was a presence inside him, a dark presence threatening to suffocate who he was. He could sense it, so he built a small mental fortress, burying himself there, away from this force of evil that was invading his body. He knew that if the dark presence found it, that he would be destroyed forever. It was his strong willpower alone that enabled him to build the place of solace, to fortify it with enough inner spirit to blanket it from the evil shadow that occupied his body. He needed to rest, and so he did as the blackness covered his inner self, leaving his body alone with the new presence.

***

Jonas came to his senses slowly, as if his mind were pushing through a dense fog into a clearing of blue sky. As his eyes adjusted to his surroundings he realized that it was not a blue sky, but a dark round room dimly lit by a wide circle of torches embedded into the ground. Benches filled with screaming, cheering people, lined one side of the room.

Jonas shook his head, trying to clear it, and as he did so he glanced down at his body. Clothed only in a metal and leather skirt resembling the garb worn by the tribes of the Sithgarin, he was otherwise virtually naked, fully exposing the pink scar in the shape of an X on his chest. As he slowly reached up to touch the wound, he noticed that he was carrying a heavy curved sword, the same blades he saw the warriors of the desert use. Where was he? Why was he standing in the middle of a room with a sword in his hand? And how could he stand with his knees having been so brutally crushed? As he gazed down at his legs he saw that both his knees were indeed gravely shattered, swollen to the size of large disfigured melons, bruised and bleeding in shades of purple, black, and red. Strangely, he felt no pain. He sought his mind for the answers and that is when he felt the presence. Then he remembered. The priests of Dykreel had placed a dark symbol in his chest, and it had embedded itself there, leeching a black force into his body.

He stumbled, feeling the presence spread out from his chest as it attempted to grip his inner self and destroy it. Jonas just caught a glimpse of two men, both wearing pieces of armor and carrying swords walk through a door on the far wall. They wore dirty brown breeches and they looked eager to fight. Was he in some sort of underground arena?

The image of the men disappeared as Jonas withdrew into himself, trying to fight off the black presence. He released control of his body and raced through the blackness of his mind. Where was he? It was an odd sensation but it felt as if he was in some empty space, but it was *his* space, somehow still him. He could feel an evil force reach towards him in the darkness as he neared the inner fortress he had built. All the strength of his mind had been compressed into this one pinpoint of light, and he saw it just ahead, like a star on a clear night.

In this strange place he had taken on the shape of himself, but he was more ethereal, like a ghost. He wore his shining armor and carried his twin swords as he shot towards the fortress of light. As he neared it, he heard the sounds of growling and howling becoming increasingly louder, though he could see nothing in the darkness. It was as if he were being pursued by thousands of screaming demons. The sound became almost deafening as he frantically flew like an arrow toward the light

As he neared the light, a black tendril lined with razor sharp hooks reached out for him from the darkness. Jonas flicked his right sword out, cutting the tendril in half just as he slammed into the light. His eyes flashed briefly and then he found himself in a floating circle of bright light. The walls were translucent and he could just make out the shapes of various demons pounding on the wall, eager to destroy him. Screaming angrily and howling in frustration, they tried to enter the sphere. But every time they touched it, there was a flash of light and they screeched in pain, retreating into the darkness. He was momentarily safe, but he had no control over his physical body, and that worried him greatly.

***

The group ran down a dark street as they followed the glowing sphere. It was almost morning and the sun was just beginning to rise in the distance. But it was still relatively dark, and the early morning rays had not yet penetrated the tall walls of the buildings that lined the roads. Though exhausted and covered with the filth of their battles, they ran on, their tired limbs fueled by thoughts of what could be happening to Jonas. He had saved them all several times, and they would repay him with their own blood if need be.

The glowing ball came to a dead end and stopped in front of an old oak door that was boarded shut with two thick pieces of wood. The area looked deserted, but the ball kept bumping into the wall as if it were knocking.

"What do you think?" Fil asked, breathing deeply.

"He must be somewhere behind this door," Allindrian replied, examining the door more closely. "I'm sure there is a hidden latch somewhere," she continued as she felt all around the door with her long delicate fingers.

"Any luck?" Addalis asked after a few moments.

"Not yet," she replied.

"Enough! We cannot waste any more time. Stand back, Blade Singer," Kromm ordered.

Allindrian stepped away from the door as the giant warrior stepped before it. He then lifted up his right leg, snapping it forward and kicking the door with incredible power. The door shook violently as wood cracked and splintered. He grunted with the effort of another powerful kick. This time one of the beams cracked, giving way and causing the door to snap at its hinges, bending inward. Kromm kicked the door one more time, putting as much effort into it as he could muster, and that was all it needed. The snapping wood echoed in the corridor and the door crashed forward, landing in the darkness.

Allindrian whispered a magical word under her breath and a glowing sphere of light appeared before her. The searching sphere created by Addalis shed some light, but not enough to see well in a large space. So she sent the light slowly creeping into the darkness as they followed the little dancing ball.

Kromm went in first, and the others followed. They had entered a large room filled with old empty pallets and various crates and barrels. It looked like an old warehouse, but it obviously had not been used recently.

"Look," Allindrian said, pointing to the floor. Everyone glanced down and saw various footprints across the dusty ground. People had been in the room recently, and by the looks of the tracks, there were many.

The ball continued to float forward and Kromm led the group through the old warehouse. The king had just stepped past a large pile of broken and discarded crates when he caught a glimpse of movement from behind them. Something very large had caught his attention.

Kromm turned, lifting up his arm in an attempt to deflect an attack. Something very large and very strong came at him, striking him a glancing blow on the shoulder with enough force to send him flying sideways. He felt a searing pain, but luckily he had succeeded in diffusing much of the power of the attack by pivoting and ducking his shoulder at the last minute.

The rest of the group reacted quickly, leaping out of the way as the king was knocked from his feet. Allindrian's light, floating above them, illuminated their attacker, a being shaped like a man, but much larger, maybe nine feet tall. But it wasn't a man, more like a non-descript statue made of gray stone. It came at Allindrian, who happened to be the closest.

"Stone Golem!" she yelled, leaping out of the way of a flying fist. Each of the golem's fists was twice as big as a man's, and they carried enough weight and force to crush bones and armor.

Fil, right behind Allindrian, swung his short sword down on top of the golem's arm. His blade bounced off it harmlessly, and the golem, nonplussed, reversed its swing, striking Fil in the shoulder, the tremendous blow tossing Fil through the air. He smashed into a nearby post, and slumped, dazed, to the floor.

"Only magical weapons can harm it!" Allindrian yelled, surging forward at the back of the golem with her silver sword.

Her blade cut into its stone body, slicing a shallow valley across its back. The beast showed no pain or reaction, it simply turned, and walked toward the retreating Blade Singer.

Durgen moved in quickly and attacked the golem from the side. His silver axe swung left and right, cutting deep into the golem's leg.

Meanwhile, Kromm had pulled himself up from the floor and grabbed his fallen sword. His shoulder hurt, but he could move it, so he assumed it wasn't broken or dislocated. He ran at the golem, attacking it from the opposite side, his huge sword coming down hard, digging a shallow valley into the golem's back. It felt like his blade had struck moist clay rather than hard rock. The golem spun, flinging a fist towards Kromm. The stone construct was strong, but not very quick. Kromm easily ducked under the blow, ramming his sword up into its belly. The point struck hard, but only penetrated the golem's tough exterior a few inches.

Allindrian then attacked the golem, this time from the front, with lighting quick flashes of her sword. Now the golem was being attacked from three sides, and every time it turned to engage another attacker, it was struck two or three times by the other two. Individually their blades did little damage, but all together, after numerous hits, the magical weapons of the warriors began to take their toll.

Finally, after several long minutes of fighting, the golem fell to its knees and crashed face first to the floor. There it froze, becoming as rigid as the stone from which it was made.

"Addalis, see to Fil," Kromm ordered, nudging the golem with his foot. His booted foot struck stone, and the giant statue didn't move at all.

"A guardian it would seem," Durgen said as he stood above the golem.

"Aye, they are often used to guard entrances," Allindrian agreed as she looked towards Addalis who was helping Fil to his feet. "How are you, Fil?" she asked.

"I'm fine, I think," Fil said, rubbing his injured shoulder. "I don't think anything is broken," he added, slowly moving his arm in a circle. He grimaced as pain shot through his shoulder. He could move it slowly, but not without substantial pain.

"You may have damaged the joint, or severely bruised it. Can you swing your sword?" Kromm asked.

"Yes, I think so. But it's painful. I'll be fine though. Let's go," he said, forcing himself to ignore the pain as he retrieved his sword from the ground.

"That noise was bound to have attracted attention, so be vigilant. I'm sure we are not alone," Allindrian warned, following Kromm after the little glowing ball.

***

Suddenly light flared and Jonas was again awake. It felt like a heavy dark blanket had been lifted from him, revealing his body to himself for the first time. All the sensations of his physical body rocked him at the same time. The sound of screaming men and women pounded in his head. Pain shot through his chest and his knees and he fell to the ground, his broken and damaged knees crumpling under him. Through his blurred vision he gradually focused on the ground. His hands were holding him up and his bloody and dirty fingers were digging into the dirt. The pain in his knees was excruciating and it was all he could do to keep himself from falling flat on his stomach.

He slowly brought his head up and his eyes found the bodies of two men sprawled near him. One of the men was dark haired and had eyes as bright as lightning. He could clearly see his wide eyes, staring at him in death, his hand still gripping his sword. Blood had pooled on the ground around his torso. He was no more than a pace away from Jonas. The other man's head was turned and he could not see his face. But Jonas knew that he was dead as well, for the back of his head was matted with blood and Jonas could see a nasty crease where a sword had struck the fighter at the base of his skull.

It was then that he realized what had happened, and the memory of it caused him to convulse and vomit on the ground. He had killed them, and there, lying next to him, was his bloody sword, the same blade he was holding in his hand before he lost consciousness. He was fighting in some sort of arena. Men were screaming, money was changing hands, and Jonas seemed to be at the center of it all.

"You killed those men, how does that make you feel?" Dakar said, squatting near Jonas.

"I have killed men before."

"But not innocent men," Dakar said as the screaming and yelling continued. Obviously, the crowd wanted more fighting.

"They chose to fight in this arena. No one made them," Jonas reasoned.

"True. But did you know that Baldar here," Dakar said as he nudged the nearest body with his foot, "was hoping to make enough money to buy his girlfriend a ring. He wanted to marry her. He was an ex-soldier and I told him that he would defeat you easily. But your skills as a cavalier surfaced, your body reacting smoothly, and you killed him quickly. Actually, you killed them both with little effort. The other man was his brother, hoping to earn some money so he could leave this town and buy some land of his own. But he won't be doing that, will he?"

"I did not kill them!" Jonas yelled. "You did! Their blood is on your hands!"

"I have lots of blood on my hands, but not the blood of these two men. I'm afraid the sword that cut them down was in your hands," Dakar said, standing up. "It was great sport watching a cavalier kill two innocent men. The crowd loved it!" With Dakar's last statement the onlookers roared and cheered loudly.

"No!" Jonas spat, "I...was not aware...I was not....in control..."

"Semantics, Cavalier...if you were not here then they would be alive. Logic dictates then that you were their cause of death," he said, kicking Jonas in the side.

"I can't even move, let alone fight," stammered Jonas. He looked around and saw that the circular room was lined with a waist high wall. Five men, attired entirely in black, stood at guard along the perimeter. There was an area of seats on one side where over fifty men were yelling and shouting out bets. The other side of the round arena had a large wood and metal door that opened into a small pen. Jonas saw another man, this one much larger than the two he had just fought, swinging a heavy axe back and forth, warming up for what Jonas guessed was the next fight. He must be in some underground arena, where men fought to the death, for a crowd's entertainment, and the chance to earn some coin.

Another kick flew at Jonas from the other side, the force of the blow knocked the air from his lungs, flipping him over on his back. He coughed violently, trying to suck in air as he looked up at his new attacker. It was the second cleric, the one called Raykin.

"Ahhh, yes, we crushed your knees, but you were standing and fighting. It is simple really. We placed a symbol of Dykreel into your chest. In that symbol sleeps a dark presence, a blackness that can take on the form of anything, deriving its power from Dykreel himself. All we need do is activate the symbol and the blackness seeps into your body, claiming it, and then it does our bidding. You have lost, Cavalier. After a while your inner self will lose the battle and your body will be an empty shell controlled by the Forsworn."

"You lie!" Jonas hissed weakly.

"Did you ever wonder how the Banthras were created? Every ounce of goodness was driven out by the Forsworn until there was nothing left. It took some time, but don't worry, we are in no hurry. You will be our slave. Correction, your body will be our slave. *You* will disappear forever," Dakar said with a laugh.

"You see," Raykin added, "when we deactivate the symbol you feel the pain of your normal flesh, but when the magic of the Forsworn is controlling you, your physical body does not follow the rules of nature."

"Shyann will protect me," Jonas whispered.

"Oh? Where is your precious goddess now?" Dakar asked. "Just like the altar room, this room is protected by Dykreel himself."

"She will find me…my friends will find me," Jonas whispered with forced conviction.

"Even if they do, you are forever tainted with Dykreel's mark. There is nothing they can do for you," Dakar said icily.

"Shyann will find a way," Jonas murmured through the pain, rolling over and turning his back in defiance of the clerics.

"No, she will not!" Dakar yelled, kicking Jonas in the face, snapping his head back and spinning his body so he was lying on his back again. Jonas groaned in pain, spitting out blood just before he lost consciousness.

***

When Jonas opened his eyes, he found himself inside a glowing sphere. He began to lose track of time and whether or not he was unconscious or awake. He assumed his physical body was unconscious, or he couldn't access it; either way he did not have control of his body. He thought of those two men he had killed and his anger began to grow. What were they trying to do to him? He would fight back against this darkness inside him. He did not want to be a prisoner in his own body…he would rather die trying to free it.

His rage grew until it began to consume him, and his body began to glow as the anger coalesced inside him. He set his chin and narrowed his eyes as he looked outside his translucent mental shield. There was nothing there, at least nothing he could see. Jonas drew both blades and took a deep breath as his anger flared even brighter. Then he pointed both blades up and flew towards the wall of the sphere.

Light exploded around him and he found himself floating just outside the protective circle, his entire body glowing with a white light.

"Come on!" Jonas yelled into the blackness. "Let us fight!"

He didn't have to wait long before he heard the howling and shrieking of the demons, or whatever they were. He didn't know. Was the dark presence inside him able to manifest itself into creatures, demons, and then hunt down and destroy what made him, *him*? And where was he? It felt like he was in a dark void, and that he, and the creatures trying to kill him, were the only ones present. And if they succeeded, if he failed, they would claim his physical body.

The sounds became louder, and he floated above the sphere, holding both his blades at the side. He didn't flinch as a hideous variety of beasts came at him, eager to put out his light.

Twelve

The Battle Within

Jonas's body pulsed with light, synchronizing to the beat of his own heart. As his anger and determination grew, so did his heart rate. His astral body, bursting with its white light, was the only illumination as the demons attacked him from the darkness. He no longer cared what happened to him. He just wanted to fight, to die with his swords in his hands, cutting into the net of evil that was trying to hold him. If he were to lose his body to this dark presence, it would not be done without a struggle.

From the blackness there emerged a purplish floating sphere with long tendrils covered with sharp spikes. The deadly tentacles, snapping like whips, sought out Jonas's flesh. Reacting on thought alone, unhindered by his physical body, he was able to move effortlessly with incredible speed, his flashing silver swords slicing through its tendrils as he spun and danced closer to the thing's abdomen.

As he was engaged in this struggle, a grey worm-like creature with a large gaping mouth shot like an arrow towards Jonas's back. But he had seen it out of the corner of his eye as he spun into the sphere-like beast, ramming his silver blade to the hilt in one of its protruding eyes. Without stopping, Jonas ripped his blade free and spun toward the other attacking demon, swinging his sword down and through the beast's mouth, slicing it all the way down its body, aided by the momentum of its attack. As they tumbled through the black void, Jonas flung the dead demon away from him, and then came to a stop, upright and ready for the next attack.

And so the fighting went, with Jonas maintaining a relentless pace, engaging demon upon demon, his blades humming as the vile creatures succumbed to his unquenchable fury. He was a glowing blur, his mind directing him without conscious thought. While his shining blades were carving up a bat-like creature, he was simultaneously adjusting his movements to defend himself and attack whatever other vermin came at him. And though he kept his mental fortress near, he knew he would never use it again. He would not remain a prisoner in his own body. He would stand and fight until he won...or until he died. Either way, he would not again retreat within himself. If he died, so be it. The thought of his body being controlled by the Forsworn sickened him. He did not want to be witness to the atrocities that his body would create when he lost control of it. He would sooner leave his shell behind and join Shyann at Ulren's palace, or join the Ru'Ach, the river of energy as the elves believed. Either option was preferable to being imprisoned in a body over which he had no control.

So, roaring his defiance, he continued to cut and slash into the horde of demons that were seeking his astral flesh.

***

They followed the little fiery ball down several corridors before entering a large round room. The floor of the room was wet and in some places covered in shallow pools of brackish water. More water dripped from various open pipes entering the circular room at the ceiling. The center of the room was occupied by another round hole about a pace wide and leading into the dark hole was an iron ladder covered in rust.

"Storm drain," Durgen grumbled, looking about. "Water drains in from the pipes above, pours into the hole here."

"Where does it go?" Fil asked.

"Could be an underground river or aquifer, depends on de design. It could be leadin' to another drainage system flowing out of de city. Not sure." Durgen gripped his silver axe and looked into the shadows for enemies.

Just as Durgen finished his sentence the glowing tracking ball moved over the drain hole and disappeared into the darkness.

"We go down," Kromm said flatly.

One at a time they carefully climbed down the rusty ladder. It looked old, but it was firmly embedded into the stone and it held them easily as they descended into the darkness. Allindrian's light continued to move up and down the tight confines, shedding enough light for each of them to see the next rung as they went steadily down.

They had not gone too far before they came to another tunnel. The corridor looked very similar to the ones they were in earlier. There was a gouge in the floor where running water had created a small drainage stream. The water was only a few inches deep in the middle and the sides of the tunnel were more or less dry, making it easy to navigate.

"I'm glad it's not the rainy season," Addalis commented, looking around at his surroundings.

"Let's go," Fil said, following the glowing ball down the dark tunnel.

"How long can you keep the light up?' Kromm asked Allindrian as they hurried to keep up with the ball.

"Several hours at least," she replied.

"Good," he said. "I have a feeling we will need it."

The tracking ball took them through many turns, and down long dark corridors, for the better part of half an hour.

"We are going deeper," Durgen said, breaking the tense silence.

"How can you tell?" Fil asked.

"I'm a dwarf," Durgen said with a humph, as if that were reason enough. Suddenly Allindrian stopped, motioning for the others to do so as well.

"What is it?" Kromm whispered, stepping closer to her.

"I hear voices ahead," she whispered back. "Addalis, can you stop the ball?"

"Yes," he said, whispering several soft words, halting the ball in midair several paces away.

"Stay here, I will go investigate," Allindrian said softly.

Kromm acknowledged her suggestion with a nod and Allindrian disappeared down the corridor, leaving her light floating just above their heads.

No one said a word as they waited in the corridor for her return. They didn't have to wait long. She materialized from the darkness like a ghost, her sudden and silent approach startling them all.

"There's an anteroom ahead. I saw several corridors leading to it, including our own. There are five guards, armed with sword and dagger, all lightly armored. They seem to be guarding one door," she said quietly.

"We need to take them out silently. We do not need to warn whatever is on the other side of the door of our presence. Any suggestions?" Kromm asked.

"What light be they usen?" Durgen asked.

"Torches, on the walls," the Blade Singer said.

"If we can extinguish them, then Allindrian and I can take them out in the darkness," The dwarf reasoned.

"Since when are dwarfs silent?" Addalis said. "I have another suggestion," he said quickly before Durgen could give a retort.

"What is it?" Kromm asked.

"Sleep spell, a few words and they all go to sleep."

"To wake up and fight us again," Durgen retorted.

"Maybe, but at least we get through that door with no one aware of our presence," Addalis countered.

"We don't even know what is beyond that door," Fil said.

"One thing at a time, Fil," Allindrian said. "I think Addalis's idea is sound."

"I concur," Kromm agreed. "Allindrian, lead Addalis closer, then come back and get us when they are asleep."

The two moved slowly down the wet corridor. Addalis had to place his hand on Allindrian's shoulder as she slowly guided him through the dark tunnel. It didn't take long before Addalis could see the light from the fiery torches and hear the sounds of talking, interspersed with sporadic laughter. It sounded as if someone was telling a story.

Addalis squeezed Allindrian's shoulder. "That is far enough," he said. "The spell will work from here".

They both stopped and Addalis began preparing the spell. He went over the words in his head several times before starting. It was not a difficult spell, and it took only a few moments before the magic of the spell was released toward the men with a casual push of his hand.

"How long will it take?" Allindrian whispered.

"Not long," and as if on cue, the voices began to slowly fade away until neither could hear a thing. "It is done," Addalis finished.

They went back, retrieving the rest of the group and entering the anteroom slowly and with caution, blades out and ready. Sure enough, all five of the guards were lying on the ground soundly asleep.

"We should kill 'em now," Durgen again suggested.

"I will not kill them in their sleep," Allindrian answered, moving silently to the door.

"They are Blackhearts," Durgen said.

"You don't know who they are. We will not kill them like this," the king stated flatly, ending the debate.

Durgen simply shrugged his shoulders and moved toward the thick door with his silver axe held in both hands. Allindrian had placed her ear to the door and was listening intently as the rest of the group came up behind her.

"I hear cheering, or some sort of commotion. Sounds like a lot of people," she said, facing the group.

"What do you suggest?" Fil asked.

Addalis had freed the ball and it was now floating next to the door, gently bumping it as if it were waiting for it to open.

"Jonas is beyond that door," Allindrian said firmly, looking at the sphere.

"Then we go in," Kromm said decisively.

Everyone nodded their heads, holding their weapons tight and ready for action. They had no idea what was beyond that wall so no real battle plan could be made. They knew that they would simply have to improvise and trust in each other's skills.

"Allindrian, open the door," Kromm said with fire in his eyes, his huge hand tightly gripping his sword. His demeanor changed instantly as mere anger and determination became a battle hungry fury.

Allindrian gently worked the handle on the door and the mechanism opened with a click. She slowly pushed the heavy door open and the group slipped silently through.

As soon as they entered the short corridor before them the sounds of loud cheers and yelling slammed into them, and there was a crazy madness in the cacophony of screaming.

Just ahead of them, maybe ten paces, was an opening filled with light. Beyond the opening they could catch glimpses of warriors fighting, moving in and out of their vision as they fought beyond the entrance.

They inched forward, noticing a passage to their left. Here, the sounds of the crowd became increasingly loud, almost deafening, and it was evident that the voices came from just inside the opening.

"That is Jonas," Fil whispered tensely.

"What?" Addalis asked.

"I saw him. He is fighting someone in there," Fil said anxiously, and he began to move forward towards his friend.

Allindrian placed a restraining hand on Fil's shoulder. "Not yet," she said, sneaking a peak around the corner. "There are maybe fifty people in that room."

"Armed?" Durgen asked.

"I can't tell. I would assume that at least some are," Allindrian reasoned. "I think this is an underground fighting arena. We might be able to just blend in with the crowd so we can see what is going on."

Addalis spoke up, "I have a spell that might help. I can send a stinking cloud of gas through the opening and into the

344

midst of the crowd while we enter the arena and free Jonas. I can use the foul mist to push the people out of the room."

"Where we will have to fight them anyway," Durgen said, always eager for the bloodier approach.

"Maybe. But they might not be Blackhearts at all, just people involved in an underground fight ring. If they do raise their weapons against us, it will be better to fight those numbers in the narrow corridor than to fight them here," Addalis said.

"Good, do it, Addalis," Kromm ordered.

"Be careful, there are bound to be clerics here. This place stinks of the Forsworn," Allindrian said.

And so Addalis began his spell. The magical words floated from his lips as he quietly recited them. The group waited tensely for him to finish, their eyes darting from Addalis to the arena opening, where they could still see Jonas and his combatant move in and out of their vision.

There was a muffled puff as bile green smoke began to billow from Addalis's hands. It spewed forth in a giant cloud and he directed the stinking mist into the chamber where the screaming men were still howling away at the fighters. They were so engrossed in what was going on that they did not notice the cloud until it was directly upon them.

Then there was chaos. The cheering turned into coughing and howls of rage as the smoke began to suffocate them.

"Now!" Addalis yelled. Everyone raced into the round chamber as Addalis continued to send the stinking cloud of smoke into the crowded stands, away from the fighting area.

The scene in the arena was one of utter confusion. There were six dead bodies on the ground and Jonas was fighting a large man wearing nothing but grey leggings and sandals. The man had been cut several times across his chest and arms, and his body was splattered with his own blood. He carried a big double bladed axe in one hand and his powerful muscular arms held the weapon easily. His torso was thick and round but he moved gracefully for a man his size. The combatant must have been a soldier at some point in his life, for he used the axe with practiced skill. His face was nondescript with no outstanding features, a plain and common looking man with graying hair, yet his features reflected a mixture of determination and strain as his older body was making a feeble attempt to keep up with Jonas.

It was Jonas that gave everyone pause. He was naked except for a metal skirt commonly worn by the tribes in the Sithgarin. He carried a curved sword that was dripping with blood. But it was his face that gave everyone alarm. His eyes were wide and dancing with maniacal glee. His chest was covered with a nasty pink scar that looked like an X, and embedded in his forehead was a glowing red sigil in the shape of a barbed halo.

Jonas spun towards them all as they ran into the arena. He was crouched over and hissing like a beast as his eyes found each one of them. He did not seem to recognize them, and they were appalled to see in his eyes, a thirst for blood, *their* blood.

"In Ulren's name, what has happened to him?" Fil asked in shock.

"Dykreel," Allindrian replied, trying to hold back her disgust.

"Very good, Blade Singer," Dakar said, stepping from the shadows. Five guards wearing all black stepped toward them from the perimeter, their weapons held before them.

Everyone spun to face the cleric just as he lifted his hands and whispered several words of power. A hot wave of complete terror crashed into them, causing them all to step back in fear. Even Allindrian felt it as Dykreel's fear covered her, chipping away at her outer being, trying to reach into her and grab her heart with the icy embrace of dread.

Kromm and Durgen shook their heads, their bodies momentarily frozen as they brushed off the magical attack as if it were a pesky mosquito. Dwarfs are inherently immune to such magical attacks, and Kromm's inner strength was virtually impregnable, allowing him to counter the fear spell within moments.

As they all hesitated in the aftermath of Dakar's attack, Jonas suddenly came at them with his blade. The attack was quick and fierce, and both warriors were startled by it.

"Jonas, what are you doing?" Kromm yelled, frantically parrying Jonas's thrust. "Wake up! You are a cavalier!"

Jonas spun from Kromm like a whirlwind and attacked Durgen who took one slash across the handle of his axe while the other sliced harmlessly across the side of his helm. Jonas howled, leaping from one to the other, his sword chopping and cutting, trying to find an opening as the two warriors frantically moved backwards, deflecting blow after blow but not pressing an attack for fear of hurting him. They were not sure they could anyway, as Jonas was attacking with such speed and precision that it was all they could do to keep his deadly blade away.

Allindrian, too, was able to snap out of the oppressive feeling of fear that had briefly overtaken her, chanting a quick spell of her own. She was a Blade Singer and mental attacks did not work well against her disciplined mind. Six glowing missiles appeared in the air at her side and she let them all fly at the Dykreel cleric, simultaneously side skirting the battling trio and coming at Dakar from the side.

But Dakar was not alone. Raykin emerged from a side door, the same door where Jonas's challengers had entered the arena. Immediately he called on Dykreel's power, and it came to him in the form of a cone of hot fire shooting from his fingers and roaring towards Allindrian. It was only her amazing agility that saved her, and even with her incredible speed the flames managed to scorch her side as she jumped out of its path. The force of the blast spun her around but she was able to maintain her footing. She kept her body moving, gripping her dagger at her belt and spinning around towards Dakar, flinging her knife towards Raykin side handed.

The move was so fast and came so quickly right after his fire spell that he was not prepared for it. Raykin had expected her to be burned into ash, so his eyes widened in shock as her dagger took him in the chest, right below Dykreel's symbol that dangled from his neck on a black chain. He clutched the knife, stumbling forward to his knees. Allindrian took no notice of the dying cleric for she was already moving towards Dakar.

It was then that the five Blackhearts surrounding them suddenly attacked.

Fil tried to move his body, but he couldn't. Dakar's spell had succeeded in gripping him with an intense fear, from which he could not seem to escape. His body began to quiver and he could not shake off the thought of dropping his sword and running, even when he saw the two guards run at him with their weapons raised to strike.

Addalis, who was more mentally practiced, struggled as well, but was faring better. The cleric was powerful; hence his spell was potent, carrying the weight of his dark heart and backed by the power of the Forsworn. But Addalis was also strong and an experienced wizard, who practiced daily to strengthen and sharpen his mind, enabling him to push back the wall of fear that was threatening him. He was visibly trembling as he fought the spell, but finally he was able to move his hand slowly toward his daggers. His brow dripped with sweat as he battled against the spell, finally winning the struggle once his hand gripped the magical hilt of the knife. It was as if a thick cloud of fear had blown away and he could suddenly breathe. His hand shot out quickly, sending two daggers flying through the air towards the two Blackhearts who were nearly on him. One dagger struck the first Blackheart in the neck, stopping him instantly, while the second dagger hit the remaining guard in the shoulder, spinning him around and halting his charge. Addalis quickly retrieved two more daggers and within two heartbeats had them flying through the air. One struck the injured guard in the chest, dropping him to the ground, and the fourth dagger flew toward the powerful cleric, Dakar.

Dakar growled and turned towards the fast approaching Blade Singer. Laughing maniacally, he summoned more power from his god. He felt his call being answered, but then the link just vanished. That was when he felt the pain. He choked as blood poured down his throat. He stumbled, clutching his neck, where a small dagger had been embedded. Then another knife slammed into his chest, penetrating his lung.

The pain didn't last long as the agile Blade Singer came in quickly, ramming her silver sword through his chest and out his back. She ripped her sword out, spinning by the cleric as he crumbled to the ground, convulsing briefly as he died.

The Blackheart guard was nearly on Fil. Only moments had passed, but to Fil it felt like an eternity. His body still wouldn't move, and for some reason his frantic eyes glanced from the attacking guard to Jonas. What he saw broke through the prison of his fear and his anger burst forth like an erupting volcano. He had no idea what they had done to his friend, but it looked to be severe, and the thought of Jonas being tortured by these vermin brought forth more anger than Fil thought possible. His boiling emotions broke through the fear just as the guard's sword was upon him. The fear spell actually worked to Fil's advantage, as the attacking Blackheart thought that Fil was still immobilized. But just when the guard thought that Fil was dead, he jumped to the side, the man's sword striking nothing but air and throwing him off balance. Fil swung his sword in a downward chop, connecting with the back of the man's neck with devastating results. He just had time to quickly parry the attack of the second guard. But this man was untrained, and it wasn't long before he too was lying dead on the dirty arena floor.

Durgen and Kromm continued to battle Jonas. It was impossible to do anything other than trying to avoid his dancing sword, at the same time taking care to keep their own weapons from injuring him. They could not keep up the evasion forever. Jonas was too skilled, something had to be done.

Finally, Addalis gave them the opportunity they needed. The wizard's two daggers disappeared from Dakar's body, reappearing back in their sheaths just as he reached for them again. Addalis knew Jonas would be a tough target to hit in the midst of the battling trio. He moved to the side for a better opening, quickly throwing two daggers towards Jonas's back, aiming for the back of his legs.

The first knife missed, but the second took Jonas in the back of the thigh. He stumbled, turning to face his attacker, giving Kromm the opening he needed. Dropping his sword, Kromm tackled Jonas, wrapping his huge arms around him as they both tumbled to the ground. The king tightened his hold, fighting to subdue the writhing body of his friend.

Jonas screamed like an animal possessed. Kromm responded by tightening his muscles even more. Like a boa constrictor, the mighty king's arms embraced him. He then wrapped his thick legs around Jonas's body while wrapping one arm around his arms and another across his neck. Kromm, his muscles straining with the effort, continued to squeeze. Jonas shook and struggled, but slowly his efforts diminished as his airway was compressed. His screams gradually turned to sharp gasps as he struggled to breathe.

"Be careful," warned Allindrian who had just joined them after quickly dispatching the fifth guard. "Do not squeeze too hard." Kromm did not answer for he was concentrating on holding on to the young warrior. Jonas was strong, and it was not easy, even for the powerful king, to hold him still. But finally Jonas stopped struggling and his eyes rolled back in his head.

Fil, having just dispatched two guards, ran towards Jonas. "Is he okay?" he asked, kneeling by the unconscious cavalier.

Kromm got to his feet, surveying the scene. Addalis was now directing his stinking cloud down the corridor after the retreating men who had been watching, and more than likely betting on the fights. Some of those men may have been Blackhearts, but there was no way of knowing. Everyone else was looking down at Jonas. "He should be fine," Kromm said. "He is merely unconscious."

"What is wrong with him?" Fil asked anxiously.

"I don't know, but by the looks of that symbol on his head, and that scarring on his chest, he has been corrupted by the Forsworn. We cannot fix him without help," Allindrian replied.

"What are we to do?" Fil asked.

Everyone looked at Kromm.

"We get out of here and we take Jonas with us. First we get away from this evil place, and then we find a way to help him," Kromm said. "Tie up Jonas's limbs in case he wakes up, but hurry. I don't want to be trapped down here when that cloud disappears and more Blackhearts come back. This entire area is bound to be crawling with more."

Allindrian pulled out a thin white rope from a small pouch at her side. It was extremely frail looking and Fil looked at it skeptically.

"He can break that easily," Fil said.

"Not this," the Blade Singer replied, "It is elven rope. Even Kromm could not break it."

Fil did not look convinced but he said nothing as Allindrian quickly secured Jonas's legs and arms. The yells and screams of the retreating men were muffled now as the dense choking fog pushed them farther away. As it turned out, most were not Blackhearts, but men who came to bet on the combatants. But the group had no idea how many Dykreel followers were about, so they quickly made haste.

Kromm reached down and picked Jonas up as if he weighed nothing more than a young child. He flung Jonas's limp form over his shoulder, turned to the rest of the group and shouted, "Let's go!"

They moved into the antechamber where the guards were still sleeping. The fog was still thick here, forcing them to stop momentarily.

"Addalis, can you control the fog?" the king asked.

"I can, where should I send it?" The wizard asked.

There were four other passageways that entered the antechamber besides the one from which they had come. He could not send the fog down them all.

"If you send the fog down the wrong one then more Blackhearts could emerge from the other tunnels and find us," Fil reasoned.

"We have no way of knowing where the vermin are," Allindrian said, "I suggest you send it down the one we came from and we follow it. That way we know nothing will attack us from the front. We will watch the rear and hope that there is no pursuit. I fear that is the best we can hope for."

There was a moment of silence as everyone digested her words. Kromm directed his gaze at the wizard. "Do as she suggests," he said.

Addalis closed his eyes, concentrating on the magical connection with the fog, and used his hands to direct the green stinking mist down the corridor from which they had entered.

Addalis followed the mist slowly into the tunnel, trailed by the rest of the group, their weapons drawn and their eyes looking back for any signs of pursuit. Luckily Allindrian's light had not gone out. It still hovered above them, enabling them to see the way, but not quite managing to alleviate the suffocating feeling of the dark corridor and the close proximity of the fog.

Fil glanced nervously at Jonas's unconscious form and then back into the darkness. He was worried for his friend. He had never seen Jonas in such a state, and the recent signs of torture on his body were impossible to miss. His mangled knees were grotesquely swollen, the color of overripe plums. How could he have stood on them? Fil wondered. Why was Jonas fighting against them? And it looked as if he had killed those men in the arena. It was clear to Fil that he had somehow been controlled and forced to do these things. He gripped his sword tighter as he tried to imagine what had happened to his friend. It would have had to be something truly terrible to have changed him so. No one deserved that kind of treatment, certainly not Jonas.

They moved through the passageway and came to the opening that led up to the drainage room. Allindrian sent her light up through the opening, grateful that it looked clear.

"Addalis, you come up last and then send the fog back here at the base of the ladder. That way no one can follow us," Kromm ordered.

"Yes, my King," Addalis replied.

"How will we get Jonas up?" Fil asked skeptically, looking up at the iron rungs embedded into the tunnel.

"I will carry him," Kromm said confidently. "Allindrian, you go first and I will follow. Then Fil, followed by Durgen, and finally Addalis will bring up the rear."

Fil didn't say a word as he had long ago tossed out his doubt regarding the king's prodigal strength. He watched the mighty king grip the first rung as he slowly, but seemingly effortlessly, followed Allindrian up the ladder. Fil and Durgen climbed up after him, aided by Allindrian's light. But just as Fil was nearing the opening he heard the sudden sounds of battle above.

Fil swore under his breath, quickly reaching up and grabbing the last rung, as he hoisted himself up through the narrow opening. The source of the din became obvious as his eyes quickly adjusted to the scene. At least a dozen Blackhearts were pouring into the chamber, their various weapons glittering from the light shed by their numerous torches.

Allindrian and Kromm fought side by side frantically keeping the men at bay as Fil, Durgen, and Addalis lifted themselves up through the hole. Kromm had dropped Jonas to the floor and Fil sprang over his inert form to block the sword of a black garbed young man who was trying to flank Allindrian.

The man's young face reflected pure evil and bloodlust as he lunged at Fil, but his facial expression soon changed to one of pain and surprise as Fil quickly parried the strike, launching a gloved fist into the man's jaw. The Blackheart's eyes rolled back and he dropped to the floor like a sack of bricks.

The fighting was fierce, and although the Blackhearts threw themselves at the line the defenders had formed, trying desperately to break through and cut them to pieces, Kromm's and Allindrian's steel formed an iron tip to a wedge that could not be moved. One Blackheart after another fell to that wedge and the ones that attempted to get around it were met by Durgen's axe and Fil's sword.

One young man managed to sneak in through a gap in the line, jabbing his long sword into Durgen's stomach. His sword hit his breast plate, deflecting harmlessly to the side.

"Dwarven steel, boy!" Durgen roared, choking up on his axe and ramming the tip of it into the Blackheart's stomach. The steel point punctured the boy's stomach and his eyes widened in surprise as Durgen quickly withdrew the point and rammed it again into the bottom of the boy's jaw and up into his brain.

Durgen flung the Blackheart away and engaged another. Kromm and Allindrian had pushed the wedge close to the opening of the room so only a few of the Blackhearts could get in at a time. They worked in perfect unison. Kromm's great sword cut into them and forced the enemy back. Any that got too close were literally destroyed and tossed aside like ragdolls. The king's great size and strength made him a monumental obstacle to overcome, and Allindrian, as she danced around him, used her singing blade like a surgeon, slicing into any men that made it past Kromm.

Some of the Blackhearts were able to squeeze by them both, and again they were met by Durgen and Fil. Addalis stayed back with Jonas's prone body in case any of them happened to get by. But none did, and soon Addalis was able to take his hand off his throwing knives and relax a little as the last of the Blackhearts were killed or ran away.

Kromm turned to them all, his body splattered by enemy blood, his giant chest heaving as he breathed heavily. Allindrian wiped her thin blade on the edge of her cloak and Addalis couldn't help but grin as he compared the two. Both were deadly, as deadly as any warriors he had ever seen, yet they were so different. The Blade Singer's petite body looked frail standing next to the giant king, but Addalis knew that she was just as lethal, perhaps more so. Kromm's eyes sparkled with adrenaline and yet Allindrian's were calm and devoid of any perceptible emotion. If anything her eyes portrayed sadness, or empathy, he could not tell. The difference between the two great warriors was stark.

Kromm moved towards the wizard and sheathed his blade on his back, hoisting Jonas's body once again over his shoulder. "Let us go," he said simply.

Everyone moved hurriedly, stepping around the many dead bodies, hastily following Allindrian's light through the dark tunnels. The continuing sounds of their pursuers kept them on the alert, but eventually the sounds became more distant. It became fairly obvious that the Blackhearts had had enough of their group for the night. But nonetheless, everyone moved with caution.

They made their way outside without further incident. It was as if the Blackhearts had climbed back into their holes, for when they emerged outside there was no one about. The alley was just as empty as it was when they entered.

"What should we do?" Fil asked.

"Go back to the inner palace," Kromm ordered.

"I mean with Jonas," Fil said, his anxiety obvious in his voice.

"We must get him to a healer, to a temple; a high priest needs to look at him. His wounds are beyond my expertise or comprehension," Allindrian said.

"What about Falstis? We should take him there," Addalis suggested.

"Very well. Let's take Jonas there. Hopefully the priest will know what to do," Kromm decided.

They made it to Ulren's temple just as the sun was beginning to rise over the buildings. The temple was still full of wounded soldiers and busy priests, but as they arrived through the front entrance they were bombarded with help. Two priests in grey robes helped Jonas from Kromm's back, laying him gently on the altar.

Just as Jonas was set upon the table his eyes bolted open and his body convulsed. Then he screamed. It did not sound like a scream that any of them had heard before. It was more of a screeching, the sound of another world, a deafening noise, carrying with it a chill that ran down everyone's spine.

Everyone around Jonas stepped back as he howled, howls that created an atmosphere of intense fear, a feeling of terror that pulsed with every scream as he thrashed upon the table like a wounded animal. The evil fear emanating from Jonas spread to the bystanders, and everyone shrunk from the sound like frightened children.

Jonas's eyes rolled back, revealing only white as he foamed at the mouth like a rabid dog. His howls continued uncontrolled, and everyone near him had to put their hands to their ears to block out the pain caused by such horrific sounds.

"What is happening?" Fil screamed. He stumbled backwards, shaking from pain and fear.

No one replied as they were all equally tormented, hands to ears trying to block out the screams that continued to pour from Jonas. It was not a normal sound; it was something of magic, something dark and born from evil.

Everyone was paralyzed with shock, everyone except Falstis, who ran through the maze of men carrying a shimmering white piece of cloth. As he got to Jonas he flung the white cloth over him, and the light material drifted out lazily, fluttering over his squirming body. As the translucent cloth touched Jonas, he went instantly still, the horrific sound disappearing. He made no move and his eyes closed completely.

It took a few moments before everyone could clear their heads. Falstis was already at Jonas's side holding onto one of his hands. His eyes were closed and he was silently moving his mouth in some sort of prayer.

"What was that?" Addalis asked, his voice strained with shock.

"I don't know, but it carried the weight of the Forsworn," Allindrian said, moving closer to Jonas. Everyone around her made the four pointed mark on their chests at the mention of the Forsworn.

"That was not Jonas," Falstis said, opening his eyes. "His body has been taken. An evil presence rests inside him and that was what reacted when his body was placed on Ulren's altar."

"What did you put on him?" Kromm asked.

"Ulren's shield, a cloth blessed by Ulren himself," Falstis replied.

"Can it heal him?" Fil asked hopefully.

"I don't think so. What happened to him?" Falstis asked.

Allindrian told the high priest what had happened and what they had seen. Just as she finished her tale, Falstis pulled back the clear cloth, inspecting Jonas's wound on his chest. He then closely examined the symbol on his forehead.

His face was a mask of concentration, but it was obvious to all watching that he was very troubled with what he saw. He slowly brought his right hand down to Jonas's chest, gently laying his hand over the scar, then instantly withdrew it as if he had touched something red hot. The high priest's eyes widened in fright.

"Something has been placed in Jonas's chest, something evil and extremely powerful. I have never felt such a strong presence of darkness. It can be none other than Dykreel's symbol, magically cursed by the Master of Torments. It is beyond my skills."

"How do we save him? How do we get it out of Jonas?" Fil asked, his eyes pleading

"I know not, young warrior," Falstis replied sadly.

Everyone was silent, taking in the priest's words. Fil looked around desperately, hoping someone else would have an answer.

Finally Falstis spoke up. "You need to get him to a kulam. The priests there might know what to do and they may have the combined power to counter whatever evil magic has befallen the young cavalier."

"Then that is what we will do," Kromm said with determination. "This young man saved my life, and my family's, and I will not abandon him. Besides, his mission was to get me to Finarth. We will go there directly and then send a convoy with Jonas to Annure."

"I will be a part of that convoy," Fil said.

"And I," Allindrian added.

"The dwarfs of Dwarf Mount will also be represented," Durgen stated firmly.

***

Jonas had not stopped fighting. He did not know where he got the strength, but somehow he kept his body moving. Demons perished all around him as his swords spun, cutting one foul beast after another. He had no concept of time. He could have been fighting for hours, or weeks, it was impossible to tell in this strange and surreal void.

Then again, it was not his physical body fighting, but his mind. His muscles would have given out long ago, but here, inside his *self*, at least that is how he thought of it, he was fighting with pure mental strength, fueled solely by his unquenchable emotions. Overwhelming anger, extreme frustration, and cold determination were his weapons, and they were proving to be lethal to the unfortunate demons that encountered him.

And as quickly as they had appeared, they suddenly disappeared, melting away into the void, leaving Jonas alone in the silence as he floated lightly above his glowing sphere of protection. Holding both blades at his side, his fiery eyes searched for more demons to kill. But none came.

He waited for what seemed like an eternity, and still no demons reached out for him from the darkness. Slowly Jonas dropped to his knees, sitting cross legged above the glowing sphere. He then laid both blades across his lap and took a deep astral breath.

"I will wait here," he said calmly, holding true to his word. He would not enter the sphere again. He would wait, fight, or die, whichever came first.

***

Everyone spent that day and night getting cleaned up, eating, and finally getting a good night's rest. Scouts had brought word the following night that a huge army, one led by the Dark One himself, was marching in their direction. This force would arrive at Cuthaine's gates in less than a month.

Kromm tried to urge the council to flee the city with the Free Legion and take as many refugees as they could to Finarth. The Free Legion army of eight thousand would be no match for the massive horde that Malbeck would bring to their gates. But they refused to shirk their duty to protect the city. They would not abandon the very people they swore to protect, leaving them to the ravages of Malbeck's minions.

No amount of persuasion could change their minds, and the group left the following morning with heavy hearts. The high council gave them food and horses for the trip, but they could not offer an escort. Nor did Kromm request one, as he knew that they would need all the men they could muster if they were to fight Malbeck.

Falstis gave them the shroud of Ulren and it seemed to keep Jonas suspended in a state of deep sleep. He did not move or open his eyes. He could not eat or drink. And though his friends were terribly worried about him, his breathing was regular and he looked no worse for the wear.

***

One week into the trip to Finarth, Fil was sitting up late into the night holding onto Jonas's hand. He looked down at his friend's inert form, taking some comfort in his slow and shallow breathing. The moon was bright and the air brisk, but the cold could not distract Fil from his worries. He looked up, scanning the tall snow covered peaks of the Tundrens and thought back to the momentous and tumultuous experiences he had shared with Jonas. Fil missed his village and his family. He couldn't help but wonder what it would have been like to have grown into a man in Manson, his village that had been destroyed four years ago. It all seemed so long ago.

Fil sighed, looking back down at Jonas. "Don't worry, my friend, I will not leave you. I will not abandon you." He gripped Jonas's hand tighter, lifting his sad eyes back to the towering mountain range. The desolate peaks were painted with the moon's blue glow, but the beauty did little to lift the sorrow from Fil's heart.

Epilogue

Tuvallis lurched up from his fur blankets, sweat dripping from his forehead in warm rivulets, disappearing in the deep confines of his heavy mustache and beard. He had been dreaming, a nightmare really, a city burned in the shadows of a cloud covered moon, while monsters howled, attacking defenseless women and children in the streets.

But something else had awoken him, tearing him from his disturbing dreams. He was lying in his bear fur blankets, sheltered by a thick timbered lean-to covered with dried brush to keep out the snow and cold. Tuvallis was a hunter and trapper, living off the meat and skins of the many animals that called the northern Tundrens their home. He had a more permanent cabin several days hike from the town of Manson, but he had constructed a number of temporary shelters throughout the mountains that he used during his long hunting trips. It was in one of these shelters that he now slept.

It had been over four years since the town of Manson had been destroyed, forcing Tuvallis to leave his cabin and venture further from the town, closer to other mountain villages where he could trade his furs and meats. He never stayed in one place long enough to take the time to build another cabin. He missed his old home. It was the only place that he had called *home* over the last fifteen years. Something evil had destroyed the village of Manson, murdering all its inhabitants to the last man, all killed except for two young boys, who, for all Tuvallis knew, were likely dead by now. He had moved further down the mountain, staying several months at a time in makeshift camps, trading his furs and meats with the various villages scattered amongst the Tundrens.

But something evil was definitely stirring. Monsters and other strange creatures were coming out of hiding, crawling from under their rocks and migrating east, down the mountain passes, as if drawn by some powerful dark force. Tuvallis had seen more orcs, ogres, and boargs over the last few years than he had seen the first fifteen years he had spent in the mountains.

He was a light sleeper, always tuned to any unusual noise that might signal danger, and he had heard something, sounds that had jerked him from his nightmare. That was another strange occurrence...he was having more frequent and vivid nightmares, so real they were like waking dreams. He could not put his finger on it, but something strange seemed to be happening to him. But he didn't have time to process the meaning of the dream as he was again alerted by the sounds of something large moving outside his shelter. He had built a basic lean-to up against a rock face. That way he was protected on one side by the high cliff, forcing any attacks to come at him from one side only. A heavy elk skin hung from the opening to keep out the night chill and hold his body heat inside the small sleeping chamber. There was only one way in, but that meant there was also only one way out.

Tuvallis ripped off his sleeping fur and gripped the handle of the long sword that was lying next to him. His bow was nearby as well, as it always was, but it would be useless in the tight confines of his shelter. For that matter, so would his sword. So he drew the long hunting knife that he carried on his hip and listened intently for any more sounds. It could be anything...a deer, raccoon, or elk, but it could also be an orc scouting party or a pack of boargs, the latter worrying him more as they were excellent night hunters.

Without warning something jumped onto the shelter above and behind him. He spun around and rammed his long sword straight up through the timber and brush covered roof, hoping his sword would find a gap through the thick logs. But luck was not with him and he felt his sword thud into a log. Whatever was on the roof was large and heavy as the logs began to bend and crack under its weight. Tuvallis backed up closer to the entrance as he withdrew his sword, readying it for another strike. Then he felt an iron grip on his ankles, and before he could even think of reacting, something yanked him through the opening and out into the darkness faster than he thought possible. Whatever it was, it must be incredibly strong, as Tuvallis was a head taller than most men and weighed nearly as much as an orc. Though wide in the shoulders and barrel chested, the years of hiking and hunting the Tundrens had kept his muscles toned and strong. He was a fast, powerful, yet silent hunter for one so large. Tuvallis could be a deadly adversary.

As he was pulled through the opening, he turned his torso and rolled onto his back, his sword arm swinging out in a deadly arc. As his eyes adjusted to the darkness of the night, the faint glow of the moon penetrated the tree tops above him, revealing his attacker. It was a boarg.

Boargs were deadly animals that inhabited the high peaks of the Tundren Mountains. They resembled the form of a man, but their arms were longer than their legs, enabling them to run on all fours at great speeds. Their gray fur was short and thick and their large bony heads resembled that of a boar, hence the name. They were equipped with an array of deadly weapons…long razor sharp claws, teeth and jaws that could crush a man's skull, boar-like tusks, and heavy curved horns. They were twice as strong as a man and capable of breaking bones with little effort.

Tuvallis watched his sword close the distance, but then he felt a powerful jerk on his leg as the beast tossed him to the side, yanking the tip of his sword away from its neck. Luckily though, his blade connected elsewhere, cutting a shallow gash across the beast's chest as Tuvallis tumbled down a slight hill and crashed into a tree trunk.

He quickly regained his footing, his sword and dagger held protectively before him. The darkness made it difficult for him to see, but he silently thanked Bandris, the god of warriors, that the moon was out and the sky was devoid of the heavy clouds that often covered the Tundren peaks. He could not see well, but he could make out the two bulky figures that were now flanking him.

Quickly scanning the area he could see no other attackers. It must be a scouting party, Tuvallis thought, and not the entire pack. Again he thanked Bandris. With two boargs, he had a chance, but with an entire pack, it would have been useless.

Both boargs rushed him, their growls echoing off the high rock wall. Tuvallis threw his knife overhand into the boarg on his left while leaping toward the other boarg, his body pivoting to the side, and his sword slashing out toward the powerful beast. He heard a grunt from the boarg to his left but had no time to survey the damage caused by his dagger. His long sword cut the other boarg across the forearm as the angry beast swung its powerful arm towards him. The boarg howled and withdrew its arm from the stinging bite of the blade, giving Tuvallus a quick moment to reverse the direction of his blade and cut the boarg a second time across its shoulder.

Tuvallis, with the wounded beast on his heels, ran up the hill with two great strides, reaching higher ground, while, out of the corner of his eye, he saw the second boarg ascend the slope just to his left. Instinctively, Tuvallis reversed direction, leaping off the high point of the hill, soaring toward the boarg to his left with this sword pointing down for the kill.

The boarg, with Tuvallis's knife embedded in its belly, and totally caught off guard, merely stared at the descending blade until it was too late. Tuvallis, landing on top of the astonished beast, rammed his sword through its chest, all the way to the hilt. They both tumbled to the ground and Tuvallis, releasing his grip on his sword, rolled out from under the dead beast.

A growl alerted Tuvallis that the last boarg had followed his lead and jumped off the rocky high ground toward him. He was still on his back and he looked up just in time to see the massive shadow of the beast fall towards him. Quickly, he rolled out of the way, his hand reaching toward his ankle where he kept his last knife.

The boarg landed where he had been, but, as quickly as a hunting cat, jumped again at Tuvallis who was now just to its left. Tuvallis kicked up violently with his right leg and connected solidly with the boarg's knee, knocking its leg out from under him. Catching itself with its long arm, the boarg roared in anger, its leg injured but still holding its weight.

Tuvallis was now up and holding his knife before him, a rather pitiful looking weapon to use against such a formidable beast. But in the hands of Tuvallis it could be lethal. The boarg roared again and reached out with its long arm, hoping to grab Tuvallis and yank him towards its deadly tusks. Instead of leaning away from the attack, Tuvallis moved forward, veering at the last minute, narrowly avoiding the attacking arm. He was now right beside the surprised creature. In a flash he thrust his knife out and low, slicing the back of the boarg's injured knee, severing tendons as it cut deeply into its flesh. The boarg howled again, this time in pain, and crumbled to the ground on its back. Before the creature could even think of defending itself, Tuvallis had fallen upon it, his knife flashing a second time, this time slashing across its exposed neck.

The boarg jerked violently, knocking Tuvallis to the side, but the beast was in its death spasms as it instinctively reached up to its neck in a vain attempt to staunch the flow of blood. Within moments, as the blood pooled around the gagging beast, its thrashing had stopped, and the stillness of the night quickly returned, as if the violence had never happened.

Tuvallis, panting with exertion, his body still shaking with the adrenaline of battle, stood up and scanned the darkness for more attackers. None came. Quietly, he collected his weapons and gear. If this was a scouting party, more boargs were sure to arrive. When they came, he would be gone. Tuvallis looked down the gentle slope. Something inside him urged him down the mountain, a trek he had not made in a long time.

With a final look at the dead beasts, he hoisted his pack, and began his long journey out of the mountains.

The End of Book Two

Book Three,

GLIMMER IN THE SHADOW

Coming Soon!

About the author

Jason McWhirter has been a history teacher for eighteen years. He lives in Washington with his wife, Jodi, and dogs, Meadow and Macallan. And yes, their new puppy was named after one of his favorite scotches. He is a certifiable fantasy freak who, when he wasn't wrestling or playing soccer, spent his childhood days immersed in books and games of fantasy. He'd tumble into bed at night with visions of heroes, dragons, and creatures of other worlds, fueling his imagination and spurring his desire to create fantasies of his own. When he isn't fly fishing the lakes and streams of the Northwest, or wine tasting and entertaining with his wife and friends, he spends his spare time sitting in front of the computer writing his next novel or screenplay.

Glossary

Ru'Ach: An elven word used to describe the source of all life…thought of as a river of energy that created all things.

Kulam: Training facility for cavaliers.

Ekahal: An elvish wizard

IshMian: Elven name for a cognivant, a person gifted with mental powers. Little is known of this power but the gifts range from telekinesis, ESP, to mind control.

Ty'erm: Sharneen term used to describe a meditative state.

Akron: Military term that means a thousand men.

Modrig: Military term that means five hundred men.

Ludus: Military term that means two hundred and fifty men.

Pandar: Military term that means fifty men.

Nock, or Nocking: The *nock* is the end of the arrow that has a crevice for the string. To nock an arrow is to put an arrow to string.

Telsirium: A form of magic use where the wizard can use the energy of the things surrounding him/her. The energy can be accessed quickly but only in small amounts, contrary to accessing the Ru'Ach directly, which gives the wizard as much power as he or she can control.

Kufura: Training facility for Blade Singers located deep in the Aur'urien Forest.

The Silvarious: Elite group of elven rangers whose job is to patrol and protect the borders of the Aur'urien forest.